Grave Reckoning

The Resurrectionist Papers

Book 1

Lisa Silverthorne

LISA SILVERTHORNE

GRAVE RECKONING

THE RESURRECTIONIST PAPERS

Left for dead in a mass grave

He awoke immortal.

Commanding rare magics.

With no memory of who he is.

Solving crimes brings him closer to the truth.

Bounty Hunter, Greysen "Blade" Mallory can find anything—except his lost memories and missing past. Left for dead in a London mass grave in 1726, he awoke immortal with a command of rare magics but no manual.

When he's hired to pursue a bounty on the Oregon Coast, Greysen awakes to find a dead man and local police scouring his rented bungalow for clues. Including beautiful, eagle-eyed Detective Harlowe Keller who labels him a person of interest. Professionally and personally.

Forced to work together, Greysen and Keller search for a killer raising the dead all along the coast as a magical war rages between the self-absorbed goddess Hecate and the quirky god of Death. The killer has clues to the fabled Resurrectionist Papers, documents that may hold information about Greyson's past. As blood magic begins to appear in dangerous and public places, Greysen Mallory and Detective Keller wage their own war to stop the destruction.

Novels by Lisa Silverthorne

Standalones:

ISABEL'S TEARS

LANDFALL

PACIFIC BLUE TATTOO

BEAUTY: CAPTURED AND FRAMED

A Game of Lost Souls series:

THE CINDERELLA HOUR

THE PRINCE CHARMING HOUR

THE EVER AFTER HOUR

THE FALLEN HEARTS SEASON

THE RISING SPIRITS SEASON

THE ETERNAL SOULS SEASON

THE ROYAL WEDDING HOUR

THE HEAVENLY HONEYMOON HOUR

THE DIVINE NEWLYWEDS SHOW

THE CELESTIAL COUPLES SHOW

THE ENOCHIAN APOCALYPSE SHOW

The Spiral series:

BETWEEN

REPRISE

AVENGE

The Resurrectionist Papers:

GRAVE RECKONING

Short Story Collections

THE SOUND OF ANGELS

THE MAGIC OF ORDINARY THINGS

Science Fiction Writing as L.S. Silverthorne

Standalones:

REDISCOVERY

Experiencing True Purple series:

RECOMBINANT, Book 1

HELIX, Book 2

SPLICE, Book 3

FORTHCOMING!

A Game of Lost Souls series:

The Angelic Anniversary Hour, Book Twelve

The Perdition Picture Show, Book Thirteen

The Spiral series:

Ruin, Book 4

Descent, Book 5

The Resurrectionist Papers:

A ROMANTIC FANTASY MYSTERY SERIES

Corpses Delicti

Stiffed Again

SHORT STORY COLLECTIONS

Timeless: 8 Time Travel Romances (January 2024)

SCIENCE FICTION WRITING AS L.S. SILVERTHORNE

Experiencing True Purple series:

Cipher, Book 4

Renascence, Book 5

1

The only bloody thing worse than being buried alive was reliving it. In flashbacks and nightmares. Like the one that just awoke me before dawn. Or maybe it was the gunshots? Great way for a bloke to start his first day hunting a bail jumper on the Oregon Coast. In a letted bungalow.

Gasping for breath, I snapped up from the bed in the dark, unfamiliar room, rubbing my eyes and mouth, trying to clear away the memory of cold dirt covering my face. Six feet of earth that had buried me alive in a mass grave.

I couldn't remember anything before the resurrectionists dug me up that evening. But that one memory was branded in my head and it had a bad habit of hijacking my dreams. Like tonight. But with startling clarity this time.

The dream always started the same way.

Shick thump of a shovel moving soil in the cold darkness. The sound reverberated. Over and over.

It had been my first awareness that I still existed.

My next moment was a gasp for air. But icy, suffocating soil covered my face, filling my mouth. It clung to my eyes in heavy, cloying darkness. The weight of it was terrifying. And so were the tangle of dead bodies around me.

Stiff. Wintry. Clammy.

So many corpses!

Surrounding me like something out of a horror film. I could barely move, my limbs unresponsive, the ache in my neck horrific where deep rope burns throbbed from my throat to the back of my neck.

And I was drowning in dirt and bodies, clawing my way through the darkness when someone sodding grabbed hold of my arm. Pulling me out, onto the wet cobblestones by lantern light.

As the echo of horse hooves and carriage wheels rose through the dark city streets, I sprawled across the cobbles, coughing, and gagging. I threw up dirt and bile as I shivered in the rain in only my small-clothes, teeth chattering, bare limbs stiff and hardly functioning. The foul stench of death and dung clung to everything and I couldn't escape from it.

"Found us a live one," someone whispered in the darkness.

Half a dozen blokes with lanterns and torches surrounded me, shadowed by dark clothing and the night. They pushed three wooden trolleys, two stacked with greying, half-naked bodies, and one empty. I couldn't see their faces. Or those of the dead on the trolleys.

The chaps dragged me across the cobblestones, the rain so cold against my skin, and tossed me onto the empty wooden trolley. The wind bit into my flesh, so frigid I thought I would turn to ice.

I tried to speak. Couldn't.

"How'd he survive a hanging?" another voice asked. "Hangman snapped his neck like a twig. I saw it."

"'Twas witchcraft, that's 'ow!" someone else whispered.

"I saw it, too. 'e was dead, 'e was. Not breavin'. Not movin'. Even when they buried 'im yesterday mornin'. Da tenth. Right 'ere. In the church poor 'ole wif all the other witches."

I couldn't tell which of the six or seven blokes in dirty shirts and dark trousers spoke. They all had long, dark hair tied with leather cords at their napes and they spoke barely above whispers. They were resurrectionists, that much I knew, working in the dead of night. Digging up bodies to sell to London hospitals and physicians. At the time, I had no idea who they were or why they were out in London's streets during second sleep, digging up bodies.

Much less why I was among those bodies. With mentions of hangings and witchcraft.

As far back as I could remember, there had been big gaps in this memory. Hazy. Out of focus. Most of it silhouettes, soil, and torchlight.

Until tonight.

Until tonight, I had no memory of their conversations. Or the fleeting, shadowy images, interspersed with painful, visceral memories of waking up in a mass grave that have haunted me ever since that night in 1726.

This time, I tried to speak to them, to ask who I was, where I came from, but only the rasp of tremendous pain came out. I couldn't talk and I had no memory of being on a scaffold much less with a hangman's noose around my neck.

Accused of performing magic—like a witch. Sod it all! I was no witch!

But the shock of the raw, horrendous ache in my neck terrified me. And the deep rope burns around my throat confirmed it. There *had* been a noose around my neck.

I couldn't breathe for a moment.

And my neck had been broken.

I felt sick all over. Whoever I was or had been, someone thought I was a witch or a wizard. Or maybe something darker?

Had I been a criminal? Sentenced to be executed by hanging all those years ago?

But somehow, my fatal execution injury had...healed. How was that bloody possible? I'd been hung like a criminal on a scaffold. I died. They buried me. But somehow—my broken neck healed?

I tried to get a look at these chaps, but the pain in my neck was substantial. I could barely turn my head. Besides, the rain and the dark and the fog made it impossible to see them in the dim light.

"Looks like 'e was young, too. Eighteen accordin' to the execution record," said one of the blokes. "Poor sod. Today's 'is eighteenth birthday. 'elluva way ta spend it."

"Rotten luck that."

"Well, 'e looks young enough, all fair-haired and lean, but 'ow do you know all that?"

"There's a number 11 still smudged on 'is forehead. It's 'is execution number. We already dug up a dozen or so with those numbers tonight. All witches they was. The crown done executed a big lot o' witches yesterday. Didn't you read the notices? Was posted all over London they was. That's why we 'ad such a big turnout tonight. Blokes eager to dig up bodies ta sell ta da 'ospital. Lots a coin made tonight, mates."

"Bloody 'ell," another voice cursed. "Not for this one. Can't exactly sell 'is body to the 'ospital now, can we?"

"Why not? Parts is parts. 'is are just—fresher. That's all."

"Shut yer gob. Resurrectionists 'ave some standards. Ya don't sell a body still breathin'."

"'e got a name? Maybe we can ransom 'im back to 'is family?"

"Can't make it out. Ink's smudged. First name's...Greysen. That's all I can make out."

"Whot we gonna do wif 'im then? Draft 'im into the resurrectionists?"

"Whot about da crimpers?"

"Now yer thinkin'. A few coins is better'n none, aye?"

I grabbed hold of one of the chap's sleeves.

"Help—me...please," I said in a raspy whisper.

It was so hard to speak.

The bloke pulled away, pointing at me, and crossing himself.

"'ave a look at those eyes, will ya? They're...glowin' violet! They was right about this one. 'e is a witch!"

One of the other chaps bent toward me with a lantern. The one that had pointed out the number smudged across my forehead. He tilted the lamp toward my face.

"Would ya look at that? 'e does have witch eyes. Crimpers gonna love this one."

"Why's that, Nigel?"

"Wif those eyes, no one'll mess wif 'im. Besides, 'e's young and obviously immortal. Just gotta get 'im on 'is feet first. Get fifty quid more for immortals."

Immortal? At the time, my brain couldn't wrap around that concept. But I'd just lived through a hanging and being buried alive (and couldn't remember either event).

"'ow we gonna do that?"

"We'll take 'im back to da pub first. Get some food and ale into 'im. Get 'im some clothes. Tad won't turn 'im down as long as 'e can run a jib. Or 'oist a sail. 'specially when 'e finds out the kid's immortal."

I had no idea who I was or what I'd done. Or why the crown thought I was a sodding wizard and executed me for it. Much less how I was still alive after being hanged and buried. I only knew my first name was Greysen, I had violet eyes, and I'd just turned eighteen at the time. And the day that they found me, the eleventh, was, apparently, my birthday.

It had been October 11, 1726. I already knew the year, but this flashback had given me the month and the day, something I hadn't known until now.

Right after that, the resurrectionists snuffed out their torches and carted me through London's frosty streets. To the back room of some dark, noisy pub that smelled like cod, flat ale, and piss. Where they forced ale laced with laudanum into me until I passed out.

Four days later, I woke up aboard the schooner, *Angry Widow* after the resurrectionists had sold me to crimpers. The *Angry Widow* had been bound for Haiti until I picked up the first mate's pipe that had fallen on the deck and told him he'd be dead by morning. After falling from one of the sails.

I'd felt it when I touched his dropped pipe. Saw it. Life and death imprinted on cherished objects and somehow, I could see those imprints. Read them.

No, it was more than that. I could suddenly reach out and touch that object's time period. Travel there and back again.

It was a strange magical gift that had grown more powerful as time passed. I had no idea where it came from or how to use it, but it had been with me ever since that misty October night in London when I awoke in a mass grave. On my birthday.

Maybe *this* gift had gotten me hanged as a witch?

When the first mate plunged to his death from the main sail the next morning, the *Angry Widow* diverted course, putting into port at New York a day later.

And dumped me there.

As I said, it was the year 1726. All in all, it had been exactly 30 days since I'd awoken in that mass grave. Marking my birthday as October eleventh. Until tonight, I'd never seen or heard any dates in these dreams before.

I had a real birthdate—at last. After nearly 300 years.

Crimpers and resurrectionists gave me the last name Mallory. A surname they gave to unfortunates without names that they shanghaied and sold to ship's crews. It meant bad luck and the crew of the *Angry Widow* would have agreed.

And maybe they were right?

I had this strange magic I didn't understand, couldn't control, and had no clue how I got it. But it helped me find things. Made me a damned good bounty hunter. I could find anything—except my own past. It was just snippets of bloody memories that taunted me in my dreams. And last night's had given me more than I'd recalled in centuries.

The knock at the front door startled me into the present.

Empress meowed and stretched, floating a foot above the bed, her long ghost fur speckled black, cream, and red tortoiseshell. She was the reason the *Angry Widow's* first mate fell off the main sail. No one knew where the fluffy tortoiseshell ghost cat had come from, but she took a liking to me and followed me off the ship to America.

And I'd been back and forth from England to America ever since.

The knock became insistent as I grabbed a pair of blue joggers and pulled them on over my black boxer briefs. My light blond hair was disheveled as I passed the hallway mirror lit by the red and blue flash of police lights as I moved toward the front door.

A fist pounded the door now. Shaking it. Hard.

"Andy?" I muttered. "About bloody time you got here."

But the muffled voice beyond the door didn't belong to Andy Keane, the bail jumper I'd been hired to hunt. Which had turned into me trying to help him disappear. Bloke had been terrified when I spoke with him at the Portland airport. And not about jumping bail.

About something supernatural.

"Oregon State Police," a loud voice shouted from outside. "Open this door! Now!"

Oregon State Police? I'd only gotten into my letted bungalow a short while ago.

I glanced behind me at the microwave clock as I reached for the doorknob. It was four thirty-one in the bloody morning—I'd been here an hour. Like I was just sitting around waiting for rozzers to show up. Instead of sleeping.

I jerked open the door and almost got a truncheon in the face.

Four uniformed cops surrounded the threshold, but I stared past them. At the body being photographed about ten feet from my doorstep. The surf roared about two hundred feet away, wind whipping sand and rain into my face.

"Sir, step outside please," said a stocky cop with a bushy dark mustache and a hand on the gun at his belt.

A nervous hand. Knuckles turning white.

I hated guns. Never carried one. I preferred a short sword or a dagger—a machete even. Anything with a blade. That's how I got the nickname Blade. Without a real last name to attach to Greysen or a past to go with it, I became Blade Mallory, bounty hunter.

"Bloody hell," I said and held my hands up in front of me. "Don't get anxious with those guns. I'm coming out."

It was bloody cold and I was barefoot with no shirt on, without my Wellies and Macintosh, but I was afraid these cops would heat things up with those guns at any moment after finding a body in my front garden. And apparently, deciding that I was the one that killed whoever it was. I saw that look in their beady eyes.

"Your name, sir," the rozzer with the baton demanded. "And identification. I'll need your passport."

"Mallory," I answered, trying my damnedest not to make any sudden moves. "Greysen Mallory. And I'm afraid my wallet's inside on the chest of drawers."

Then I felt Empress rubbing back and forth against my legs. Nervous. She hissed and swiped at the cops surrounding me, a low feral growl rumbling, fur puffed up.

The baton cop motioned toward another nervous-looking cop. Like I'd just slain a whole sodding police department one town over.

"Go get it." He turned back to me. "Vacationing here, Mr. Mallory? From Great Britain?"

I frowned. I'd been in this country since 1726, thank you. Rather permanent at this point. Even though I also had a flat in London and spent a lot of time there, too.

But being immortal complicated paperwork.

Every sixty years or so, I had to work with a specialist to fix my identity. Become my heir who inherited my own property. And it got harder as the technology advanced. But right now, I had dual citizenship, a New York birth certificate, and a New York driver's license, putting me at about 23. I looked almost that age even though I was over 300 years old. Next time, now that I knew my real birthday thanks to last night's dreams, I'd use it.

"New York," I replied in my thick British accent.

The cop frowned. "New York? But the British accent—"

"Was born in New York but live in London part of the year."

The cop walked out of my bungalow, carrying my old brown

leather wallet. He handed it to the baton cop. I had 20 quid in there. If it got nicked, there'd be trouble. Uniform or not.

Normally, I contacted the local police whenever I worked a job. I'd intended to call them today before I started hunting Andy Keane. Until my New Jersey bail jumper contacted me, asking for help. But the dead body in my front garden had derailed that plan rather handsomely.

The baton cop opened my wallet and kept glancing from my driver's license to me and back again.

"That's him," said baton cop, slapping my wallet closed.

Like he was judge and jury. Of course, who else's picture would be on my sodding license? Prince William?

I frowned. "Excuse me?"

Baton cop pointed behind him toward the dead body and advanced toward me. But the cop that had nicked my wallet off the chest of drawers was suddenly behind me, pulling my arms behind my back, cuffing my hands. Like it was my bloody fault that some tourist got merked by a rogue wave on the beach.

"What are you doing?" I snapped, glaring at baton cop.

"Afraid you'll need to come down to the station and answer some questions, Mr. Mallory."

"Are you charging me with something?" I demanded, glaring at the cop.

"Somebody get Detective Keller over here to handle this," Baton cop said into the radio on his belt.

"You'd bloody well better read me my rights or cut me loose," I said with a growl. "Otherwise, my barrister will read you a declaration for a very large claim, er, lawsuit."

But my anger disappeared along with every thought in my head when Detective Keller stepped around the other cops like a gathering storm and stopped in front of me.

She wore a purple leather motorbike jacket, black form-fitting T-shirt, and black trousers that hugged her long legs. Her hair was a lengthy, thick sable braid that hung down her back, big, smoky light blue eyes piercing as she stared at me, a gold detective badge fastened to the bottom of her jacket. With those black pumps on, she was about five-foot-ten to my six-foot-two height.

The wind carried her intoxicating scent of warm jasmine and cool musk and I wanted to drown in it as I felt the electricity in the air. Felt the heat of her presence.

Suddenly, I didn't mind going to the station.

I couldn't stop the smile that had obliterated my tough bloke's mask. Bollocks.

Regardless, Detective Keller could interrogate me all she wanted.

Empress rubbed against my legs again and I felt her rumbling purr this time against my gooseflesh as the wind sharpened across my bare chest. She seemed to like this detective.

"Greysen Mallory," said the female detective with a stony expression and emotionless but smoky tone, her eyes like blue flames in the wash of police lights as she stared unblinking at me. "I'm Detective Harlowe Keller with the Oregon State Police."

Her alto voice was warm like cinnamon. Sharp like a Bowie knife. She squinted at me, that piercing blue stare feeling like a deep scan. Like she was strip-searching me.

Like that was difficult. I was barefoot in a thin blue pair of joggers. Even my mobile was back on the chest of drawers, my trainers beside it. And my boots.

"Planning to read me my rights, detective?" I asked. "I'd like to call my barrister and find out what I'm being charged with. And maybe have him bring me a jumper and my trainers. It's cold as bollocks on the coast."

The corners of her mouth lifted, her pupils widening as she kept staring at me. I hoped she liked more than just the view of the ocean behind me.

"It's the wind off the ocean," she said in a quiet voice, motioning behind me. "Makes it—cold as...bollocks."

Her deadpan delivery of bollocks made me smile again, almost forgetting I was about to be arrested for murder.

"All right, Smitty," said the beautiful Detective Keller, that long sable braid falling over her left shoulder as she turned toward Smitty the baton cop. "Let's get Mr. Mallory down to the station for questioning and the victim to the morgue. Search every inch of this bungalow."

"Please don't mix up those orders, Smitty," I replied as two cops yanked me across the icy, sandy ground toward a state police car. "I've already had a bad night. Let's not bugger the rest of it by dropping me off at the morgue instead of the station."

For a brief moment, Detective Harlowe Keller's stony cop façade faded into a laugh as she turned toward my letted bungalow. To tear through all my belongings. Look for a murder weapon. See if I was a cross-dresser or slept with a teddy bear. Something to leak to TikTok or whisper to the barman who then posts it to TikTok. That kind of fun with cops.

I'd already had enough fun with them for lifetimes. And that included a rather smashing evening on the gallows with constables, followed by a blackout without the drunk, and waking up in a mass grave. Quite the party that I hadn't enjoyed one bit.

The two cops shoved me into the back seat.

I smacked my forehead against the top of the doorframe and face-planted into the seat. The pain throbbed hot against my fevered brain and I felt a trickle of blood into my hair as the rozzers piled into the front seat. The car squealed onto the dark motorway and headed into the night toward some isolated state police post. Where they could beat a confession out of me with no tourists watching.

At least they couldn't kill me. But they could make me wish I were dead. I may be immortal, but I bled, bruised, and broke like mortals. It hurt like hell and then it healed.

Like my broken neck.

I hoped they found something interesting at my letted bungalow, something about me that even I didn't know. And maybe they could even decipher the strange book someone had tucked into my rucksack in that London pub long ago—or was it aboard the *Angry Widow*?

After centuries, I could only read one page that referenced something called shadowmancy, whatever that was.

One of the pages glowed red when I first touched it and then I felt wisps of a power awaken in me. Like the first line of a song I couldn't remember the rest of. Wouldn't the cops lose their little blue minds over witnessing that? Or learning that I was immortal?

How would Detective Harlowe Keller handle that news?

I sighed and slumped against the cold, fogged-up window, my hands and fingers growing numb from these damned cuffs. This was the worst bounty hunt I'd ever worked and this one hadn't even started yet.

2

THE SKY WAS GETTING LIGHT BY THE TIME THE OREGON STATE Police dragged me into the state police post at Newport, nearly forty minutes away. The squat grey building with windows facing the highway and the coast looked like it was a house of some kind. The car park was small and had been given a fresh covering of asphalt, the warm sulfury smell still hanging above the salt air. In the predawn darkness, the cops didn't mind shoving me around a bit before hustling me inside into an austere interrogation room at the back of the building.

And left me there for what felt like hours.

At least they had the decency to remove those damned cuffs from my wrists.

Grey walls, grey ceramic tile, and a bare lightbulb above a black square table. Two metal chairs. And no windows. Just a large one-way mirror on the back wall.

Like I didn't know they were watching everything I did. So certain that I'd killed whoever was lying dead in the front garden of my letted beach bungalow.

I distinctly recall telling the letting agency that I wanted an unobstructed view of the ocean and absolutely no dead bodies in the front garden. I was working for God's sake and didn't need another case to solve while dealing with Andy Keane. Who hadn't shown up. Poor bloke had been terrified. Probably still in hiding and blowing up my mobile right now to come find him.

The room was cold and smelled like bleach and pine needles. Like someone was trying to erase Christmas. Which was about five weeks away. These rozzers didn't seem like the holiday type to me anyway. Probably hated candy canes and reindeer, too. Taking the piss out of the entire holiday.

Well, I wasn't about to wrap up a nice, neat little confession for them. I had no idea who that dead bloke in the sand was or why he or she chose to die at my holiday bungalow.

My forehead still ached and I felt the blood drying against the side of my face. A minor injury. And I knew that within the hour, the wound would heal itself. The deeper the wound, the longer it took to heal, of course. An interesting aspect of my unexplained immortality.

I padded across the frosty tiles and stared into the one-way mirror, a hand against the side of my face. Hoping my glare was centimeters away from some bloody inspector's face.

"Bet they told you I got this for obstruction," I said, squinting as I pointed at the blood on the side of my face. "Wrong. I got it for being six-two around insecure five-eight cops."

I crossed my arms against my chest, feeling the first stages of hypothermia setting in. I held out my arms, turning in a circle.

"It's monkeys in here! Bloody freezing! Anyone got a parka on hand? Some Wellies? A tauntaun? No?"

When no one responded, I turned and walked away, back toward the icy metal chair to huddle under the bare lightbulb's warmth. November at the bloody Oregon coast was cold as bollocks.

"Fine," I snapped and sat down. "Don't blame me when you have another body on your hands. I'll just freeze to death quietly beneath this bulb and dream of the Caribbean. Unless we can get this Antarctic interrogation over already! Or give me my one bloody phone call and I'll call Amazon and have an electric heater delivered."

At last, the door into the interrogation room opened and Detective Harlowe Keller sauntered inside. Smiling. She carried a large manila envelope in one hand.

"Five stars, Mr. Mallory. This police post already voted your interrogation as their favorite of 2023. Unless you have more closing remarks, another monologue, we can get this over with as quickly as possible."

She sat down at the table across from me.

"Am I being charged?" I asked, leaning across the table toward her.

The detective gave me that noncommittal look, looking all warm and cozy in her purple leather jacket.

"Am I being detained?"

Again, she was silent.

I snapped up from the chair. "Well, unless you're charging or detaining me, I think we're done here."

The detective was on her feet now. She reached out and gripped my bare arm. Her fingers were hot enough to sting. They sent a burst of heat through my body, almost stopping the chattering of my teeth.

"Mr. Mallory," she said in a quiet voice. "Greysen. I have questions that I need to ask you. A man was murdered in front of your bungalow. You know we have to question you about it." She motioned toward the chair. "Please. Sit."

The forthrightness of her tone and her honest delivery momentarily halted the smart-arse in me. Along with her polite courtesy.

Sighing, I turned back toward the chair and sat down. We exchanged a few awkward glances.

"I ran a check on you, Mr. Mallory. Greysen. You're a bounty hunter by profession, correct?"

I nodded. "Licensed in four states including New York. But I also own a small antique shop in upstate New York. Lost Time Antiques."

Except that I had moved it to the internet. Being immortal gave me an edge in the antiques business. I had a huge storage facility filled with antiques. It paid the bills when bounty hunting didn't. But not nearly as much fun.

"Are you aware that bounty hunting in Oregon is prohibited? Apprehending fugitives from other states and taking them across state lines is considered kidnapping."

The detective's words cut through me like a knife blade. I'd been set up. But I couldn't let this eagle-eyed detective know that.

"Detective, I'm on holiday, not hunting bounties," I countered, studying Detective Keller's expression.

"Then why did fugitive Andy Keane, the bounty you were hired to hunt, turn up dead in front of your rented bungalow, Mr. Mallory? With an email from you still open on his phone."

This time, I couldn't hold back my shock.

"The dead man was Andy Keane?" I asked.

No...not Andy. He was guilty of poor judgment at most. And he certainly hadn't deserved to be murdered for it.

"Yes, Mr. Mallory."

She stared at me for a moment or two, letting that little news flash settle into my sleep-starved brain.

"That makes you a person of interest in this case."

Bugger. Checkmate. Someone set me up big time. To take the fall for a murder rap, one I didn't commit. Who wanted Andy Keane dead? And me convicted of his murder? I had to figure that out fast. Life in prison would be a long stint for an immortal.

I had to start with the bail bondsman who called and hired me to hunt down Keane in the first place and bring him back to New Jersey for trial. Brian Beckerman. Beckerman probably thought I'd blunder right into a kidnapping and confinement charge at the very least. Murder charges at the worst. I'd never met the man, but in my book, he was a real knobber. He was the one who told me that Andy had fled to Oregon. Had he wanted Andy Keane dead? If so, why?

Bet he never expected me to befriend Andy Keane and try to help him either.

"Did you hear what I said, Mr. Mallory?" said the detective in her warm cinnamon voice, smelling like warm jasmine and cool musk. "You're a person of interest in the case, but you haven't been officially charged with a crime. Yet."

I returned my attention to the detective. Beautiful, coal-black hair in a thick braid down her back. Big blue eyes. A body that shamed that purple leather motorbike jacket she wore. She was positively heart-stopping.

But she didn't need to know that I'd met with Andy Keane yesterday.

"I may be many things, Detective Keller, but I am not a murderer. I didn't kill Andy Keane, but I'll find out who did."

"Don't leave town, Mr. Mallory," said Detective Keller, rising from the hard metal chair. "We'll be in touch."

"I'm sure you will," I snapped and got to my bare feet. I pointed to the wound on my forehead. "I just hope it doesn't hurt as bad as this next time."

This time, she looked genuinely concerned.

"I'm sorry about that," she said. "Sometimes, our officers get a bit...overzealous. I'll remind them that people are still innocent until proven guilty." She squinted at me. "You should see a doctor for that —it might need stitches. There's a twenty-four-hour urgent care here in Newport. I'd be happy to drive you there and take care of the cost."

"Would someone be happy to drive me back to my bungalow instead? Since I have no wallet, no mobile, and no trainers."

"Of course," she said, nodding, and motioned me toward the door.

She opened it out into the narrow hallway that led out the back of the building and I followed. The hallway smelled like over-warmed coffee and vanilla. When we got to the back door, she handed me that manila envelope. It had my name on it and the word, *evidence* in big black letters.

Like I was already guilty.

"Your wallet's in there along with the key to your bungalow," she said and held the back door open. "Are you sure I can't drive you to urgent care?"

The sky was a deep grey, fog hanging low, the sun obscured. Like London in winter. That sulfury asphalt smell rose on the wind, with warm jasmine traces of the detective's perfume.

"No, but thank you," I muttered as she led me over to a shiny red Honda CR-V and opened the passenger side door.

I ducked my head and climbed inside, clicking my seatbelt into place as Detective Keller slid her long, shapely legs underneath the steering wheel and belted into the black leather seat. She pushed that long, thick braid of sable hair over her shoulder and slid the key into the ignition. The heater huffed through the vehicle and I wanted to sink into the warming leather seat.

"Seat warmers," I said with a gasp, closing my eyes a moment and sighing. "I've died and gone to Hell."

She smiled, her gaze flicking from the mirror to me and back again. I caught her squinting at the mirror once. Was she still doing police work or was she curious about me from another angle?

Regardless, these heated seats didn't hold a candle to Harlowe Keller. Long legs, slender body, and a face that Michelangelo could have sculpted. Chiseled pert nose, large piercing powder blue eyes, softly curving chin, and long graceful neck. There was a strength and a delicateness to her. And this close to her, I couldn't help but fall under the spell of her warm jasmine and cool musk scent.

Then I noticed the silver chain bracelet draped across the cupholder in the console between us.

I should have kept my distance.

Should have stayed disconnected and ambivalent, but the magic within me stirred. I could feel all the walls she'd put up around an old hurt. Covering it in armor, ready to push away anyone that dared scale those walls or cut through that protection.

In that moment, I understood her. I had those very same walls. And they were very old. Back when walls were made of wood and stone. As the centuries slipped away, I upgraded them to concrete, rebar, and steel. I had so little of myself, not even a last name or past for comfort (or pain), so I was very careful about who I let behind those walls.

Again, that bracelet made my magic spark.

I couldn't help myself. I wanted to understand this detective who might arrest me for murder.

I reached over and picked up the bracelet. It sparked against my fingers.

Like a slingshot, it slammed images through my brain as I white-knuckled the seat, holding my body in place. It had taken immense practice over the centuries to only allow my consciousness to travel through the timestream. And not my entire being. If I'd let it, it would have propelled me, body and soul, backward in time. But I rode out the force waves, letting my consciousness surge along the timestream.

May 2015. Al-Amr Syria. Special forces raid. A younger Detective Keller crouches on a desert hill above a village, sniper rifle at her shoulder, pointed toward a group of blokes dressed in white kaftans.

Wind is hot and gritty. Sand sparkles in the baking sun above the din of a small outdoor market, wooden stalls and posts draped in brightly colored silks. Fuchsia, emerald, citrine, amethyst, and sapphire fabrics flutter in the breeze.

The air is thick with sweat, black pepper, dust, and cardamon strong as she lifts her rifle to her shoulder. Targeting.

At the edge of the market, the five blokes in white kaftans congregate. Voices hushed and anxious. Robes hide something from view.

Keller's demeanor is cool. Calculated. Laid back as she scopes her target, a short, stocky chap with a long, wispy grey beard and leathery cheeks.

She pulls in a long, deep breath, shoulder frozen, rifle like stone as her finger slides deftly to the trigger. Silver bracelet sparkles on her wrist.

The chap jerks his gaze up toward a sudden flicker of light. Panicked.

In an instant, everything changes.

The bracelet has given away her position.

As she pulls the trigger, the man shoves a dirty-faced boy with dusty clothes in front of him.

She gasps, shoulder jerking, hands shoving the rifle barrel downward. But nothing halts the bullet that whispers across the market. Silent. Deadly. Striking the child.

"No..." Her voice aches in the silence above the market. "No!"

The color drains from her face. The boy's on the ground now.

"I shot a kid," she whispers over and over in disbelief and I can feel every icy cold moment of fear and every sick feeling roiling in her stomach.

Screams erupt through the market. People scatter. Vegetables fall into the sand. Crates break, spilling fruit and jars of oil.

The group of men carries the boy out of the sun as tears flood Detective Keller's face.

Six months later, she walks away from the military.

Even though the lad lived.

And she has been running from that memory ever since, moving from job to job, state to state. Until she lands here on the Oregon Coast in 2018. And stays, becoming a cop.

That bracelet had been a gift from her parents when she passed basic training.

"Put that back," Detective Keller snapped. "Now."

It took me a moment to acclimate back to present time. It always took a little time when my magic ignited. Usually, I initiated it, helping people find something—or someone—they lost. I'd always been careful about guarding the magic, not letting it just pop off on every object I came into contact with. That took some practice and some willpower, too, but this time, I'd let the magic control me.

"Forgive me," I said and quickly laid the bracelet back into the cupholder. "I shouldn't be messing with your things like that. My apologies."

Her gaze was a mixture of anger and surprise. What had she seen just now? Had I been that careless? Letting her catch a glimpse of my magic when it fired on her bracelet?

"Next time ask," she said in a calmer tone and backed the SUV out of the parking spot.

She cast a strange look at me, put the SUV in gear, and pulled onto the coastal motorway—heading back north. Back toward Lincoln City and my letted bungalow.

Next time? Implying that I'd be seeing her again before she charged me with murder? Professionally or personally, I wondered.

"So, you were born in the U.S.?" she asked, her gaze on the road.

"Yes," I lied. "Despite the accent. But I grew up in England and still have a flat in London. And dual citizenship. Didn't return here until I was eighteen."

Same story I'd told for centuries. But my British accent was ingrained. And the centuries had only sharpened it. I couldn't explain it away, so I had to have a story—and credentials—that supported it. And Keller was a cop. She'd tear apart anything that wasn't professionally...developed. I knew absolutely nothing about who I was. For centuries, all I had were hazy memories of a mass grave, London's dark streets, and a ship. Until last night when parts of that evening returned to me with startling clarity.

For the very first time.

Now, I wanted to know why. Why after centuries had some of those memories returned? Did that mean I'd start reclaiming more of my memories? My past? Who I was?

I'd researched witchcraft executions, scouring lists of names and actual records. But I hadn't found the watery parchment from that night in 1726, the one bearing my name. And I hadn't found the information listed in some university archives database either. Much less the execution record for that October day in 1726. I'd tried going back to that time period through objects, but they never put me on the right date. The night I died and awoke immortal in a mass grave. Now that I knew the exact date in 1726, I might have a chance to find more information.

Unless I stumbled on the descendants of those resurrectionists who were notoriously secretive and kept all manner of written records. I'd been looking for their hidden caches of documents since I arrived in America.

"You have family in Oregon?" the detective asked as rain buffeted the SUV, the coast so dramatic and stark with its steep rocky cliffs and wild surf, softened by mist and a blanket of evergreens.

Reminded me a bit of south Cornwall.

"No family," I replied.

She glanced at the console between us and then slid her hand into her motorbike jacket pocket. Right then left.

"What about back in New York?"

So, the main part of the interrogation was happening now rather than the back at the police post. Just as well. I didn't have much to hide. Only the bits that might set the detective's brain on fire.

Like being immortal. And having a strange magical gift.

Then I realized she hadn't turned up much on me in those databases, so she was trying to gather information about my family from me. I smiled. Her person of interest was too big of a mystery.

"Sorry, detective," I said as she rounded a curve and stopped at a traffic light. "No family there either. It's just me, I'm afraid."

Unfortunately, I didn't have a clue whether that was true or not. I'm sure there was a polygraph in my future when they got annoyed at my lack of database records. Or a match or two on those online DNA services, but I didn't trust those either.

The sky looked stormy. I didn't know much about the Pacific

Northwest coast, but it looked like a storm was coming. More than one since Andy Keane decided to jump bail and then got himself killed in my front garden.

I'd tried to help him and his family. Sod it all! Who wanted to kill a scared little burglar that had never hurt anyone? I sighed. The bail bondsman that lost all that bail money when Andy Keane buggered off from New Jersey? The one that set me up?

Who else could it be?

"Looks like a storm's coming," I said, pointing toward the western horizon.

"That's what the weather report says. High surf and strong winds. Any family in Great Britain, Mr. Mallory?" she asked, glancing over at me as the light changed.

She eased the SUV forward, following a line of traffic headed north. Probably caravanners going back toward Portland or Salem.

This time, she slid her hand into her front pants pockets. Left then right.

I looked away from her. "I wouldn't know."

"What does that mean?" she asked.

I didn't even have a last name. How would I know?

"What's the matter, detective? Didn't find enough personal contacts to interrogate on my mobile?"

It had been unlocked. They had access to everything. And plenty of time to sort through everything while I was stuck here in Newport.

"What mobile—er, phone?" she asked, glancing over at me again.

"Don't insult my intelligence," I snapped. "Your police force woke me out of a sound sleep at four thirty this morning. I didn't have a chance to even take a piss much less lock my mobile. Then you hauled my arse a half hour away to interrogate me while Smitty and his mates took a baton to my letted bungalow. Bolloxed it and took a bloody microscope to everything I had."

She didn't miss a beat. "That's standard procedure for any police department, Mr. Mallory. Especially at a murder scene. As a bounty hunter, even you must know that."

I shook my head. Shooting that kid had turned whatever was left of her heart to stone. She had zero compassion left for anyone. Including herself.

"I also know that you're playing good cop right now," I added, my gaze narrowing.

The SUV rounded a curve into Lincoln City, slipping past a furniture store and the North by Northwest Bookstore. Had it already been forty minutes?

"And after you assure me that you cops are running every lead and every angle, I'll wake up to a squad car early tomorrow morning. Taking me in for a polygraph. Because we both know a holiday weekend at the coast is coming up fast and this murder's bad for business. It's got to be solved fast. And with no other leads, your department's under serious pressure. You're going to crucify me."

She didn't even flinch. "American Thanksgiving," she said matter-of-factly.

"Well, thanks for giving me a royal railroading."

She pulled into the bungalow driveway and shut off the SUV motor. She glanced down at her feet. She'd misplaced something.

The sky had turned soot-grey, making it look more like night than day. She whirled around in the seat, her powder blue eyes penetrating.

"Look, Mr. Mallory," she said, her tone sharp. "We both know that you had means, motive, and opportunity to kill Andy Keane."

I glared at her, shaking my head as wind buffeted the motorway and lightning cracked open the dark clouds above it.

"What's the motive, detective?"

She smiled like she was glad I had asked that question and then glanced over the console to my feet.

"You found Andy Keane yesterday and dragged him out to this isolated bungalow," she began, unblinking as she described the scene. Like a news article. She had seen my email on Andy's mobile. "But he informs you that bounty hunting is illegal in Oregon. He threatens to call the cops and you kill him before he can turn you in."

I couldn't help rolling my eyes. Apparently, she hadn't read all my emails to Andy.

"First, detective," I began. "I hadn't even had a chance to skip trace Andy, so I had no idea where he was staying yet. Besides, my flight had been delayed six hours yesterday, so I didn't even get to the coast until 3:30 this morning. You can check my car hire agreement and the car's mileage."

Okay, that was a lie.

I met Andy Keane yesterday at the Portland airport where he agreed to come here to my bungalow. To hide because someone besides me was after him. He said he'd tell me more then, but not until he was safe. And I'd offered to protect him.

But that never happened. I had no idea why Andy was so scared or why someone was after him beyond that jumping bail bit.

Her expression didn't change as her hands tightened on the steering wheel, the wind rocking the SUV from side to side.

"Takes only a moment to pull a trigger, Mr. Mallory. By the way, have you seen my phone?"

Detective Keller had been an army sniper, so she knew how long it took to kill someone.

"No, I haven't. And second," I continued, glancing at her unfazed expression. "I hate guns and refuse to own or carry one. And three, Andy Keane had a wife and two small lads. He jumped bail on a B and E charge because it was his third offense. He isn't dangerous. He's scared. Scared for his family because someone besides me was after him."

I watched for a shift in her emotions, but if she'd had a change of heart, she didn't show it.

Thunder rumbled again as the daylight darkened.

"I've met my share of bounty hunters, Mr. Mallory," she said, turning to stare at me. "Never met one with a heart. Just a wallet that needed filling."

She handed me the evidence envelope again.

So condescending. So sure she had the right suspect.

"Like cops, right?" I asked with a smirk. "I mean we're all criminal scum that should be behind bars. The public, I mean. Why even bother reading us our rights? Why not just put us all down like the rabid gits we are?"

I took my wallet out of the envelope and shoved it in the back pocket of my joggers.

"And my twenty quid better be in here."

The detective looked annoyed now, crossing her arms.

"We'll be in touch, Mr. Mallory," she said and unlocked the SUV doors.

And now, I was being formally dismissed.

"I can't wait," I said with a growl and threw open the door, climbing out of the CR-V.

I turned toward the bungalow's front door and hurried down the short, winding sidewalk toward the entrance.

To the left, a Japanese Maple flamed red with butterfly-like frilly leaves, and across from it, on the right, an overgrown rhododendron covered half the walkway. It touched the roof, casting a rich, deep shadow across the entryway as I moved toward the front door, key out.

The flash was like lightning. The gunshot like a thunderclap.

In the gloomy twilight of an approaching storm, a bullet hit me square in the chest.

The detective swung open the door to her CR-V, using it as a shield as she extended a Glock around it, pointing it toward the bungalow.

"Oregon State Police! Drop your weapon and step out slowly. Keep your hands up where I can see them. Now!"

Thunder rumbled. Lightning crackled.

Cold wind scraped across the beach and the bungalow as I fell to my knees on the driveway, my heart racing. Blood trickled down my bare chest and dripped onto the asphalt.

No one stepped out from the shadowy abyss surrounding the bungalow's front door.

A shower of sparks lit the darkening sky along the motorway and like a rolling wave, lights went out along both sides of the street. Bathing the coast in growing darkness.

"This is Detective Keller, Priority E. Repeat, Priority E," Keller said into her handheld radio. "Requesting backup at the Jameson bungalow in Nelscott, highway one oh one."

The crackle of dead air was profound.

Lightning had hit a transformer, knocking out power. Probably knocked out the transmission tower for Keller's radio, too.

"I said come out!" she shouted toward the bungalow. "Hands where I can see them. Now!"

Bushes rustled.

"Mallory, are you all right?" the detective called out to me in a steady voice.

"I'll live," I muttered.

Gripping the Glock in her right fist, Keller darted to the side of the house and pressed her body flat against it as wind moaned, blowing over the landscape with hurricane force as she edged around the bungalow toward the front door. She was off to my left, inching toward the Japanese Maple.

She seemed to know there would be no backup coming either.

I struggled to get my feet under me, my chest on fire. Bugger. Today's bullets hurt like hell. I had to be ready to spring at the shooter, so Keller wouldn't get herself killed trying to protect me.

She'd go bonkers if she knew I was immortal.

Detective Keller moved closer. Soon, she'd be at the entryway, facing...I had no clue who had shot me. And I needed to know what this person was thinking right now.

The bullet!

I reached my hand to my chest and summoned my magic toward the wound. The shooter had touched the bullet. Maybe I could draw out some small thing about him or her?

Enough to keep Detective Keller from getting herself killed.

Red sparks churned at my fingertips as I pressed my right hand against the wound that still bled profusely. And searched for a thread from the past, one I could follow long enough to find out who shot me.

But I wasn't prepared for the chilling time loop that wound toward a young bloke about twenty-five, once a local high school football star. Dylan Akers. Died in a car crash three months ago.

I groaned. His corpse was stolen out of a remote cemetery about a week ago.

Bollocks! That meant there was a bloody necromancer at work out here. Supported by corpse stealers. I sighed. Modern-day resurrectionists. I'm not sure which one I hated more: necromancers or body snatchers. But it looked like I'd be dealing with both now.

And a reanimated corpse.

Headshot or decapitation was the only way to kill it. Or burn it up with fire.

Still, the big question remained: how did necromancers and body snatchers connect to Andy Keane? And his killer? And the big money question...why was a coffin dodger sent to kill him? Or me for that matter? With a bloody gun.

"Detective," I said in a quiet, careful voice. "Do you ever watch The Walking Dead?"

"You're asking me about my streaming habits right now? With an active shooter on the premises? And you with a bullet in your chest?"

"Active is rather subjective at the moment, detective," I said as the rhododendron rustled, branches of the Japanese Maple swaying in the hurricane-force winds. "A better word for it is reanimated."

"Cartoons?"

This woman was infuriating.

"Do you believe in evil, Detective Keller?" I asked.

"Of course, I do. I'm a cop, aren't I?"

She had a point there.

"What are you getting at, Mallory?"

"What if I told you there were much darker things than murderers and rapists?"

"Politicians?"

"Darker," I said with a hiss. "Like horror-movie dark."

"Jokes, Mallory? Do I really need to remind you there's—"

I groaned. "An active shooter. Yes, I'm aware. I've got the bloody slug in my chest to remind me. Would you listen? The thing in those bushes isn't a criminal. It's a reanimated corpse. And if you use standard cop protocol, you'll be torn to bits. It wants you to pursue it, detective. It hasn't eaten in months and it's quite hungry."

Her laughter made me bonkers.

"You're hilarious, Mallory," she said. "Last chance, dirt ball! Toss the gun on the sidewalk and come out with your hands over your head. Now!"

Did I have to do everything?

I struggled up from my knees as Detective Keller slid 'round the corner of the bungalow. Glock pointed toward the Japanese Maple, its branches shaking in the high winds.

Across the walkway, the rhododendron bush shuddered.

I stumbled back to the driveway, to the little white Fiat parked there. My hired auto. With half my stuff still in the backseat. I lifted the handle on the back door and reached behind the driver's seat, grabbing a bundle of black cloth in my right hand.

And then turned toward the walkway. I'd have to draw it back to me before Detective Keller got chewed up by that coffin dodger. It had come here after me, so I'd give it a shot at the title.

Every step toward the front door was an experiment in pain, the bullet lodged beneath my collarbone radiating agony. My skin was beyond gooseflesh and I could barely speak I felt so frozen, my bare feet like blocks of ice as I approached the rhododendron bush. Detective Keller didn't even realize that was where the undead crouched, ready to feed.

On her.

I had to hurry. She'd already reached the Japanese Maple.

"Dylan, if you're still in there somewhere, listen to me," I said, moving toward the shuddering bush with waxy green leaves and shriveled brown blossoms that had been lavender only a month ago. "Some wanker nicked your corpse. They're using it to do evil shite. Fight back and confuse it. I have to kill it in order to release you."

"Mallory, stand down," the detective shouted, throwing an angry glance my way. "Now!"

I was between her and the rhododendron bush now.

"Dylan, hear me," I said. "Help me release you. Take back your body, so I can recorpse it."

Detective Keller frowned. "Recorpse it?"

"Yes, detective," I snarled, getting tired of being interrupted. "The act of turning a reanimated corpse into an unanimated corpse. Noun. Verb. Source, Blade Mallory's dictionary of magical creatures he's fought. Second edition. Audiobook pending. Ebook available at your favorite online bookseller."

The undead corpse of Dylan Akers screeched and launched itself at me, grabbing me 'round the neck.

"Stop!" Detective Keller shouted. "Now! Or I'll shoot!"

"Don't shoot, detective," I said with a sigh, trying to break the decaying monster's hold on me. "You'll just annoy it."

It stunk of mold and decay, its wild neon green eyes burning in the storm's darkness, its sharp, pointed teeth gnashing together as it tried to take a big bite out of my shoulder.

For a brief moment, it halted, freezing in place.

I grinned, rolling free of its stinking grasp. Dylan was still in there, fighting against it.

I threw down the black cloth, freeing my machete.

Snapping it up over my head, I swung it hard at the coffin dodger's neck. Severing its head from its decaying shoulders. The head bounced and rolled against the front wheel of Detective Keller's CR-V. The body collapsed like someone had cut its puppet strings.

Still gripping the machete, I dropped to my knees, feeling fresh hot blood leak across my bare chest. Detective Keller was beside me now, staring at the remains of Dylan Akers.

"You killed it," she said, sounding surprised.

"I only told you half the story back at the police station, detective," I said with a sigh, huffing for breath. "My bounties aren't always alive in the traditional sense. Or human."

Her blue gaze softened when she saw the blood running down my chest. But that soft look turned quizzical. I'd taken the bullet to my left side. Right where the heart resided. For a mortal, it was a killing blow.

"Power's out until the storm passes," said the detective, taking hold of my arm and gently pulling me to my feet. "Radio's out. Let's get you to a hospital. Get this wound treated before it kills you."

She slid her arm 'round my waist and I wanted to melt into her warmth. Or maybe that leather jacket. Too bad it wouldn't fit me.

Each step toward the SUV ached through my chest.

"Wouldn't that tie up your case with a giant red bow, detective?"

"It would," she said, her arm around my waist tightening as I began to sink. "But I want the truth, not another collar."

Her statement brought a smile to my lips as she took the key from my bloodied, shaking left hand. And gently took the machete from my right hand. I'd been white-knuckling it since I pulled it out of the hired auto.

"Don't think you'll need that at the hospital," she said with a smile. "Blade. That's how Andy Keane had you listed in his phone contacts, by the way. Seems awfully strange for a bail jumper to have his bounty hunter's contact information entered into his contacts. Wouldn't you say?"

Because I hadn't been hunting Andy Keane. I'd been trying to help him ever since we spoke. And according to Andy, Brian Beckerman wasn't a typical bail bondsman. He dealt with supernatural and mundane clients. I wasn't sure what had been pursuing Andy Keane, but it wasn't human. And Andy had been terrified. I offered him a place to sleep last night and he accepted. But when he didn't show, I went out to hunt for him, getting to my bungalow 'round 3:30 A.M. I never dreamed I'd wake up and find Andy dead on my doorstep.

Okay, I lied to the cops.

My flight was delayed six hours and I didn't get to the bungalow until 3:30 A.M. Because I was out searching for Andy once my flight landed. After we met, he stopped responding to my texts and ignored my calls.

I gave him my contact information at the airport, telling him I'd meet him at a pub in downtown Portland. He never showed and he stopped responding to my texts—even the one with directions to my bungalow. That's why he had my contact information and an email open on his mobile. He was probably texting me to open the bloody bungalow door when those undead monsters got him.

I'd failed Andy. But I wouldn't fail his family. I'd make sure his wife and two lads survived this ordeal. I'd make sure they were taken care of—something Andy couldn't do now.

"My contact information...very strange," I said as the detective unlocked the SUV with her key fob.

The growl came from behind Detective Keller's CR-V.

A raspy, sandpapery snarl that could only be made by something mummy-level dehydrated and missing a working set of vocal cords.

Another bloody coffin dodger.

But a second voice joined it in tandem. Looked like more corpses had been stolen from nearby cemeteries to shut me up permanently. Sent by whoever killed Andy Keane. Not realizing I was immortal.

But Detective Keller wasn't.

We needed to get inside the bungalow and barricade the doors. Wait for morning. With this storm, it was almost like night. The sun always slowed them down. Increased the decay rate. Made them easier to kill.

But they moved faster at night.

Detective Keller looked more than a little gobsmacked as I slid my machete out of her hand.

"Let's get inside," I said in a quiet voice, motioning her toward the bungalow door. "No telling how many more are out here."

The detective nodded and took hold of my right arm, backing

toward the bungalow as the wind buffeted the structure. With her back to the door, Keller reached over to the doorknob with the key still in her hand and unlocked it. She helped me inside as three coffin dodgers rushed toward the door. She slammed it shut.

An undead herd. Bugger. It was going to be a long day.

3

"What are those things?" Detective Keller demanded as the bloody coffin dodgers pounded against the front door.

She backed away from the heavy, shuddering wooden door, her gaze transfixed on it. She couldn't look away.

"Bollocks," I muttered, gripping the machete. "More undead."

I didn't want to wait for those things to splinter the bungalow's front door.

"My mobile's on the chest of drawers in the first bedroom," I said. "Since yours is missing, have a go at mine. Get a bit of backup while I brace the door."

Nodding, she turned toward the bedroom doorway.

As soon as she was out of sight, I swung open the front door and slammed it behind me.

Two undead rushed down the sidewalk at me, wind whipping all around us. They moved fast for being dead.

I swung the machete in a quick, wide arc, catching one of them in the shoulder. Knocking it into the Japanese Maple.

The other one slammed me against the wall and then tossed me into the rhododendron bush. The machete bounced out of my hand.

With shriveled, leathery grey flesh and wisps of wiry white hair, it looked fresh from the grave as it came at me again.

I scrambled underneath the waxy rhododendron leaves, crawling toward the machete that glinted in the mulch. The wind was wild and I struggled against its force to grab hold of the handle.

My fingers had just closed around the grip when razor sharp teeth punctured my calf.

Sod it all!

I screamed and kicked the undead hard, caving in its face. Its skin and bones crumbled around my foot, leaving a gaping hole where its sinus cavities used to be.

Lurching forward, I dived for the machete again and snatched it out of the mulch as the relentless undead thing came at me again. I rolled onto my back as it lunged at me.

With both hands, I swung that machete with everything I had and decapitated the hissing monster. A clean cut that scattered corpse dust, bone fragments, and teeth like confetti along the walkway.

Its head rolled under the rhododendron, its body collapsing into powder. The older the corpse, the faster undead faded to dust. This one was instant. That meant this necromancer didn't have a lot of choices for fresh corpses. Took what was available, apparently. Must have been in quite the hurry to kill me.

The wanker.

The other undead grabbed me by the ankles and dragged me out from beneath the rhododendron. These bodies may not have been fresh, but they had a ton of strength, meaning this wasn't a common, everyday necromancer. This one was powerful.

And that worried me. A lot.

The other coffin dodger was an emaciated old woman with long, stringy white curls, paper-thin grey skin, dead eyes, and a big hunger. She lunged toward my arm, trying to feed on my flesh, but I blocked her bite with my machete blade.

"Sorry, buffet's closed," I said with a snarl and kicked her in the teeth, scattering a handful of them like nicotine-tinted pearls across the sidewalk. "But I do have an iron supplement for you. Or rather steel."

I swung the machete as hard as I could propel it.

The blade severed her head from her shoulders. The body hit the sidewalk with a dull thump. The head rolled underneath the Japanese Maple. Another heartbeat later, she turned to dust and the wind carried her away.

My blood was all over the sidewalk now, the bullet lodged high in my chest, wound still bleeding. But I was immortal. It would heal.

At that moment, the sky opened up and torrential rain pounded the sidewalk. Drenching me in cold November rain.

"Mallory!"

Hands grabbed hold of my shoulders, but I slid out of the detective's grip when I dropped to my hands and knees, lightheaded, and struggling to stand.

She wrapped her arms around my waist and dragged me back toward the door. Those long, shapely legs kicked the door open and hauled me back into the bungalow. Still holding me upright against the wall, she slammed the door, locking it.

"Are you crazy?" she shouted, turning back to me, anger blue flames in her big, piercing eyes.

"The mobile work?" I asked, panting as I slid down the wall and collapsed against the rain-slicked hardwood floor.

Her eyes narrowed, mouth pressing into an angry line. She propped her hands on her hips, that long, sable hair drenched and clinging to her face, braid dripping, black T-shirt soaked. Her leather jacket creaked. She smelled like sea spray and jasmine.

"You knew that phone would work," she said with a glare. "You were deliberately keeping me out of that fight. Why?"

"Didn't figure you'd had experience fighting undead, detective. Didn't think they taught cops how to fight undead at the police academy."

"Those things could have killed you while I was calling for backup!"

I smiled. Was that concern I detected?

"Would have closed your case nice and tight, though, wouldn't it? Cleaned up this mess and gotten the Oregon governor off your back, too. Just in time for holiday."

Those blue eyes turned fierce. "As much as the idea of burying your corpse pleases me right now, Mr. Mallory, I want justice for Andy Keane. Not a closed case just in time for Thanksgiving weekend on the coast."

So, the detective had more integrity than I'd given her credit for... that meant she wouldn't trump up evidence against me and do her best to lock me up for eternity. And she was handling her first undead case like a bloody professional. All wrapped up in an incredibly hot package of sable hair, long legs, lithe body, and grit that I hadn't encountered in a long time. I admired that.

"I didn't want you getting hurt," I admitted as I struggled to my feet, my blond hair dripping wet and plastered against my face. "That Glock of yours is useless against the undead. I was just trying to—"

"Protect me?" she said with a growl. "Because I'm a woman?"

"Because you didn't have a machete," I replied. "And sniper fire won't work on undead."

Her face turned pale and I groaned. Hadn't meant to say that. I wasn't trying to insult her. Only show her that she needed training to fight the undead. She needed me.

"Sniper fire? How did you know about that?"

I stared at her a moment, my mouth bobbing open like a halfwit. "You must have mentioned it."

She shook her head. "I never mentioned I was an army sniper. Ever. I don't talk about that with anyone. Ever. Especially a person of interest that I've known for only hours."

Well, that was incredibly thick. I couldn't explain to her how I knew that. Without revealing my magic and alienating her forever. If she didn't have me committed first.

She got quiet, squinting at me.

"Forgive me," I said finally, bowing my head. "I must have misheard that information at the police post."

But the room began to rise.

I didn't realize that I was sliding down the wall again until I hit the floor face first. Hard.

For a moment, everything went white and all sound went away.

"Mallory!"

Her voice cut through the nothingness and I was back again. Still face-planting on the maple hardwood floor.

She was beside me now, kneeling, her arm around my waist, helping me up from the floor.

"I've got backup and an ambulance on the way."

"Ambulance?" I said in a dark tone. "I'll be fine in a day or two."

"We'll just see what the paramedics say about that bullet wound. Won't we?"

Was that a bloody challenge? I knew what they'd say. They'd say I was dying and try to shove me into some hospital that cost more than a brand-new Aston Martin.

Using the torch on my mobile, she helped me into the bedroom and sat me down on the bed, the covers still akimbo from when I crawled out of them at four thirty this morning. She hurried into the washroom and grabbed a small blue flannel. She folded it twice and pressed it to the bullet wound on the left side of my chest.

"All I could find was a wash cloth," she said in a softer but still commanding voice. "Now, you need to stay still until the paramedics get here, or you're going to bleed worse. Can't believe you're even upright after taking a 9-millimeter slug to the chest. Much less fighting undead in the middle of hurricane-force winds." She sighed, shaking her head. "Can't believe I just said that. I don't know if you're batshit crazy or crazy fearless."

"A little of both, I'm afraid," I said as I slumped against the wall at the head of the bed. "Lucky for me, that bullet missed my heart."

"How do you know?" she asked, glancing from the wound to my

face, her eyes getting bigger as she realized exactly where the entry wound was in relation to my heart.

Right in front of it.

"Because obviously, I'd be dead right now," I replied, trying to play it off.

But this time, her gaze was locked onto my face. Staring like she'd just seen a meteor shoot across the sky. Why would she look at me like that?

"Your eyes," she said in a quiet voice, gazing into them like they were a bottomless lake. "You any relation to Elizabeth Taylor?"

I frowned. "Don't think so. Why?"

"Because," she said, the hint of a smile on her lips. "She had violet eyes, but not so light or vibrant like yours. Amazing. I've never seen eyes like yours before. Are those contacts?"

I shook my head. No, they were a sign that some sort of wild magic apparently inhabited my body. One I couldn't control and didn't understand. Something well beyond my temporal magic. Something that might have made me immortal.

Her hand was gentle against my bare chest this time, keeping firm pressure on the wound, but I felt her fingers trail across my skin and leanly defined muscles. At six foot two, I was a bit wiry. Had trouble putting on weight, but I'd done my best to keep in shape these last three hundred years or so.

She reached down and slid the quilt across my body. I was shaking from the rain and cold, still barefoot and wearing only joggers, but some of it came from her touch against my bare skin.

I swallowed a breath, closing my eyes a moment, her touch sizzling across my skin, something I hadn't felt in a very long time. Connection. Attraction. Two things I'd avoided after my Elizabeth died so very long ago.

One of the resurrectionists had called my eyes witch eyes. I'd never met anyone else with the same color eyes. The hue was connected to this strange magic I possessed. And couldn't control. I had no idea if I was related to Elizabeth Taylor or not (or anyone, for that matter), but one thing I knew for certain. I wanted to get to know Detective Harlowe Keller better. Much better.

"Why'd you do that?" I asked in a soft, sleepy voice, feeling dizzy. She looked confused.

"The quilt."

"Can't have you going into shock, Mr. Mallory," she said in a quiet voice. "Besides, you've got to be freezing after that soaking rain."

"Please," I said, brushing my fingers across her hand. "Call me Greysen." I smirked. "Or Blade."

She was smiling at me like I talked too much. Because I did. Nearly everyone said so. I shook my head.

"Oh, bollocks, call me whatever you like, just...call me. It's not like you don't have my number. Ring me when you find your phone."

The smile faded from her face, replaced by a troubled look.

Bugger. I'd taken it too far. Too soon.

I wasn't usually this forward—or interested—but Detective Keller had ignited something in me that I thought had died when Elizabeth passed away. Normally, the concept of grafting (flirting for you Yanks) eluded me. But it seemed to come naturally when I was in Detective Keller's presence.

Keller didn't have to say a word though because I knew exactly what she was thinking. It was written all over her face.

Huge conflict of interest. And I wouldn't jeopardize her investigation.

Besides that, I was a sodding tourist in her eyes. On holiday. In two weeks at most, I'd be gone—back in New York.

Bugger. I hadn't had anything but a rare shag or two for more than a century. It hurt too much to watch someone I loved grow old and die. Immortal or not, that pain didn't heal. I'd just learned to live with it. But I was so incredibly attracted to this fit but standoffish cop that kept her distance. She was smart, tidy (that's hot for you Yanks) and fearless. And she didn't put up with my shite.

Despite what she projected, she felt this strange spark between us. Just like I did. I know she did.

Any woman who didn't bat an eye the first time she saw undead and instead of running, drew her Glock, was a woman I wanted to get to know better.

A loud knock thumped against the front door as the wind moaned around the bungalow, the glow of red and blue lights pulsing against the darkness.

Ambulance was here.

Detective Keller hurried out of the bedroom to the front door.

She opened the door and soon, the sound of several pairs of trainers traipsed down the hall toward the bedroom.

I'd refuse the ride no matter what the detective said. It had been a long day and I wouldn't spend the evening in hospital, trying to explain how I'm still alive after a 9-millimeter slug went through my heart and lodged under my collarbone.

At least the coffin dodgers had turned to dust and blown away, their heads underneath the rhododendron, so I didn't have to explain why the heads of three corpses were decorating the front garden.

Two paramedics dressed in dark blue Macintoshes, light blue shirts, and dark trousers entered, carrying what looked like a large grey tackle box.

"Sir, I'm just going to evaluate your condition, all right?" said a young bloke with shaggy ginger hair and a kind smile.

"If you must," I replied and pulled off the quilt.

His brown eyes got huge when he saw the gunshot wound. Right over my heart.

A short, stocky brunette stood beside him and opened the tackle box, looking like a doe caught in headlamps.

The bloke kept glancing at my face and then back to the wound. Did he expect me to just keel over or maybe he wondered how I was sitting upright at all?

I did my best to play it off, so the detective wouldn't get suspicious. She'd already found out that undead were real and that I wasn't a typical bounty hunter. If she saw me use my magic, her head might explode.

Or maybe she had already seen it when I picked up her bracelet? That possibility still nagged at me.

In a moment, two uniformed cops trudged into the bedroom and spoke to Detective Keller in low voices while the paramedics tried to figure out how to bandage a bullet wound through the heart.

"Sir, we're applying a pressure bandage to staunch the bleeding and then we'll be on route to the hospital," said the young chap as the brunette brought in a transport board.

I waved them off.

"I appreciate the concern," I said. "But obviously, this isn't as bad as it seems or I'd have already bled out and the coroner would be handling this instead of paramedics."

The young bloke sighed. "Can't argue with that, sir, but I really think you need to be in the hospital. There's no exit wound, so the bullet's still in there."

"How about you bandage it up tight for tonight? And I'll head 'round to hospital tomorrow."

"You shouldn't wait," said the brunette. "That bullet needs to come out right away. If you get septic—"

They had a point about the bullet needing to come out. It did need to come out, but I wouldn't go to hospital for it. There were immortal communities all over the country. Yes, there were a lot of us. No one knows why exactly—beyond the usual assortment of vampires, werewolves, gods, goddesses, the typical lot of magical beings, and the undead. I was an enigma even among immortals, according to my best friend, Cash—a vampire. Because I was none of those things. And like the rest of the States, the Oregon Coast was no different. I'd find an immortal to patch me up, one that wouldn't ask a million questions or make a big deal about a bullet passing through my heart.

Besides, I had questions about a very powerful necromancer that had reanimated three corpses to come and kill me. And how that connected to the murder of a New Jersey bail jumper running from something much worse than his third breaking and entering charge.

The paramedics were very uncomfortable with my decision, but they bandaged the wound across my chest and back, looping it over my left shoulder until it was trussed up, and urged me to get to hospital right away to have that bullet removed. I assured them I would and they quickly faded into the storm and the darkness of the coastal power outage.

Only when the two cops left the bedroom did Detective Keller move back to me. She studied me for a moment, a worried expression deepening across her face. She had her phone in her hand. Those rozzers must have brought it to her.

"What's the matter?" I asked.

Was she going to lecture me about not going to hospital, too? Or was her worry about something else?

"Got three reports tonight of graveyard defacing in and around Newport," she said, looking a little disturbed. "Three graves were dug up at three local cemeteries. Corpses stolen."

I did my best not to look smug as I gave her a knowing look.

"Detective, you realize that you're not just dealing with grave robbers," I said and took a deep breath that hurt from my collarbone to my navel.

She looked unsettled.

"Ask yourself what was taken," I said. "It wasn't flowers or tombstones, detective. Bodies were stolen. And not for buried valuables. For the bodies. Because there is a very powerful necromancer behind these thefts. We've already seen his or her handiwork."

I rubbed my leg where one of the bastards had bitten me. At least they were undead and not bloody zombies. Then we'd have a whole different set of problems.

"There could be a million reasons for stealing corpses," said Detective Keller, slapping her hand against her side. "Why do you have to immediately jump to the supernatural?"

I sighed. "Because I decapitated three undead in my front garden tonight, detective."

I knew what it meant to be dead and awaken again. I felt a little like these reanimated corpses, except I awoke immortal and they awoke because of a spell. That would eventually wear off and render them into dust. And the undead weren't the same people that had died. They were dark spirits called forth by a necromancer and sent to inhabit a dead body in order to do that necromancer's bidding.

"And because it isn't a coincidence that three undead show up to try and kill me and three bodies are stolen from nearby cemeteries. So, forgive me for proposing the undead angle, detective. But the maths add up."

She sighed and sank down beside me on the bed.

"I know it's been a really long day for you," she said. "And you've been shot in the chest. But right now, you're the only person I know with any clue about this undead supernatural stuff. Would you mind...riding along to the cemeteries? You might catch something we would miss."

"Me?" I replied, laying my hand against my chest, holding in a grin. "Your person of interest in Andy Keane's murder?"

She gave me a sideways look and rolled her eyes. "It's not like you wouldn't be with a trained officer the whole time. And under surveillance."

Bugger. She had a point there.

"You're not going to cuff me, are you?" I asked, giving her a warning look.

"Not unless you give me a reason to cuff you," she said in a flat tone.

Well, then. Challenge accepted.

"Could I at least get dressed first?"

She chuckled and rose from the bed. "I'll be waiting at the door."

I sighed and rose from the bed, moving toward my luggage. Here we go again.

4

Worst holiday season ever at the coast! Especially for a police detective.

I shifted my braid off my shoulder, hand against my Glock, and leaned against the wall beside the front door of the Jameson bungalow, waiting for the most mysterious, frustrating—and definitely the hottest—man I'd ever met. Waiting for him to get dressed to investigate three body snatchings from local cemeteries.

Here! On the Oregon Coast. With power out all along the shoreline and a storm blowing ashore.

It was bad. Bargain bin movie bad and I was starring in it. Alongside the biggest smart-ass I'd ever encountered. Smokin' hot though. With the most amazing British accent I'd ever heard. And he smelled...divine. Not like those guys whose aftershave arrived a minute before they did—and overstayed its welcome. Or like someone had dropped a can of Axe in the drugstore aisle. Four days ago. No, his scent was subtle and...sexy as hell. I first noticed it at the police post and then in the car. An earthy, woody scent with a touch of...something I couldn't put my finger on—soft and warm. Sort of like smoky vanilla and oak. Very heady.

I sighed. And very distracting—like Greysen Mallory.

But right now, I had no idea if he killed Andy Keane or not. And that ate at me.

Just my luck that the hottest guy I'd met since I left the army was my primary murder suspect. At the very least, person of interest.

This was officially the worst Friday night on the job ever. And it would be nightfall by 4:30 P.M. A night in a dark graveyard investigating stolen corpses with a gorgeous murder suspect carrying a machete who smelled like Heaven. Perfect!

To say that he bothered me was an understatement.

More like unsettled. There was something so strange and otherworldly about him. Especially the way he handled my bracelet on the drive back to the bungalow. And suddenly knew all about my past.

I winced, the heels of my black pumps scraping against the wet maple hardwood. No one on the police force here in Oregon knew I'd been a special forces sniper. I'd quit the day my target put a kid between his cowardly ass and my rifle. So, no one here on the coast knew that.

The little boy lived, thank God, but it rattled me to my core. After that, I couldn't pursue targets, always afraid another human shield would pop up in my scope. So, I walked away. No one back home in North Carolina could believe it.

Least of all, my father.

A suitcase zipper whispered in the quiet bungalow, traces of that heady cologne or aftershave hanging in the air. I closed my eyes a moment, wanting to bathe in it. Clothes rustled. Bed frame squeaked. Something thumped against the hardwood.

What was I doing here? On the Oregon Coast? At the farthest ragged edge of the world.

Harlowe Winter Keller, daughter of the multi-decorated Colonel Busby "Buzz" Keller, multi-decorated Army special forces, had walked away from the military. Left family and friends on the opposite coast. I was an only child and Dad wanted a boy, so he'd treated me like one my whole life. Taught me everything he knew. It had always suited me, too.

Until that day in Syria.

Dad and I hadn't spoken since the day I told him I'd quit the military. Four years ago last month. Guess I'd always had an expiration date as his kid. The moment I broke the spell and became his daughter instead of Busby Junior, I was dead to him.

His loss.

I wasn't going to cry over a man that had never even hugged me. Afraid it would make me soft, he'd said. No danger there. It had turned me to stone instead. I hadn't felt anything for a long time. Not even anger.

But I was good at my job, at police work. At the forensics—and thinking like the criminals I hunted. I'd always fought for justice and tried to uphold the law. It had been my uninterrupted focus for four years now. Trying to blot out that moment in Syria. Until four-thirty this morning. When bounty hunter Greysen "Blade" Mallory stepped into in my world view. And turned it all upside down and inside out.

But what a view!

I couldn't help but smile. I'd known him for almost a day, but already, he'd totally upended my world.

The six foot two, leanly muscled blond Brit was all quick-witted smart-ass, that luscious accent wrapping every word in velvet and dark chocolate. I could listen to him talk all night while I ran my fingers through those thick waves of light blond hair. While the scent of his aftershave permeated my brain.

But those eyes... I pulled in a breath.

Violet! They were actually a light violet. And they almost glowed like a flame lit them from the inside. I'd never seen anything like them in all my twenty-seven years. Completely intoxicating.

He was a person of interest all right. And not just in this murder case.

No, Greysen Mallory—or whatever his real name was—had

something to hide. A lot of somethings. Unlike Andy Keane's records which were a mess. We were still struggling to get a positive ID on his corpse. Hadn't even notified his family yet because we lacked those records. But Greysen had the most carefully crafted records I'd ever seen. They were too perfect and they bothered the hell out of me. Like he did, turning up the heat to almost flashpoint. I had to keep my distance though.

Person of interest, I reminded myself again. Not in the way I wanted him to be. Regardless, he was a temporary distraction at best and he'd be leaving by Christmas at the latest. I had to keep telling myself that.

Because I could get lost in those eyes. In a heartbeat.

But I couldn't forget what I'd seen on the drive here. A couple of times, I would have sworn that I saw red sparks at his fingertips. Almost like...magic. But that was crazy, right? There was no such thing as magic.

Yet...I couldn't quite discount what I saw here tonight—much less explain it. Undead? With a late fall storm blowing in from the Pacific?

And those undead were after Greysen Mallory. My person of interest in a murder case. My only suspect.

But he knew right away that they were reanimated corpses and he knew exactly how to take them down. Even carried the tools to do it. Who carried a machete? Was upstate New York that dangerous? Did he think Portland at Christmas required a machete? Or the I-5 North a week before Thanksgiving? Maybe. He insisted that there was some dark thing around here grabbing corpses and bringing them back to life. What'd he call it? A necromancer? Made me laugh until Smitty reported the graveyard thefts.

Mallory unzipped another suitcase in the bedroom, the sound sharp and abrupt. More clothes rustled and shifted. Was he putting on layers? Or everything he owned?

I tried not to be impatient. After all, the man had a 9-millimeter slug in his chest. I needed to go easy on him until I could convince him to go to the hospital.

And that was another thing.

That bullet's trajectory was so close to his heart that I needed a photo finish to make sure it had missed. According to Mallory, it had lodged underneath his collarbone, yet he refused the ambulance to the hospital. Why?

It wasn't just the cost.

No, the only thing I could conclude was the bullet's path was deceiving. If it had taken the obvious path, it would have gone right through his heart and killed him. Exploded his heart or he'd have bled out. Or both.

Of course, that was impossible, right? Because the man was up and walking around like he'd cut himself shaving A little unsteady, but looking fine otherwise. Very fine.

So many things just didn't add up here, but lacking evidence, I couldn't conclude anything other than Greysen Mallory would recover.

I folded my arms against my chest, leather jacket creaking, my breath fogging the air as my phone shifted in my jacket pocket. The uniforms had been nice enough to bring it to me. My black T-shirt and pants were still rain-soaked from dragging Greysen's ass back into the bungalow. Otherwise, he was going to make a career out of fighting undead. If he hadn't already.

Still, I couldn't get it out of my head. He'd said that many of his bounties involved supernatural situations. And he'd said it like it was perfectly normal. Of course, we deal with the supernatural. Was the perp a male, female, or undead, sir? A ghost? Necromancer maybe? Okay, then, where was the last place it was haunting—or raising the dead—before the crime was committed?

I couldn't wrap my brain around all of this supernatural stuff, but I'd just seen three undead right in front of me. Like they'd stepped off a movie screen.

I shivered. The bungalow was freezing. He hadn't even been in it long enough to turn on the heat before the power went out on the whole coast. But I had on a leather jacket. It would keep me warm enough until I got into my SUV. And to my seat warmers.

At last, he stepped into the hallway, wearing heavy black boots. They were either hiking boots or work boots, I couldn't tell. He had on a pair of dark jeans, knees ripped out, that hugged his lean frame like he'd stepped out of a Levi's commercial. One I wouldn't mind looping on repeat. He wore a light grey, long-sleeved thermal shirt underneath a charcoal grey T-shirt and was pulling on a dark brown leather bomber jacket softened with age and that intoxicating smoky vanilla oak scent.

God, he was sexy and he hadn't even opened his mouth yet. He looked younger than twenty-three, confirmed by his driver's license, but he acted much older. He had a quiet maturity about him that seemed to match his experience with the world—despite what his age said. And distance, something I understood well. But he also carried a huge chip on his shoulder. To mask past hurts? Relationship gone bad? Or was he just angry at the world?

His records said he was single, but did he have a girlfriend? I had to know.

I didn't know if he'd be on the coast long enough to answer those questions, but I'd enjoy trying to find those answers. I could always find a reason to detain him. Would give me more time to peel back the layers on his credentials and database records.

"Sorry, that took much longer than I'd expected," he said, brushing a long sweep of blond bangs out of those hypnotic violet eyes. "Bloody TSA must have dumped out my luggage and then had the bomb-sniffing mutt put everything back again."

I did my best not to chuckle, holding onto my detective's façade. I couldn't let him know that his demeanor was hot enough to melt steel. Or that he was as funny as he thought he was.

"You sure you're okay to travel, Mallory?" I asked, looking him up and down five or six times because the view, y'know...making sure he wasn't wobbly in those tight jeans.

Or about to pass out. I couldn't carry his Brit arse if he passed out on me. But I'd welcome a few dozen more looks at him in those Levi's. I'd make him go first.

"I'm fine," he said in a clipped tone, those violet eyes narrowing as he gazed around at the dark, cold bungalow.

It was cold in here long before the power went out.

"You planning to get a doctor to take out that bullet or are you planning to bring a case of sepsis back from Oregon when you leave?"

He seemed distracted, deep in thought. He'd barely heard a word I said.

"What?" he said, his gaze snapping to my face. "Oh, right—the bullet. No, I'll take care of it tomorrow."

I sighed. Getting a bullet removed was buried somewhere on his To Do List. He was either one of the toughest men I'd known or it didn't hurt enough to warrant high placement on his list. Which I found shocking. Either way, that worried me. Reminded me of my dad.

Never show weakness, Winter (he always called me by my middle name). *Even if you're dying. Just suck it up.*

They'd called me Ice in the special forces because of my middle name and because I never got rattled. Until that little boy got shoved into my scope sight.

And I wanted no part of another tough guy/suck it up routine.

In the wash of blue light from my phone in my jacket pocket, I handed him his phone. "Just like that? Take out the trash. Find the local necromancer. Get 9-millimeter slug removed."

He considered my list for a moment as he slid his phone in his jeans pocket.

"Let's put taking out the rubbish after finding the local necromancer."

I rolled my eyes. "Have it your way, Mallory," I said with a sigh and opened the door. "Let's go."

Tough guy routine it is. Yes, I was disappointed. I liked guys that weren't afraid to show a little vulnerability. Meant they were human and could handle a little emotion. And it meant they weren't alpha male dickheads.

The wind almost blew the door out of my hands, but I held onto it, ducking my head as the rain fell sideways, and sprinted for my SUV.

He closed the door behind him and moved slower than I'd expected toward the vehicle, hands in his pockets. I wasn't carrying his Brit arse back inside this bungalow again.

I unlocked the SUV doors and slid into the driver's seat as he opened the passenger side door. As rain pattered against the vehicle, I pretended to be focused on the dashboard, but I kept one eye on Mallory, watching him sit down gingerly and fumble with the seatbelt. I started the engine and turned on the heated seats as he leaned his elbow against the window.

"Bugger, I forgot my machete," he said in a sad voice, like it was a dear friend.

"I hope to hell you don't need it," I said. "We're going to investigate the desecrated cemeteries for clues. Not fight more undead."

"Not sure we've got a choice in that matter, detective."

Sighing, he opened the car door and trotted back toward the bungalow's front door. He was hurting. I could see it, but he was pretending he was fine. Just like my father would have. Dammit!

Greysen bent over with effort and picked up the machete from the bungalow's front stoop. He was definitely hurting more than he let on. I knew I'd better go easy on him or I wouldn't have anyone to arrest for Keane's murder.

God, that made me hurt all over.

I didn't want to arrest Greysen Mallory for jaywalking much less murder. I wanted to drink wine and eat supper with him. Sit by the shore and watch the waves roll onto the beach beside him. Get to know him.

And my gut was telling me he had nothing to do with Andy Keane's murder, but right now, he was our only suspect. And I had to treat him as such. Because of protocol...procedure...and my reputation as a tough as nails cop. Couldn't let some hot blond Brit walk in and ruin my rep. Besides, so much about Greysen Mallory just didn't add up. He was the biggest mystery I'd ever encountered and I wanted to solve it. Prove that I'd seen this man doing magic.

That was crazy enough without adding in undead and necromancers.

But right now, we had body snatchers and three corpses to find. And Mallory's necromancer. Were the missing corpses the same three we'd already fought or had there actually been six corpses snatched?

Holy hell, this was the weirdest day ever.

By the time he got back to the SUV, his blond hair was dripping. He laid the machete across his lap and refastened his seatbelt.

"Ready when you are," he said, looking straight ahead.

I put the CR-V in reverse and backed out of the driveway, onto the dark highway. I shifted into drive and headed south, dodging tree limbs and trash cans. Back through the dark toward Newport. I flicked on my police radio and got Smitty.

"Smitty, need those cemetery locations," I said.

His nasal voice crackled through the radio. "All three?"

I groaned. There were three separate locations? Couldn't this necromancer at least dig up three from the same damned place? Make my investigation easier?

"Of course," I answered, casting a glance at Mallory who was frowning. "Start with the closest one," I said, pulling over when I couldn't see the road because of a rain burst.

Mallory was unusually quiet. Well, unusually quiet for the one day that I'd known him.

"That would be...Taft Pioneer Cemetery," said Smitty. "But I'd start with South Beach. It's the smallest. And it's really a pioneer cemetery."

He was right. It was a small, old burial place. Most of those graves were over two hundred years old. Not much left. Easier to investigate.

"And the other two?" I asked and waited for Smitty's response. Radio crackled.

"I'd hit Taft on the way back. After the Toledo cemetery. Only one of the graveyards is really old and historical. And that includes Toledo."

"Ohio?" Mallory replied, raising an eyebrow. "That will be a long drive."

He was warming up again with the wit. I'd actually missed it.

"Might make things go faster," Smitty continued. "No families to contact. Just need to alert Iris at the historical association."

Iris Cline. I stiffened.

Tall, leggy blonde with perfectly bobbed hair who dressed in New York chic skirts and tight sweaters that showed off her t—taste in turtlenecks. Had men from Cannon Beach to Coos Bay salivating over the area's historical records. I groaned. One look at Iris and Greysen would be much more interested in historical records than police work. Guaranteed. I was so not giving him her name unless I absolutely had no choice.

"Thanks, Smitty. We'll start with South Beach. Keller out."

When the rain let up, I pulled back onto 101 and headed out of Lincoln City, headed south toward Newport. Another forty-minute drive.

"Why would a necromancer reanimate two pioneer-era corpses and a former high school football star's corpse? Seems not very random to me." Mallory asked, staring out the window like he was only half-listening for an answer.

"Football star?" I cried, shooting a confused glance at him. "How did you know that?"

Mallory hesitated a moment. "I spent some quality time with his corpse while it was trying to bite my legs off. He wore the remains of an old varsity letter jacket. Had a big blue T on it. With a football patch behind it." He smiled. "I got a very good look at it while he was trying to crush my skull against the sidewalk."

I didn't get a good look at the first reanimated corpse. I was too busy screaming inside because I'd seen a reanimated corpse and failed to notice what it had been wearing.

"Regardless, that's very strange," said Mallory, a hand on his chin, the other one holding onto that machete. "Makes no sense right now."

Well, we agreed on that.

"Were the corpses chosen based on opportunity?" I asked.

Frowning, he turned to stare at me. "Opportunity?"

I nodded. "Maybe those three cemeteries were directly on our necromancer's route home—or to your bungalow? So, he or she picked them because they were easily accessible. And on the way."

"That makes a lot of sense," Mallory replied.

But that dark, brooding expression returned. He wasn't telling me something. Or everything. I felt like he was only skimming the surface of what was really happening out there. Like every conversation I'd had with him so far. Granted, all of them had been interrogations, but maybe this time, with me and him on equal footing (investigating these body snatchings), he would be more open with what he knew.

He seemed disturbed by this sudden turn of events. The desecrated graves and the body snatching. Like it was something personal. That he didn't want to talk about. I'd give it a shot, try to get him to talk about it, and see what happened.

"Greysen," I began, struggling to find the right words. I was a cop not a therapist. "You seem bothered by all this."

Talking to people wasn't my strong suit. Interrogating them? Talking at them? I had that down to an art form, but empathy was hard for me.

He scoffed. "Bothered by the undead? Detective, more than half my bounty cases have involved the supernatural. Like coffin dodgers and necromancers. Bail jumpers are a nice change from these wankers, I assure you."

Played that right off. He was an expert at steering people away from things he didn't want to draw attention to—or handle. Like the body snatching. He hadn't acted affected until the body snatching cases came up.

No tensing or flexing or nervous ticks. No shifting position, but lots of trying to change the subject.

"No, I don't mean the supernatural stuff," I said, casting a quick glance at him to gauge his agitation. "I mean the body snatching. Three bodies were dug up tonight and stolen from three different cemeteries."

Greysen visibly shuddered and focused his attention on the machete in his lap. His fingers beat out a tense rhythm against the door's armrest.

It was the body snatching that had unsettled him. And I wanted to know why. When he didn't seem fazed by necromancers and undead. It made no sense.

"Necromancers deal in corpses," he said, matter-of-factly, staring straight ahead now, still acting unaffected. "So, it's no surprise that three of them were taken from local cemeteries after three undead showed up at my bungalow trying to kill me. It's mere maths after all."

"That may be true," I said, pushing back at his unconcerned tone. "But that's not what's bothering you. It's the body snatching that's unnerving you and I want to know why."

His face pinched into a grimace and he pulled in a deep breath. He was breathing faster than he had been. Suggesting a fear response. Maybe it wasn't so much the body snatching as the burials and the graves?

"Oh, so you aren't bothered by the fact that some knobber's out there digging up the dead and giving them a new lease on life as a necromancer's personal assistant?"

Deflection. Waving his hand, so I wouldn't see his visceral reaction to graves and burial. But I had seen it. He looked a little shell-shocked, like he was remembering something very traumatic. And I admit, it tugged on my heart a little. There was something so strange about him. He'd put forth this invincible, armored image, but this reaction made him...vulnerable. Like something out of his past was a huge issue for him. But I didn't know how it all connected together with body snatching and burials.

"Talk to me, Mallory," I said.

"Person of interest, detective," he fired back at me. "Anything I say can and will be used against me in a court of law."

Well, that killed our conversation all the way to Newport.

When I got to the turnaround, I turned on a narrow lane that led toward the beach where the little sandy trail led onto a bluff and into the small cemetery. I turned away from the highway, toward the ocean, and past a few sprawling expensive houses with wraparound porches and beach access. With their lights on. Either they had generators or Pacific Power had already gotten some of the coast's power back on.

I parked my CR-V along the dark road that had a small paved turnaround and places for three or four cars to park. In front of the beach that sloped toward the wild ocean below. The little sandy path was just past the turnaround to the south. It wound through beach grass and onto the bluff overlooking the Pacific Ocean. Where the tiny cemetery nestled among the beach grass with only a couple dozen grave plots. Newport Cemetery at Yaquina, Smitty had said. But it had been renamed to South Beach Cemetery some time ago.

I turned off the motor and unfastened my seatbelt, whipping around to glare at Greysen as the wind pounded the shore and rocked the SUV. Hoping to intimidate the story out of him.

But there was something vulnerable shining in those glassy violet eyes. Not blue not purple, but a beautiful light and shimmery mix of both. Giving his eyes an almost bioluminescence that hit me hard. God, he was so hot.

"Greysen," I said, but he was staring down at the machete, not looking at me again.

I reached out and gently laid my hand on his for a brief moment.

"Greysen," I repeated, trying a softer approach. "You've obviously been through something deeply traumatic and somehow, it connects with burials and body snatching. And I just want to help. That's all. I'm not asking as a cop. You don't have to say a word. You don't have to tell me anything, but believe it or not, I'm a damned good listener. And anything you tell me right now in this vehicle, is considered strictly off the record. Okay?"

He jerked his head up, lips parting as he fixed me with that electric, hypnotic violet gaze. Like he wanted to share something with me.

Still, he hesitated.

"I know it's hard to trust people," I continued, "especially when so many screw us over. I'll start by telling you something about me." I reached down and picked up my bracelet from the cupholder and held it out to him. "This bracelet. It's not just some piece of jewelry I own that I took off and tossed into the cupholder."

His gaze didn't leave my face as he nodded slowly.

"I gathered that by your reaction to when I picked it up without asking."

I sighed, shaking my head. "It wasn't about asking permission," I said. "It's a very painful reminder from my past. And sometimes, it gets to be too much, so I take it off."

His eyes narrowed. "Why wear something that causes you pain?" he asked.

"Because," I said. "It helps me keep things into perspective when I'm having a bad day or things aren't going well." I held up the bracelet again. "This bracelet reminds me how much worse things can get."

He was nodding now, like he understood.

I squinted at him. No, it was more than understanding. He empathized with it. Almost like he'd experienced something similar. I felt a rush of cold air brush across the nape of my neck. Or he'd somehow seen what had happened to me that day in Syria. The magic... Had he actually cast magic? Was there really such a thing that existed in the world?

"See, I used to be in the army special forces," I said, my gaze somewhere between the bracelet and his hypnotic violet eyes. "I was a sniper like my dad. He was so proud. But one day, my target saw the glint of this bracelet when the sun hit it." I pulled in a breath, trying to get through the story without choking up or tears running down my face. "He used a kid as a human shield, Greysen. Just as I squeezed off the shot."

"My God..." he said, his voice barely a whisper as he reached out and laid his hand on top of mine. "That's horrible."

I bowed my head. "After that, I couldn't concentrate on a target. I kept expecting another kid to pop up in my scope. And I couldn't help but feel it was my fault. I shouldn't have been wearing that bracelet. Non-regulation and all that. That boy lived, but what about next time? I couldn't let there be a next time. Not with me behind that scope."

"What did you do?" he asked in a warm, quiet voice, so compassionate that it took me by surprise.

I hadn't felt that kind of compassion from another soul for a very long time.

Wind whistled around the SUV, the rain pounding it, and everything around us.

"I left the military. Left North Carolina—became a cop. My dad stopped talking to me. I'm his only child, so to say he was displeased is candy coating it. That was four years ago."

"He's a daft prat," Greysen snapped and even if I didn't understand what he'd said, I was surprised at the sharpness of his tone.

The anger.

"A what?" I asked.

"He's bloody stupid!"

"Why do you say that?"

His eyes flashed with rage.

"He doesn't know how lucky he was to have his only child admire him so much that his dream became hers. And then when something that terrible happened, all he thought about was himself. Not how something like that left a lifetime of scars on his daughter. Bloody narcissist."

Wow, he not only understood, he empathized. He felt all of it. I sat back in my seat, stunned.

"You sound like you're talking from experience," I said.

He nodded.

God, he was impossible!

He was just going to sit there in silence and not share a damned thing with me. I'd only told him the story because one, he already knew it, and two, because I thought it would convince him to trust me with one of those mysterious, murky things from his past. I held onto my anger.

"Care to share with me why you bristle every time I talk about digging up corpses and body snatching?"

He tried his damnedest not to react, but I saw those words hit him right in the chest until he had to pull in a deep breath, his pupils widening, nostrils flaring. And for a few moments, I felt him travel a million miles away from the SUV as something dark and disturbing passed over his eyes. He swallowed a breath. Another one. Finally, his gaze flicked toward me and he sighed. But his hands were shaking now.

"Greysen..."

I struggled, trying to find the right thing to say to him. Something that would get him to open up.

"Nothing leaves this SUV," I said, holding up my hand. "I give you my solemn promise. This isn't part of my investigation."

He bowed his head, pulling in another breath, his chest rising and falling faster. He wasn't looking at me now.

"Back in London..." He stumbled over the words, fighting hard to hold them back and say them at the same time. "I...was left for dead."

His words hit hard. Sobering. Painful. I felt the ache as he got each word out.

"They buried me in—in a mass grave." He shuddered, fingers gripping the edges of his bomber jacket, twisting them as he spoke.

"Bodies. Soil filling my—eyes a-and mouth. Couldn't breathe." He pulled in another aching breath. "And then...body snatchers dug me up. Found me alive." He winced, his whole face pinched with pain. "Sold me to slavers. But I got away."

Stunned, I couldn't speak for a moment.

My God...what a deeply traumatic and painful thing to have shared with a stranger. A cop that had labeled him a person of interest in a murder investigation. And somehow, for some reason, he'd trusted me—of all people—with that deeply painful memory. I was taken aback. I wasn't expecting his story to be so traumatic.

"So, I understand post-traumatic stress disorder, detective," he said, retreating, pulling back now. "All too well."

I couldn't help myself. I was horrified but deeply moved by his story. I laid my hand against his shoulder and rubbed it. I needed to show him some comfort, to let him know that he was safe, and that someone gave a shit. Even if it was some strange cop on the western-most edge of the country in the middle of an autumn coastal storm.

"What you went through was horrific, Greysen," I said finally. "I can't even imagine the terror you went through. And almost dying in the process. Have you been in treatment for your ordeal?"

Slowly, he shook his head.

"I understand," I said, nodding. "Therapy is a very big and personal decision and—"

But he was staring past me now, his eyes getting bigger, those pupils blotting out most of that glimmery violet hue.

"Detective..." he said, pointing as his other hand went to the machete in his lap. "I don't think we need to go to the cemetery."

I frowned. "Why?"

"Because it's coming to us."

5

Bollocks! I'd just opened up my heart and poured out the most intensely personal tragedy of my life. That I could remember. To a beautiful woman that I'd felt the first connection with in a century. Even though she was a cop on the verge of arresting me for a murder I didn't commit. And the goddamned undead had to pick this moment to leave their bloody cemetery to join in the bloody conversation.

This necromancer had just moved up to the number one slot on my shite list and I was going to lay waste to his or her operation after I finished slaying these undead pioneers. Why pioneers? It didn't make any sodding sense!

The dozen or so undead seemed unfazed by the wind and the rain. They were mostly bits of leathery grey skin wrapped tight around bones that clacked and ticked against the evil hiss of bone against bone as they surrounded the SUV that was already rocking in the storm.

"Right," I said and slapped my hands against the torn knees of my jeans. "Time to send these undead pioneers back to the prairie. I always hated that show, Little House on the Prairie, anyway. Be back."

"What?" Detective Keller shouted above the rain and the undead moans surrounding the CR-V. "You're not going out there! They'll overwhelm you!"

I gave her a curt smile.

"Well, if they do, then I won't need to get this bullet removed, will I? One more thing off the ol' To Do List, aye?"

I tried to open the door, but she was faster. Locking it.

I unlocked it and shoved it open before she could lock it again.

With machete in hand, I careened out of the SUV into the rain and storm of undead, machete raised.

Three of them rushed me, the other dozen surging around the SUV on both sides.

I swung the machete as hard as I could propel it. Taking all three of their scraggly grey heads off. They bounced and rolled in the torrent as skeletal hands grabbed me from behind, the others rounding the front of the SUV. They were mostly bones, scraps of leathery grey skin here and there, stringy locks of black and brown hair on top of their heads.

The CR-V door jerked open as Detective Keller hit them with the door and closed it quickly. Knocking them backward into the street.

I could see her shouting inside the SUV as the coffin dodgers overpowered me, knocking me to the ground. Gathering around me to feast on my flesh as the handful of undead in the street moved toward me.

Screaming, I swung the machete right and left as the sounds of gunshots exploded above me. Knocking them away like bowling pins.

I couldn't believe it. Detective Keller was out of her vehicle, firing at these monsters like they were typical dangerous criminals. I'd expected her to stay in the vehicle. She had guts, this bird. Saved me from a lot of painful wounds and substantial recovery time.

I beheaded one after another until I had nine heads on the ground.

Another gunshot startled me. I looked up.

Six undead had the detective surrounded. She swung her purple leather jacket in a wild arc around her, keeping them just out of reach.

"Keller!" I shouted and leaped at the nearest undead.

I tackled it, separating its head from its shoulders and then threw myself in front of Keller as the remaining five lunged for her. I pushed her behind me, covering her with my body and swung my machete like a cricket bat, scattering heads across the pitch.

One after another, the undead fell. I took dozens of bites before I'd lopped off the remaining five heads.

When the last head skittered across the street, all sixteen bodies turned to dust and melted into the rain and wind.

"Detective!" I cried and helped her to her feet. "Are you all right?"

Her black pants and black T-shirt were torn and soaked as she shivered, pulling on her purple motorbike jacket. Making me a little sad. I quite enjoyed seeing her in that wet T-shirt.

She nodded and grabbed my arm, pulling me toward the SUV. She threw open the door to the back seat, shoved me inside, and climbed in behind me. Locking the doors.

Her chest heaved as she gulped air, trying to get her breath. Most of her long sable braid had fallen free of its holder and she slid it off, letting her gorgeous black hair fall into long curly waves that made my breath catch. She was breathtakingly beautiful with all those damp waves of shiny black hair. I wanted to run my fingers through all that silk.

"Do you have a death wish?" she demanded, those powder blue eyes steely and burning with fury.

I squinted at her. I wasn't sure yet. After four centuries of continuous existence, and no memory of who I was, I thought about it sometimes. But she had no idea I was immortal. She looked terrified and not because of those reanimated corpses. She stared at me, a mixture of anger and fear alight in her eyes.

"You were surrounded!" I shouted, motioning out the window. "I wasn't going to stand there and watch them take you apart, Keller."

She punched my left shoulder with her fist, hard, the leather bomber jacket absorbing some of it.

"You went out there and threw yourself at sixteen undead like a rawhide chew toy!" She waved her arms, her voice loud and biting against my eardrums.

"I had a machete," I countered.

"Oh, well—that makes it all right then, doesn't it?" She hit my shoulder again. "You aren't trained to handle situations like this!"

"Like there's a sodding course on cop procedure for handling the undead? This I've got to see."

Her eyes narrowed. "Don't get cute. For handling that many dangerous perpetrators. You almost got yourself killed with me helpless to stop it."

Had she been worried about me? Or worried about her case?

I chuckled. "Well, no worries, detective," I said with a sneer. "There's plenty of me left to charge with murder. You can put your case to bed just in time to sit down with family to a Thanksgiving feast. I'm sure the county jail only serves the finest powdered eggs and...what do you Yanks call it—Wonder bread. Because I wonder what the bloody hell it's made of? Sponges? Pudding? Because it's not bread."

She was glaring at me again. "Do you really think this is about a collar, Mallory?"

Bollocks. She'd reverted back to Mallory again. She was really cheesed off at me.

"Call me Greysen," I replied.

I'd never gotten used to Mallory because it had been forced on me. The only name I was sure of was Greysen. And Blade, a nickname I'd earned, at least. But she didn't know any of that. Besides, Americans tended to call people by their last names.

"Don't change the subject when I'm yelling at you!" she continued, clearly narked, and I did my best to hide my amusement as she shook her hand at the SUV window again and then back at me. "I watched more than a dozen of those monsters overwhelm you and I couldn't stop them or you. I've never felt so helpless."

I couldn't help but smile. She'd been worried about me. But she hadn't known me long enough to worry. Sadly, it had to be about dealing with the mess I'd have caused her if I'd gotten myself merked. Her department would have been mired in paperwork and investigations for weeks.

"Didn't stop you from taking on half a dozen yourself," I said with a wry smile. "Without a machete."

Her blue eyes narrowed. She was not amused.

"From now on, if you're part of one of my investigations, you wait for instructions. No kamikaze tactics and no dead heroes, Greysen. Is that clear?"

I nodded. Back to Greysen at least. Things were looking up.

I wished I could explain to her that I was immortal, but I doubt she'd have believed me. To her, I probably looked like a barmy headcase, diving into the middle of a herd of undead like that. But someone had to or we would have been trapped here until morning. Or longer with the power out and this bloody storm pounding the coast.

"All right, are we ready to investigate this graveyard now?" I asked, reaching for the door handle.

She grabbed my arm. "Wait, why would you bother now that all its residents have walked out? There were only about fifteen or so graves in that cemetery."

"Ah, but that's the interesting thing about necromancers," I said and picked up the machete in my lap. "Some of them are powerful enough to raise undead spirits separate from the bodies. We need to be certain that these graves were dug up and bodies taken."

She looked positively kettled. Understandable to be confused. Her first time dealing with undead and all.

"Do you see any bodies on the ground outside your SUV?" I asked.

"No, they all turned to dust," she said with a shake of her head, that silky black hair looking so soft. I wanted to tangle my fingers in its beautiful waves and press my face against it.

"If there are no bodies—or heads—then that means we were fighting undead spirits, detective, and not the physically raised corpses. Like the ones at my bungalow. So, we need to investigate the graves, see if bodies have been taken or not. Like the three reported. And how they were taken is just as important as if they were taken."

She crossed her arms against her leather jacket as she pondered the situation, looking kettled again.

"So, we need to see if these graves have been disturbed?"

"Exactly, detective," I responded. "And we need to see if the bodies were just dug up or if there are necromancy symbols surrounding the graves. Written in blood, fragrant ash, or fire."

"Blood, fragrant ash, or fire?" she repeated, frowning. "Why does it matter?"

"I'm glad you asked that question," I said with a cheeky smirk and took hold of her hand, placing it flat in front of me, palm up. "If it's blood," I said and touched the veins at her wrist. "Then it means a living sacrifice had to be made in order to reanimate the corpse. Spilling their blood, usually at the wrists or the throat."

"What about fragrant ash or fire?" she asked, looking wide-eyed and concerned.

"Fragrant ash," I said, tapping her palm, "means that our necromancer made a god offering to reanimate the corpse. Meaning humans had to carry in and burn sacred incense specific to that deity. And fire means that our necromancer summoned a demon to inhabit the newly dug up corpse. Which means humans had to burn an effigy of that demon inscribed with its real name. The presence of those elements will also tell us how powerful of a necromancer we're dealing with."

Her face scrunched, that kettled expression returning as she stared at me.

"How?" she asked, shaking her head.

"The higher up the demon, the more powerful the necromancer," I said and finally let go of her hand. "If our necromancer simply dug up a body and used his or her dark magic to reanimate it, that means there's a great deal of power in this dark wizard's hands already. But if the necromancer called on a god, a demon, or made a living sacrifice, that means he or she required help to reanimate those corpses."

To my surprise, Detective Keller was smiling at me.

"Wow, you really do know your stuff, don't you, Greysen?"

A compliment from the detective? I was chuffed to bits. This day was definitely looking up.

"I've dealt with these creatures for a long time," I said with a shrug, like it was nothing.

"Do you have a theory about Andy Keane's murder?" she asked.

She wanted to know what I thought about the murder? That meant she was starting to doubt my involvement or she had her own theory that she wanted to test on me.

"I don't think that Andy Keane jumped bail at all, detective," I said and her eyes got huge. "He ran from New Jersey because he was scared. He wouldn't say anything until he was safe—and sadly, that never happened. No, I think he ran because of something that happened at Beckerman Bonds maybe? Done something he shouldn't have done there—or saw something perhaps? Wrong place wrong time maybe?"

I swallowed a breath, realizing the truth for the first time.

"My God...detective...he ran because he saw something that he shouldn't have. Something dark and twisted—like necromancy—and to protect his family, he fled. The only thing he would say was that something dangerous and evil was after him."

Keller's expression hardened.

"We're still trying to get hold of Andy Keane's records to confirm his identity, so we can contact his family," said the detective. "It's hell getting out of state records right before a big holiday."

"His poor wife and lads will be devastated," I said. "I hope no one goes after them, too."

Andy had shown me a picture of them. A pretty, short-haired brunette wrapping her arms around two young, rambunctious lads. Summer time. A field of sunflowers. Blue skies. Big grins on all three beaming faces. Almost like a work of art.

"As soon as we have a positive ID, we can get the local police there to provide some protection for them," said Keller.

"I hope so. If Andy witnessed someone at the bail bondsman's shop perform a conjuring ritual, there might be undead stumbling around New Jersey, too. More undead than usual, at any rate."

"Is that why we're suddenly encountering all these undead here on the coast? Because Andy Keane saw them perform some dark ritual in New Jersey? And it followed him here?"

I nodded. And then it hit me.

Beckerman didn't hire me to bring Andy back to New Jersey. He hired me to find Andy here in Oregon, blazing a trail so his people could step in and kill Andy. After conjuring up a few undead to cover their tracks. Of course, I'd take the blame for all of it. Sod it all.

Andy saw something and they killed him for it. And now, Beckerman was trying to pin that murder on me.

"Detective..." I said in a wary voice. "Beckerman Bonds didn't hire me to bring Andy back to New Jersey for the bounty."

She frowned. "What? You lied about that, too?"

"No," I snapped. "Of course, I didn't lie about the bounty! The bounty was the bait to hire me. Their true goal was for me to flush Andy out of hiding—because that's what I do best. My reputation was built on bloody well finding anything. So, I find Andy quickly. Beckerman's people kill him—or kill me outright alongside him—and pin his death on me. Cleaning up all the loose ends."

I frowned. Somehow, Beckerman was connected to the supernatural community like I was—but he was a dark, dangerous mortal fool who played with forces he didn't understand and couldn't completely control. Like demons. Gods. And necromancers. The whole lot of them. I was connected as a bounty hunter that knew how to handle supernatural creatures. None of them knew I was immortal. Only that I had a strange magic that helped me find things quickly. That's why Beckerman hired me. Maybe the bondsman knew more about my past than he'd let on? And he'd planned to kill two birds with one stone.

Beckerman figured I'd be an easy kill like Andy. Not realizing that he was playing with fire.

"You really think this bail bondsman tried to frame you for Andy's murder?" Detective Keller said finally.

I nodded. "They thought I'd be another easy kill. Figured I'd be terrified of Beckerman after finding Andy dead in my front garden. Maybe he figured I'd tried to run, too—so he convinced the local necromancer to conjure a small undead army to make me disappear. Problem solved—and he didn't even have to pay me—bloody bastard. But he didn't realize that I don't die easily."

The detective was silent for several moments and I could almost see the wheels turning in her head. She'd taken my theory to heart and was running scenarios in her head. I felt it.

"Tell me what you're thinking, detective," I said. "There's some sort of connection between Beckerman and this Oregon Coast necromancer. I'm certain of it."

Now, I just had to prove that. To myself and to Detective Keller.

"You think that Beckerman Bonds in New Jersey was practicing some sort of dark art—that Andy Keane witnessed? So, they hired a bounty hunter with supernatural experience to find him fast, shut him up. And you. Leave behind no loose ends?"

She was good at this!

"So, you lied to me about having contact with Andy Keane yesterday. And that contact inadvertently led this supernatural mafia right to Andy."

"Lied?" I cried, sounding indignant, but sod-it-all, she was right.

With a sigh, I nodded. "All right, I lied. I did meet Andy yesterday. Back at the airport. He was terrified. Said something dangerous and evil was after him now. Must have been whatever he saw conjured back in New Jersey. So, I gave him some readies and offered him a safe place to stay."

"Some what?" Keller asked, frowning.

"Readies," I said. "Cash. Money ready to spend."

"And this safe place?" said Keller. "It was the bungalow?"

I nodded. "I didn't know what he was running from, but I thought I could handle it here—at the bungalow. But I didn't realize that in a few hours, he would be dead. And I didn't know Beckerman had set me up. I never met the man. We spoke once. By mobile."

Beckerman had Andy killed. And now, they were coming after me since Beckerman's undead assassins failed to do their job. And now, they were using some local necromancer to do it. Throwing off suspicion from Beckerman and onto some *barmy local*. But now, I felt terrible.

It was my fault that Andy Keane got merked. And somehow, I had to find the people that did it. Even if it meant facing down the most powerful necromancer I'd ever encountered.

Wincing, I bowed my head.

"Keller, it's my fault that Andy's dead. And somehow, I need to bring these wankers to justice for killing him. I've got to make this right. For his family."

I hit the door with my fist, angry at myself for letting Beckerman use me to get to Andy Keane.

Then I felt Detective Keller's hand on my shoulder, squeezing.

"Greysen," she said in a quiet voice. "This isn't your fault. You had no way of knowing what Beckerman was planning when you took this job. You probably thought you were helping Andy."

I nodded and leaned my head against the cold, rain-slicked window. Of course, I thought I was helping Andy. I thought I could get him back to his wife and lads safe and sound after I figured out exactly what Andy had seen. And dealt with it. But Andy had been too terrified to tell me and would only say that Beckerman was playing with deadly forces that he didn't understand. Using them in his bail bonds business was insanity! Andy claimed that what was chasing him was horrifying. The darkest of forces and they were anything but human.

Whatever Beckerman summoned back in New Jersey either escaped his control or was sent here after Andy. To the Oregon Coast.

"And I got him killed trying to help him," I shouted through gritted teeth, feeling fury surge through my veins. "He didn't deserve this. And neither did his family. I've got to find who did this and make them answer for it."

She kneaded my shoulder. It was a comfort I hadn't known in such a long time. I hadn't allowed myself to get close to anyone for so long. It was too painful and I was weary of burying people that I loved.

"That's why I became a cop," she said in that smoky alto voice. "To help people who didn't deserve the bad things that happened to them. To find justice for those people. For the ones without a voice and for the ones left behind. Like Andy Keane's family."

I turned toward her. "And that's why I became a bounty hunter. To find things thought lost forever. Including people—living and dead."

At last, she smiled, those soft blue eyes so bright against the dashboard lights, rain pounding against the SUV's roof with a soothing tinny percussion. That matched my racing heart. When her hand slid off my shoulder, I suddenly felt cold. And so lonely.

"I think we're finally on the same page, Greysen Mallory," she said and pointed through the rear window. "Ready to go see this graveyard? Find out what we're dealing with? Then we'll head to Yaquina and Toledo." She glanced at the digital watch on her wrist, a cheeky expression on her flawless oval face. "Should be back by four thirty."

I laughed. I was immortal, but I needed sleep like anyone else.

After an entire day of traveling just to get to the coast, and a gunshot to the chest, I was already knackered. I'd be dead on my feet by the time I got back to my letted bungalow. If I was dead on my feet, I couldn't think of any place more appropriate than a graveyard—or three—to investigate. Beside Detective Keller.

Keller and I got out of the SUV and turned toward the graveyard. In the driving rain and fog, I saw the roiling black mist twisting through the graveyard like a ghostly serpent. My stomach dropped, knowing there was only one kind of entity with that startling appearance.

Death.

6

With Death running amok, the South Beach cemetery by torchlight was much creepier than I'd expected, especially with the remnants of the storm still skittering along the coast, splattering rain, and scouring the beach and inlands with high winds during a blackout. The bluff was so dark, the sun having set while the coast was being beaten down by the storm. And with the power out, and Death prowling, I'd had no idea what time it was until I saw the clock on the detective's SUV.

This day had gone from too early in the bloody morning to afternoon to the next day in record time, all of it spent with Detective Harlowe Keller. Something I had begun to enjoy more than anything else in my life.

She was a step behind me as I followed the dark trail through hilly sand and beach grass, moving toward high ground and the forbidding image of two-hundred-year-old tombstones in the fog and rain. Cracked, scoured by wind and sand, they were difficult to read.

But the presence of Death in the graveyard made my skin turn to gooseflesh. Not the entity I'd been expecting to encounter tonight. Or wanted to encounter on any night.

But the symbols glowing around a dug-up grave weren't difficult to read at all. And they were disturbing. Bloody red symbols that looked part magical and part alchemical oozed dark red along the edge of the deep hole in the earth. I stepped over the glowing red symbols, scent of rusty iron strong in the air, and leaned over the hole, holding up my mobile's torchlight to see into it.

A decayed pine box had once been lowered into that hole and had long turned to dust. Remnants of some sort of dark cloth littered the bottom. Had that been the lining of a coffin?

As I stood staring into this hole, knowing that those glowing symbols meant a god had been summoned with a living sacrifice to raise the dead here, flashbacks shuddered through my head.

I gasped. Flashes of bodies. Cold earth covers my face. Stiff frozen limbs. Dead eyes staring past me.

Can't breathe.

Soil is smothering, weighs down my arms, my legs. Clings to my eyelids, fills my mouth and nose. I dig. Claw. Scrape. Desperate to escape this mass grave. Why can't I remember who I am? Or anything before this moment? Why?

I sucked in another breath, my chest heaving. The *shick, thump* of a shovel is steady. Almost comforting. Drawing closer.

I. Can't. Breathe.

I pulled in a deep, hoarse breath, choking as at last, my lungs expanded, and the images dissipated.

Detective Keller was beside me now, her hand kneading my shoulder again. My chest hurt with every deep breath, the bullet reminding me it was still there, and needed to be removed.

"Slow, deep breaths," she said in a quiet, gentle voice. "You're all right."

Her touch sent a jolt of warmth through my body as her steady, rhythmic touch pushed away the flashback. I wanted to take her in my arms, feel her heart beating against my chest. The need ached through me. But I had to let it fade away.

After a moment or two, I could breathe again, the memory of

waking up in that mass grave dissipating at last. Only when the image had faded into blackness did I return my attention to the opened grave and the burning symbols summoning a god.

"The bullet?" she asked, studying my face with concern.

I didn't think. I reacted.

"Flashbacks," I whispered.

She rubbed my shoulder once more and then her hand fell away. And suddenly, I was cold again.

"You were right, Greysen," she said, moving in front of the row of glowing blood-drenched symbols in the sand and grass that framed the grave hole.

She bent closer to examine the symbols.

"Whoever opened this grave and awoke its inhabitant used blood. Just like you said."

I nodded. All the graves had been opened, but only one body was missing. The rest were still intact, meaning they'd raised them in spirit and not in body. The fact that this necromancer raised the whole cemetery in one way or another disturbed me. Way more powerful than I'd dealt with before, but I wasn't sure if it was the god or the necromancer.

And I needed an answer to that question before things got worse. Much worse.

"They used a living sacrifice and summoned a god to raise this occupant," I said, pointing at the grave missing a body. "The other graves were opened and infused with spirits to raise them. That's why the bodies still remain in those graves. Probably turned their living sacrifice into an undead as well."

"So, now, we're dealing with undead, necromancers, and a god?" Detective Keller asked matter-of-factly. Like I'd just added a purse snatcher to the list of murder suspects.

This woman had nerves of steel and the longer I dealt with her, the more enchanted with her I became. I mean, how impressed I was with her detective abilities.

"Yes," I said, nodding again. "This daft necromancer is playing with blood magic now, in addition to various undead raising rituals. And bringing another god into our world. Not smart."

We already had enough of those.

Detective Keller frowned, glancing from the glowing symbols to my face.

"What kind of god are we talking about here, Greysen?" she asked finally and rolled her eyes. "I can't believe I'm asking this question."

"Old world gods," I replied. "There was a great walkout among these lesser gods and most of them walked away from their positions as gods. During the Great Resignation. They still have all their powers, but they have relinquished their god responsibilities."

She was smiling at me now, shaking her head, arms crossed. Giving me that, you've got to be kidding look of hers. I'd started being able to identify her expressions. We *had* been spending a lot of time together. Had it really only been one day since I'd met her? I felt like I'd always known her. Always.

"Unemployed old gods?" she asked, giving me that look again. "Okay, now we have undead or coffin dodgers as you call them, necromancers, blood magic, god summoning rituals, and now unemployed old gods. Greysen, this gets stranger every time you open your mouth."

At least she was still listening to me.

"It does," I said, pointing to the symbols. "But the presence of these blood-drenched symbols means our necromancer may not be so powerful. He or she summoned a god, so I don't know if all these bodies were raised by the god or the necromancer. Still, if they've brought a god to the area, there may be big problems ahead. Depending on which one they've called."

"Like who?" Keller asked, eyes narrowing as she waited for my response.

"Lesser-known gods we'll be able to handle, perhaps even reason with, but if they've summoned a god like Hecate or even...Death, you may have huge problems to deal with on this coast—much worse than a murder at a letted bungalow."

I didn't have the heart to tell her that Death was already roaming through the cemetery, so most likely, these window-licking prats had used those blood symbols to summon Death. For what purpose, I hadn't a clue. But the black, smoky trails snaking around grave stones and turning gently in the wind was unmistakable.

"What kind of problems?" the detective asked.

I glanced past the open grave, watching as a black-robed figure floated up and out of the hole.

Death. In his business form.

Helluva god to call up at a cemetery. With no containment magic to keep them from wreaking havoc on the summoners and their location. Or wandering off to the next bloody town without any supervision. Like an angry supernatural toddler with a nuclear warhead. Yes, it could be that dire if done wrong.

Like this. But I couldn't discount the possibility that this lack of safeguards had been intentional.

"Problems like that," I said with a moan, pointing at Death. "This necromancer went full-tilt emo goth and summoned Death. For what purpose, I haven't a clue yet, but it looks like he has no interest in leaving. This is bad, Keller. Really, really bad."

Marvelous. My first dealing with a god since I first encountered Mars, former god of war, during the Civil War, and it has to be Death. The universe had a bloody awful sense of humor.

Keller squinted at Death's smoky dark image. Yes, she could see him, too, now.

"What is that?"

The detective pulled her Glock from her side holster and I couldn't help it—it made me laugh.

"You're laughing?"

She gave me an angry glare, but I couldn't help myself. Cops. The embodiment of Death floated in this graveyard and her first bloody reaction is to grab a tool responsible for calling Death to thousands and thousands of corpses created by the aftermath of using that thing.

"It really is funny," I said and motioned at the deadly figure. "Especially when I tell you what or who that is."

She frowned. "Who is it?" she demanded, Glock pointed at Death as the figure moved about the graveyard, ignoring both of us.

We weren't dead or dying, so we were outside this god's realm. Thankfully. He or she didn't give jack all about our presence right now. But he would. When I cheesed him off by speaking to him. I'd heard about the Great Resignation. Most of the gods that remained among humans now were pissy and short-tempered. And they had nothing but contempt for humans, now that humans no longer worshiped these gods and no longer brought them tributes. Forcing these gods to go to work. Shill for a living like the rest of us.

Times were tough—even for former gods.

"Hard cheese for us," I said and ran my hand through my unruly blond bangs, still wet from the rain and sliding into my eyes. "Detective Keller, meet Death. Not sure where he put his scythe, but I'd feel that dark vibe anywhere. Let's try not to hack him off, aye?"

The detective studied the black figure that floated in a trail of black smoke through the graveyard. He looked a bit lost, truth be told. Probably cheesed off at being summoned to such a small cemetery, too. And for being called out in the middle of the night during a storm.

"I take it you're planning to talk to him?"

I gave her a deep nod.

"Only he can tell us about our necromancer. He might not know their identity, but he can tell us more than we know right now. Which is nothing."

"Or he can kill us," she said with a wary gaze on the spectral figure moving about the cemetery like a harmless spirit.

I gripped her by the shoulders.

"That's why you're going to stay right here and I'm going to go talk to him. I'll keep him within earshot, so you can hear him."

Her hands flew to her hips, the fury igniting in those powder blue eyes.

"I'm getting tired of your sexist bullshit, Greysen," she said. "I'm not a helpless damsel in distress that needs you—or any man—to rush in and rescue me. I can handle myself with you and with Death himself, so don't you dare try to mansplain to me how dangerous the world is—including this spirit out of a Hollywood special effects studio."

That was a lot of anger thrown in my direction. I wasn't trying to be her white knight or anything of the sort. But she didn't know I was immortal and I wasn't about to tell her that. She already thought I was from nutterville. But I didn't want her to think I was a sexist bellend to boot.

"Forgive me, detective," I said, laying a hand against my chest as I gave her my most apologetic look. "I apologize if that sounded like a sexist attempt to ride in on a white horse and manhandle the situation. You're a trained sniper and a trained cop with years of experience. I only wanted to handle the situation because I have years of experience dealing with the supernatural. That's all."

Her eyes narrowed. She wasn't buying it. And I was laying it on way too thick, I admit.

"You're twenty-three," she said, sounding annoyed now.

Bollocks! That bloody driver's license always got me in trouble. I might look twenty-three (if that), but I was over three hundred years old.

"Six years of experience must count for something," I said finally. "It's just that I've dealt with most of these creatures before and—"

"You've never dealt with a god," she said, holstering her Glock. "You said so yourself."

"Well, not one this powerful, I—"

"Regardless, we're going to approach this—this entity as a team."

"Good cop bad cop?" I asked. "Please let me be the bad cop this time!"

She sighed, arms crossing. "You done?"

"Quite," I said, feeling defeated. "Just be careful, aye? And remember, that figure out there is Death and he can end your life in a heartbeat."

"Caution noted." She nodded toward Death. "Let's go."

This was going to bloody suck.

She stepped over the blood-soaked symbols and moved across the graveyard like she owned it, head held high, hand on that Glock. I followed, letting my machete hang at my side. I had no talisman, no spells, and not even a bloody enchanted staff to protect her from Death's touch. That's all it took. One touch from Death to her heart and it was over.

The best I could do was step between her and this god if he even acted like touching her. Call it sexist, chauvinistic, what bloody ever...I wasn't about to let her get within an arm's reach of Death and not protect her from herself.

But I couldn't be certain that Death would even acknowledge us. Somehow, I had to pique his interest or tap into those symbols. Since I wasn't leaving Detective Keller's side, that only left me the option of saying something interesting that might excite Death. Something besides the fact that I was immortal. Detective Keller was not going to learn about that. It was bad enough that she knew about all of this supernatural activity—and had even fought undead.

What could I say to Death, in front of Detective Keller, that he'd want to know about or handle?

"What do we say to it?" she whispered to me. "To him?"

"May I give it a go?"

She looked annoyed, but motioned me forward.

I gratefully took the opportunity to step in front of her, doing my best to shield her from the deadliest god walking the Earth right now. Hecate was a close second.

"What necromancer dares to summon Death himself to raise one corpse?" I shouted.

The black, smoky figure shifted, turning toward me as a trail of black smoke coiled around my body and back to Death. I felt relieved that it hadn't entangled the detective. I had no idea if she even noticed.

Death looked right through me and turned away.

"Well, that went well," Keller snapped.

This god didn't even give me a second look. If he'd bothered to look closely, he might have seen my immortality and took more interest in me. But I couldn't risk having that conversation in front of the good detective. So, I had to appeal to him in some other way. Mars had once told me that there was quite a rivalry between Hecate and Death. Maybe I could use that? I hadn't seen Mars since Vietnam. Or was it the Falklands? I couldn't remember.

"Another necromancer summoned Hecate and she raised the whole bloody cemetery," I shouted into the wind. "Two hundred coffin dodgers running amok. This dodgy operation seems so minor by comparison."

Death whirled around and grabbed me by the throat.

"That pathetic hearth witch doesn't begin to compare with Death. Real Death. That you're about to experience, boy."

That got his attention.

I heard the detective gasp beside me.

I hadn't been this close to death since that night in London at the end of a noose. That I thankfully couldn't remember. But the longer he clutched my throat, the better the look I got at him.

As the air began to sparkle around me, I noticed that the black robe that Death wore was actually a black dressing-gown. A bloody bathrobe? With Statler Hotels embroidered in gold letters across the left breast. I remembered that old hotel chain. Opened in 1907 in Buffalo. I had stayed there several times, hunting bounties—and other things.

"A bathrobe?" I sputtered. "What kind of god are you?"

"A cheap one," he said with a snarl and dropped me.

I tumbled to the ground and Keller was beside me again, putting her body in front of me. One hand was on her Glock, the other on my shoulder.

"Are you all right?" she asked.

I nodded. "Should have let the expert handle it apparently," I said with a sigh.

That made her chuckle.

"You fickle humans," said Death, darting around me. "One minute you're worshipping us, bringing tribute, and pouring out your respect and appreciation, and the next, you hear the word god and yawn. Or giggle."

"It's a bloody bathrobe," I snapped. "What did you expect?"

He shot across the ground and stopped an inch from my face. I could smell the mildew clinging to his dressing-gown along with grave dust and the scent of dried flowers.

"Proper tribute," Death said with a growl. "And a little respect."

It was hard to respect an entity hiding his bathrobe in an aura of black smoke.

"Where are your regular robes?" I asked.

"Times are tough," he said, wilting, turning smoky around me. "With no tributes coming in, I was forced to find a job."

I tried to keep a straight face.

"Funeral parlor director?" I asked.

"Bagger at Safeway."

I couldn't help myself. I started laughing until Keller elbowed me in the gut.

"Laugh it up, kid," he said and then he was in my face again, all black smoke and glowing red eyes, a hand squeezing my throat until he'd cut off all the air. "Still laughing? Will you be laughing when I pull your spirit from your body?"

Poor sod. Thought his powers were misfiring because I wasn't dying in his grasp. Guess he still didn't realize that I was immortal.

"Let him go," Keller demanded, Glock pointed at Death. "Now."

"Or what?" Death asked, looking bored. "It's not like anyone will miss him."

"Good point," Keller replied. "But do it for me. Please? Don't kill him. I know you could in an instant, but I'm asking you to stay your terrible powers and spare him."

Nice work, Keller. She was appealing to his ego and as a female, it had far more traction than anything I could have said. Although, for all I knew, Death swung that scythe both ways. Lots of ways. And that was kind of sexy.

Death stared at me as I continued to flail and choke and then at Keller.

"All right, detective," he said. "For you."

He dropped me like a rotten melon and I sucked in a breath, my head feeling like it would explode.

She cast a smug look at me and returned her attention to Death.

"So, whoever summoned you to this graveyard has been reanimating corpses all along the coast," said Keller. "And three bodies from three different cemeteries have been dug up and stolen. I would be honored if you could help us locate this monster."

Death frowned, rubbing his smooth, pointed chin.

"Why would a necromancer be randomly reanimated corpses like this?"

Keller shook her head and then pointed at me as I got to my feet, feeling a little unsteady now.

"All of the undead were sent to kill Greysen Mallory there."

Death chuckled. "If I'd thought of it, I'd have sent some to kill him, too."

Keller was grinning now.

"See, Greysen, you're even on Death's shit list tonight."

"Not my day," I said with a hoarse groan. "Is everyone out to get me here on the coast?"

Death and Keller looked at each other.

"Yes," they both said in unison.

I pushed my bangs out of my eyes and struggled to stay on my feet.

"I didn't think you'd talk to me unless you were interested. Figured there might be a rivalry between you and Hecate."

"Right on all three counts, kid," said Death, black smoky trails roiling around him now, those red eyes flaring as he leaned toward me, hands on his hips. "Pissing off Death is very bad idea, you know. If it wasn't for your attractive lady friend here, I would have ended you just now. Do you understand how close you came to dying tonight?"

I admit, I was still kettled by his inability to sense my immortality. I found it strange, but I couldn't broach the subject with Keller standing here.

And she looked smug as hell right now, that gloating little smile lighting up her beautifully sculpted face, those big powder blue eyes filled with laughter. At me.

"I was just trying to find the wanker that's been raising the dead for no good reason. And those bloody symbols are the first connection we've found."

Death glanced over his shoulder at the symbols still glowing in the rain and wind, still oozing blood.

"Oh, those?" he said with a shrug. "Left his calling card when he summoned me with them."

Keller's eyes got wide and she glanced at me and then back at Death.

"Do you know who summoned you?" she asked.

He smiled, his chest puffing out. "Of course, I do. Name was Ryan. Gilbert Ryan."

Keller's face went pale and she turned away, folding her arms against her chest.

"Keller?" I said, moving toward her.

I laid my hand on her back as she stood there in the rain and wind, staring at the waves crashing on the beach below.

"What's the matter? You look gobsmacked."

She frowned, her brow furrowing, and then looked up at me, an almost panicked look on her face.

"Do you know a Gilbert Ryan?" I asked.

She nodded, her blue eyes turning glassy.

"Personally?" I asked.

Maybe it was her lover? Wouldn't that take the piss out of everything? I knew almost nothing about her life. Just that her father was Colonel Busby Keller and she was an only child. From North Carolina. She went from Army sniper to detective. That was it. All I knew.

She nodded and finally turned toward me. She was shivering as she put her hand on my sleeve.

"Greysen, he's the superintendent. Controls the Oregon State Police. His brother is Evan Ryan. Mayor of Newport."

Well, that was unexpected. The superintendent of police was a bloody necromancer. And his brother was the city's mayor.

"That's incredible," I muttered.

She shook me. Hard.

"Don't you understand?" she said, gripping my arm so tight I thought she'd cut off the circulation. "The superintendent knew everything about Andy Keane's case. We were made aware of his arrival in the state the day you arrived and were told a bounty hunter was illegally hunting him. There was a BOLO out on you yesterday, before your flight ever landed."

I shook my head and held up my machete. "This is a bolo."

"No, Greysen, a notice to be on the lookout. For you, in this case. And then the report of a body came in at four seventeen A.M."

I groaned. This whole situation stunk like a three-day-old cod.

"Hang on, at four seventeen?"

She nodded.

"I was sound asleep, detective," I said with a growl. "And do you know who the most likely person to report that body at four seventeen was?"

"Who?" she asked.

"The killer."

She stared at me, the thoughts rushing across her eyes as she started putting pieces together.

"Andy Keane died shortly after 4 A.M.—heard your cops discussing the details. Four oh six or seven…I can't remember which. That means someone called to report a body just ten minutes after Andy died. And considering it was at a newly letted bungalow—by me—there was no one else around on that deserted beach at 4 A.M. I noticed a security camera nearby. Perhaps you can get the footage to know for certain, but I'd bet my life that our killer is the one that reported the body."

The superintendent of the Oregon State Police was a necromancer and quite possibly a killer—or he sent someone else to kill Andy. Giving him an airtight alibi. He was the only person with access to the entire puzzle. And he would have been notified first about Andy's whereabouts. He had means and opportunity, but honestly…what was his motive?

"Oh, no…"

A horrible thought slid into my head, that name Ryan suddenly so familiar. I fumbled my mobile out of my pocket.

"What is it, Greysen?"

"No, no, no!"

"What?" Keller cried. "What's the matter?"

I pulled up the newspaper website from Andy Keane's hometown. Where Beckerman Bonds was located. Where Andy's wife and two sons lived. I lived close. In New York. That's why I remember seeing it.

I pulled up the wedding announcements from last week. There, at the top of the column, was a smiling bride in white satin and lace. The headline read, Kerrie Alexis Ryan Weds Brian David Beckerman. Witness to the marriage was listed as Gilbert Ryan, brother.

I turned my mobile toward Keller. She stared at the headline.

"What about these people, Greysen?" she asked.

"Brian Beckerman hired me to find Andy Keane," I said. "And Beckerman just married a woman named Kerrie Ryan. Brother Gilbert witnessed the marriage."

Stunned, Keller and I stared back at each other, unsure what happened next. Gobsmacked again.

"He's the police superintendent, Greysen," she said again in almost a whisper.

"He's a feckin' necromancer!" I fired back at her. "And he probably marked Andy Keane, too—or ordered it done. If so, then why bring me into it? With the whole bloody state police in your pocket, don't tell me he couldn't find one New Jersey bail jumper. And someone here to blame for the murder."

Her silence confirmed that she didn't disagree with my statement. That meant this thing went all the way up the chain. On both coasts. But why? What tied them all to Andy Keane and the Oregon Coast? Other than to get him arrested, why send him to a state where bounty hunting was illegal? Andy told me that Beckerman had always joked about bail jumpers running to Oregon.

"Maybe it has something to do with this?" Death said.

I whirled around.

"With what?" I asked.

He pointed a bone-pale finger toward the open grave and I hurried back to the edge of the deep hole. All I saw was decayed fabric and grave dust.

I shrugged. "I don't see anything."

Rolling his eyes, Death shot across the cemetery in a trail of black smoke and into the dug-up grave. He pointed at the fabric and black smoke coiled around it, tossing it aside.

Underneath it was an old piece of folded parchment. I slid into the hole and retrieved it.

My entire body froze, the shock of the words chilling me to the bone.

The Resurrectionist Papers!

It was a page out of the legendary papers kept by the London resurrectionists. Thought to be much more than body snatchers. They had been keepers of the dark magics. Of necromancy and other strange enchantments. And keepers of the original records of every execution for witchcraft in Great Britain. They created their own protected spell books and passed them down to chosen members. Powerful magic.

"It's part of the Resurrectionist Papers," I said with reverence, staring up at Death.

Death pointed at the tombstone.

"Looks like someone's also searching pioneer graves for those papers."

But the horrible truth slid into my brain.

"Or...our necromancer found this page and reanimated the corpse to interrogate them about those papers."

"What's so special about these papers?" Keller asked, peering over top of the hole.

Death smiled and turned toward her as I felt smoke expand beneath my feet, lifting me out of the grave. I landed beside it on the edge of the dark hole.

"Resurrectionists were body snatchers," said Death as he floated over the grave. "Worked all over England, but most prevalent in London. But the stories persist about them being necromancers and dark wizards, cultivating dark magics, and using the dead to conjure the unspeakable."

"Unspeakable?"

Keller looked intrigued and horrified at the same time.

"Demons. Undead. Monsters—even gods. That sort of thing. But also taking magical control of time."

"Temporal magic," I offered.

It was what other supernaturals called my magic. The strange energy that allowed me to touch objects and follow them through the time-stream. It's what made me a good bounty hunter.

"They passed down their spell books and papers to chosen few," Death continued. "Most of their writings are hidden away in private collections. Some say they continue their work in present day. Hidden in secret societies."

What? Continued their work? Did that mean there were descendants of the resurrectionists that had carried on the magic and traditions of those London body snatchers that had dug me up that cold October night in 1726?

"I told you we should have summoned Hecate instead," said a voice behind me. "She doesn't talk much. She just kills."

I turned around, putting myself in front of Keller. I know it cheesed her off, but too bad. She couldn't stop a bullet and live without a Kevlar vest. And I could.

She tried to step around me, but I grabbed hold of her arms and held her behind me.

A bloke with two male sidekicks stood in the dark and wind and rain, all three of them pointing guns at me and Keller.

And Death.

Death rushed at them in a burst of black smoke, but a silvery glint held him back about a foot from the three men.

"A magical ward," said the bloke. "Sorry to disappoint you."

It was too dark to make out their features. But the main chap that spoke was tall, stocky, and carried some sort of high-powered pistol like the one Keller carried. A nine-millimeter? I had no clue. I hated guns.

Keller pointed the barrel of her gun around my right side, training it on the chap, trying to shove me aside, but I stood my ground.

"Now then, cop," said the bloke. "You're going to turn your back and forget you saw us and your person of interest. Not sure how you got to that bungalow so fast, but if you'd been ten minutes later, you'd have had two bodies. And an open and shut case. No questions. No loose ends."

So, Andy Keane hadn't been the only target last night. Apparently, I *was* supposed to die with him. But who called in the body? If it wasn't the killer, then who?

But now, they were back to finish the job. And that meant killing me.

"If you think I'm just going to let you take Mallory off and kill him, you're crazy!"

Keller glared at them. She wasn't going to back down.

"That's a real shame, detective," said the chap, moving closer.

Death kept pounding against the silvery ward surrounding the blokes, but he couldn't penetrate it.

"See, if you don't walk away right now, there's gonna be two bodies instead of one here tonight."

"You're playing with fire, sonny," said Death. "Deciding who lives and dies is my territory."

"And Hecate's," said the strange assassin.

"Detective, get out of here," I said. "Now. There's no reason for you to die tonight. Not for me."

"Trust me, lady," said the assassin. "He's not worth dying for."

I wasn't. Apparently, I was a criminal who'd been hanged and somehow awoke immortal. But I didn't know this bloke. How did he know anything about me?

"I'm not leaving you here to die, Greysen!" she shouted.

I felt her hand against my back, gripping my bomber jacket in her fist.

The first shot was a pop, like a cork. The second like a car backfiring.

Taking the assassin by surprise.

Both killers on either side of him dropped. Dead. Head shots. Keller was a sniper after all.

The remaining assassin held up his hand and Keller's Glock flew across the distance. Into his hand.

"Reanimates," he said with a shrug. "I'll get more. Last chance, detective."

"Keller, go," I said in a sharp whisper. "I won't be responsible for getting you killed."

"And I won't let them kill you, Greysen."

Suddenly, the strange assassin was inches away from us. The barrel of his gun lifted toward my chest and then tilted toward Keller.

"Fine, cop," said the lead killer with the blackest eyes I'd ever seen, matching his stringy black hair. He had a pale, angular face and jutting chin. "You can die first then."

"Keller, run!" I shouted, turning my body toward the gun.

The flash of orange startled me, the muzzle burning. The bloke fired again. Over and over.

My body was in front of Keller as the barrage of bullets pounded into my chest.

Three. Four. Five!

7

THICK BLACK COILS OF SMOKE ROLLED OVER THE GRASS, obscuring us from the gunman. Death had decided to help me out after all.

Keller knocked the gun away and the man looked surprised, fleeing into the fog and night.

"Oh, my God—Greysen!"

Keller's voice was frantic as she dropped to the ground beside me.

My mobile fell out of my hand and into the frosty, wet grass as I hit the ground, blood soaking through my grey T-shirt and onto my jeans. The icy wind scraped across my body, rain still falling in stinging sheets.

Bollocks, that hurt!

Three of the slugs hit me high in the chest, joining the one from earlier. The other two had lodged lower. In my gut.

Bugger. I'd just bought these jeans.

"Oh, no, no, no...Greysen, hang on! Please hang on."

Keller pressed one hand against the gunshots in my belly where blood trickled out like a leaky faucet. She gripped her mobile in her other hand. Calling 9-9-9 or whatever you Yanks dialed.

My wounds looked really, really bad.

Nevertheless, I was immortal. I didn't need an ambulance, but I couldn't tell her that.

"You need me to shepherd your spirit off this mortal coil, kid?" Death asked, hopeful as he leaned over me and Keller. "I'm saving up for a scythe, but I've got a knife. Will that do?"

"No!" Both Keller and I shouted in unison.

"Fine. Just doing my job."

He looked like he was pouting now as he held out that silver knife like a scepter.

I squinted at it, seeing the word Ginsu engraved into the blade. Hold up! Ginsu? Really? Did he carry a Cap Snaffler and a ShamWow, too? Dodgiest god I'd ever encountered.

"Well, do your job someplace else," I choked out, the pain getting to me now. "You're not helping."

"Stay with me now, Greysen," said Keller, her voice quivering as she put her mobile in her jacket pocket and kept pressure on my wounds.

Damn that pistol hurt! I hated guns. Especially when the bad guys all carried them. Although, I had to admit, I'd never had a bad guy unload a pistol into my chest like this before.

It was a whole new experience in pain.

Keller reached down and brushed my unruly blond bangs out of my eyes.

"Greysen, you saved my life just now. You know that, don't you?"

I nodded. It was hard to talk. And it would take a while to heal from this, but I wasn't going anywhere. At least not with this barmy god of Death.

Her eyes got glassy as she reached down and gripped my hand.

"I've only known you for a day, but I feel like I've known you a lot longer. I don't usually...click with people. But you and I just...well—clicked. I can't explain it."

"A connection?" I asked in a weak, pained voice.

She smiled. "Maybe."

I'd take all five of those bullets all over again to hear her say that.

"I liked—being your partner," I said, my voice thinner than I'd expected.

"I've never worked with a partner before," she said, her eyes getting misty. "Guess I'm still that Special Forces sniper, working alone, scoping my targets on my own. Having a partner was...nice."

Shaking, she pressed the back of her hand against her forehead, clearly rattled now.

"No," she snapped and fixed me with her gaze, her hand returning to keep pressure on my belly wounds. "Having you as a partner was nice." She pulled in a heavy breath. "So, dammit, Greysen Mallory—Blade—you stay with me, now. You hold on with everything you've got because I need you to help me hunt down these dirtbag necromancers."

Had I made that big of an impression on this tough-as-nails detective? I smiled and reached over, laying my hand on hers.

"I'm not going anywhere, detective," I said with a crooked smile. "And I'll be there when you solve this case."

She swiped at her eyes. "You promise?"

"I promise."

The distant wail of an ambulance rose on the wind as it moved closer along the motorway.

"Stay with me now...help's coming," she assured me and glanced over at Death.

The ghostly creature floated beside me, making me nervous. Last thing I wanted hovering at my shoulder was Death. Even if he was wearing a bloody hotel bathrobe and carrying a Ginsu knife. I wondered if Ginsu made a scythe. Would make a lovely Christmas gift for this hardworking but clearly bonkers god.

"The closest Level II trauma center is in Corvallis to the east," said Keller. "Over the Cascades. I called for a MedEvac heli. Two squad cars are en route, too."

"I don't need a helicopter," I said, grumbling as blood continued to soak through my new jeans and both shirts.

"You took five nine-millimeter shots to the chest, Greysen," she said with wide-eyes, voice rising. "At close range. I can't believe you're still conscious and that I'm not straddling you doing CPR right now."

Hmmm. I stared over at her, imagining that scene in a different way. I needed to take acting lessons. If I'd done a better job of playing into these gunshots, she might have thought I was dying and started CPR. With my luck, it would have been only compressions and she'd have broken my ribs instead of putting her mouth over mine.

Still, another missed opportunity.

"What's that look about?" she asked, studying me.

"Nothing," I said.

A cough rattled through my chest. My lungs were on fire and it was hard to pull air in and out. Considering that they'd been riddled with holes like a screen door by that strange black-eyed necromancer's minion, I wasn't surprised.

Just what the bloody hell did Andy Keane see anyway? What would have been so important that he and I both had to die for knowing about it? Didn't exactly need the supernatural to merc a couple of mortals. Had Hecate really sent these assassins? Or were they acting on their own? Or through someone else? I'd expected a shooter to come after me but not a necromancer.

Had we found more here in this cemetery than we'd realized?

I sucked in a breath, but my lungs didn't want to expand. And there was so much blood covering my clothes. I'll admit, I felt rattled by so much of my own blood spilling into the grass like a broken tea kettle.

Keller let go of my hand. She gently lifted my head and shoulders and slid her legs underneath, keeping my airway elevated and clear.

"That should help. Come on, Greysen," she urged. "Fight! The paramedics are almost here. Don't let go now."

"I'd...planned to be here only five days," I said.

I didn't think it would take that long to find Andy and help him disappear. But not like this. And I hadn't anticipated meeting a beautiful, commanding police detective either.

"Just five days?" Keller blurted out.

Her mouth flattened. She didn't seem to like that number. Was it because she wanted me to stay longer? Or that it would take longer than that to arrest me for murder?

"Planned to—fly out...day before...Thanksgiving."

It was getting hard to talk. And for the first time in four centuries, I felt scared. Maybe I wasn't immortal anymore? Maybe it just took a lot of bullets to take me down? Like a grizzly bear or someone on angel dust.

Was I dying at last? After 314 years?

"Keller?"

I stared up at her a moment, feeling nothing but regret. She was the first woman since my Elizabeth that I'd wanted to spend some serious time with and not just shag, or hookup as they say in the States.

I'll admit, hooking up was less painful. Spending decades with someone and then losing them broke me into little pieces. And the last time I allowed love to break me into shards was when I married sweet, angelic Elizabeth James. In 1727. She died of Yellow Fever in 1729. I had to bury her in an iron casket to keep from spreading the fever—because no one understood at the time that mosquitos spread it not contact.

Was I about to join her at last?

"Don't try to talk," Keller said in a quiet, shaky voice as her hand rubbed my shoulder, the other still pressing against the belly wounds.

"Am I dying?" I asked.

Like all humans, I didn't know what death felt like. And I had never seen the god, Death before. Lingering beside me in his black Statler Hotel bathrobe, clutching that Ginsu knife, and waiting to pull my soul out of my body like a hungry magpie.

I'd died once in 1726, or come as close as a man could come to death, but either way, I had no memory of it.

"I don't know," said Keller, her voice quivering.

She stopped rubbing my shoulder and reached down to my right hand, gripping it.

"But you fight it with everything you've got and hold on, okay?"

Blood trickled from the corner of my mouth and I spat out a mouthful of warm, salty blood. Coming from my lungs.

When I glanced up, Death sat beside my left shoulder, chin propped in his left hand, elbow balancing on his leg as Empress appeared beside him. She mewed and rubbed against my hip.

Death looked bored, fiddling with that damned Ginsu knife like it was a bloody fidget spinner.

I reached out to Empress, but my fingers passed through her. She was in her ghost form and wouldn't allow me to touch her. Was it because I was about to cross over into her realm? And become a ghost bounty hunter?

"How you're still breathing with all those slugs in your chest, I'll never know, kid," said Death, his voice loud and gravelly and the god nodded toward Keller. "She know you got five that cut a path of destruction through your torso?"

"She does," I said.

Keller frowned. "Who are you talking to?"

"Death," I said and nodded to my left. "He's at my left shoulder."

She glanced to her left and right several times, but shook her head.

"I don't see anybody." Then her face went pale. "Does that mean he's here just for you?"

"Hope not," I sputtered.

"She's a sharp one, isn't she?" Death said, smiling. "Easy on the eyes, too. I like her. She keeps you honest."

"Kept," I corrected him, mumbling. "I'm dying, aren't I?"

Death frowned and chewed his bottom lip.

"Now, see, at first, I thought you were a goner. Thought I should take your soul and put your out of your misery. Because mortals don't last long with these kinds of injuries, kid. And you're going on fifteen minutes or so. That's a record with five slugs in your chest."

Obviously. Didn't take Death to make that observation. But I didn't say anything. Didn't want to cheese him off and have him pull my soul out through my nostrils. Or someplace worse.

"Sometimes they last longer," I said, coughing. "Don't they?"

Death shook his head, spinning that Ginsu knife in the grass.

"None that I've seen. Then I thought maybe you had on one of those bulletproof vests. Until I saw all this blood."

He pointed at my grey shirt, with holes in it, that was covered in blood along with the left leg of my jeans. And the congealing pool of blood beside me in the cold grass.

"Saw all this blood and figured you wouldn't be here long enough to tell her bye."

He nodded at Keller again and then fixed me with his gaze.

"But here you are, still breathing. Other mortals would have bled out several minutes ago. So, tell me, Greysen Mallory," he said. "Blade. How is it that you haven't bled out? How are you still kicking?"

I shook my head. I had no idea. Every part of my body was on fire and throbbing with the worst pain I could remember.

Death pressed his index finger against his forehead.

"Because there's something different about you."

He scooted closer and reached out toward my forehead.

I violently pulled back from him.

"Easy," said Keller.

Death chuckled. "Relax. I'm not going to snatch your soul from you. I'd warn you first."

My whole body shrieked as his ghostly hand slid toward my forehead. It was cold as the grave, fingers pressed against my skin like blocks of ice. I had no idea what he was doing or why it was necessary to touch my forehead. I was still terrified that he was tricking me into taking my soul.

"There's something inside you," he said with a hiss. "A power of some kind. Powers, I should say."

He frowned and finally drew his hand away as a smile rose on his pallid lips.

"Kid, I don't know how or why, but you're immortal."

So, he'd uncovered my immortality after all.

"Am I dying?" I whispered.

"Don't you let go of my hand, Greysen," Keller said, her voice cracking. "You hear me? Promise me you won't let go."

Death shook his head. "Looks like you're gonna get to keep that promise, kid."

"How do you know?" I asked.

"'Cause your body's starting to react to those bullets. It's starting to fight back against them. To heal itself."

"Isn't that a normal human reaction?" I asked.

"Who are you talking to, Greysen?" Keller asked, squeezing my hand.

"Death," I said. "We're discussing whether or not my body can heal this mess."

"There's so much damage," she whispered.

I needed to change the subject.

"Keller...the letting company—said my bungalow's—for sale," I said and wheezed, coughing up more blood. "I thought I'd—"

"Here!" Keller shouted, waving her arm. "Over here!"

Long, lean shadows rushed ahead of their torches as voices approached. I saw three shadows. Paramedics?

A bright light washed over me.

"Let's see what we've got here," said the tall, lanky paramedic, her hair in a tight brown ponytail.

Wearing blue scrubs, two others gathered around me as Keller slid her hand back from my belly. Her hands were at my shoulders, peeling off my bomber jacket.

"He took five shots at close range," said Keller to the lead paramedic. "Point blank. Nine-millimeter."

"Five?" The paramedic looked shocked. "And he hasn't bled out? That's—miraculous. C'mon, people—this one's critical. Let's move!"

"Did you hear me, Keller?" I asked.

The lead paramedic had bandage scissors in her hand and started cutting away my clothes. And my brand-new jeans. Sod it all.

Death took hold of my chin and turned my face back toward him.

"Now that I've got your attention," said Death. "I realize who you are."

Death knew *my* identity? I held my breath for a moment.

"You know who I am?" I said in a weak voice.

"Is Greysen Mallory an alias?" Keller asked me. "Please tell me it's not an alias."

But I was looking past her. At Death. Would this powerful spirit, this god be the one to finally tell me who I am? Tell me about my past?

Then Keller's words filtered into the back of my brain. Greysen wasn't an alias, but Mallory sure was—given to me by crimpers as they shanghaied me aboard the *Angry Widow*.

I shook my head. If I had other names, I didn't know them, but maybe Death did?

"No, Keller," I said. "That's my—real name."

I felt some of the tension leave her. She must have been terrified that I had a poster up at the Post Office with a bunch of aliases on it. Or a massive file at the FBI with several names attached to it.

"Do you know who I am?" I repeated to Death, coughing up more blood.

"You're that immortal bounty hunter from New York," Death said with a grin, sitting up in the grass.

He reached out and patted my shoulder.

"The one that can do some peculiar magic to find things. Find people."

I bristled. He didn't know who I was—not really. Not like Death should know all of the souls he takes, but I must admit, I felt very disappointed.

"They said you'd be on the Oregon Coast. And that I should look you up. See, there's this person I need to find and—"

My eyes narrowed and I glared at Death.

"And I'm lying here with six slugs in my chest, bleeding out in a bloody pioneer graveyard, and you want me to find someone for you! I thought you knew who I was."

"Who's he talking to?" asked the paramedic.

Keller smiled. "Not sure," she said. "I think he's hallucinating."

She was covering for me. So, these paramedics didn't think I belonged in an asylum.

"Do you know anything about my past?" I demanded.

"Sorry, kid," Death said and bowed his head. "Just heard about you at Wraith's and thought you could help me out. I'd like to hire you once you deal with these necromancers. But I will tell you one thing."

Death held up the page from the Resurrectionist Papers. The one from the opened pioneer grave. It glowed blue in his hand. He pointed to my right hand where I'd held the page.

"See that glow on your hand?"

I moved my fingers, shocked by the bright blue glow clinging to them now. I thought that had been the light from my mobile. Until I realized that I'd dropped it in the grass.

"They can't see that glow, but it's proof that you have some sort of connection to those papers. I'm not exactly sure what it all means, but you take this paper with you. You may be able to decipher the page and know what it means. Use it to find more pages. Or lead you to a descendant of these people."

He reached over to my jacket lying in the wet grass and tucked the page into the inside breast pocket.

"It'll be there when you need it, kid."

Yawning, he stood up and stretched.

"Where are you going?" I asked, my voice hoarse and broken.

"We're not going anywhere yet, Greysen," said Keller. "It's okay. Just stay with me now."

"I'm heading back to Wraith's. You aren't going to be needing my services tonight. Even the ghost cat wandered off because you weren't coming to play with her in her realm."

"What's this Wraith's?" I asked.

"He's really out of his head," said the lead paramedic, still trying to get the bleeding under control. "Understandable, considering he took five shots to the chest."

"I know," said Keller, sounding so scared and worried.

About me. A bloke she met barely a day ago. Things were looking up.

"Wraith's a bar, kid," said Death, a cheeky grin on his face as he gripped that Ginsu knife in his right fist. "Well, a bar slash hotel. And not just any bar though. It's a magical place where immortals, gods, and enchanters drink. Sorceresses, wizards, witches—and yes, necromancers—all hang out there. It's between the worlds and connects to a lot of other places. A lot!"

"How do I find it?" I asked, my voice barely above a whisper.

There were places all over the world where immortals found other immortals. Clubs. Restaurants. Hotels. And pubs. Even online. But nothing like this bar that Death was describing. A place like that might help me find out about my past.

Death chuckled and tied the belt tighter on his black bathrobe.

"That's part of the initiation, kid. You gotta find it. It's between the worlds." He pointed at me. "That temporal magic as you call it is your ticket to Wraith's. I'll be there waiting. Like I said, I want to hire you to find someone." He scrutinized me a moment. "You sure you're old enough? Drinkin' age in the States is 21, kid."

"I'm twenty-three, thank you very much."

"You sure?" he asked, squinting. "You look eighteen."

Death had kept me distracted from all the mundane medical procedures as the paramedics and Keller fought to stop me from bleeding out. None of them knew that my body was beginning to turn the tide on that hail of bullets that the necromancer's stooge had fired at me. Trying to kill Keller first. And then me.

"Mick, check on the status of that MedEvac heli," said the lead paramedic to one of the others I couldn't see. "He needs immediate critical transport to Good Sam trauma center in Corvallis. I can't get the bleeding stopped in the middle of a graveyard in a storm. He's gonna bleed out unless I get him to Corvallis, stat."

I felt Keller's arms tighten around my shoulders.

"Is Bad Sam's closer?" I asked. "I'm not picky."

The paramedics chuckled. "Impressed that you can joke with five bullets in your chest."

"Heli's still en route," said Mick.

"Six," I said and spat out blood. "There's one from this morning under my collarbone."

The lead paramedic gave an *are you serious* look at Keller who nodded.

"He stepped in front of a gun about to unload on me."

"On purpose?" the paramedic called Mick asked.

"Of course, on purpose," I sputtered. "They were trying to kill her."

The lead paramedic held another pressure bandage against my gut.

"Detective, you'd better hold onto this one," she said. "He's got the selfless bit down, but teach him to duck next time."

"Wish I could," said Keller as the *whup, whup* of a helicopter whirred overhead. "He's only here until Wednesday."

The lead paramedic shook her head.

"Not with these wounds. Gonna need to reschedule that return flight, Mr. Mallory. You won't be traveling for a few weeks, I'm afraid. If then."

"Weeks?" I cried.

A big smile rose on Keller's lips and then disappeared. So, she liked the idea of me staying longer. Things were definitely looking up, gunshot wounds or not.

They tried to put a cervical collar around my neck and I fought it, feeling trapped.

"No! Don't—need that thing."

"It's required," said the lead paramedic and the three of them forced me into it.

I felt trapped, claustrophobic, wanting to tear it off.

"On three," said the lead paramedic as the three of them slid hands underneath me. "One, two, three."

The three paramedics lifted me out of the wet grass and slid me onto a stiff transport board. Away from Detective Keller.

She pulled a plastic bag out of her pocket and bent toward the ground, picking up my mobile. She used a stick to lift what looked like a gun and slid it into the bag. She shoved my mobile into her jacket pocket.

Somewhere behind me, the helicopter landed as the paramedics lifted me on the transport board and carried me out of the cemetery as the lead paramedic kept pressure on my wounds. Keller hurried behind me, carrying the plastic bag with the gunman's pistol and my bomber jacket draped over her arm.

"Hurry," ordered the lead paramedic and they ran with the board. "He's getting shock."

Keller reached out and gripped my hand, running alongside them.

"Hang on, Greysen," she said, biting her lip, her blue eyes so glassy.

I squeezed her hand as she climbed into the helicopter beside the paramedics, still holding my hand.

We barely knew each other, but in that moment, I didn't want her to let go. I'd been alone in the world for so very long and I was knackered. Tired of waking up alone. Tired of holidays that made me ache all over because I had no one to share them with me. Tired of the numbness that had permeated my body and soul after so much time in self-appointed exile. Connections caused pain, especially when suddenly severed, but after centuries, I wanted to feel something again. And not feel so alone.

I hadn't felt that electric spark of connection in so long that it scared me. Keller scared me. Because I felt something. And I didn't want to because it always ended in pain.

"He's alone out here," Keller said to the paramedics. "No next of kin. So, I'd like to stay with him if that's all right."

The lead paramedic started to respond, but Keller cut her off.

"If you say no to that, I'm going to pull my detective card and cite that I'm protecting a person of interest that cannot be out of my sight."

The lead paramedic smiled. "I get it. Just stay out of the way, okay?"

Keller nodded and kept holding my hand as they tried to keep me from bleeding out. Not realizing that my body was beginning to compensate for the damage. Being immortal and all.

"I'll take it from here, people," said the stocky, brown-haired pilot as he got out of his seat and ushered the paramedics off the helicopter.

Wait. What?

"What are you doing?" the lead paramedic demanded. "That's our patient! He's shocky and bleeding profusely!"

"Got a weight issue, so we'll meet you in Corvallis," said the pilot, slamming the helicopter door closed.

The pilot rushed back to his seat, paramedics pounding on the door.

"Wait!" Keller cried, looking gobsmacked as she moved toward the locked helicopter door. "He needs support to get to the hospital. You can't—"

The helicopter lifted off in the rain and wind and darkness, almost knocking Keller to the floor.

She grabbed hold of my transport board to keep upright, fear burning in those big, powder blue eyes.

I stared at her. Why did the MedEvac heli pilot just lock out the paramedics and take off? With absolutely no medical personnel aboard?

The helicopter lurched over the motorway and soared into the darkness, skirting the mountains that stood between us and Corvallis.

Keller thrust her hand against the bandage around my belly, trying to staunch the bleeding. The bandage was already turning rusty.

"What just happened?" I asked and winced at the pressure against my stomach.

"I don't know," said the detective, turning toward the helicopter pilot that seemed ambivalent about his critically injured medical passenger.

But that look told me she intended to find out.

"Look!" she shouted at the pilot. "This man has multiple gunshot wounds. You need to go back and get those paramedics right now or he won't make it alive to Corvallis!" She flashed her badge. "This MedEvac was a priority E request from the Oregon State Police and you just dismissed the team working on him. Why?"

Something was very wrong here.

The pilot ignored her, instead squawking his departure information over the radio.

"MedEvac helo NC23158 en route to L2 in Corvallis. Over. ETA is about eight minutes. Johnson out."

"Did you just completely ignore a direct order from the Oregon State Police?" Keller demanded. "Land this copter immediately."

No response.

"I said land. Immediately!"

Keller pulled her Glock, but the pilot trained a semi-automatic rifle on her.

"Afraid I can't do that," he said, swiveling around in the pilot's seat, a cheeky smile that made my skin crawl. "We're over the weight requirement. So, who we transporting there, detective?" the pilot asked, flicking the barrel of the rifle toward me in the back of the helicopter. "That murder suspect of yours?"

How would this pilot know anything about the detective's cases?

In the dull glow of the helicopter's instrument lights, the pilot's hair looked light brown and windblown. He was stocky and about average height. But those eyes! They were the darkest brown I had ever seen. Almost black. That was because his irises had been blotted out by darkness.

My skin turned icy. This pilot wasn't entirely human. Or he was possessed. My gut instinct leaned toward the demonic. Something I hadn't dealt with as a rule.

Until tonight.

"There's something very off here," I whispered to Keller who nodded at me.

"You mean besides the AR-15 he's pointing at me?" she asked.

I was more afraid of those eyes than that bloody rifle.

"Look at his eyes."

She hadn't taken her gaze off this pilot. Couldn't she see that his eyes were solid black now?

Why was this demon so interested in her murder case? Then I felt like a stupid prat. It was me he was after. Finishing the job his demon partner started in the cemetery.

Because they were both demons.

It made me shudder as I struggled to breathe. Especially with no medic aboard the helicopter. I felt Keller's grip on my hand tighten.

"What murder suspect are you referring to?" Keller asked in a nonchalant voice. "There are several ongoing investigations currently. And I don't discuss them outside the department."

"Look at his eyes," I whispered again. "They're all black."

It had been a little over a day since Andy Keane was shot dead in the front garden of my letted bungalow. No names had been released to the public yet. Keller mentioned something about delays in getting his records in order to identify the body. Andy's wife and two lads didn't even know he was dead yet. But this demon did, summoned by our friendly neighborhood necromancer.

The superintendent of police.

And his demon-spawn happened to be piloting our medical helicopter at the moment. Now, I was terrified.

Keller was playing along with it.

"He looks familiar," she whispered to me.

Must have seen his picture on the Post Office wall or in some dictionary of the demonic.

"Heard about the guy shot up in Nelscott yesterday," said our demon pilot as the helicopter lurched over the thick blanket of Douglas Firs below. "Heard you arrested a suspect tonight. Down here at South Beach Cemetery after some gunfire."

I glanced at Keller. Really? This demon was the most talkative one I'd ever met.

Why did it keep talking like this? It made no sense.

I struggled against the cervical collar immobilizing my head and neck. Trying to get loose. Keller had no idea what she was dealing with right now. This wasn't some surly criminal. This demon could carve her to ribbons in moments. Much worse than some hungry coffin dodgers. That Glock was useless against the supernatural. But it was a bloody insult to the demonic.

Shooting it would just piss it off more. And we were thousands of feet off the ground at the moment. Not a good place to cheese off a demon.

Besides, it carried an AR-15 out of spite.

"Why are you asking me questions when you already know the answers?" Keller asked.

"Just making sure everything's in order, detective," said the pilot, that stupid cheeky smile pasted across his smug demonic face.

"You were there in the cemetery," I said, struggling against that damned collar. "Why so careful now? Is your boss watching?"

The local necromancer slash police superintendent probably heard the call for a MedEvac helicopter, realized his minions had failed to end Keller and me, and sent this one back to finish us.

Keller's gaze snapped to me, some sort of revelation hitting her cop senses. Judging by the look on her face, she knew something that I didn't.

"You look familiar to me," said Keller to the pilot. "Do I know you from somewhere?"

Familiar? Did that mean this pilot was merely possessed and not an actual demon conjured from the underworld and placed in a reanimated body? That made a big difference in how to handle this pilot. What was Keller doing? Keeping him distracted so he wouldn't use that rifle?

"You ever serve in the military?" the man asked with a chuckle.

A condescending tone like she couldn't have possibly served. It made me bristle.

"Army. Special forces," she said. "Served in Syria."

The man went quiet for a few moments. There. Take that, ya bloody knob. He was nothing more than a demon ride-share and he had the gall to think that Detective Keller couldn't handle the military? Please.

"Wow, special forces, huh?" the bloke said finally. "I was air force. Flew copters in Iraq."

At last, the look on Keller's face changed, turning to recognition.

"You were part of the Newport veteran's parade last year," said Keller. "Riding on a flatbed truck with other veterans. But you carried the flag."

"You recognize me?" he asked, frowning.

Her excitement quickly turned to dread as she gave me an *oh, shit* look.

"Neville Ryan, right?" she said, giving me a panicked look. "You had long hair and a beard, but I still recognize you."

Oh, bollocks. Another bloody Ryan.

That meant he was either a necromancer that had fecked up his magic or he'd intentionally invited a demon in for tea. Either way, he was bloody stupid.

And now, we were in its crossfire.

I was still strapped to a transport board and cervical collar. I couldn't move. Even if I could, I had six slugs in my chest. I wouldn't be any help to her.

Keller's eyes got as big as saucers.

I squeezed her hand. "Detective, another Ryan?" I whispered. "They're like bloody roaches around here."

She nodded, looking ill.

"Gilbert Ryan's oldest son," she whispered as the radio squawked. "The superintendent, remember?"

Oh, bugger. The superintendent's son was either possessed or a demon that had taken his form. Or why not both? That's how they knew where I was tonight. And Keller. That gunman hadn't been sent by a god. He'd been sent by the superintendent. To cleanup this mess. Which included killing me and now, Detective Keller.

And apparently, the superintendent's son—a helicopter pilot—was the backup cleaner. How bloody convenient.

I didn't get a chance to ponder that horrible turn of events because the helicopter rocked forward, its blades whipping like a washer out of round. Until a thick fog of black smoke trailed out from both sides and the tail.

As it began to lose altitude. Over the mountains.

The pilot, Neville Ryan, bounced out of his seat and strapped on a parachute.

A parachute?

Bollocks. This wouldn't end well, would it?

Neville Ryan pushed open the helicopter door. Wind roared through the cockpit, rotors churning like buzz saws.

"I'm sorry you recognized me, detective," said Neville Ryan, AR-15 balanced on his hip as the tops of evergreens floated underneath the shimmying helicopter. "Now, I'm afraid you and Mallory need to go down with the copter in a tragic accident." He paused on the lip of the door, glancing back at us, wind whistling past the helicopter. "Give my regards to Andy Keane. In Hell, Mallory."

Neville Ryan leaped out the door, leaving me and Keller to go down with the helicopter.

Bollocks.

8

Lurching away from Greysen's transport board, I stumbled, then threw myself into the pilot's seat as the helicopter threatened to spin.

After our pilot, Neville Ryan, had just parachuted out of it.

My heart hammered my rib cage and for a moment, I couldn't breathe. This wasn't happening.

Grabbing for the controls, I called back the dozens and dozens of hours I'd logged flying a military helicopter in Syria. Part of my special forces training. But that felt like a lifetime ago.

I flicked on the radio.

"Mayday!" I shouted. "Repeat, mayday! This is Detective Harlowe Keller with the Oregon State Police. Pilot has bailed, leaving me and the in-bound patient aboard this copter in danger. We're not going to make it to Corvallis in eight minutes. Or ever. More like we'll be in the middle of the pass when this thing goes down. Over!"

An alarm began to wail through the shuddering copter as I fought to keep it level. But with the storm, the wind, and the rain made it almost impossible. I could barely hold the stick halfway level with both hands.

Something thumped against the back wall of the helicopter. I winced.

Greysen's transport board.

Poor guy was still strapped in with his head and neck immobilized in one of those collars. But I couldn't help him right now. I had to keep us from crashing.

"Greysen, hold on!" I called out. "I'm trying to get us out of the sky. Gently."

"Do whatever you have to do," he replied in a tired voice. "By the way, detective, do you know how to fly this thing?"

Greysen's voice was thin and sounded weaker than it had before we'd boarded this deathtrap. He'd needed those paramedics beside him for the ride, to keep him from bleeding out or going into shock. If this MedEvac copter went down, things would go from critical to fatal. Infinitely worse now that our evil bastard pilot parachuting to safety. Leaving us to flail up here.

I'd shred him like cabbage when I caught up to him again.

Why weren't they answering my distress call?

Greysen kept telling me to look at his eyes, but it was too dark to get a good look. They were so black though. No color to them. But I still recognized him as Neville Ryan, Superintendent Gilbert Ryan's son—even without the beard and long hair he'd had during the veteran's parade. Had something evil and twisted possessed Neville Ryan —like Greysen Mallory claimed? Or was he just a callous bastard?

Great! That's all this ridiculous case needed. A demonic possession. It was already a three-ring circus with monkeys and dancing bears. Might as well complete it with demons and a high wire act.

Somehow, I had to get this copter out of the sky and both me and Greysen down in one piece.

"I had some training in the army," I answered Greysen finally, doing my best to stay calm for him and me. "But it's been a while."

"That's reassuring," he said in that warm, velvety British accent. "I think."

"You concentrate on not bleeding out while I concentrate on bringing this copter down gently. Without killing both of us."

"Deal, detective," he said in a weary voice. "And when we're back on the ground, I propose that we beat the piss out of Neville Ryan."

I grinned.

"Oh, I am so holding you to that, Greysen," I said with a chuckle.

His voice wasn't as bright as it had been before the graveyard. He was getting weak from blood loss. And I was worried. No, worried was six gunshots ago. Now, I was bordering on distraught.

I glanced over my shoulder at him.

The transport board was pressed against the aft wall of the copter and he struggled to keep it from flipping over. In the dim light, those hypnotic violet eyes looked frail as he weathered pain and all that bleeding, trying to keep himself upright, struggling against that cervical collar. Making him look stiff and annoyed. I would have laughed, but the blood still seeping into his clothes terrified me.

I'd never seen someone bleed so much and still be conscious. And not go into shock. Not even in Syria.

Something was off about Greysen Mallory, but I had no idea what. Something was different. Something I hadn't encountered before. Like remaining upright and alive after taking five slugs to the chest. I groaned. Like dealing with necromancers, Death, and a possessed helicopter pilot all on the same case. And a few hours ago, I'd swear I saw him cast magic. Not that I'd ever seen anyone use magic before. I never believed it existed until I met Greysen Mallory. But I'd swear I saw him cast magic.

I just had to prove it. Somehow.

Regardless, I'd have to sort all that out later. The fact that the police superintendent's son had commandeered a MedEvac helicopter, intent on killing me and Greysen, was still in the forefront of my thoughts.

The police superintendent's son. It boggled my mind and set every detective's instinct I had on fire. Why hadn't someone stopped him? How did he get this far with this messed up plan?

"Mayday! Mayday!" I shouted into the comm again. "Repeat, this is the MedEvac heli inbound to Corvallis from South Beach Cemetery. Over."

The superintendent—and his son—weren't working alone. That much I knew now.

Did the superintendent think his cops wouldn't find out? Did the Ryans think they'd just ignore killing a cop? How deep did this go? And were those black eyes to blame? Making anyone and everyone do his bidding. With a demon.

No. The Ryans thought we were going to crash and die tonight. Problem solved. And they had planned to play it off as a tragic accident to the department. After all, it was hard to tell the world about the superintendent's unbridled corruption when you were dead.

How deep was the State police force involved in Andy Keane's murder? And in the stacking of Greysen's murder charge. Or just murdering him in his sleep like they'd planned. Then none of these incidents would have happened.

How many cops on the payroll had looked the other way? Cops I worked with every day. Counted on to watch my back in the field.

Now, they were trying to kill both of us.

Trying to kill a bounty hunter and a cop wasn't very smart. Both of us had a big network of colleagues. People that would know that the Ryans' concocted stories were a load of horseshit.

This wouldn't end here if Greysen and I died. At least that was a small comfort. Very small.

"MedEvac helicopter NC23158, this is command base," said the calm male voice through the radio as it crackled through the cockpit above the helicopter's buzz and ticking. "Could you repeat? Where's Johnson? Did you say that he bailed? Over?"

"Affirmative," I replied, struggling to level out the helicopter as it shuddered high over the treetops—barely missing them. "His name wasn't really Johnson, but he was piloting the copter and then parachuted out over the pass. Leaving me and a critically injured trauma victim aboard to die in a crash. Over."

"That's insane! NC23158, please identify yourself again. Did you say you were a cop?"

"Detective Harlowe Keller, Oregon State Police. With a critically wounded civilian aboard. Multiple gunshot wounds to the chest."

"The flight plan indicates you're en route to Good Samaritan level two trauma center in Corvallis. Detective, is there anyone aboard that can fly a helicopter?" the man asked.

What'd he think *I* was doing? Streaming YouTube cat videos on my phone?

I gripped the stick and eased the helicopter away from the mountains. It shuddered and chugged, the trail of curling black smoke widening around us, leaving plumes of thick clouds against the stormy, dark sky. Stench of leaking fuel was pungent.

"Had some helicopter training in Syria. Former Army special forces. Only logged a couple hundred hours or so on one model. I'm trying to hold her steady long enough to land. Anywhere. We're not going to reach Corvallis. This copter's shuddering and threatening to stall. Thick black smoke is trailing out and its leaking fuel. And I've got to get this civilian with five slugs in his chest to the hospital."

"Five?" the radio operator cried.

"Five. Nine-millimeter slugs. Civilian is bleeding profusely. Shocky."

"Where are the paramedics?"

"Pilot kicked them off this bird and took off without them."

"My God...that patient doesn't stand a chance."

"Yes, he does," Greysen announced from the back of the copter.

It made me laugh.

The heavy black smoke reminded me of the dark, smoky trails that Death had left behind him. And that was no comfort.

"My civilian is hanging on as best he can, but he needs immediate medical attention. Probably a transfusion and surgery. Over."

"Detective, you land that copter wherever you think you can land it. Sending out a reconnaissance bird using your locator beacon. We'll find you. And we'll get your patient to Good Sam's, stat. We'll need a heads up on blood type."

"Greysen, what's your blood type?"

"I'm told it's a bit rare," he replied. "AB negative."

"Command base, the patient has rare blood. AB negative. Over."

"Wow, you weren't kidding, were you? Trauma center should have units available. Somehow. Command base out."

Of course, he had rare blood. Everything about Greysen Mallory was rare and different and—and exciting. Electric. Wondrous. In a way I hadn't felt for a long time. There were moments when it gave me chills, goosebumps, and made my heart flutter.

In a good way. Unlike this failing chopper.

The copter sputtered and started swaying back and forth.

I gripped the stick with both hands, trying so hard to hold it steady, but the wind and the rain and whatever mechanical issue (or sabotage) made it threaten to stall.

It bucked. Shimmied. Tried to roll and spin.

I fought it with everything I had, trying to keep it steady and level. Hoping I wouldn't slam us into the side of a mountain. But I'd never flown a copter in the dark. Much less in a storm. Over a mountain range.

Ahead, a clear-cut patch of forest loomed beneath a lone security light. Lots of tree stumps to hit and flip the chopper, but the wide dirt logging road that carved through it was clear. Empty. It was night. Work wouldn't resume for a few hours.

I hoped.

"Command base, we're headed toward a clear-cut logging area. There's a logging road cutting through the center. I'm turning the copter toward it. It's our best chance. Over."

"Roger, NC23158," said the man. "Based on the flight plan and your trajectory, we've pinpointed the logging camp and the manmade road in question. Another MedEvac helicopter's headed that way from Corvallis. With two mountain rescue copters flanking it. And paramedics aboard. ETA is five minutes forty-nine seconds from your position. Over."

"Roger that, command base," I said, fighting the stick, trying to hold the copter steady, but the wind howled and buffeted the copter, overwhelming it as it steadily lost power. And fuel.

And altitude.

If Greysen's transport board flipped again, it could kill him in his condition. I had to get him and me on the ground safely.

In one piece. Fast.

Wind whistled past the copter, its lights winking red, white, and green over the dark terrain, trees thinning into a balding patch of stark tree stumps that the loggers would grind down and plant another forest around them after the crew had finished harvesting trees.

The copter sputtered, shook, and the engine died as I cleared the top of the old growth trees.

For a moment, everything was deathly quiet. An eerie silence punctuated by the rush of wind and patter of rain against the cockpit. Eerie glow of a red warning light, indicating a stall, flashed on the control panel.

"Greysen, brace for impact," I announced. "We're going down, but I'm still going to try and land her."

"Warning. Stall." *Whoop, whoop!*

The intense male voice filled the cockpit from the copter's warning system, looping as the chopper started to fall out of the sky.

"I would brace for impact except some bloody wanker tied me to a surfboard and put my head and shoulders in this sodding pillory. I swear to God, if I hang ten down the side of this mountain, someone's going to hear about it."

I tried not to laugh, but I couldn't help it. He was hilarious when he got pissed. And I needed that laugh.

The dead copter swayed back and forth, wind buffeting the hull.

I held my breath as branches scraped the tail and the copter tilted forward.

Greysen's transport board slid to the back of the copter again.

His muffled cry of pain was the only sound in the copter except the pounding of blood in my ears that kept the rhythm of my heart in high gear, my breath coming in gasps as the dirt logging road swayed into view.

"I'd planned to learn to snowboard one day," he announced. "Today was not the day I had in mind."

I fought the stick, trying to control the descent as I tapped the rotor brake pedal.

The copter barely responded now that the engine was in full stall. But if I let the stick go, the copter might fall into a wild spin and we'd go over a rocky cliff face. Or roll down the side of a mountain. Or hit it head on. The stick couldn't help us land either. I just hoped the wind didn't flip the copter and send us sliding down into a deep crevasse.

That would be certain death.

I pumped the rotor brake pedal and kept trying to relight the engines as the chopper dropped below the tree line, passing over rows of stumps, gliding toward the dirt logging road to the right.

I angled the stick, slamming it hard to the right, stomping the rotor brake as I tried with all my willpower to steer us onto the flat, level logging road.

The first thump against dirt startled me as the copter ricocheted off it, bouncing up and down as I tried my damnedest to land it. Trying to hold it steady. Foot crunching the rotor brake pedal to the floor. To get us down onto this dirt road alive.

The copter bounced three more times and then tipped onto its side, sliding to a stop on top of the rise.

I held onto the seat, fighting the momentum as the copter lay smoking on its side.

A few hundred feet more and we'd have tumbled over the mountainside into oblivion.

"Greysen!" I cried and crept across the dark copter floor toward the back, only the faint blue light of my phone to guide me.

I heard his groans, a sound I'd never been happier to hear. That meant he was still alive. Still fighting to survive five gunshot wounds. And that he hadn't bled out.

Then I bumped into him.

The transport board had cracked in half and he'd rolled off it, that cervical collar keeping him from a worse injury. Like breaking his neck. But even the cervical collar had come loose now, freeing him.

I sat him up against me, feeling warm stickiness against my palms. He was still bleeding.

"Hang on, Greysen," I said as the distant *whup, whup* of helicopters punctured the thick silence. "Hear that? Help's coming."

Until the door of the copter trundled open.

Neville Ryan stepped inside, AR-15 pointed at me and Greysen, parachute and leads trailing behind him.

"I was afraid when you said something about special forces that you'd manage to land this bird, detective. So, I had to make sure there were no witnesses. And please understand that Mallory has to die. It's nothing personal. Those copters aren't going to get here in time to save you either, detective."

Neville Ryan shuffled closer, parachute still dragging along behind him. He fumbled over the pieces of the broken transport board and stood over me and Greysen. I slid my hand underneath my jacket.

"Should have been smarter, Mallory," said Neville Ryan. "Investigated before agreeing to help someone like Andy Keane. You might have lived through this."

"Why did Andy have to die?" Greysen demanded. "He was just

a harmless burglar, trying to take care of his family. Scared out of his mind. And I never got a chance to find out why."

"Liar!" Neville shouted and poked the barrel of his rifle against Greysen's cheek. "We both know that's a lie, Mallory. You know what he saw that night at Beckerman's. And I'm sure you've told the detective about it, too. That's why both of you have to die."

Neville shoved the rifle barrel against Greysen's left temple, finger poised on the trigger.

My fingers coiled around the butt of my Glock and I slowly slid it free of its holster. But I had to distract him from that trigger. Fast!

"Tell me, Neville," said Greysen, holding out his right hand. "Was this what he saw?"

He held a ball of writhing red flame in his hand. What the hell?

Neville's eyes got huge.

"What?" His mouth gaped.

Greysen flung the fire in Neville's face and grabbed the rifle, pointing the barrel up toward the ceiling.

Neville fired off four shots, but Greysen kept the barrel pointed away as they fought for control of the gun.

I yanked the Glock from my holster and launched myself at Neville.

Slamming my knee into his back, I tackled him to the floor of the helicopter, pointing my Glock at his head.

"Drop the gun, Neville," I growled. "Now. You're so under arrest, dirtbag. And I don't give a damn that your dad's the superintendent."

Greysen yanked the rifle out of Neville's hands as I read him his rights. And cuffed the bastard. Hands and feet.

Collapsing against the wall, Greysen slid down it.

But searchlights passed above the dead helicopter as three more copters roared overhead, circling the downed MedEvac copter. They landed around us and climbed into the dark hull. Three paramedics. Two air marshals. And SAR personnel dressed for mountainous rescue.

The air marshals took Neville Ryan into custody. Along with the rifle. To my right, paramedics had swarmed Greysen. They had a gurney and lifted him onto it while trying to stop the bleeding.

"Let's go!" I shouted, following them out into frigid temperatures, the rain turning to snow.

"We've got to get out of here fast," said one of the SAR guys in a dark blue parka. "Weather's turned. We've got to get off this mountain while we still can."

I nodded and ran behind the gurney as the paramedics lifted it into the other awaiting MedEvac copter. I climbed in behind them and held Greysen's left hand while paramedics ran an IV and hung fluids and two bags of AB negative blood for him.

The MedEvac helicopter lifted off and soared over the treetops, the mountaintop lit with personnel and the downed copter, and we headed toward Corvallis.

"ETA is six point two minutes," the pilot announced as the copter's steady *whup, whup, whup* filled the cockpit.

Greysen smiled and squeezed my hand.

"If this is what the first twenty-four hours or so of being your partner is like, I can't wait for tomorrow."

I laughed. But despite his joking, that twinkle in those hypnotic violet eyes told me that he'd meant every word.

"We made a good team, Mallory," I said with a wry smile.

"Make," he corrected me. "We make a good team. When they kick me out of hospital, we'll look deeper into Andy Keane's murder. That's a promise."

Wasn't he leaving next week? I hated the sound of that.

"In five days, you'll be on a plane back to New York," I said, my gaze narrowing.

The thought of that made me really, really sad.

He sighed. "Listen, detective," he began, staring down at the gurney.

Avoiding my gaze.

My heart started to race. He couldn't look me in the eye now.

That meant this was the goodbye speech. Here it comes. But dammit, I wasn't ready to hear it. It was too soon.

I wanted more time. To see if there was something between the two of us after the electricity wore off from being thrown together and chased by tons of bad guys.

No, I needed it. Five days wasn't enough time to tell me anything.

"The owner of my bungalow informed me that he's put it up for sale."

"What? The Jameson place is for sale?"

He fidgeted, pulling at the edge of the gurney with his strong, squared fingers. He had sexy hands.

"Was." His gaze flicked up from the gurney and hit me with a swirl of emotion.

And those violet eyes burned with animation. Was it attraction? Dammit, I needed more time. To find out.

"Was?" I said, frowning.

He hesitated.

"I have no idea how long I'll be in hospital," he said, beginning to stammer a little. "And—I couldn't be sure that he'd allow me extra days, so I..."

His voice trailed off.

I squinted at him. "So, you what?"

"I...I bought the bungalow."

His voice was barely above a whisper. He bought the bungalow?

My heart raced again and I couldn't hold back the smile.

Was that embarrassment burning across his face? Or fear? I couldn't tell. He wasn't looking at me now, like he was afraid of how I'd react.

I was still trying to process everything, but that message cut through the confusion like a machete. Greysen Mallory had bought the Jameson bungalow.

That meant he'd be staying awhile. I couldn't stop the grin from curving across my face. Greysen "Blade" Mallory would be staying awhile on the coast.

"So, looks like you're going to be staying on the coast for a while," I said.

His gaze slid back to my face and for a moment, we stared at each other. Did he sense my excitement that this partnership wasn't over?

"As a person of interest, you weren't allowed to leave the state," I countered. "You know that, don't you?"

I held back my laugh at the confusion and surprise in his gaze as he tried to rein it back in, so I wouldn't see it.

"Person of interest," he said with a scoff. "Fine. Go ahead and arrest me, detective. Just get it over with already."

I crossed my arms, shaking my head.

"Not so fast, Mallory. I said you were a person of interest. Not a suspect. And I'm interested in seeing how this investigation pans out. Besides, I still need a partner. This case is far too complex for one detective. Especially with...necromancers involved."

His face brightened. "You still—"

"You heard me," I said and let go of his hand as the paramedics moved around the gurney. "I'm not letting you get out of this investigation that easily. I still need your—particular brand of expertise."

"I look forward to it, detective," he said and sat up on the gurney.

The paramedics tried to force him back down, but he resisted.

"Mr. Mallory, please—you'll make the bleeding worse. Please lie back down."

"How is he even on his feet?" One of the paramedics asked.

I shrugged. I had no idea and it was one of the biggest questions in my personal investigation of Greysen Mallory.

He finally gave in and laid back down, but he seemed almost restless now. Had the paramedics stopped the bleeding? If they had, they'd be pissed at him for trying to get up and move around.

They had just gotten him settled back against the gurney when the helicopter landed at the hospital.

The MedEvac team slid open the helicopter door and the paramedics whisked Greysen out into the rain and chill. Onto the helo pad.

I ran alongside them into the brightly lit hospital with its cream-colored walls and tan floors that smelled like soap and bitter antiseptic. They wheeled Greysen into emergency and I couldn't go back with him.

I drank three cups of coffee and paced the waiting room, floor covered in tan and cream striped carpet squares. I watched the army of blue-scrubbed nurses and doctors in white coats hurry in and out of those double doors beside a small, brightly lit front desk.

As waiting room television blared the local news that ran a weather report on the storm and power outages, a nurse with short brown hair called me to the desk.

"Detective Keller?"

I tossed my coffee cup and rushed to the desk.

"How is he?"

She smiled. A good sign.

"We rushed Mr. Mallory into surgery and the surgeon removed all six bullets. He spent an hour in recovery and was doing so well that the doctor discharged him to home care."

Suddenly, the relief hit me all at once and I felt exhausted. Greysen Mallory was going to be okay.

But then it sank in that they were releasing him. And that didn't sound right at all. The man had six slugs in his chest. No hospital would release him to home care the same day as surgery. Especially with that many chest wounds.

Something was wrong.

"Wait, what? You're not admitting him? Or at least holding him for observation?"

The nurse shook her head. "Believe me, detective, even the doctor was surprised when Mr. Mallory met all the criteria for release. I've never seen anyone bounce back so fast. Based on his numbers, insurance wouldn't cover his stay if we kept him. So, as soon as I receive his discharge papers, we'll release him to you."

Behind me, the television blared the end of the ten A.M. newscast and someone changed the channel.

Confused, I stood there, staring at the E.R. doors, and tried to process everything that had happened over the last day.

So, Police Superintendent Gilbert Ryan was a necromancer that apparently summoned demons and reanimated corpses on slow nights at the office. Summoned gods when business picked up. And ordered bail jumpers and bounty hunters murdered on the coast for fun. That was good for the tourism trade. And so was digging up corpses from coastal graveyards and reanimating them.

And then there was bounty hunter, Greysen Mallory. Who I'd watched summon a fireball in his hand tonight. A fireball.

Magic? Um, yeah. What else could it be? Honestly, after necromancers, the undead, and seeing Death, was it such a stretch to think that Greysen Mallory had some sort of magical skills?

Not now. Yesterday, yes. Today? Not. At. All.

For a half hour, I paced the waiting room with the intoxicating scent of Greysen's smoky vanilla and oak aftershave clinging to my clothes. My leather jacket was spattered with his blood, so I took it off, not realizing my shirt would smell like him. His bomber jacket got left in the graveyard, but I had his machete. In the car. He'd carried it in a long, narrow pocket inside his bomber jacket . The blade had been bloodied from the gunshots to his chest. I would worry about getting back his jacket and cleaning up blood later.

But the warm traces of that unusual scent he wore made me light-headed. Wood smoke, oak, and vanilla. Sandalwood. A touch of something else I couldn't identify.

For a moment, I pressed my sleeve against my face and let the heady and cozy scent wash over me like a balmy summer breeze.

When I couldn't stand the wait for Greysen's discharge any longer, I went over to the desk and flashed my badge at an older nurse with steel grey hair. Detectives had to have some perks.

"Detective Keller, Oregon State Police," I said and put away my badge. "I need another update on Greysen Mallory's release."

"I'm sorry, detective," she said, looking confused, and my heart skipped a beat. "But they treated him and released him into that other detective's custody."

"What?" I wanted to punch a wall. "What other detective?"

She shrugged and typed something into the computer on the desk. Squinting, she wrote down a name on a yellow sticky note.

"A detective Hikatte," she said and slid the note across the desk to me. "She said you'd already been informed."

I picked up the note and my heart shuddered into overdrive. I couldn't breathe for a moment, staring at the name in shock. It was badly misspelled, but the translation was instant.

Hecate.

9

I TRIED TO RISE FROM THE BLOODY GURNEY AGAIN, THE emergency room in high gear, crowded with patients. But the staff kept putting me flat on my back. All I could see was the blue curtain surrounding my bed and shoes rushing back and forth beneath it. The noise was a steady din of shoes, beeps of monitors, and roar of voices.

I swear I never saw that curtain move, but suddenly, a nurse in tight-fitting black scrubs was beside me, checking my IV stand where that third bag of blood had almost emptied into my veins.

Shivering underneath a thin white sheet and an even thinner white blanket, I only had on a pair of grey boxer briefs. They'd cut away all my clothes. And I was freezing.

They'd already taken me into surgery and removed the slugs from my chest. All six of them. Sewn up the holes and bandaged me right up. Giving me painkillers and antibiotics—and blood. Apparently, they were about to discharge me. Said the bullets had miraculously missed vital organs and blood vessels.

Despite all the blood I'd lost.

It was a nice story at any rate. And if it got me out of this place faster, I'd tell them anything else they wanted to hear. They had no idea that in the hours after that gunman had filled me full of metal, my immortal body had kicked into overdrive, healing the destruction to major organs and repairing the savaged arteries and veins. Replenishing blood. By the time I got to hospital, four and a half hours had already passed.

Enough time and healing to keep me out of the ICU. And I was chuffed to bits about it.

Now, I waited for my discharge papers. Not someone to mess with my IV—unless they were removing it. The last bag of blood they'd hung was almost empty. They promised to remove the IV line when they brought in the papers. But I had no idea what this nurse was doing.

"Did you need something?" I asked the raven-haired woman as she examined the IV stand.

She turned toward me, holding my IV line in her hands. She had blood-red nails that were at least two inches long. That ended in points. Her piercing gold eyes were smoky and smudged from eyebrow to cheekbone with black shadow. Like some bloody goth nurse out of nightmare. Her skin was the color of moonlight. And her hair was the color of night and if I looked closely, I'd swear that I saw stars floating in its shiny blackness.

"Yes," said the strange nurse. "You."

She chuckled and shot something into the line.

The alarm bells screeched in my head and I tried to rip out the IV line. Couldn't move. My voice strangled in my throat and I couldn't speak. Muscles felt locked. Frozen. Only a squeak came out.

"There now," she said with a condescending smile and patted me on the head like I was her pet chihuahua. "Let's get you dressed, Blade. It's time to go."

She pulled me out of the bed. I stood there, unable to move, wearing only my boxer briefs. Her gaze was invasive, studying every part of my body. Every curve, every sinew. Every muscle. It was miserable, but I couldn't speak and I couldn't move.

"No one told me how delicious you were," she said, giving me one last invasive look. "Such a lovely surprise. Never mind about the clothes. We'll be leaving now."

I tried to shake my head and grab hold of the bed frame, but no part of my body responded. Like I was paralyzed. I had no idea who this woman was or what she'd just done to me. I had no idea where Detective Keller was either or where this strange woman planned to take me. Or why.

She chuckled again.

"Now, now, don't resist, Blade," she said in a voice she might use with a small child. "It'll be harder on you if you resist. Fighting me has never ended well for any of you mortals over the centuries. Know your place."

I shrugged my shoulders, already unable to lift my arms, and made my best *you've got to be feckin' kidding me* face.

Amused, she tossed her head back and laughed, the sound chilling.

"You don't know who I am? How adorable. Well, we'll discuss all of that soon enough. Come along now, Blade. We've got a lot to talk about."

She laid her taloned hand against my bare chest and stroked my bandages. My skin.

"Like these gunshot wounds for starters. And why they didn't kill you." She clicked her tongue and shook her head. "Someone was trying to kill you and didn't do their job."

She walked her index and middle fingers playfully across my shoulder and pecked my cheek.

"Now, I need to know just who that someone was, Blade Mallory," she said like I was still a young child. "West Coast or East Coast? And then you're free to go."

West Coast or East Coast? Like I was bloody Facebook friends with these people? With her arrogance, she had to be a goddess. But which one?

And I only had one name because Keller recognized him on that helicopter ride of death. And I had no idea about the bloke that had unloaded his pistol into my chest. It had been pitch-dark. In a windy graveyard filled with undead and Death. With a storm blowing ashore.

And the arrogant prat had demon eyes! Like the other one. I couldn't bloody well tell any of those black-eyed wastes of space apart in the dark, now, could I?

All demons looked alike to me. Like these sodding necromancers taking the piss out of magic. Making it their bitch as the Americans said. I wasn't in the mood for playing Jeopardy with a goddess either. No one had bothered to raise Alex Trebek from the dead, so I didn't know the questions or the answers at this moment.

Getting shot multiple times in the chest made me grumpy. I wasn't in the mood for games or grafting with a goddess (remember, that's flirting for all you Yanks, just go with the alliteration already!). And I was tired of getting the Saturday night square up at every turn.

I pulled away from her and she laughed.

"Have to do better than that, you sexy little mortal."

Then it hit my fevered brain hard as I lost my grip on the bed. Judging by the starry black hair and moon-pale skin, I had one guess.

Hecate.

Goddess of the moon and the supernatural. Goddess of the night, magic, and doorways. The one who apparently had her own stable of necromancers here on the coast. And she thought I knew something about this dumpster fire?

Regardless, she knew who I was and seemed to think I knew all about these window-licking gits raising the dead with wanton abandonment. Like freeing animals from a zoo. And I had no clue why they were raising the dead any more than I knew who was sending them my way.

In 314 years, I'd only encountered one god. Mars. Former Roman god of war. Then I fly out to the Oregon Coast and run into two of them in the same bloody day. Gods high up the chain. Death and

Hecate. Didn't get much higher than that. And she either wanted to shag or merc me—maybe both?

Did she even realize that I was immortal yet?

Obviously not if she kept calling me mortal, but maybe that was just habit when dealing with humans.

I couldn't resist her. Couldn't fight back. She'd shot something into my IV line, paralyzing my limbs and my voice. I couldn't tell anyone. Couldn't even write S.O.S. or the words, *help me* on the discharge paperwork as the acute care nurse slid open the curtain, dressed in beige scrubs.

Hecate reached over to the clipboard that the nurse set down beside me and touched it with her red taloned fingers. I watched my signature coil across the page.

I was horrified, but I couldn't stop it.

She handed the clipboard back to the nurse.

"I'm Detective Hecate," said the goddess with a smug smile. "I'll be assuming custody of the suspect upon release. Detective Keller has already been informed."

"Thank you, detective. Please make sure he sees a physician in a week to have those sutures and wounds checked. And make sure these bandages get changed twice a day. The instructions are all here on the discharge papers. Good luck, Mr. Mallory."

My frustration level was off the charts.

Hecate turned around, holding a silky midnight blue robe in her hand. It looked like a wizard's robe. Wonder where she'd retrieved that robe from—on second thought, maybe I didn't want to know.

She slid my arms into the sleeves and tied it around my waist. It was long, hitting the tops of my bare feet.

"Time to go, Blade," she said, gripping my arms.

My legs responded to her magic, forcing me to follow alongside her. I was powerless to fight back. Couldn't counteract her spells or resist them. I wanted to scream, but my voice had been paralyzed.

She leaned toward me as we passed through the acute care center's double doors to the front desk. A maple wood desk tucked into the corner of the cream and tan entryway beside the automatic doors that led outside.

She leaned against me and pressed her lips to my ear.

"Make even a teeny little scene, Blade," she whispered, "and I'll zap Detective Keller completely out of existence. Is that clear?"

I couldn't halt the murderous glare that burned across my face and laser-focused my hatred on her.

It made her laugh.

"Such rage," she said. "Means there's a lot of spirit in you." She ran her fingers through my hair. "And passion. Wish my minions would take a lesson from you. Come along now. And don't try to fight me. You'll lose. Mortal."

She led me outside the hospital. Into the late morning's bright blue sky, the sun climbing higher toward zenith.

With the wave of her hand, we vanished from the present, tunneling through darkness and shadow until it abruptly halted in front of a place that looked like the Palace Versailles. A sprawling estate with a black French mansard roof and marble stone walls. That gleamed with a field of stars overhead in the darkness, the rest of it glowing with magic like neon lights.

In big, gold letters that burned with starlight above the rooftop, a single word gently flashed there in delicate script. Wraith's.

She held out her arms. "Welcome to Wraith's, Blade," she said as I stood there shivering in the cold, my chest aching, and my throat clamped so tight I couldn't speak.

Wraith's? Hold on. That was the club where immortals, gods, and enchanters gathered, according to Death. A club between the worlds where the magic congregated. And gods drank away their sorrow after the Great Resignation when they all walked away from their godhood. And gathered together to commiserate and figure out their next moves.

The worst thing I could think of was a place where bored enchanters, immortals, and gods got together. No wonder humanity was so screwed up. Nothing worse—or more dangerous—than bored gods.

"I'll bet you're wondering why I've brought you to Wraith's."

I tried to nod. Couldn't. Why would she bring me here? Why didn't she just take me out of hospital and kill me, like everyone else was trying to do? Was my death what she was after? Finish the job that those nutjob necromancers had started a few hours earlier.

I wanted to lay my hand against my chest and ease the pain. Soften the throbbing ache from the healing bullet wounds. But I couldn't move. I may be immortal, but things still bloody well hurt. And I still bled like a mortal. I just didn't die.

She giggled. "Of course, you're wondering why."

She held out her arms and turned in a circle in front of the double black doors leading inside Wraith's, and then she whirled around and slapped my face. Hard.

"You started a war, Blade. Shame on you."

Shocked, my face stinging, I mouthed the word, *me?* I gave her the most confused look I could muster.

Me? Started a war? How?

She shook her head, clicking her tongue at me again.

"You have no idea what you've done, do you? Silly, naive boy. But oh, so beautiful."

"Leave the kid alone, Hecate."

The familiar voice behind me went right through me and slapped Hecate in the face.

I smiled. Death.

He fluttered past me, trailing black smoke, that black Statler Hotel dressing-gown fluttering in the breeze as he floated between me and Hecate.

"How did you get past my people?" she demanded, a hand on her hip as those black scrubs shifted into a flowing, midnight purple dress that glimmered with stars.

He shrugged. "I'm Death. After I touched one of your people and he...well—expired, the rest of them magically got out of my way."

Hecate didn't look amused.

"The kid has no idea what you're talking about," Death said with a growl.

"He starts a war between the magics and he has no idea what I'm talking about?"

Hecate looked furious, but I had no idea about a war—especially a magic one. I think if I'd started a war, I'd have known about it beforehand. And it would have been intentional.

I tried to shake my head at Death, but my bloody neck was still frozen in place. Instead, I mouthed the word *no* over and over until he understood. His eyes narrowed and he returned his gaze to Hecate.

"What'd you do to him?" he demanded, fingers curling around that Ginsu knife tucked into his bathrobe pocket.

"Paralyzed his limbs and vocal cords," Hecate said with a dismissive wave. "He'll recover soon enough."

Death looked horrified and furious.

"It's only temporary. Had to get him here without a fight."

"Why?" Death demanded.

She crossed her arms against her chest and chewed her bottom lip.

"So, he can answer for what he's done. It's the talk of the entire bar tonight. No one's even heard of this kid and tonight, it's like he's the Genghis Khan of magic or something. As one of the few working goddesses left in the world, I should have been telling them this story. Not hearing it second and third hand from Mars, former Roman god of war."

I mouthed the word, *no* again. I was more an Alexander the Great than a Genghis Khan type. I had no idea what she was talking about. What war? How did I start a magical war? And if I did do that, then I wanted to know how to stop it, too.

Bollocks. This was turning out to be the worst day of my life. I sighed. Second worst. Then there was the night that they hung me in London for practicing witchcraft, something I thankfully couldn't remember.

Death turned toward me.

"Kid, do you know anything about a war?"

I tried to shake my head again. Couldn't. I mouthed the word, *no*. Again.

"A likely story," Hecate said with a growl. "Mortals. Always lying."

At that comment, Death smiled.

"Kid, does she know that you're not a mortal?"

I mouthed the word, *no* and rolled my eyes. Since I only knew who she was because Death had called her Hecate (confirming my suspicions), I had no idea what she knew and didn't know about me.

Hecate crossed her arms again and glared at me.

"What do you mean Blade's not a mortal? Of course, he's a mortal. He's the one that caused that big mess in New Jersey. The one that's causing ripples all the way out here."

"New Jersey?" Death frowned. "Hecate, what in blazes are you talking about? Will you make some sense already?"

"Summoned the entity." Her eyes burned with fury. "Remember? The entity that everyone in the bar is talking about? Got that terrified mortal that ran from it killed. Woke the dead all along the coast. Set a war between Night and Death in motion. That's you and me, Bob." She pointed at me. "Of course, it was Blade. Pesky mortals are always messing with things beyond their understanding and cause havoc. Then expect their former gods and goddesses to return—without tribute—to save their mortal keisters."

Death started laughing. "You think the kid here caused all of that? It'd be pretty damned impressive if he had."

"Of course, he did! It's all over the bar."

The bar. What was this bar and why was I suddenly the subject of their bloody conversations?

"Look closer oh, Queen of the Night and Spells," Death said with a lilting delivery. "He's an immortal. And he has no memory of his past. Has no idea who he is or what he is for that matter. I've been asking around. No one else seems to know either. That's why I wanted him to find his way to Wraith's. I was hoping that someone here knew something and could help him find out those answers."

Answers! If I had use of my arms, I would have hugged Death. Everything he said was spot on—everything. But for some reason, Hecate thought I'd started a magical war along the coast. What did she mean about someone summoning an entity in New Jersey? What sort of entity? And why?

Was that what Andy saw that night when he went to Beckerman's Bail Bonds? Was that why Beckerman married Kerrie Ryan in the first place? Sister to two necromancers. Hell, maybe it ran in the whole bloody family and she was one, too.

I felt a chill dance between my shoulder blades. That had to be why Brian Beckerman married her. Together, had they summoned some deadly and powerful entity that night? Something they couldn't control? And poor Andy happened to be in the wrong place at the wrong time. Saw everything. And they had him killed for it? Now, they were trying to eliminate me, the last loose end.

Had whatever they summoned broken its bonds and escaped? Maybe it was making its way back to the other coast? Back to its true source? The Ryans here on the Oregon Coast. And because I'd flown in from New York, all the immortals and gods were blaming me for it. Bollocks.

A horrible thought slid into my head.

Did whatever they summoned kill Andy? Was the killer I hunted supernatural rather than human after all? An immortal or a god? I shuddered. Or a demon?

I was way out of my league right now.

Hecate groaned and rolled her eyes, pointing at me. "Damn it all. Now, that little mortal detective he's teamed up with is busting up Corvallis looking for him."

She was? Maybe she did have a thing for me?

Then reality returned to my brain. More likely that she needed her person of interest back. So, she could wrap this case up just in time for Thanksgiving. So she could have a happy Christmas. And I could spend eternity in the nearest supermax. For a murder I didn't commit.

Hecate's comment made Death smile.

"You seem surprised. Kid here is a person of interest in that detective's murder investigation."

"Oh, that one. With the small-time necromancers. That think they can compete with a god. Or an entity they summoned? They're gnats. I should swat them and stop all this raising undead nonsense right now. And concentrate on whatever those morons unleashed in New Jersey. Before it shows up here. On the Oregon Coast."

First thing she said that I agreed with and I hoped that these gods wouldn't leave this monstrosity all to me for cleanup.

"They're raising the dead to try and kill the kid here," said Death. "I know. I dealt with one of your minions in a graveyard just last night. They dug up corpses and raised all kinds of dead. And hell. In my territory."

Hecate laid a hand against her chest. "My minions did that? I can't imagine why. I certainly didn't order it. I thought I'd made it clear to them that I had the northern coast and you had the southern. Looks like I need to smack down my humans again."

"Tell them to stay out of my territory next time, Hecate. One of them put five slugs in the kid."

"That's why you were in the hospital, Blade?" she said, looking surprised. "And here I thought it was just trouble with those mundanes you've been hanging out with since you arrived."

I wanted to nod. Couldn't. Was everyone watching me since I'd arrived on the Oregon Coast? But then I watched Death's words sink into her brain and she finally realized the part Death had been highlighting.

"Oh...and you lived?" Her eyebrows lifted, her dark blue eyes brightening with surprise. "With five gunshots to the chest?"

I glared at her. Put there by her barmy prat followers. Caused me to waste my entire evening dealing with those gunshots. Not to mention almost killing us in a helicopter ride from hell. Her minions had royally cheesed me off by shooting me that many times. The one bright spot was that I got to spend my evening with Detective Keller. That made up for all the pain and nuisance these gunshot wounds had caused. But not the helicopter nightmare—that was a fresh new hell that would stay with me a while yet. And Keller.

Then I began to wonder if Hecate's minions were moonlighting in her employ. Necromancing their own projects after hours. I was quite certain that Hecate would end them if that were true.

Were the Ryans part of her minions? I didn't know yet.

"I told you, the kid's immortal," said Death. "Your minions just pissed him off with those slugs. Besides, with your necromancers running amok, we can't tell them apart from the New Jersey necromancers. Much less some entity."

Hecate frowned. "What other necromancers?"

"The ones from New Jersey! Aren't you listening?"

Looking flustered, Hecate adjusted the folds of her dress and turned toward the black double doors into Wraith's.

"All right, Death, I'll talk to my people." She pointed at Death. "Keep Blade Mallory on a short leash this time. And send him back to his handler so that detective will get out of my town. And stop busting up everything to find him."

Corvallis belonged to Hecate? She mentioned something about territories, but I thought she'd said hers was north. It wasn't like I'd seen a map or anything. Bloody hell, this immortal and gods stuff was complicated on the West Coast. Made gerrymandering look ordered and clear. Made my head throb.

She pointed a finger at me next and took back her silky blue robe. Leaving me only in my smallclothes again.

"And you, find out who started this magical war in New Jersey. We need to know what was summoned and why. And then we need to send it back to its realm. Shut down this war. And punish the mortals responsible. Stop all these wild bar rumors, too." In a moment, a smile stretched across her face. "You know what? It feels a little like the rebellious good ol' days. I've missed that. Maybe

Dionysus will start having parties again? Maybe I'll even get tribute? For handling this mess."

"We'll handle it, Hecate—don't you worry," said Death, taking hold of me and backing away from Wraith's, its sign with gold script letters still flashing bright gold neon in the cold night.

"I want you to report back here, Blade, Death." Hecate ordered, not turning back around. "Find out what this entity is and what they plan to do with it. Soon. I don't want it spoiling Kronia. Or Saturnalia, or whatever."

"Christmas, Hecate," Death corrected her. "They call it Christmas now."

She waved her hands around.

"Everything is so inclusive these days. Yes, Christmas. Before Christmas. And that stupid mortal holiday before it. Thanksgiving."

I had no use for Thanksgiving either. Eating a turkey sandwich alone while the rest of the sodding country ate a huge home-cooked meal with family always made me feel awful every November. Maybe it was time to visit my adopted family? The clan of vampires that took me in that first Christmas in New York. Moira Dupree was like a mum to me and Cash Cattrell was my best friend. I hadn't seen either of them in some time.

"Not that you're in charge of...anything, now, Hecate," said Death with a growl. "But if it will foster a truce between us, the kid and I will investigate and let you know what's happening out there."

In a rush of black smoke, Death yanked me into a shadowy tunnel that bore between the worlds like a Mongolian Death worm. And returned me to the hospital car park. Right in front of the entrance to acute care.

And bloody left me there.

In broad daylight no less. In only my grey boxer briefs. Bastard.

10

I still couldn't move my legs or speak, but I felt the muscles in my neck and shoulders begin to relax. My arms responded a little, too. Detective Keller would throw a wobbly, thinking I'd run from hospital and left her holding the bag on this whole supernatural fiasco.

Didn't even have my mobile. It was somewhere between the coast and Corvallis.

It felt like an eternity, but after a few minutes, I had command of my limbs again. And my voice. What had Hecate given me anyway?

I gazed around the car park in the warm sunlight, casting bold fuchsia and peach streaks across the grey sky. Bloody hell, I was freezing.

Every time a car drove up, I slid away from the automatic doors and clung to the shadows. Baltic, chilly shadows, but at least people couldn't stare at me in my smallclothes.

And then a familiar voice turned the corner. Shouting my name.

"Greysen Mallory! He couldn't have gotten far with five bullet wounds in his chest."

Taking a deep breath, I slipped out of the shadows, my face burning. Still in my smalls—and nothing else.

"Detective," I called in a rusty voice and struggled to motion her over to me.

It took a moment, but her expression went from relief to cheesed. She stormed down the sidewalk toward me, black pumps ticking against concrete.

"Greysen Mallory!" she shouted and closed the distance between us.

She grabbed me by the arms, shaking me.

"Where have you been? And where's Hecate? I've been searching for you everywhere! For over an hour!"

"Long story," I said in a weary voice and tried to sound unconcerned.

For a moment, she looked upset.

"Your skin's like ice."

But the detective's momentary concern morphed into fury again. At me.

Something shiny glinted against the pale sun and snapped against my right wrist. Handcuffs.

"Handcuffs?" I cried, shaking my head. "Why are you handcuffing me? Am I being charged or detained—"

"You're being held accountable for slipping out of the hospital before being discharged."

Her eyes were blue flames, mouth taut as she slapped the other cuff onto my left wrist.

"It wasn't me," I said barely above a whisper. "I mean I didn't wander off. I was taken out of acute care."

She propped her hands on her waist, glaring at me, giving me her best, *you expect me to believe that load of bollocks* look.

"I swear it, detective," I said, holding up my cuffed hands. "First, I would have put on some clothes before absconding from hospital."

Her gaze traveled to my boxer briefs, slid past my bare chest, and back again. Finally, she focused on my face, her cheeks turning red.

Did she like what she saw or was she just being a cop and studying every clue presented to her. And I was presenting a lot at that moment.

Like she was surprised to suddenly discover I was standing there in my smalls. I sighed. That meant she hadn't even noticed. Apparently, I had that effect on most women.

"Why are you standing out here in only your underwear?" she asked finally. "It's freezing out here."

Like I bloody well didn't know that?

I couldn't halt my upper lip from curling into a snarl.

"Because the goddess Hecate paralyzed my voice and my muscles and then nicked me right out of hospital. That's why."

"Hecate," said the detective, sounding unconvinced. "The goddess? Then that hospital clerk wasn't deluded."

I nodded and began to pace, wanting only to crawl back into my jeans and shirt. Except that the paramedics had cut them into streamers in that pioneer graveyard. This was all I had to wear at the moment.

Every time someone approached the acute care center, they turned around and stared at me.

Then I remembered that I'd worn my bomber jacket out to that remote cemetery. I hoped that the detective had grabbed it—and hopefully not the paramedics. I'd give anything to have a jacket right now. Or even a bloody tauntaun.

"Think we could discuss this out of the wind and chill?" I asked, shaking my cuffed hands at her. "I don't exactly have any clothes to put back on, detective."

"Oh—sorry," she said with a gasp and turned me away from the hospital entrance.

Toward a black sedan in the car park—a letted sedan. Had to be.

"Let's get out of here," she said. "We need to talk."

"And I need some clothes."

She glanced at me one last time and then we hurried away from the acute care entrance. Into the car park and toward that black

Toyota sedan. It was parked in the second row as the greyness burned away from the world, the brief sunlight giving everything a warm, ethereal glow (except me, because I was freezing and it was still cold as bollocks outside). Blotting out Hecate's threats. This car looked too shiny to be anything but letted.

I had no idea what entity Hecate had been talking about. Especially back in New Jersey. Andy hadn't gone into details. And I wished I'd had more time to talk to him. He'd been reluctant to tell me anything the day I landed. Kept looking over his shoulder the whole time. Told me the less I knew, the safer I'd stay, but by that point, someone had already ordered me marked alongside Andy Keane.

I knew that there was only one way to find out what Andy saw that night. One way to find out what Brian Beckerman and Kerrie Ryan—or whomever— raised in the cellar of Beckerman Bail Bonds— or wherever one raises an entity on their premises.

To find out, I had to use my magic.

But to use it, I needed some object or thing that had been present in the bail bonds office that night. Something that had also belonged to Andy. Only something like that would allow me to use my magic and reach back through time, touching the moment when they'd summoned this entity. The moment that Andy saw it and ran.

But how would I get hold of something like that?

Even if I did manage to find something, I'd still have to explain my magic to Detective Keller. Something I wasn't ready or willing to do. Right now, she wasn't exactly sure what I was and keeping her off-kilter and uncertain might preserve this incredible partnership between us for a few more days.

I worried that the moment she saw that I had a strange magic at my fingertips, she'd get as far away from me as she could humanly travel. Forget she knew me.

Right now, the detective thought I was just some strange bloke from New York and London. That had taken a hail of bullets to the chest and lived to tell the tale.

When the M word came up, I was fairly certain that Detective Harlowe Keller would lose her cop mind. She didn't seem to like things she couldn't see and even the thought of necromancers, undead, and strange magics had terrified her. With good reason, of course, but if I told her about my magic, she might shut down and take our precarious partnership with her. Shut me out of the investigation completely.

Keller unlocked the black sedan and I scrambled into the passenger seat, shivering, arms folded against my bare chest.

She climbed into the car and started the engine.

I couldn't just walk away from Hecate's threat. She could find me anywhere. Granted, she couldn't kill me, but she could make me wish I was dead.

Besides, she'd already threatened Detective Keller once. If I didn't return to Wraith's and report something about this entity, Hecate would hunt me down. And probably harm the detective.

I couldn't let that happen.

"All right, Mallory," Keller snapped and turned around to glare at me.

Those piercing powder blue eyes bore holes through me.

"All right what?" I said, still shivering as the heater huffed on, blowing warm air across my bare skin and bandages.

Those metal cuffs still sent a chill through my body.

"Oh, God that feels good."

"Now, spill it. What just happened to you? I have been searching for you for over an hour. How did you just suddenly pop up in the hospital parking lot?" She motioned toward my bare chest. "And how is it that you took all those shots to the chest and walked away like it was nothing? Something is very wrong here and I don't know how you're up and walking around."

She sighed, gripping the bridge of her nose with thumb and forefinger.

I started to respond, but she cut me off. Bollocking me again.

"And another thing!" she shouted. "How are there reanimated

corpses traipsing up and down the coast alongside Death and this goddess he's at war with? And the fact that the police superintendent and his family are apparently a bunch of necromancers that think having a good time involves a six pack and raising corpses. I'm totally losing my mind."

Keller looked frazzled. About to throw a wobbly—at me. And I had no answers for her. None that she would believe. She wanted some nice and neat response that she could file away under murder solved. Case closed.

And I couldn't give her any of that. Much less a plausible answer to any of her questions. I didn't know how I took six shots to the chest either. I also didn't know how or why I was hung for being a witch in 1726, buried in a mass grave, and then awoke the next evening alive and kicking. I didn't know how I became immortal and I didn't know what Andy Keane saw. Or rather what entity got conjured back in New Jersey.

And I had no idea who had reported the body in my front garden. At 4:17 A.M. Who made that phone call? And why?

Regardless, that call got the cops out to the bungalow fast. If I'd been mortal, that call would have saved my life. Instead, it saved me from a few more gunshot wounds.

Since Andy Keane couldn't tell me what he saw in New Jersey (his body was still in the local morgue), the only way I could find out was through my temporal magic. Touch something of his. Something that he'd carried into Beckerman Bail Bonds that night. To place me in the space. So I could see it for myself.

But that required getting hold of evidence from the police lock up. And with the police superintendent probably still gunning for me (like everyone else), the only way that could happen was if Detective Keller helped me.

And she would never help me unless I leveled with her, one hundred percent, what I needed it for, and what I hoped to accomplish with it.

Both of those explanations meant explaining about my magic. And that would set her hair and brain on fire.

"Dammit, Greysen!" she shouted. "Are you even listening to me?" She grabbed hold of my shoulders, sending a deep ache through the bandaged wounds across my chest. "You tell me what's going on! I got thrown into the middle of the craziest paranormal clown show that's ever performed on the Oregon Coast!"

I sighed, hanging my head. "Sorry, detective," I said and squinted at her. "I don't think you're ready to hear any of it. But ask yourself why I survived those gunshots. Ask yourself why Death didn't end me like he'd been ending other people right and left around him. And finally, ask yourself why everyone is trying to kill me."

Her eyes narrowed. "Because you're the biggest pain in the ass I've ever met. Bar none."

"That's probably true, but beside the point."

I winced when she let go of me and settled back against the seat, still staring at me, watching every move. But I couldn't tell her I was immortal any more than I could tell her about my temporal magic.

Still, I felt her pulling away from me now. Mentally and physically. A touch of fear burned against her apprehension and confusion now, something that hadn't been there until today.

"Hecate, the goddess of night and magic, walked into my cubicle in acute care and shot something into my IV line. Paralyzing me."

Keller got quiet. "Are you serious?"

I nodded. "And then she impersonated another detective, signed my discharge papers for me. Without my consent. And then she walked me out through the front doors. With you in the waiting room."

Keller shook her head. "Where did this—this goddess take you?"

"She called it traveling between the worlds."

The detective chuckled and pushed her long black braid off her shoulder.

"Traveling between the worlds? Sounds like some old pulp story."

I shrugged. "I didn't get a chance to think about it. She waved her hand and we entered a shadowy tunnel. When we came out the other side, we were standing in front of some strange nightclub. A huge chateau that looked like Versailles."

"Versailles, huh?" she said, the hint of a smile touching the corners of her mouth. "Sounds like some sort of historic building or estate."

"Maybe? All I know is it was some sort of nightclub called Wraith's. Said it could only be reached between the worlds."

"Right," said Keller. "Of course. Some sort of private, exclusive club."

Of the supernatural kind. She had no idea how accurate that statement had been.

"Hecate insisted that I had started a magical war along the coast."

"You?" Keller scoffed. "A New York bounty hunter?"

I nodded. She didn't seem to think much of me. I had no idea what transpired here in Corvallis when Hecate was threatening to take me apart in little pieces. But based on how Keller had said bounty hunter, pond scum and Ebola ranked higher on her list than I did. Keller acted like I was one step (or more) beneath the gutter.

"No, because of something that Andy Keane saw." I frowned at Keller. "But detective, everyone thinks I know what Andy saw, but I don't. He never got to tell me. Now, I have to find out what that was. It's the only way to get this goddess off my back. She demanded I return in a week with an update."

Keller shoved the sedan's stick into reverse and pulled out of the space.

"Hate to break it to you, Mallory," she said and slid the stick into drive. "But Andy Keane is still dead."

"Although I'm shocked that Andy's still metaphysically challenged at the moment, there is a way to find out what he saw that night in New Jersey."

"There is?" Keller looked shocked, most of her nonchalant approach receding.

I stared down at my cuffed hands. "Yes, but...you're not going to like it."

"Spill it, Mallory."

I turned toward her, studying her angry expression and sullen demeanor. Couldn't say that I blamed her. She'd been through enough and now, I was about to dump magic onto her. I had to make sure I completely left that word out of my vocabulary.

"I have a...well, a gift. A talent. By touching an object that has been in someone's possession, I can sort of...see into that moment. See what happened. So, with something that had been in Andy's possession that night, I can see what happened. Satisfy Hecate's demand and find out why they killed him."

To my surprise, she didn't roll her eyes or laugh. I could see the thoughts racing across her eyes as she pondered my statements.

I'd intentionally left out the word magic. I didn't want to call it that yet. Keller's melon would explode if I did.

"You talk like you're a psychic or something." Keller chuckled and pulled out of the car park, driving past the helipad and headed south down Highway 99.

A sign said something about U.S. 20 and the coast. Somewhere ahead that would take us back to Newport. And up the coast to my bungalow.

"Are you like those scammers on television? Doing cold readings until something fits?"

I glared at her, shaking my head. "It's not a trick, detective. Or a parlor game. I have an unusual ability to read images from things that were in the space during the time that the event happened. That ability connects me to the people, too."

But I refused to call it magic. Calling it that might just make Keller walk away. Or have me arrested and forget I existed. I had no idea where it came from or how to use it, for that matter. It was all trial and error. But when there was a strong need to uncover something, I always gave my magic a try. To see what I could see. From being right there in the room with whatever had ignited the fuse on my magic. Or at least to see it in my brain.

Keller sighed as she followed the exit ramp for U.S. 20 and merged onto the motorway headed west toward the coast.

"And how would you use this...this ability?"

I glanced at her badge still fastened to her leather coat. She was going to especially hate this part.

"I need to hold something that belonged to Andy."

The detective almost threw on the brakes right there on the motorway, but she kept her foot on the accelerator, gritting her teeth.

"And what would that be, Mallory?" she demanded as she merged onto the motorway.

Traffic was light. The rain had finally stopped.

"We just need to go into the lockup and get a piece of his personal property," I insisted. "Something he'd carried around in New Jersey—that was in his hand or pocket at the time."

Keller glanced at me again, fighting not to slam on the breaks this time.

"Dammit, Mallory!" she shouted, both hands white-knuckling the steering wheel. "You're talking about evidence in a murder case."

I smiled. "I'm talking about taking something from the police lockup that belonged to Andy Keane. Nothing more. Besides, it's not like we can't put it back."

She slapped the steering wheel with the palm of her hand, glaring at me.

"Great," she snapped. "Just great. Now, I have to break into my own post's lockup because if the superintendent's involved, I won't have access to any of that now." She gritted her teeth, speed increasing. "And steal something that belonged to a murder victim. So, you can do some New Agey mumbo jumbo with it."

Definitely about to throw a wobbly.

I leaned back in the seat.

"Could we please stop at my bungalow for some clothes before we burgle the evidence lockup and nick something of Andy's?"

"I can't believe we're about to do this." Her voice trailed off.

Wonderful. Just out of hospital and on the way to Newport's police post to nick some of Andy Keane's personal effects. Without getting arrested.

"The only other option is for me to return to New Jersey and go to the bail bonds location," I said and gazed out the window at the other cars headed along the two-lane motorway toward the coast. "With no guarantee that's where Andy saw whatever it was he saw."

She didn't say anything.

"All right," I said. "I'll exchange my return ticket for tomorrow morning."

She turned toward me, amusement brightening her eyes.

"Nice try, Mallory," she said and nodded at the handcuffs on my hands. "You're not leaving my sight, person of interest. You fly out of Portland and I'll have to have you extradited back to Oregon for the murder of Andy Keane. By the time you land at JFK."

"Dammit, detective!" I shouted, jerking my gaze toward her. "When are you and every bloody cop on this coast going to figure out that I did not kill Andy Keane? I was trying to help him disappear."

"Just didn't get a chance to dispose of the body, did you?" she said and cast a quick glance at me.

I slammed my cuffed hands against the dashboard. "I! Did not! Kill! Andy Keane! I may be many things, detective, but I am not a murderer!" I glared at her now, not caring anymore. I was fed up. Tired of being bollocked for killing a man I'd been trying to help.

"Andy Keane had a wife and two small lads. He was scared out of his bloody mind because of something that happened at Beckerman Bail Bonds. He begged me to help him disappear from Beckerman's radar, detective. To protect his wife and boys. For all I know, they're all three in grave sodding danger right now!"

Keller glanced at me, but didn't say a word.

I kicked the dash with my bare foot. "Dammit, detective! Those two boys may be in terrible danger—along with Andy's wife. And I refuse to stand by and not try and save them. From what, I haven't a bloody clue!

But something terrible happened that night. And Andy Keane saw it. I don't know if these undead chasing me belong to Beckerman, your crooked police superintendent, or the goddess, Hecate. Either way, Beckerman married your super's sister, so it's from the same bloody source! So, either help me or arrest me because I no longer care."

She let the silence settle through the car, the heater still on high, seats heating.

"Fine. Arrest me then," I said, dropping my cuffed hands into my lap. "My bloody barrister will either get it thrown out of court or me into prison. Regardless, you'll be stuck at the post on Thanksbloodygiving. I hear the Colorado supermax has an excellent tofurkey feast on that day."

At last, she smiled.

"Nice monologue, Mallory," she said. "I've been trying to get you mad enough to spout off your true feelings since that morning at the bungalow. But you're so damned laid back that I couldn't get you angry enough. So, now I know that your focus is really on protecting Andy Keane's family. Not collecting a bounty. Not some grudge. We're on the same page. I want to help Andy's family, too. If you say they may be in grave sodding danger, then I believe you."

Sounded odd coming from her lips. Sodding. But it made me chuckle. Now, I needed to teach her how to properly say bollocks. Noun, verb, it was all about context really.

She nodded toward me. "And as much as I enjoy the scenery, let's get you some clothes and break into the lockup. For something you can use to connect to that night in New Jersey. We have to know what Andy saw—and if you can get a glimpse of it, then we have to try. So, yes, I'm in. Partner."

Couldn't stop the grin as I bowed my head, still parsing her previous statement.

She enjoyed the scenery? So, maybe there was a connection between us after all? And here I thought she had barely noticed my lack of clothing.

"Good," I muttered. "I just want to protect Andy's family. And bring in whoever killed him."

"Same," she replied. "Just glad to hear you wanting to bring them in instead of...dealing with them."

"Like with my machete?" I asked. "Tempting. But no, I'd rather the authorities deal with them."

Highway 20 was a lovely drive with its forests of pine trees and remnants of autumn leaves still falling along the two-lane motorway. Occasionally, it became three lanes, allowing faster vehicles to pass slower ones as it wound through wilderness and past creeks, passing little towns along the way until the motorway meandered past a carpet store and a bank and a realtor's office in a small strip mall. But instead of turning north toward Lincoln City, the detective turned left. Going south.

"Where are we headed, detective?" I asked.

"My place," she said. "It's just a couple of minutes south. Overlooks the ocean."

Well, that moved quickly. From admiring the scenery to her place? I raised an eyebrow.

"Why?" I asked, glancing over at her.

She looked me up and down again. Bandaged, handcuffed, in my boxer briefs. I had to look a sight.

"We need to get you some clothes," she said.

"As much as I admire your fashion choices, detective, I don't think they'll fit me."

She smiled. "I've got some men's clothes that might fit you."

I frowned, my spirits sinking. That meant she had a boyfriend. Or worse—a fiancé or husband. Dammit, I hated it when people didn't wear their wedding rings these days. How could she be married? Taken.

I tried to hide it, but dammit, I was gutted. I didn't even know why. I'd only known this woman a few days. What was the matter with me?

"Won't your husband get a bit mardy if you bring a strange bloke home in just pants and take some of his clothes?"

"Husband?" she said with a confused look. "Mardy?"

"Boyfriend?" I offered. "Fiancé? Last date still cuffed in the basement? You are a cop after all—with an apparent handcuff fetish." I held up my cuffed hands. "And Mardy is like—being grumpy."

"You're not good at this game, are you, Mallory," she said with a chuckle. "I was engaged for a while, but we broke up. He left some of his clothes behind. It was amicable."

I felt relief wash over me. "Is that what you told everyone? After burying him in the backyard."

She laughed. "Might have been easier if we'd hated each other. But we both realized that we were more friends than lovers. He was former Army like me. We had so much in common. Too much. There were times when I felt like we were the same person. We're still friends, but there was just something missing."

"A spark," I said.

She turned right into a car park behind a concrete and glass building with pale blue and green accents. Five floors that faced the ocean. She pulled into a numbered spot and turned off the sedan's engine.

"What do you mean, a spark?" she asked, turning to face me.

"You know," I said with a smile. "A spark. Fireworks. Flames. Something that burns through you so hot and so bright that you can't imagine being apart from them. Because nothing else matters but being with that person. That the worst thing you could go through is being away from them."

She stared at me for a moment or two. I had no idea what was going through her head as she shuffled that thick sable braid off her left shoulder. It fell against her back as her gaze never left my face. My eyes.

"Yes," she said in a quiet voice. "Exactly. I want that person to be my best friend, but I also want to ache all over without that person. That all I want to do is rush home and hear their voice. See their smile. Feel the warmth of their presence." She chuckled. "God, that sounds more like a Golden Retriever than a spouse, doesn't it?"

I shook my head. "No. Not at all. I want that person to be the first and last thought in my head even after I've been with them for a decade. And that after ten years, they still make me burn for them if they're away for the weekend."

A funny look touched the detective's face and then there was that familiar distance pushing her back again.

"Bet she didn't like you leaving for a whole week, did she?" said Keller as she slid the keys out of the ignition and opened the door.

"Who?" I asked, frowning. "My imaginary girlfriend? Oh...she threw a huge wobbly when I said I was leaving for a week. She's probably run off with the tosser that mows my lawn. Oh, wait—he's imaginary, too. Like my lawn. Sorry, detective. It's just me and my wild imagination."

She chuckled. "Imaginary girlfriend?"

I nodded. "Maybe someday I'll have a real one?"

"Can't believe that someone hasn't already snatched you up."

An interesting observation.

"Shocking, isn't it?" I said and held up my handcuffed hands. "With my suave style and sedate personality? And quiet demeanor. Who could resist all this?"

She pressed her hand to her mouth, laughing out loud as she opened the car door for me (my hands being cuffed made it difficult).

"Come on, Greysen," she said and leaned over, grabbing the cuffs, and unlocking them. "Let's get you dressed for success."

I pointed a finger at her. "I swear to God, if you put me in some dungarees, someone's gonna get hurt."

She squinted at me. "Dungarees?"

"I believe you Yanks call them...overalls."

She laughed and motioned me out of the car and I followed her toward an aqua door. That led to the entryway of her building. Just past the front desk on the left was a lift to the right. The cream-colored tile floor clicked as she walked over to the lift and pressed the button. The tiles were like blocks of ice against my bare feet, but I followed her to the lift.

Thankfully, the person at the desk was on the telephone and never looked up as we got into the lift and Keller pressed the button for the fifth floor. In a moment or two, a pleasing woman's voice announced we were on the fifth floor. I followed Keller down a hallway painted a serene pale blue with gold-framed prints of the beach and ocean. She stopped at 5 1 4 and slid a key into the white door's lock.

She pushed open the door and it opened into a shot-gun style condo. Kitchen on the left with a sand-colored quartz countertop and white lacquer cabinets. Stainless steel appliances. The condo was painted a pale mint green and had maple hardwood floors.

In front of a massive picture window that overlooked the ocean stood a teal sofa with two matching loveseats and ottoman that flanked a huge big screen telly on a glass table. Behind the sofa was a round glass table with four aqua-colored chairs. The room was soft with the scent of gardenias and lavender. It was a soothing space and well-decorated with cobalt vases, silk lavender flowers, and a small grouping of abstract paintings on each wall. The chandeliers dripped crystals and scattered the light, giving the room an almost ethereal glow.

"You have excellent taste, detective," I said and leaned against the back of the sofa.

"Thank you," she said and stepped into a room to the right. "I'll be right back."

I stood there analyzing the space, trying to learn something about her. Something more than the detective's façade she presented.

There were two bottles of red wine, Malbecs, on the countertop with two crystal wine goblets beside them. Two paperback books sat beside a stack of mail. History of Medieval London. History of the New World. A history buff? A catalog of gourmet foods with things like grilled artichokes in olive oil, smoked salmon, fair trade coffee beans, and hand-painted chocolates sat beside the books along with a gift card for Bob's Books.

Either she was picking out Christmas gifts or she enjoyed gourmet food, wine, and books about history.

Keller returned to the living area, carrying a stack of clothes. She set them on the kitchen counter bar.

"Nathan left a few pairs of Levi's, some flannel shirts, and some long-sleeved T-shirts. And a pair of white socks and sneakers. You're taller and thinner than he is, so I don't know if any of these will fit you or not." She pointed at the door behind her. "The bathroom's right there. Go ahead and try them on."

"Thank you," I said and picked up the pile of clothes.

I carried them into the loo and grabbed the first pair of Levi's. Way too big. The second pair was smaller, so I tried them on. Way too short. The third pair was long and a little loose in the waist. But they would do.

Next, I pulled on one of the long-sleeved T-shirts. A baseball-sleeved shirt. Long blue sleeves. Said California with West Coast underneath it. It was loose, but it hid my bandages and it was warm.

The white trainers were size eleven and a half. I wore an eleven, so that was a lucky break. They were like loafers, no laces. I pulled on the socks and slid my feet into the trainers.

And already, I felt ten degrees warmer.

I took the rest of the clothes out and set them on Keller's countertop.

"Much better," I said. "Thank you."

She smiled. "They look way better on you than they ever did on Nathan."

A compliment from the detective? Before I could thank her, she pressed ahead.

"Sorry, that didn't come out right," she said, a hand to her face. "I meant that Nathan wasn't really a casual dresser. He preferred dress pants and dress shirts to jeans and T-shirts. He always looked awkward in jeans."

She tossed a red and black flannel shirt at me. "Might want to put that on, too. It's still windy after that storm. Until I can get your jacket back from my department, you'll need more than that T-shirt today."

I slid it over the T-shirt.

"Thank you, detective. Now, let's go break the law."

"All right," she said and motioned me toward the door. "But when we get to the lockup, you let me do the talking."

"Of course," I said, following her.

She opened the door.

A man stood in front of the threshold. With a gun. Pointed at Keller's face.

11

I couldn't believe it! Ricky Rawlins was at my door. With a Ruger pointed in my face. I'd busted him for B and E three years ago. And he'd picked today—this moment—to find where I live and pay me back for arresting him.

His dark brown hair was shaved up the sides and long on top with a side part that fell over his left eye. He had a few days of stubble on his angular face, his jeans and steel-toed work boots dusty. He wore a faded green Oregon Ducks hooded sweatshirt splattered with flecks of white and yellow paint. He'd barely finished high school and worked at a package distribution center near Salem after getting out of prison a few months ago. It wasn't a glamorous life, but it was stable.

Why would he risk going back to jail for this?

Rawlins flicked the barrel of the gun at me and Greysen, motioning us back inside.

"Did you think I forgot about you, Keller? Bet you forgot about me in my cramped Walla Walla prison cell. Until now."

His gaze was hard, angry as he backed me and Greysen into the living area.

"And I bet you put yourself in prison," Greysen snapped, anger in that smooth British accent. "So, don't blame her for your poor choices."

Rawlins looked surprised. He swiveled the barrel of his gun toward Greysen.

"What'd you say to me?"

Greysen's gaze narrowed, anger sparking in those hypnotic violet eyes.

Oh, no. I swear, I'd kill him if he took one more bullet today.

I was not rushing him off to another trauma center. But if he got killed standing up to this revenge-seeking thief, I'd never forgive myself.

Still, his bravado was hot. I liked that he was taking up for me and he had way too much courage for such a young guy. But his lack of respect for guns and the people that put them in his face infuriated me. He was bandaged all over from taking six in the chest today and now, here he was, standing up to another man with a gun.

Unfortunately, today wouldn't be the day Greysen learned that lesson.

"You heard me," said Greysen in a sharp tone. "Own up to your mistake and move on. Otherwise, there's a supermax cell with your name on it."

A horrified look washed over Rawlins' face.

"Supermax cell? What the hell do you mean?"

Greysen nodded toward the gun.

"You fire that gun. Kill Keller and me. And you're going to supermax for the rest of your life. Is that worth your freedom? Sure, you're cheesed off, but only because you got caught. Deal with your own shite and stop whinging about the people that arrested you."

Rawlins' eyes glazed for a moment and then narrowed. He looked confused and angry as he glared at Greysen.

"Tell your boyfriend to shut his face, Keller," Rawlins said through gritted teeth. "Or get a bullet in it."

Greysen rolled his eyes.

"All right, I'm sick of people pointing guns in my face. And shooting me. It's really taking the piss out of being a bounty hunter!"

Before I could even open my mouth, Greysen grabbed Rawlins' gun and turned the barrel toward the ceiling as he wrestled it out of the man's hands. He pointed the gun at Rawlins.

"Now then, let's see how you like having a bloody gun pointed in your face."

"Don't!" Rawlins cried, throwing his arms over his head. "Please —don't!"

"So, it's all begging and manners, now, is it?"

Greysen sighed and turned toward me, lowering the gun. He handed it to me, grip first.

"All yours, detective."

He shoved his hands in his jeans pockets and turned away toward the window that overlooked the Pacific Ocean. Jeans that looked great on his lean body—model perfect with every curve and stretch. Much better than they ever looked on Nathan.

I grabbed Rawlins' arm and shoved him against the wall, gun still trained on him as I fished my handcuffs out of the back pocket of my black pants. I held up the cuffs.

"We've got two choices here, Ricky," I said, shaking the handcuffs in his face. "Either you walk away and deal with the fact that you got caught breaking into other people's apartments for two years and stealing whatever you wanted. Walk away from the fact that you spent three years in prison for it. Because it was your second offense. Or I can haul your ass down to the station and rebook you. Your choice? How'd you like to spend the holidays?"

"Please," said Ricky, trembling against the wall. "I made a mistake, okay? I'm mad because I have a shit job and nobody will hire me because of my record."

I shook my head. "So, your response to that was to come after me? A cop? With a gun?"

"It was a stupid mistake and I'm sorry," he said, holding up his hands.

I sighed. I didn't have time to deal with this guy, but I didn't want to be responsible for him killing someone either. One call from me to his parole officer and he'd be back in prison. I picked up one of my AirTags off the counter, one I'd been meaning to stick on the TV remote, and held it in my right fist.

"Ricky, one call to your parole officer and you're going back to the slammer. You know that, don't you?"

His eyes got glassy as a pleading look scrunched up his features.

"Please—don't call my parole officer. A guy paid me to come here and scare you, all right? Gave me the gun and everything. I'm sorry. I really needed the money."

I grabbed him by the sweatshirt and shook him, sliding the AirTag into the kangaroo pocket of his sweatshirt.

"All right, Ricky. You tell me who paid you. Now!"

"He didn't give me a name," Rawlins replied, voice quivering, "but I saw his phone screen when someone texted him. Called him Nev. That's all I know."

Nev. Short for Neville Ryan. Now, I was seeing red.

"Please," said Ricky, his gaze pleading with me. "I wasn't going to hurt you."

I pointed a finger in his face. "You promise me that the next time this guy contacts you, you let me know. Otherwise, I pick up the phone and call your parole officer."

"Okay, okay! I promise."

"Now, get out," I said with a growl.

Rawlins ran to the door, flung it open, and pounded into the hallway.

"You let him go?" Greysen cried, moving toward the open door.

I nodded but gave him my best smirk.

"I put an AirTag in his sweatshirt pocket. He'll go back to Neville or whoever hired him and the AirTag will lead us right to him."

Greysen grinned and grabbed hold of my arms.

"Detective, you're brilliant!"

His compliment burned right through me. I stared into his

mesmerizing violet eyes, still feeling that heat. Was this the spark that Greysen had talked about? God, I wanted to know. Because whenever I saw Greysen Mallory, I felt fireworks.

I reached out and squeezed his arm. Then I slid my phone out of my back pocket and held it up.

"Let's track our minion to the lair."

"You're on, detective," said Greysen, grinning.

Together, we hurried toward the door. I grabbed a small cardboard box off the kitchen counter as Greysen carefully opened the door. He glanced both ways and then stepped into the hall. I closed and locked the door behind me and then we hurried to the elevator. It beeped, opening, and carried us to the first floor.

Greysen and I rushed out to the rented Toyota Avalon sedan and climbed inside. I set the box in the backseat's floorboard behind me and put my phone in its hands-free holder on the dash beside my dash-cam and started the engine. The camera snapped on as I pulled out of the parking lot and turned left onto the highway. I headed south, following the AirTag to who knew where. It flashed across the map, moving away from the coast. Into the wilderness beyond the shoreline.

Until it suddenly stopped moving.

"Greysen, where did it stop? I wasn't expecting our bad guy to be so close."

His face looked pale.

"The map says...Coastal Mausoleums."

I felt my skin crawl. We called that place Crypt City. A 1950s collection of mausoleums where wealthy people who didn't want to be buried had been interred. The corporation went bankrupt in 1962, leaving Crypt City overgrown and forgotten. The forest grew up around it, swallowing it up. Hiding it from sight.

Until today.

Greysen groaned. "Another bloody graveyard?"

I nodded, knowing how he felt. But we had to follow Rawlins. It was the only way to find Neville Ryan after the dozens of laws he broke commandeering that MedEvac helicopter and trying to kill me and Greysen. I put out a BOLO on Neville as soon as I got to Corvallis, but a lot of good that did. After all, his dad, the police superintendent, knew how to hide people.

But what frightened me most was the fact that Neville Ryan didn't need to hide in a forgotten place like Crypt City. He had money and connections. No, he was in that nightmare land because he'd chosen to be there.

And the real question was why.

Was it because Neville Ryan really was a necromancer? Or was that just a cover for some non-supernatural crimes that this entitled scumbag was perpetrating.

I glanced at my phone and turned left down a lonely, winding road that faded into the fog and wilds nestled between the coast and the Cascade Mountains.

I drove for several minutes and then swerved right when I saw the unmarked road that snaked deeper into the thick, old growth forest shrouded with mist and moss. Somewhere in the solitude and shadow of this forgotten resting place, Neville Ryan was up to something dark and disturbing.

Following the road to its end point, the pavement faded to dirt and fanned out beneath rich black silhouettes of stone and marble mausoleums that cast long, forbidding shadows through the thin wash of sunlight filtering through the trees.

I shut off the engine and swiveled toward Greysen who had been unusually quiet. Wide-eyed, he stared at this strange world of the dead stretching out through the forest like some old horror movie set.

"We're going in there?" he asked. "Isn't that just asking for undead?"

"Afraid so," I said and slid my phone out of its holder. "The tag's moved to the center of Crypt City, so we've got to follow it."

I pulled my Glock out of its holster and reached over Greysen to retrieve my flashlight out of the glove compartment.

"And don't you dare get shot again, Greysen."

A smile curved across his face. "I'll do my best."

I set the black metal flashlight on the console and then reached into the cardboard box in the backseat, rifling through a collection of things that Nathan had never come and gotten. Like this long knife in a sheath that he hadn't reclaimed. It was a little shorter than Greysen's machete, but it would do the job. It was sharp enough.

I handed the brown leather sheath over to him.

"What's this?" he asked, his eyes brightening when he realized it was a blade.

"Something Nathan didn't want. Thought you could use it. Since your machete went AWOL while I looked for you in Corvallis. I think it's in the trunk."

"Smashing," he said. "I was afraid you were handing me a gun."

I chuckled. "You'd just shoot yourself."

"I would not," he said with a frown as he attached the blade's sheath to the belt loops on his Levi's.

"An undead would end up shooting you with it then."

"Much more accurate," he said, smiling, and patted the sheath. "Let's go find that AirTag."

I grabbed the flashlight and unfastened the safety on my Glock, sliding it back into the side holster underneath my purple leather jacket. And stepped out of the sedan.

When Greysen slid out of the sedan, I locked it.

I'd just put away the keys when I heard a twig snap behind me.

I turned, Glock drawn.

But something hit me in the head and I crumpled into blackness.

12

"Detective!"

Bollocks.

I hit the ground and rolled around to the back of the sedan. Scrambling around it, I found an undead standing over Keller, about to take her gun.

With long knife raised above my head, I catapulted over the car's boot and launched myself at the shriveled, decaying thing. I swung the long knife at the undead's head. Lopping it clean off.

Sharp blade.

The head rolled across the leaf-strewn ground and disappeared in the thick overgrowth of weeds.

Birds twittered in the trees above the sedan in the undisturbed forest—until the head hit the brush. The birds scattered like I'd tossed a hand grenade at them. No one had probably been in here for years.

Until Rawlins and Neville Ryan.

I hadn't a clue what they were doing out here, but whatever it was, it had disturbed the dead. Or raised them. Maybe both? I wasn't certain.

"Keller, wake up," I whispered in her ear as I gripped the borrowed knife in my right fist.

The air smelled cool and thick with the scent of burning leaves as I gathered her in my arms and crouched beside the sedan. I held out the knife, watching for movement. Then I saw her phone in the grass.

I stretched across her, retrieving her phone, and searched the map for that bloody AirTag.

I could see the blip still in motion across the map on her phone. Rawlins was moving around the crypts in the center of this place. I felt the hairs on the back of my neck stand up.

Like he was going door to door to awaken the dead. Or in this case, crypt to crypt.

The swish of grass echoed on the wind as stones rasped against marble. Abruptly, all the birdsong died away.

Bugger. That wasn't good.

"Keller," I whispered, shaking her again. "I think they know we're here. And by they, I mean the entire population of corpses. Because they've graduated to undead and are shambling this way."

I wanted to punch something.

Of course, they were undead. Neville Ryan had counted on me and Keller following Rawlins right to this place. Isolated. Empty of humans. Deep in the forest. Perfect place to kill a nosy cop and the last loose end from the New Jersey debacle.

I picked up Keller and her phone, placing both in the sedan's back seat. I locked the doors and shoved the keys deep into my jeans pocket.

The sound of dragging and shuffling through grass made me turn, long knife raised.

About fifty undead lumbered out of the city of mausoleums toward me. Bugger! I was severely outnumbered!

I held my blade aloft and jumped onto the bonnet of the sedan, waiting for them to get close enough.

"Nice try, Neville!" I shouted into the still, dark forest as the undead moved closer. "They'll just slow me down a bit."

Something cold as death grabbed hold of my ankles.

My gaze shot downward.

Two coffin dodgers were already at the bonnet, grabbing hold of my legs.

I swung the knife blade hard, decapitating the nearest undead. It took another swing to take out the one beside it.

And still they kept coming.

I'd swing the knife, take down one, and three more would approach from the left. Or the right. With more behind them.

I needed something with more power than this knife. I needed to send them back to where they came from.

Then an idea slipped into my head.

I grabbed hold of a headless corpse draped over the bonnet and yanked free a gold chain that had been around its neck.

Holding up the chain, I focused my temporal magic onto the necklace.

Hands grabbed hold of my ankles. Trying to pull me off the sedan.

I fought their hold, concentrating on the chain and my magic until red swirls of light shot from my fingertips and coiled around the chain.

There were too many undead now, pulling hard until I pitched head first off the bonnet and landed in the middle of the horde of undead. I hit the ground hard and rolled, but the army of undead surrounded me.

The knife bounced out of my hand when I hit the ground.

They were swarming me now.

I gritted my teeth against the bites and the tearing, focusing every last breath of magic I had on that chain.

Until smoke churned around me.

That's when I felt the pull. So strong. I could barely resist it as the sea of undead overwhelmed me.

And like a tornado, the past swirled in neon red tangles, rotating faster and faster until the light tangled around all of the undead trying to turn me into a breakfast bar. In a burst of red light, the world exploded into a torrent of heat and time and light.

When the smoke cleared, I collapsed onto the ground, panting.

"Mallory!" a voice screamed from somewhere in the center of the dark, hazy mausoleums. "What'd you do?"

I gazed around me, laughing.

I'd used my temporal magic to wrap up the whole lot of undead and send them back to the day that this city of crypts opened. Resetting Neville's necromancy timer. He couldn't call up these particular undead until they'd been in the grave a while. Buying us some time to get out of here. Because, to the supernatural, it was the 1950s right now.

"This isn't over, y'know!" Neville shouted, stepping out from behind a mausoleum about fifteen meters from the sedan.

He threw Rawlins in front of him and the thief hit the ground hard. A popping sound echoed through the trees.

And Rawlins didn't get up.

I felt terrible now. That monster had just shot and killed the bloke. Tying up loose ends as it were. Like he or someone in that pioneer graveyard was trying to do to Keller and me.

A smoky blackness hung above Rawlins.

Bugger! Neville Ryan was turning that thief into another undead. Time to go. But this one disturbed me. Rawlins knew where Keller lived. She couldn't go home until Rawlins was dealt with —permanently.

Couldn't wait to have that conversation with the detective.

Quickly, I used the fob to unlock the sedan and threw myself into the driver's seat. I shoved the keys into the ignition and sped away from Crypt City, kicking up soil, and leaves in my wake.

"Greysen?" Keller called from the back seat, sounding groggy and out of it. "What's happening?"

"I know you'll be shocked to hear this, but it was a trap," I said as the sedan hit asphalt.

Only then did I slow down and find my way back to the motorway that led to the coast.

Keller sat up in the back seat, holding her hand to the back of her neck, rubbing it.

"Something hit me in the head," she said, staring around at the trees rushing past as I burned asphalt back to civilization.

"An undead came up from behind you. Almost got your gun, but I took off its head. Putting it down. Neville summoned every last corpse from their tombs."

Her face looked pale, her mouth open, eyebrows raised. Even shocked to her core, Harlowe Keller was beautiful. I did my best to hold back my smile, her powder blue gaze burning right through me.

"That had to be sixty or so undead." She frowned, brow shadowing. "You just faced that many undead alone?"

"Only for a minute or two," I replied. "When I heard the birds stop singing, I knew it was bad. So, I put you in the sedan, hoping to face that coward, Neville. Only he sent fifty or so undead to negotiate for him." I sighed. "Oh, he also killed Rawlins. Probably tying up loose ends. And made him undead. I'm sorry."

She looked concerned now. "Without a body, Rawlins will only be reported missing. Dammit. It will be days before they open a missing persons case."

"Until he lumbers into a Safeway and starts gnawing on the nearest shopper. At least they're not zombies, biting, and turning half the population. But still, they could tear someone apart."

"Neville knows exactly how to get around our investigations," she continued. "Even if he didn't, his father does. Regardless, I'll call the tip line and anonymously report the location of Rawlins' body." She squinted at me. "How'd you get away from all those undead anyway?"

"I ran," I said.

It was true. I did run. After I'd cast temporal magic on the whole bloody lot of them and sent them back to the start of their interment. But I wouldn't tell her about that part. Maybe Hecate was right?

Maybe I did start a magical war here on the coast, but according to my interactions, these necromancers and sorcerers had been battling each other long before I got here. Maybe I didn't start it, but I sure turned up the heat on it.

Now, they were all gunning for me. And after throwing a shite-load of magic at Neville Ryan's little undead playpen, he would no doubt focus all his efforts on taking me out. If Hecate didn't decide to merc me first. Or Death, but he seemed to be the only one on my side.

I needed to get into Wraith's and plead my case.

But before I could do that, I had to get hold of a piece of Andy's personal effects. Cast my temporal magic on it. And see what he saw that night at Beckerman's Bail Bonds.

Only knowing what he saw would tell me what these necromancers were trying to accomplish. So far, they'd managed to keep Keller and me at least an arm's distance from their operation. But something connected them to this entity summoned in New Jersey. I needed to know what this thing was and why they'd summoned it.

Then I could go to Wraith's and plead my case. With Death on my side, maybe the patrons would keep Hecate from zapping me out of existence?

"How's your head?" I asked the detective.

She looked a little unsteady, but she still had her gun and phone and I hadn't gotten riddled with bullets again.

In a week, most of the damage would heal. It always did. Even six shots to the chest. I hope she didn't get curious about how those bullet wounds healed so fast. But by that time, I would probably be back in New York. Unfortunately.

That thought really bothered me now as I glanced into the rearview mirror—at Detective Keller. I didn't want to go back there now. I had...other interests.

"There's a guy in there with a sledgehammer that I wish would go away," she said with a groan. "Otherwise, I'm okay. Thanks for getting me out of there, Greysen."

I smiled at her in the rearview mirror. "It was my turn. But you're welcome."

She laughed.

"Now that we've survived Neville Ryan's trap, are we still headed to the evidence lockup?" I asked, glancing up at the rearview mirror as I stopped at the traffic light on the motorway.

She slouched against the back of my seat and peered around it at the dashboard for a moment.

"Since Rawlins is dead, er undead, and Crypt City was a trap—who knew—let's head to the lockup."

"By the way, detective," I began. Might as well break the bad news about her place not being safe right now. "Since Neville turned Rawlins into an undead minion, you can't go home until he's been dealt with."

She frowned. "Why not?"

"Detective," I said, glancing over my shoulder at her. "He knows where you live."

She went quiet. "I'll deal with it," she said finally.

She had no place to go. I knew because that's what I would have said if I hadn't had another option. She was trying to look unaffected by it.

"My bungalow has a second bedroom," I offered. "You're more than welcome to use it until we take care of undead Rawlins."

"No," she said, an edge in her voice.

"Detective, the door locks and it has its own on-suite loo. Complete with shower and soaking tub." I glanced into the rearview mirror. "And I give you my word that I will be a gentleman the entire time. I'd go to a hotel, but I don't want to leave you alone in case Neville sends another cemetery of undead at you. Us. And you can't trust your mates at the police post because their superintendent is a necromancer."

She was quiet for a long time.

"We have to fight them together, Keller," I insisted, my voice rising. "If they catch you alone, they could overwhelm you. And kill you. Don't forget, your Glock is worthless against undead."

I waited for her response, but she didn't make a sound. Finally, I heard a heavy sigh in the back seat. A reaction I got a lot from women.

"All right, Greysen," she said, sounding defeated. "I keep trying to come up with a reason why this is a bad idea, but I can't. Because you're right. Rawlins knows where I live and he probably knows how to find your bungalow, too. But I can't fight him with familiar tools. And I've never even swung a knife before. You'll have to teach me."

"Deal," I said. "There's nothing to it—especially for a cop and former Army special forces. Just need a spot of practice. And someone to watch your back while you lop their little grey heads off."

This time, she chuckled.

"All right. We'll head back to my place after the lockup. After I retrieve my CR-V from the pioneer cemetery and drop off this sedan. I'll rent something else, something Rawlins won't recognize. I'll need you to drive my CR-V back to my place before we return the sedan though."

"Certainly," I replied. "Anything I can do to help."

"After we get my vehicle back to my place," she continued. "We'll head to your bungalow and fortify it. Having it north of here might be a good thing."

Things were looking up.

I'd have to send Neville Ryan a Hallmark card, thanking him for sending Detective Keller to stay with me for a few days. I wondered if they had a card for this occasion. A *sorry you're undead* card. Or *congratulations on escaping your crypt* celebration card. No matter. A generic thank you would do nicely.

"Now then, where's this police lockup located?" I asked Keller.

"It's a little tan building about a block north of the police post. On the right."

"Shall I head there now?" I stared into the rearview mirror, waiting for her to respond.

She nodded. "Yes. Drive past the building and turn right. There's a gravel lot behind it. Pull in and park. I'll take it from there." Her gaze narrowed. "And make sure you do everything I tell you or we'll both be in jail."

"I have no desire to sit behind bars, detective," I said. Especially with Detective Keller coming to stay with me for a few days. "I'll do exactly what you tell me."

She gave me an unconvinced look, eyebrows pressing into a frown.

"Since when?"

"No time like the present," I added with a smirk.

She shook her head and looked away.

I followed the traffic headed north along the coast with its restaurants, whale-watching tour signs posted along the piers, and shops nestled along the beach's misty edges. The sky was grey and thick with clouds, winds gusting across the motorway as I passed the police post. Keller watched it slide past as I drove north another block or two.

"There, Greysen," she said, pointing at the square tan building with a black roof and two small windows in front.

The rest of the building had no windows. A narrow, cracked sidewalk wound up to the heavy, maple wood front door.

I turned right at the street past the building that had no signs or outward markings. And pulled into the small gravel car park behind it. Fit about four cars. I turned off the motor and turned around in the driver's seat, studying Keller's beautiful blue eyes and pert mouth.

Waiting for the lecture.

"All right, Greysen, you are going to stay right here while I go inside and negotiate with the clerk."

"What?" I cried. "Stay here?"

"Yes, because if this goes south, I should still be able to cover for myself. But if you're there, they'll arrest us both if it goes bad."

As annoying as that was, she had a point. I was an outsider at best. A person of interest at worst. Either way, I had no business going into that building. Like it or not, it was best to let Keller handle it.

"You're right," I said and leaned back in the seat.

"Wait, what did you say?" she asked with a chuckle.

"I said you're right, detective," I replied. "But don't expect those words to be bronzed and mounted as a trophy any time soon. You're right this time."

She was still smiling. "Oh, that hurt, didn't it, Mallory?"

"A bit," I said, chewing my bottom lip. "Do you think there's anything left of Andy's in lockup? If they sent everything back to New Jersey, then I'll have no choice but to fly back there and break into Beckerman's myself."

Keller slapped her hands over her ears,

"I don't want to know that," she said. "We're still waiting for records to identify Andy Keane's body, so nothing's been sent back yet. Regardless, you won't be able to leave the state, Greysen. You're still a person of interest, remember?"

"Even with Neville Ryan nicking medical air ambulances and trying to kill us both? You still think there's motive, means, and opportunity to keep me as the prime suspect?"

She hung her head.

"No. If it was up to me, you'd be off that list. But Neville's father has other ideas. Until you're officially charged with Andy's murder or something irrefutable removes you from the list, he'll make sure you're still considered the prime suspect."

"Or I'm dead," I snapped.

"Well, that's why I'm keeping you under police protection."

"So, Smitty and his sidekick, Buster, are going to follow me around the coast? Observe while Neville Ryan tries to kill me at every opportunity."

She chuckled. "No. Until we have enough evidence—showing probable cause—and indict the Ryans for murder, you're my partner on this investigation, Greysen." She poked my shoulder with her fist. "Blade."

I couldn't stop the smile from curling across my lips. She finally believed I was innocent.

"All right," I said and nodded toward the building. "Get something we can work with. We'll take it back to my bungalow and I'll use my abilities on it. See if I can see what Andy saw that night."

She got out of the sedan and opened the passenger side door. Opening the glove box, she took out her badge then grabbed something off the dash. She closed the door but turned around abruptly, gaze narrowed as she pointed at me.

"Stay in the car," she mouthed.

I rolled my eyes. Like I was a sodding five-year-old. I nodded and then leaned against the driver side window, locking the doors, and waited for her to return. Hopefully, she'd come up with something of Andy's that would work with my temporal magic.

Rain pattered against the window, lulling me to sleep. When I opened my eyes, the afternoon had grown darker, the rain harder until I realized that the pounding I heard was Keller knocking on the window.

I unlocked the passenger side door and Keller opened it. She dropped into the passenger seat, my bomber jacket in her arms. I frowned. It looked like she hadn't gotten anything that had been with Andy Keane's belongings. Just my bomber jacket that paramedics must have dropped off to the police post and entered into their system as evidence.

"Go," she whispered. "Now."

I fired up the engine and pulled out of the car park as she put on her seatbelt. I rolled out of the car park and turned left onto the motorway. Headed out toward the pioneer cemetery to pick up her CR-V and things from her condo before we dropped off this black sedan. I made a mental note to get my machete out of the boot and then we were headed to my bungalow.

<h1 style="text-align:center">13</h1>

After Greysen got my CR-V back to my condo, I pulled a tan duffle bag out of my closet and packed for a few days. Including work clothes. I was still on duty, trying to solve Andy Keane's murder.

Working with a partner on this one was nice (even if it was unofficially), but I had to keep reminding myself that in a week—two at the most—he'd be gone. Back to the East Coast. Even if sparks flew on both sides (who am I kidding...more sparks), a coast-to-coast, long-distance relationship would be almost impossible. Even worse, he was a bounty hunter and never knew where he'd be on a case.

No matter how hard it was, I had to pull back from this possibility. Throw on the brakes. To keep it from causing pain on both sides.

A lot of pain.

When we got to my condo, nothing had been touched inside. But I couldn't shake Greysen's warning. Rawlins was undead now and he knew where I lived. And all Rawlins had was time now. I could come home one night, open my closet, and he'd be there. To rip out my throat at Neville Ryan's command.

I'd never used a knife for defense before, not like Greysen

anyway. Sure, I'd had basic training in the army on using a knife to take down an enemy, but no training on how to lop off the heads of undead. With a much longer, sword-like blade.

In the lockup building, I'd gotten back Greysen's bomber jacket and a flashlight. The two black and whites that arrived on the scene at South Beach Cemetery had taken everything we'd left behind to lockup for me to retrieve. Which I appreciated.

The items were safe that way. And they gave me a good reason to be at the evidence lockup building. Long enough to grab an old silver Zippo lighter that had belonged to thirty-something Andy Keane. It was the only personal item left on the body besides a wallet.

Lifted it while I talked to Jared Atwood, the lockup clerk on duty. When he handed me Greysen's bomber jacket and my flashlight, I slid the bagged lighter into Greysen's jacket pocket. I asked Jared to thank the other officers for recovering the jacket and my flashlight all the way out at that cemetery. Said he'd pass along mine and Greysen's thanks. Greysen would be thrilled to get his jacket back.

And after Greysen was done with this lighter, I had to get it back to lockup. Fast. Before anyone (like the police superintendent) found out.

I glanced over at Greysen as he drove the rental car—a white Kia Soul—back up the coast to Lincoln City. I'd gotten his machete out of the sedan's trunk before we returned the car. The machete leaned against the console on the driver's side now and he wore his bomber jacket. God, he was so hot.

"Bet you're glad to have your jacket and machete back," I said.

He nodded. "Please thank the officers that turned in my jacket for me. And thanks for keeping up with my machete. I feel more comfortable fighting undead with it. And I've had that jacket a very long time. It's an original World War II bomber jacket."

It was a bona fide antique. Way older than Greysen. "Wow, a family heirloom?" I asked.

He shook his head. "I uh, own an antique shop back in New York."

I glanced down at the dashboard. At my dash-cam.

He had no idea that my dash-cam had captured the entire fight at Crypt City while I was knocked out. Recorded everything to my cloud account, but I didn't want to leave the camera behind in the other rental. It was in my duffle bag now, but I couldn't wait to watch the footage on my phone. See what really happened out there.

I had a feeling that Greysen wasn't telling me everything.

Or more importantly, he was hiding something. Something he didn't want me to know about him. He was still a person of interest, personally and professionally. One more question I had about his sparse background from a list that was already long. But the top question on that list was still about those gunshot wounds. Granted, he was a young guy—only 23—but I still couldn't wrap my brain around the fact that was he up walking around like nothing happened a day after taking six bullets to the chest. Six!

He was four years younger than me.

I admit, I felt a little uncomfortable about that. That made him fourteen when I graduated high school. But after 21, it was just a number. Right? And I couldn't deny that I was attracted to him. He was sexy as hell with that thick blond hair, warm velvet British accent, and those hypnotic violet eyes. Tall and lean and fearless. God, he was so my type! Except for the fact that we lived on opposite coasts. And he hated guns.

But I couldn't dismiss the gunshot wounds. Or how he'd survived fifty or so undead attacking him at once. None of it added up.

And what was this ability that he had? That allowed him to see the past through an object that belonged to someone else. Like that would be admissible in court. Was he lying to me about all of this? Was he one of those cold reading experts that could play a whole room and make them think he was psychic? I'd always been skeptical of psychics. Especially the ones that claimed to talk to the dead. I'll never forget one insisting she had a message from my grandmother. I lied and told her Nana wasn't dead, she was just in Fresno. Like the dead were all just standing around, waiting for some psychic to run into someone they knew?

No, I didn't believe in psychics.

But after what I'd seen with Greysen, I wasn't sure anymore. I saw Death in a graveyard. I'd seen a bunch of undead. And I watched a man take six bullets to the chest and walk around like nothing had happened.

That's why I needed to see the dash-cam footage. See what really happened out there—see how much truth he'd told me.

Nevertheless, I had to work hard to cover my excitement at spending the weekend at his bungalow. So much for putting on the brakes. I'd learn more about him, but it was a good excuse to get closer to him. Get to know him better. Although, I felt like I'd known him a while—just not the fine details.

I would never tell him any of this, but I was excited. And I tried to push it out of my mind again that he would only be here a week or two. He'd originally planned to leave Wednesday, but I knew that police superintendent Gil Ryan would never let him leave so soon. Greysen Mallory had nothing to do with Andy Keane's murder. I was certain of that now.

But I still didn't know who reported the body that morning. Saved Greysen's life. At least on that day. And I didn't know who'd pulled the trigger on the gun that killed Andy Keane. In fact, I didn't even have a murder weapon.

As the light began to retreat from the grey overcast sky, the pallid sun sinking into the ocean to the west, Greysen pulled the Kia Soul into the bungalow's driveway.

I grabbed my tan duffle bag out of the backseat. He tossed me the keys and I locked the rental car as he moved toward the front door. The car rental was in my name. Greysen didn't think I should drive my own vehicle right now, in case Rawlins (and the Ryans) knew what I drove. But a quick records check would reveal my rental reservation. With the police superintendent involved, nothing was safe and information was cheap.

I studied Greysen a moment. He seemed on edge, glancing around the sand and beach grass that surrounded the little cedar bungalow that stood about two hundred feet from the beach. And then toward the road that led up to Highway 101. There were so many shadows around the bungalow. So many nooks and corners to hide behind.

When he got to the bungalow's front door, he turned around with his back to the door, looking around again, those violet eyes narrowed, a frown on his face as he surveyed everything before unlocking the door. Like he'd felt something nearby. Or saw something out of the corner of his eye. He carried his machete in his right hand.

He had good instincts and I bet he was a very good bounty hunter. He wasn't ruthless and he had compassion. That made a big difference.

Even then, he didn't open the door and go inside. He stared at the door for a few moments, checking to see if anything had been disturbed. But I was tired and cold.

"You planning to stay out here long?" I asked as I reached out and turned the door handle.

He stepped in front of me, entering the dark bungalow ahead of me. I turned on the flashlight on my phone, my hand falling to the butt of my Glock in its side holster beneath my leather jacket.

His footsteps were quiet. Slow. Deliberate as he made his way down the hallway.

He paused in front of the dark living area. Studying it like he was planning to recreate it from memory. Then he reached for the light switch. Flicked it on.

The ceiling light came on, warm gold light illuminating the living area. At least the power was back on again.

"Anything out of place?" I asked. "Or missing?"

He shook his head, not saying a word as he moved toward the bedroom door on the right. He gripped the door handle a moment and then shoved it open.

A black suitcase sat on a folding metal luggage rack inside the open closet beside the queen-sized bed with a disheveled blue comforter. A Navy blue duffle bag set underneath a white wicker chair on the other side of a cheap pine dresser across from the bed. The chair nestled in the corner and looked odd all by itself—like it was missing another chair and a small table. An olive-green backpack sat in the wicker chair. To the right, opposite the wicker chair, a door led into the on-suite bathroom. Dark.

He crept past the bed and moved toward the white tile bathroom door. After flicking on the lights, he pushed back the blue and green pastel shower curtain.

Lights were bright. But no shadow stood behind the shower curtain. It was clear.

When he came back to the bedroom, he dropped to the floor and looked underneath the bed. Then he got to his feet, not acting at all like a guy who'd taken six slugs to the chest yesterday.

"It's clear in here," he said and moved toward the bedroom door. "Let's check the other room and the kitchen."

I nodded and followed him into the hallway, hand still on my Glock. Turning left into a small but modern L-shaped kitchen with those typical oak standard builder's cabinets but painted a pale sea glass green gave the cabinets a 1920s feel. The appliances had been upgraded to stainless-steel. The countertop was a cream-colored quartz that surrounded a large ivory farmhouse sink. A dark wood pantry door stood against the wall by a window that faced north.

He flung open the pantry door. Empty.

"Kitchen's clear," he said.

He went back down the hall and I followed him through a short hallway with a set of double doors concealing a side-by-side washer and dryer. At the end of the hallway, through the living room, and into a short hall was the second bedroom. The room was dark, the walnut four-paneled door wide open.

He turned on the lights, checked the closet, underneath the queen-sized bed, and the other on-suite bathroom. Nothing lurked behind the lavender-flowered shower curtain or behind the door.

"All right," he said, sighing in relief. "Guest room is clear, too. I'll leave you to get settled and your things sorted."

"We'll have to figure out something for dinner," I said and set my tan duffle bag on the bed.

It was a cream-colored room with maple hardwood floors, dark wood trim, and a lavender comforter draping the bed. Still had that 1920s feel to it like the rest of the bungalow. Another one of those white wicker chairs sat in the corner beside an old pine dresser that matched the one in Greysen's room.

"I'll cook something while you're getting settled," he said.

"You cook?" I couldn't help the smile.

I loved a man that cooked. And didn't destroy the kitchen doing it.

He shrugged. "I've got groceries. I'll whip up some fettuccine Alfredo. Do you like mushrooms and sun-dried tomatoes?"

"I like both." Wow, impressive.

"Red or white wine?"

"Either one is fine," I said. "Whatever you want to open."

I wasn't picky, but I was impressed that he'd offered to cook.

"Vinaigrette okay on your salad?" he asked.

I nodded.

"No problem with garlic bread?" he asked. "Any food allergies I should know about?"

I smiled. "Love garlic bread and no food allergies."

"All right then," he said, the hint of a smile on his face. "One fake Italian dinner coming up. After I check all the locks on the windows and doors. Check yours."

"I will."

I didn't want any surprise undead in my room tonight.

He closed the door and left me to decompress. Which I appreciated. God, he was so easy on the eyes—and the nerves when he wasn't diving headfirst into trouble.

I unzipped my duffle bag and pulled out a bag of toiletries and a hairbrush, putting them in the white bathroom, the lavender shower curtain and purple towels the only color in the space. The room smelled like lavender oil and lemons. I checked the lock on the bathroom window, making sure the window didn't pull up. I went out to the bedroom and checked the window with a view of the ocean. Lock was tight and the window didn't budge.

Satisfied, I plopped down on the bed and slid my phone out of my leather jacket pocket. The heat in the bungalow hadn't been turned on yet, so it still had a chill in the air. I opened up my dashcam app to review the footage. Couldn't wait to see what really happened out at Crypt City.

I started up the video, but I wasn't prepared for what I saw. Not by a long shot.

Watching him leap over the sedan's trunk to trounce that undead that almost killed me was hot. Intoxicating. And I couldn't help but grin as I watched him pick me up and protect me. Defend me. But my heart bounced into my throat when he put me inside the sedan and locked it. Taking on fifty or so undead alone. To protect me.

It choked me up. I had no idea he was that selfless. Because he had no idea that I would ever see what happened out there. And he wasn't about to tell me about it either. He wasn't the type.

In the video, he fought off a massive number of undead at first, but they just kept coming.

I couldn't stand it when they grabbed hold of him and pulled him off the hood of the car. But that long knife cut through them over and over, rolling heads across the ground, until he'd fought his way out of the barrage of undead.

Then he yanked off a gold chain from one of the decapitated bodies and held it up to his face as—I gasped—as red flames coiled around his fingers.

The undead were pulling him down into the swarm that was overwhelming him, but he held onto that chain until flames coiled around his hands and arms, growing brighter and roiling in the dimlit city of mausoleums.

In a sudden burst of red fire that spread out like an explosion, all of the undead vanished.

My mouth hung open. Where'd they go? How'd he do that? Was that...magic?

My God...how could Greysen Mallory do that? It looked like something out of a special effects movie.

But at the same time, it frightened me.

Seeing Death had already made me uncomfortable. VERY uncomfortable. I didn't like things that defied explanation. Things that didn't have straightforward answers. Clear reasons for how and why they happened. And Greysen Mallory defied all explanation. There were no straightforward answers about him.

That had been magic.

He'd summoned some sort of magic. But how? I never believed in the supernatural much less magic, but in just a couple of days, Greysen Mallory had shown me undead, the supernatural spirit of Death, and whispers of magic. Like my bracelet revealing my past to him. Until this dash-cam footage caught him casting something powerful enough to destroy fifty or so undead. Or something?

I had no idea what happened to them.

Or what Greysen Mallory was—exactly. He was smokin' hot, but what had I just witnessed him do in that video?

At some point, I had to bring up the dash-cam video with him. See what he said about it. See if he confessed to me what he was— and what this red magic was that coiled all through the video.

How would I bring this up though? *So, Mallory, how long you been a wizard?* I had no idea how to broach this subject with him. But I needed to know who and what he was. He had to level with me.

But at the same time, I didn't want to know. I didn't want it to ruin this attraction I felt for the smokin' hot bounty hunter. Even though he was leaving as soon as he was allowed to leave the state. He was so damned hot, but I wanted more than just a hookup.

If it ever got that far.

The heavenly scent of garlic and parmesan cheese filtered

through the bungalow. Making my stomach growl. I left the room and wandered into the kitchen. His bomber jacket was draped over one of the kitchen table chairs, machete leaning against the wall.

He had pasta boiling on the stainless-steel stove and a pan of Alfredo sauce with mushrooms and sun-dried tomatoes simmering. An empty carton of heavy cream sat on the counter beside the remnants of a block of parmesan cheese. He'd even grated the cheese fresh!

The oven was on, thick slices of garlic bread filling a baking sheet, slathered in garlic butter, and toasting in the oven.

A big glass bowl of lettuce, croutons, cherry tomatoes, and carrot slivers set on the counter beside a bottle of balsamic vinaigrette. And an open bottle of merlot.

I moved over to the cream-colored countertop and opened the pale green kitchen cabinets above the stainless-steel sink until I located two wine glasses. I set them beside the opened bottle and poured garnet-colored wine into them. I handed one to Greysen.

"Thanks," he said, turning down the burner on his Alfredo sauce as he took a sip of merlot.

"I had no idea you were making the Alfredo sauce from scratch," I said. "I figured it was from a jar."

"A jar," he scoffed. "It's so much better from scratch. Like grating the cheese when you're ready to use it."

"I have no doubt."

The timer on his noodles went off and he turned off the burner, using a spaghetti strainer to divide the hot, dripping noodles between two plates.

"A bit of pasta water lets the sauce coat the noodles," he said as he lifted the pan of sauce off the heat.

He ladled sauce onto both plates and grated more parmesan on top. He'd already set the small table in the corner of the kitchen with ivory cloth napkins and silverware.

Oh, my...this man was so handy in the kitchen. I smiled. And he cleaned up as he cooked.

I grabbed two big serving forks out of the silverware drawer and filled two small bowls with salad. I carried them over to the table along with the bottle of dressing. Then I came back for my Alfredo and wine glass.

He carried his plate and glass to the table and I sat down across from him with mine. He set down his plate and then slid into the wooden chair. After I put my napkin in my lap, he lifted his wine glass to me.

"A toast," he said, still smiling. "To bringing down the entire Ryan necromancy before Thanksgiving."

I clinked my glass with his.

"I'll definitely drink to that."

I took a sip of the wine. It was mellow and rich, a hint of blackberries and cherries. I would definitely find out what wine this was and add it to my list of favorites. It was delicious.

"I really like this wine," I said.

"Good. I was hoping you would. It's one of my favorites."

But when I ate a forkful of his Alfredo, all conversation stopped. The garlic warm and fresh, the sun-dried tomatoes giving it a little tang, and the Alfredo sauce was so creamy I could have poured it into a glass and drank it.

"Greysen...this is the best Alfredo I've ever had."

"The garlic bread!" he cried and jumped up from the chair.

Just as the timer went off.

He grabbed an oven mitt and pulled out the browned slices of garlic bread. He put the six slices into a small wire basket draped with a black cloth napkin, turned off the oven, and carried the basket to the table.

I snatched a hot piece of bread and dipped it into the Alfredo sauce, the garlic overload amazing.

"Wow, you can cook for me anytime," I said between bites.

His smile widened, watching me over the top of his wine glass with a steamy expression that made me struggle to focus on my pasta.

"Glad you like it," he said in a warm, velvety voice that was so sultry I felt the heat burn my cheeks.

I could get used to this. I felt like I'd known him for a long time and had to keep reminding myself that I'd only known him since Friday. How'd that happen anyway?

He picked up the bottle of vinaigrette, shook it up, and drizzled it over his salad.

"Dressing?" he asked, holding up the bottle.

"Thanks," I said and sprinkled a little of the balsamic vinaigrette over my salad, careful not to put too much.

And then I took another slice of garlic bread. It had a little bit of a tang to it, something I didn't recognize.

"Garlic bread's amazing," I said. "What's that other ingredient I'm tasting?"

A twinkle lit those violet eyes, his smile turning coy.

"Secret ingredient," he said with a chuckle. "If we live through this case, I'll tell you."

Dammit...I wanted to know now.

"Come on, Greysen," I said with a laugh. "Tell me. I don't want to wait until we catch Andy Keane's killer."

His eyebrows quirked up for a moment and his voice got low and dramatic.

"What if you're sitting across from his killer right now?" he asked in a dark, dramatic voice. "What if I've been gaslighting you this entire time?"

I stared into his eyes. He had a point. I'd only known him three days. Had he managed to charm me that completely? That quickly? Enough to let my guard down? A cop for crying out loud.

I felt a chill brush across my skin.

Was Greysen Mallory—if that was even his real name—Andy Keane's killer? Had everything he'd ever said to me been a lie?

But the chill receded quickly when I remembered the dash-cam footage. Everything he'd done on that video was to protect me. No.

Greysen Mallory may not be his real name, but one thing I knew in my heart. He was not Andy Keane's killer.

"Nope," I snapped. "Sorry. You haven't been gaslighting me and you didn't kill Andy Keane."

"Dammit!" he cried, laughing. "I was trying so hard to see if you still thought I'd killed Andy." He exhaled sharply and picked up his wine glass. "You've only known me a few days and have no reason to trust me. About anything. But I still hope to prove to you that I didn't kill Andy by finding the person who did."

I felt the tension drain from my body and I snatched up my wine glass, taking a long drink.

"And I plan to start with that item you got from lockup," he said and then he frowned. "You were able to get something, weren't you?"

I nodded. "Yes. After we've loaded the dishwasher, you can take a shot at it. See if it tells you what you need to know."

He settled back against the wooden chair, wine glass in hand.

"Excellent. Thank you, detective. I appreciate your belief in me." He took a sip of his wine. "Even if it only extends three days."

Like it or not, he was right. He was a realist. He felt the connection we had, but he understood that only a few days had passed. He wasn't going to make any assumptions or take any liberties.

I held up my wine glass.

"A toast," I said. "To more time."

"And more partnership," he added, clinking his glass against mine.

He watched me over his wine glass again as he took a long sip.

I drank another mouthful, intoxicated by him. His looks. His accent. His honesty.

I just hoped there wasn't a deal-breaking lie in there somewhere.

He set down his glass and reached for his fork. But something divided his attention for a moment.

Frowning, he looked up from his plate, scanning the room.

The kitchen was open to the living room, so if anyone was at the front window or the door, we would have seen them. But everything seemed still and quiet beyond the warm kitchen.

"Greysen, what is it?" I asked as I cleaned my plate, eating the last bite of noodles, sun-dried tomatoes, mushrooms, and Alfredo sauce.

He was still frowning. "Thought I heard something."

"What did you hear?" I asked.

I hadn't heard anything, but honestly, I'd been distracted by Greysen Mallory and hadn't been paying attention. Not like he had apparently.

"It was a really soft sound," he said, glancing around the kitchen and the living area. "Like a hiss."

A hiss? "You mean like the sound a cat makes?"

"Softer," he said, his gaze still traveling around the room. "Like a breath. A shuffle of feet. Something shifting."

Then I heard it.

It was the softest of sounds. Like a blanket rustling. Or the wind whispering across leaves. But not quite.

"I hear it, too," I whispered.

Greysen was on his feet now, grabbing his machete that leaned against the wall.

He moved into the living area. I followed.

His expression was intense. Concerned. As he shifted toward his bedroom.

The door was open and he stepped into the room. More cream-colored walls. A tangled blue comforter that hadn't been moved on the queen-size bed.

He checked the windows. Checked under the bed. Checked the closet and then the bathroom. He shook his head at me and we moved back into the hallway. Passing the washer and dryer closet.

He opened it. It was clear. Then he moved through the living room and down the short hallway to my room. Door was still open.

With quiet, determined footsteps, he entered my bedroom and I was no more than two steps behind him. He checked the bathroom, making sure the window was locked. Then he checked the bedroom window. Locked. Checked the closet. Empty.

With a nervous inhale, he slid down to the floor, pulled in a breath, and looked under the bed. I felt my hands beginning to shake, but he shrugged at me.

"Nothing under the bed," he said, getting to his feet.

But his eyes got huge and he stared straight ahead. Scaring the hell out of me.

"What is it?" I asked in a whisper.

Slowly, he pointed toward the closet.

I turned toward where he was pointing. And saw nothing.

"Greysen," I whispered. "I don't see anything."

He moved over to the closet and lifted his arm, pointing.

A chill shuddered down my spine when I finally saw what he was pointing to beside the closet.

Up on the ceiling. Where the trapdoor into the attic stood. The pull-down rope gently swayed back and forth in the air.

Someone had opened the trapdoor.

No heat or cooling blew through the space. No fans.

Again, that hiss-like sound whispered through the room. Hushed. Subtle. A sound I would have missed without Greysen Mallory.

My skin began to crawl and I moved closer to him.

The sound was the same one that the few undead I'd seen made as they moved, a little hiss of air. Like a sigh.

Like the sound above our heads. In the attic.

14

It was a horrid sound. One I knew by heart and dreaded hearing as a bounty hunter. It was the sound undead made when they moved and air passed through their dead lungs. Like a wheeze— or a last death rattle. A quiet, almost imperceptible sound. Unless you'd heard it before. And knew what it was.

And I had. More times than I cared to remember. I even heard it in my dreams whenever I had my recurring nightmare about waking up in a mass grave.

But that sound meant Rawlins was above our heads right now. Waiting for Keller to fall asleep so he could climb down from the loft and kill her.

"Rawlins!" I called out and grabbed hold of the cable, pulling open the trapdoor stairs that led into the loft. "I know you're up there."

"Greysen, please don't go up there," Keller replied. "What if there's a horde of them in the attic?"

"Then I'll be up there awhile," I said. "Decapitating the lot of them."

When the creaky steps unfolded, I climbed them into the dark loft.

The drafty space was murky and smelled musty. The long attic space that ran the length of the bungalow was empty and laden with dust, only bare studs and joists visible. And insulation. A small louvered window at the end of the loft let in slivers of light. Illuminating the lone grey figure standing in the middle of the room.

Ricky Rawlins.

I raised my machete and moved toward him.

He turned around, holding up his hands. Protecting his face that was already beginning to look hollowed, skin starting to stretch. Terror glimmered in his black eyes.

"No! Don't—please!"

I drew back the blade over my right shoulder.

"What possible reason would I have for not ending you right now, Rawlins?"

"Because Neville Ryan betrayed me, too," he said, his pitch rising. "He betrays everybody. He used me to get you and Keller out to that abandoned mausoleum. To kill you both. And when things didn't go his way, he killed me and made me undead after you wiped out his army."

Why would Rawlins come here? Even if Neville Ryan had betrayed him.

"Still doesn't explain why you're lying-in-wait above Keller's room, ready to kill her in her sleep. And how did you know she'd be here?"

Rawlins ran his bony fingers through his thick brown hair, looking panicked. As much as an undead could look panicked as the muscles in his face had already begun to deteriorate.

"Heard Neville talking to his dad. He thought you might come back here. With her. Look, I don't have nowheres to go now. I couldn't go back to my place at the halfway house. My life's over now —thanks to that bastard."

"Why not go back there?" I asked. "At least it's a place to stay for a while. One you know well."

He shook his head. "You don't understand—it's a halfway house. Temporary. And there are other people there. Besides, everything's so different now. What I see walking around now that I'm undead. It's terrifying. You have no idea what's out there!"

As an immortal, I knew what lurked at the edges of comfortable and safe. I'd dealt with the supernatural for centuries.

"You can't see it until you're dead either. I didn't know where else to go, so I came here. Thought if I could hide up here for a while and then maybe, I could help you take this sonofabitch down. Because he will show up here. He doesn't care about anybody but himself. Trying to impress Hecate with his—battle prowess, so she'll put him in charge of her army. His words, not mine. Hecate's smart enough to see that he's an idiot. Neville and his family only see other people as fodder for their undead army. Whenever they need them."

I had to admit, I felt a little sorry for Rawlins. Bloke needed money. Trusted the wrong chap. And not only did it get him merked, but it got him undead, too. That had to be hard to take. And after he saw me lop off undead heads to kill them all, he no doubt realized that he was just one more decaying body to Neville Ryan and his family. A necromantic number if you will.

But if he could offer me and Keller something we needed—like the location of the Ryans' necromancing empire—then I might not chop off his undead head in return.

He probably didn't have a choice, but I still couldn't trust him. For one, he was undead now. They were hungry all the time—for someone to command them and for the human flesh that had already decayed from their own bones. Or was decaying, as in Rawlins' case. In another day, I would have smelled Rawlins in the loft long before I heard him.

Nevertheless, Rawlins might have information we need. Or maybe he was just trying to save his own skin? Literally.

Either way, I had to talk it over with the detective. But I had to ask him about Andy.

"Rawlins," I said, lowering my machete. "Do you know what Andy Keane saw in New Jersey?"

"Who?" Rawlins replied, fidgeting more.

Who? Bloody hell. Keane started this whole debacle. Rawlins had to know who Andy was...and maybe what the young bloke saw that night.

"Andy Keane!" I shouted. "The bloke from New Jersey. He's the whole sodding reason the Ryans are after me. Saw the Ryans' sister conjure some entity. Now, what did he see?"

Rawlins frowned, thinking for a moment.

"Heard Kerrie on the phone to her brother. She whispered something about demons," said Rawlins finally. "A general, maybe?"

My blood began to chill. A Hell general? No wonder the immortals on this Coast were nervous. Hadn't expected that.

"All right, Rawlins," I said. "Sit tight and I'll discuss this with the detective. Just don't...try to eat anyone, all right?"

He nodded. "I mean, I could go for a burger, but not—people. That's disgusting."

Finally, an undead with a discerning palate. He began to pace again. Poor chap looked desperate.

I climbed back down and Keller looked frantic. She rushed toward me grabbing hold of my arms. The heat of her hands against my skin shot through me like a hot breath against my neck. And I wanted to touch her. Hold her. Kiss her. It took me a moment to sort my thoughts, but I didn't react to her touch—as difficult as that was.

"What's up there?" she asked, wide-eyed. "Are you all right?"

I nodded, pulling in a quick breath.

"Fine. It is Rawlins."

Fear lit those piercing blue eyes and for a moment, she looked like a doe caught in headlamps. Unusual for the detective. Then she recovered, that cool, hard-edged look brushing away any trace of weakness.

"He waiting for me to go to sleep?" she asked, anger sparking in those beautiful blue eyes. "So he could kill me?"

"Actually, I think he's feeling a bit lost because Neville Ryan betrayed him. Made him undead. He says he came here because he didn't know where else to go."

"Bullshit!" Keller snapped.

"He also said that he wanted to pay Neville back for taking his life from him. He wants to tell us what he knows about Neville and his family. Help us take him down. He said that the Ryans were betting that we'd come back here. And that the Ryans would show up here after us. Because Neville was apparently trying to impress Hecate enough to join her army."

Keller looked surprised and I felt cold when she let go of my forearms. She fixed me with those incredible light blue eyes as the fearless, analytical detective took over. And so did her distance, pushing me back to arm's length again.

I couldn't hold in the sigh that escaped my lips.

"I told him I had to discuss it with you first."

"You did?" she asked and stopped in mid-pace to stare at me.

Like she couldn't believe I hadn't just barged on ahead and made a decision for both of us. I wished she could see that I wasn't like that.

Only when it was a split-second life or death situation.

"Okay," she said, hands pressed against her face as she began to pace again. "Pros and cons to having an undead in the attic."

I chuckled. "We don't have to sift a litter box or give him kibble. Well, maybe a burger or two."

"All true," she said. "But immaterial. C'mon, Greysen—pros and cons."

"He was with Neville long enough to know what the Ryans' end game is," I offered.

"True," she said, still pacing. "And he's angry at being made undead, so no loyalty to Neville or the Ryans."

I nodded and pointed up at the loft.

"He can inform us about the whole undead experience. Like

numbers of undead. How large is their army. Where they were gathered from and how they were made undead. The necromancer's process."

"Yes, I like that." She continued pacing. "But con, he's going to get hungry soon and try to gnaw on you and me. And anybody else he can get near."

"A definite con," I said with a nod and stared down at my machete. "It's only a matter of time. But right now, he's sickened by eating human flesh. Mentioned wanting a burger."

"Con," she said and turned toward me, waving her hand in the air. "The smell."

I wrinkled my nose. "Yes, the smell will get worse."

"Definite con." She resumed her pacing. "There's also a possibility that Neville Ryan sent him here to gain our trust. Distract us long enough to end us."

That was my biggest concern.

"This is by far the most frightening con of the lot, detective. And I'm worried that Rawlins is the advance scout that will draw Neville's undead army to the bungalow like a searchlight. And we have no idea how many that might be."

She stopped pacing again, turning to stare at me. Nodding.

"That's my biggest worry, too."

Then I knew what we had to do.

It wasn't safe here for Keller and me. We had to take Rawlins and go find Death. Get him to take us to Wraith's. There, I could use my magic on whatever Keller got from lockup. So, I'd know what Andy Keane saw. And Wraith's was neutral ground. Even if the Ryans could find immortals to take them there (like Hecate).

Keller would also be safe at the immortals nightclub. Allowing me to find out how to deal with whatever entity Beckerman and his wife summoned that night at the bail bonds office. Kerrie Beckerman was a Ryan after all. And if she summoned a Hell general, we had bigger problems than necromancers.

Only the beings at Wraith's would know how to deal with a Hell general. I sure didn't. Again, keeping me and Keller safe. And putting Rawlins in a place where there were others like him. Giving him a bit of comfort.

What was it with the Ryan family and necromancy anyway? A bit of a strange tradition to pass down rather than Mum's tea set. But...maybe they were that good at it? They'd certainly done a bang-up job of it here along Oregon's coast. Working their way into Hecate's good graces.

One undead at a time.

But if she knew that a Hell general was involved, would she be that amenable to the Ryans?

I stepped in front of Keller and took her by the shoulders. She stared at me a moment or two, not saying a word.

The contact made me a little lightheaded. Made me feel warm all over.

"Keller," I said, studying her intoxicatingly beautiful face. "I think the best course of action is to take Rawlins and go find Death. Get him to take us to Wraith's."

She frowned, her brow scrunching. "Where?"

"Wraith's." I sighed. "The bar between the worlds. Hotel, too."

"The place where that goddess took you?" she said, looking amused.

"Abducted would be a better word choice, detective," I said, eyes narrowing.

"Those events were probably E.R. hallucinations, Greysen. You lost a lot of blood from those gunshots and they had you on morphine. You sure this place even exists?"

I nodded emphatically. "Yes, of course, it exists. I saw it with my own eyes."

She stared at me a moment, studying my eyes, my expression with her cop senses.

"You were under some pretty potent painkillers during all of that, Greysen. Not sure it's a good plan to go looking for Death for starters. And then try to go someplace that may or may not exist?"

"You believe Death exists, don't you?" I asked. "You saw him right there in that pioneer cemetery."

A faraway look touched her gaze as it slid away from my face.

"Honestly, Greysen—I'm not exactly sure what we saw in that graveyard. It was certainly something strange. But was it truly Death? I don't know."

I should have known she was a hardcore skeptic. I'd been one, too, until the night I woke up immortal in that mass grave. I couldn't exactly fault her for that. But Wraith's was the only neutral ground where I felt safe enough to use my magic. To confirm this nonsense about a Hell general conjured in New Jersey.

Magic had a strange effect on the real world. It left tons of evidence behind. And any being that had mastered any of those forbidden arts could detect it from quite a distance. I had no idea who was watching this bungalow. Or Keller's condo. Well, beyond Neville Ryan and his father, Gil.

Either way, if I went triggering my temporal magic and entered the time stream to see what Andy Keane saw, they'd know it. And the consequences could be dire.

No, Wraith's was the only neutral ground I trusted. And Detective Keller had no idea about any of this. Much less what I was. And I couldn't tell her. No matter how I felt about her, I couldn't afford to trust someone with that information after only a few days.

I couldn't risk it. Besides, it wasn't safe. And in a week, I'd probably be back in New York anyway.

All right, that was a lie. The bloody bungalow was for sale at an incredible price. And the seller had granted me the right of first refusal. I'd already bought it. So, I could stay here indefinitely. With no reason to go back to New York.

I didn't want her to cut contact with me! Okay? The moment she knew I was immortal, that would be the end of this incredible partnership. Of the sparks between us.

And that made me ache all over.

Sighing, I let go of her and turned away.

"Detective, what if I ask you to suspend your overly suspicious, skeptical cop senses for a bit?"

"My what?" she asked with a chuckle.

"You didn't believe in undead until we were attacked by them. Try to stretch your sense of wonder a bit further. Enough to believe that Death is a real supernatural entity and Wraith's is a real nightclub where supernaturals hang out. Between the worlds."

"You're really focused on this place," she said, standing at my shoulder. "Why?"

"Because it's the only place I can think of that will keep you safe," I said, turning toward her. "Safe when I use my ability on Andy's personal possession."

How could I explain this in a vaguer way and not come right out and tell her that I was immortal and I could summon a strange magic I didn't understand? And couldn't control.

She was quiet again, the thoughts flashing past her eyes.

"Well, I'm starting to agree about things not being safe here. Or anywhere along the coast." She motioned toward the loft. "If Rawlins got in, so could any of Neville Ryan's...creations. And besides, Rawlins said that Neville and his family will be coming here soon."

And I hadn't even told her about the Hell general yet. I wouldn't, I decided. Not until I was certain.

"Exactly!" I said, turning toward her. "The only being brave enough to tangle with Death is Hecate, but the two of them will honor a truce at this bar. At least they did the only time I was there. And our necromancers will have to find a goddess or entity like Death to follow us there. Unfortunately, that means teaming up with a god or a witch. Even if the Ryans do follow us, they wouldn't dare try anything in a room full of gods and sorceresses. Even if they joined forces with Hecate herself."

"And being necromancers isn't enough to get them to this place on their own?" Keller asked.

I shook my head.

"Correct. Necromancy rarely involves an independent power to raise the dead. Most of the time, it involves summoning spirits or demons into bodies. Transferring ancient energy from artifacts to bodies in awful rituals that involve blood, fire, or fragrant ash. Now, if they had a rare necromancer's power, they could bring themselves here. But most of them are like those novice hackers on the internet that download software kits that they don't understand to break into websites."

Keller crossed her arms against her chest.

"I swear, this is the craziest thing I've ever done." She glanced at me. "Since I met you. You've turned my life upside down, Greysen, you know that, don't you?"

I gave her my most charming smile. "In a good way," I said and poked her shoulder. "Admit it. You'd be so bored without me."

At last, she smiled. "Gotta admit, things have definitely been interesting since you arrived and shook up the coast."

"Me?" I cried, a hand on my chest. "I'm not the one reanimating corpses in every cemetery from here to California. Much less, summoning gods to run my errands."

Then she got quiet and turned away, toward the loo. She stood there a moment and finally whirled around.

"All right," she said with a sigh. "I've only known you for three whole days, so I can't say I one hundred percent trust you."

I hated that statement. It bore right through my chest. But she was right. She wouldn't be the eagle-eyed detective that she was if she trusted me (or anyone) after three days. But I had to admit, her statement stung.

I nodded and focused on my feet.

"I get it. That's fair."

"You didn't know I had a dash-cam rolling when we went out to Crypt City, did you?"

A cold chill danced along my skin. A dash-cam? Dear God...what had she seen me do out there? Had she captured me casting magic on digital media? Bloody hell.

"You look unnerved, Greysen," she said, unblinking as she studied me with that cop's gaze.

That cop's suspicion. Like she was about to read me my rights.

"I don't like being recorded without my knowledge or permission, detective," I snapped, unable to take the anger out of my tone. "I guess we're back to person of interest again, aren't we?"

I turned and walked out of the room. She could sort things out with Rawlins herself. I was done.

"Greysen!" she called after me, but I kept walking.

I went into the kitchen and picked up my wine glass. Drained it. And poured another one.

She caught up to me as I set down the bottle. Her hand was on mine now, the heat intoxicating.

I shuddered, wanting to wrap her in my arms and carry her into the bedroom, but it wasn't enough to overpower the pain I felt in that moment. Except for my old friend, Cash Cattrel (who was in New York), I had no one I could trust. No one I could tell that I was immortal. That I could cast magic. Even though our time together had been much too short, not even Elizabeth knew those things about me. I couldn't tell her. Couldn't break her mortal heart, knowing that she would grow old and die and I'd look eighteen forever. Even though it had eaten me up inside every day, knowing that was our future together. And the future of anyone else I made the mistake of fancying.

At times, the pain was unbearable.

"Did you bring your cuffs?" I snarled, glaring at Keller as I pulled away, turning toward the kitchen table.

I had a mess to clean up. And I couldn't wait to leave it behind for New York again. Selling this bungalow would be easy peasy given its proximity to the ocean, but I'd let a realtor handle that.

From New York.

"Greysen, stop!" she shouted. "And listen for a moment. Please."

"Is this good cop or bad cop, detective?" I asked with all the sarcasm I could muster, but didn't turn around.

I felt her hand gently press against my arm. The heat of her skin enveloped me like a guttering winter hearth and I wanted to drown in her warmth.

"This is just Harlowe Keller, Greysen," she said, her voice a little shaky now, a little unsure. "No cops. No agendas."

I was surprised, but not convinced I wasn't being played. I didn't turn around.

"You saved my life out in that abandoned mausoleum."

Her voice was gentle and a little emotional. Vulnerable. It surprised me.

"It was my turn," I said in a quiet voice.

"No," she said. "I don't believe that. Because I watched you leap over the back of that sedan and decapitate that undead about to kill me. I saw you pick me up and stand guard over me. And then I watched you put me inside the car, lock it, and face all those undead. Alone."

That was mostly accurate. The one thing she left out was the part when I summoned my temporal magic and sent them all back to the day they were first interred in their mausoleums. She had me using magic on a recording. She had me dead to rights. I couldn't deny it. And I couldn't argue it away. Every time I used my temporal magic, it gave off a red glow that surrounded my fingers and hands. Sometimes, my entire body.

She had the footage, so I was no longer a who. I was a what. A freak. A curiosity. A complication that couldn't be explained away by the modern world. One she didn't want any part of—she'd said so herself—like the rest of this supernatural piss-parade she'd already seen.

"I wasn't about to let you get killed, detective," I said in a weary voice. "Not on my watch."

"Why?" she asked.

Why? A damned good question. One I wasn't quite able to put into words just yet. Okay, it bloody scared me—happy now?

Because I had feelings for her. Strong feelings that I hadn't had since…since—ever. Not even Elizabeth shot sparks through my body the way that Detective Harlowe Keller did.

And that terrified me.

"Why, Greysen?" she repeated. "You're the main suspect in my murder case."

I whirled around, unable to hide my shock.

She'd just told me that she didn't believe I had anything to do with Andy Keane's murder. But this whole time, I've been her main suspect.

My God, she had been playing me the whole time. And I'd supplied all the harmonies.

"So, I've been your main suspect the whole time?" I said, glaring at her, anger hot at my temples. "I distinctly recall you telling me that you didn't think I had anything to do with Andy's murder."

She moved toward me and grabbed my left arm, shaking me. Almost spilling merlot down the front of my shirt.

"Let me finish," she said, voice clipped with anger. "You're the main suspect, so leaving me to die in that abandoned mausoleum would have helped your case immensely." She loosened her grip on my arm. "That's when I knew you were one hundred percent innocent, Greysen Mallory. Not only did you not do that, but you risked your own life to protect mine. You fought off fifty or sixty undead to keep them from killing me. That's when I also knew that you had my back."

I stared at her now. Surprised. So, she didn't think I killed Andy Keane and she knew that I'd risked my life to protect her.

"I'm sorry," she said, her eyes turning watery. "That all came out wrong. I wanted you to know that I saw what you did to protect me out there. And I wanted to thank you, because most people wouldn't have bothered."

I bowed my head, covering my eyes, feeling embarrassed that I'd gotten so angry. I just couldn't believe that she still thought I was a person of interest after everything we'd been through these past few days.

Had it only been three days? Seemed like weeks. Months. Keller was comfortable. And the heat between us was heady. Feelings I'd never felt before.

Forgive me, Elizabeth. I loved you, but I walked on eggshells the whole time we were married. At the first whiff of magic, you'd have fled from me in terror. After being hung by the crown for witchcraft, I couldn't take seeing that hysteria burning in your eyes. Every day, I feared you'd find out and leave me. Turn me into the church for heresy.

"I'm sorry, too," I replied. "I thought you believed that I had nothing to do with Andy's death. And after I faced down all those undead, I couldn't believe you thought I was still a person of interest." I pulled in a breath. "I overreacted. I'm sorry."

She rubbed my arm. "You're apologizing when I'm the one that should apologize. Greysen, you risked your life for me. More than once. I wanted to thank you." She paused a moment. "But I have to ask..."

I stiffened. Here it comes. The magic.

"What happened to all those undead? What...did you do —exactly?"

How could I possibly explain this to her? Without using the M word. Magic.

I studied her face, her expression. She couldn't wrap her head around the fact that Death had been in that cemetery and that necromancy was real. How could I possibly explain to her that magic was real, too? I think her melon would explode if I even hinted at that. But she clearly had footage of me doing magic. I couldn't explain that away.

But I was going to try.

"I grabbed a necklace off one of the undead I'd decapitated," I said, trying to find a neutral way to explain this to her. "Personal effects can really foul up a necromancer's control. My picking it up sort of...reset the necromancer's timer on his undead army. Sending them back to the day they were entombed."

Her eyes widened. "Are you serious? How is that possible?"

I shrugged. Feign ignorance. It was all I could do.

"I'm not sure, but it has something to do with past and present conflicting. I'd heard it was possible, but until I picked up the necklace, I had no clue that would actually work."

She looked a little confused, but like me, she didn't understand enough about necromancy to argue the point. I knew very little about necromancy, only the evidence it left behind, and I only knew a bit about temporal magic. Enough to use the magic—from a lot of trial and error. Unfortunately, it hadn't come with a manual.

"Regardless, I wanted to thank you."

I managed a smile this time. "Any time, detective."

"So, that still leaves us with Rawlins and Andy Keane's lighter."

"What?" I replied, frowning.

She leaned against the kitchen counter and crossed her arms.

"If you think we should find Death and go to this strange bar for goddesses, I'll trust you. I trusted you with my life back at that mausoleum, so I'm going to trust you now. With Rawlins and Andy Keane's lighter."

She reached into the pocket of her leather jacket and held up the bag with a silver rectangular object to me.

I took it. And opened the plastic bag. Removing the lighter.

The metal was warm against my fingers, stirring up my powers. I turned it toward the light. It was a Zippo lighter. An old one. Chrome finish. A little scuffed up. But the longer I held it, the more likely my temporal magic would fire up.

Right in front of the detective.

And I couldn't deny that it was magic if the red waves of energy wrapped around my fingers and Andy Keane's lighter. Right in front of her. She couldn't witness me using my magic. It would scare the bloody hell out of her and then she'd want nothing to do with me.

I dropped back into the plastic bag.

"I'll let you hold onto it," I said, pressing the bag back into her hand. "Chain of custody and all that lot."

"You're probably right," she said.

If I got Death to take us to Wraith's, she wouldn't know that I could take myself there now. That I was an immortal with magic.

I'd kept it from Elizabeth for two years. She'd been terrified of a local voodoo priestess and anything otherworldly that didn't come out of the Catholic church. She'd have been terrified of me if she'd learned I had magic. And I couldn't bear that thought any more than I could stand Detective Keller being frightened of me.

"Does that mean we're going to go find Death?" I asked.

She nodded. "But only if Rawlins rides way in the back. Or drenches himself with a boatload of Febreze." She waved her hand in front of her nose.

I laughed, but I understood. Undead smelled like...well, death. Rotting. Decay. Compost.

"All right," I said. "I'll get my jacket and Rawlins."

"Where do we find Death?"

I shrugged. "Let's try the pioneer cemetery again. And with our undead friend in tow, that might be good bait to lure Death out. But we'll have to make sure he doesn't take out Rawlins yet. I don't think he's quite ready to cross over just now. Unfinished business and all that. I may need to get a takeaway burger though. So he doesn't get hungry."

"You get Rawlins and I'll get my phone. We'll meet..."

Keller's voice trailed off as her gaze shot to the kitchen window.

I turned toward it.

Shadows moved past, the night beginning to settle along the beach, wind rising. Stiff, lumbering shadows. Clumsy against the sand and beach grass.

Bollocks! Neville had sent another wave of undead after us. Not even the bungalow was safe right now. So much for the evening with Detective Keller I'd had in my head.

"This wanker's really done my head in," I said and grabbed my machete. "And I'm about to throw an epic wobbler. With my machete."

"A what?" Keller replied, looking completely kettled.

"A wobbler!" I shouted. "A bloody tantrum. I've had it with these wankers."

The sudden smell of decay made my nose wrinkle. I turned, machete raised.

Rawlins lumbered into the kitchen, looking gobsmacked.

"Neville and his family sent another army of undead after you two!" the undead thief cried, pointing toward the back door. "And I think he did a graveyard sacrifice, too. Summoning a god. Hecate, I think."

My blood turned to ice. Hecate? Again?

"So, he's managed to team up with Hecate after all?"

That was terrible news.

"Think so," said Rawlins. "After he heard that Death had freed you from her clutches. Figured she'd be his best ally now. Since she's all kinds of pissed at you."

Groaning and scritching scraped along the kitchen window. Back doorknob began to rattle.

Keller's eyes glinted, looking anxious as her gaze darted from me to Rawlins to the window. Then the door.

"We need to get out of here," Rawlins said with a hiss. "Now. He's probably not far behind them. And what if Hecate's with him?"

"Or what?" I demanded. "Be knee-deep in undead heads? Because I'm going to get machete elbow lopping all of them off tonight." I turned to Keller. "Bloody hell! Where's he getting all of them? Has he been raiding every cemetery along the coast? Like someone isn't going to notice that all their cemeteries are empty? Is he ordering them online? From Etsy? Half-Price Corpses? Undead dot com?"

"He's going to empty every cemetery near here," said Keller, frowning. "And then what happens?"

I shrugged as I drained my wine glass again and set it on the table.

"All right, let's fight our way to the Kia Soul—how appropriate—and go find Death."

"What? Death!" Rawlins grabbed hold of the kitchen counter and huddled there, cowering. "Why you gonna do that? Man, I was straight with you!"

"Relax, my whingy undead friend," I said, patting him on the back, careful not to knock anything loose. Like a shoulder blade—or his rib cage. "Death is going to take us to a place that's safe. Including you."

"You sure?" Rawlins asked, squinting at me.

Even the sodding undead were questioning my motivations now. Fine.

"I'm positive," I said and motioned the detective out of the kitchen. "And you have my word. He'll know that you have unfinished business."

"How?" Rawlins asked in a quiet voice.

"Because I'm going to tell him, that's how," I insisted. "Now, come on. Before those wankers get inside and I end up with a huge cleaning bill after they've completely bollocked my bungalow. We'll get you a nice takeaway burger to tide you over and go find death."

"Fries, too?" Rawlins asked in a quiet voice.

"Yes, I'll spring for bloody chips, too. Now, let's get out of here."

Something crashed hard against the back door. Hissing rose above the wind, bones rattling above the swish of beach grass.

Keller grabbed my arm and jerked me into the hallway. Toward the front door. Rawlins shuffled behind us.

15

With the detective and Rawlins behind me, I swung my machete in a wide arc and mowed down several undead as we moved toward the Kia Soul. Keller had the keys and used the remote starter on the key fob, but she kept it locked until we got close. Didn't want any unwanted undead passengers stowing away and surprising us later.

We got past the bungalow's entryway. Past the overgrown rhododendron bush and the Japanese Maple, leaving a dozen or so headless undead in our wake. Down the narrow walkway to the driveway.

The vehicle was no more than fifteen meters or so away. But at least two dozen undead stood between us and the Soul. That I could see in the darkness anyway.

I rushed ahead with my machete and cut through the center of the undead line, felling a bunch of coffin dodgers. I motioned Keller and Rawlins past me.

"Go!" I shouted at them. "Get in the car. Now!"

Keller sprinted past them, moving toward the white Kia Soul. Rawlins shambled behind her.

I swung the machete again, taking off the head of an undead trying to gnaw on my arm. As more came at me from all sides.

Dammit! Too many to take down with one machete. I needed one in each hand.

Shoving one undead into a big group, I whirled around and slammed my elbow into another one's face.

Undead fragile bones crumbled. Papery skin tore.

But three coffin dodgers grabbed me from behind, jerking me backward. As the rest of them advanced on me.

"Greysen!" Keller shouted.

I hit the ground as six or seven of them pounced on me. Evidently, they thought the buffet was open. Had some very bad news for them.

I kicked two of them. Bones snapped. Skin turned to dust.

Swinging my machete like a buzz saw, I lopped off two of their heads. But four more leaped on top of me. Biting. Tearing. Clawing.

I whipped the blade around, taking off another head. But they were dragging me down. Rending my clothes. Slicing into my skin.

Overpowered, I dropped to my knees. As they swarmed me.

This was going to hurt.

But the Kia Soul slammed into them. Rolling over two. Knocking the others backward.

I decapitated another one trying to snack on my shoulder as Keller threw open the front passenger door.

"Greysen! Get in!"

I swung my arm, knocking a coffin dodger backward.

Scrambling up from the ground, my body aching all over, I ran around the Kia, and jumped into the passenger seat as Keller peeled out of the driveway. Doors locked when I slammed the door and she put it into drive. Chest heaving, I laid my head back against the headrest.

"Thank God they're not zombies," she said and gently touched my left shoulder where my shirt had been torn open.

Part of it hung off my chest, revealing bare skin and wounds. And blood. I wondered if she'd notice that the gunshot wounds were barely noticeable now.

"Very good point," I said between breaths. "You'd have your hands full, wouldn't you?"

She looked unnerved by that comment as she turned right onto the 101 motorway and headed south. Toward the pioneer cemetery where we'd first found Death.

"Are you sure you're all right?" she asked, glancing from me to the road.

I nodded. "Fine. There were just too many of them for one machete."

"That was close," said Rawlins, wide-eyed. "Next time, I—I could help. If you had another machete."

I laughed. An undead taking out his own kind with a machete? That thought entertained me.

"You'd be comfortable decapitating your own kind, Rawlins?"

"Why not?" he said with a shrug. "It's them or me."

Bloke had a point.

Keller motioned toward the back seat. "There's a box with a long knife in it, Rawlins. And Greysen, your bomber jacket is back there, too. It looks authentic. Was that passed down to you by your great grandfather or something?"

Actually, it was mine. I'd fought in many American and English wars since I got put ashore in 1726. And that included World War II. I'd earned that bomber jacket. It even had Corporal Mallory embroidered inside.

"Yes," I lied. "It's been in the family for a long time."

"That's really something," she said. "I figured it was pretty important to you."

I nodded. Honestly, I felt ambivalent about the jacket. Other than the fact that I'd earned it—for better or worse. Like my American militia coat from the early 1800s. But that was another story.

Rawlins screamed and threw himself back against the seat. Startling the bloody hell out of Keller and me.

I jerked my gaze toward the back.

Empress sat on the seat behind me. Licking her front paw, her long tortoiseshell fur almost transparent. She glanced up at me, sniffed the air, and mewed her disdain. Apparently, she didn't care for the smell of undead either.

"What's wrong?" Keller cried, glancing in the rearview mirror and then over at me.

"I haven't a clue," I responded, still staring at Empress who settled into the seat behind me and began to purr.

A loud, pigeon-like purr that was strangely soothing.

"Nuthin'," Rawlins muttered, glancing from Empress to Keller. "Just got startled. I'm good."

Guess he figured that she and I couldn't see the ghost cat, so why bother mentioning it. I liked that about him. For an undead, he was rather calm and likable.

Keller gave Rawlins a look that was part annoyance and part confusion. She glanced at me again, like she was checking to make sure everything was still okay. I gave her my best kettled expression and shrugged.

The drive to the pioneer cemetery was almost forty minutes, after we stopped at a takeaway and got Rawlins his burger and chips. Keller was unusually quiet and Rawlins kept to himself. Empress continued to purr. I had no idea what might be going through Rawlins' head right now. The other undead had been dead for quite some time, but Rawlins had been alive and then suddenly dead and then undead.

I admit, I felt sorry for the bloke. He hadn't had a chance to deal with the fact that he was even dead and now, he was undead.

But my head was spinning with all sorts of other possibilities. What if we couldn't find Death? How could I get us to Wraith's without Keller asking a million questions? And I wanted desperately to know what had been conjured up or summoned at the bail bonds-man's place.

At least this possible Hell general was all the way back in New Jersey. Still, I didn't understand why a bail bondsman would summon something supernatural into his place of business. Especially from Hell. Even if it had been after hours. Why? It didn't make any sense. Maybe the bail bonds office was just a front for something else? The West Coast immortal community was certainly riled up by whatever had happened out there. So, it had to be a major summons.

Something really bad. I sighed. Like a Hell general.

That made me uneasy. Bail bondsmen got a lot of troubled people through those doors. And they paid out a lot of funds. If someone skipped out on their court date, the bail bondsman lost a lot of quid.

Had they intended to summon something formidable to hunt down these bail jumpers? Or were they somehow luring people into their shop? Using them for something else? Something that involved demons?

Regardless, I had a personal stake in this.

And the biggest question: how did this operation in New Jersey connect back here? To the Oregon Coast? Was it solely because of the Ryans or was it some orchestrated plan? For what end, I had no idea.

By the time Keller drove us to that little side road near the beach, where the path led through the grass and sand, it was completely dark outside.

Keller parked the Kia Soul along the curb. I opened the glovebox, grinning at my find. I snatched it out of the glovebox and piled out of the Kia Soul as Rawlins got out, too. Empress stretched out in the back seat and slept. Rawlins gripped the long knife in his bony hands, looking nervous, glancing about. Behind him, around him.

"Here, Rawlins," I said, grinning. "This might help you make more friends at Wraith's."

I handed him a green tree car air freshener. Pine scented. To cover the coffin rot.

He frowned.

"What's this for?" Rawlins asked.

"To cover the undead smell," I said. "Looks like someone wanted to hide the spiff smell in this letted vehicle."

Keller's nose scrunched as Rawlins shrugged and put the little green tree in his jeans pocket.

"Spiff?" said Keller. "Is that slang for—"

"Weed?" I replied and then nodded.

She smiled. "I'll have to add that one to my lexicon. It's legal here, by the way."

My eyes widened. "What? Legal here? Good to know. Now, let's go find Death."

Keller had her hand on the Glock in her shoulder holster. I grabbed my bomber jacket from the back and slid it over my torn and bloodied shirt. And petted Empress, scratching behind her ears. She stretched her paws out and rolled onto her back.

With the machete gripped in my fist, I closed the door and stepped away from the car as Keller locked it. And pocketed the keys.

"All right," she said, looking around in the darkness, the sound of the ocean waves soothing. "Let's look for Death."

Didn't like the sound of that any more than I liked being here.

The last time I was in this dark, old cemetery, I took five bullets to the chest and almost died in a helicopter crash. Didn't want to repeat that adventure. And I think it would break Keller to see that again. Besides, how would I explain that to her?

The moon hadn't risen yet, so the world felt very dark tonight. I sighed, wrinkling my nose. At the stink of decay rising from Rawlins. I felt uneasy now. Especially with an undead brandishing a long knife behind me. Smelling like last week's rubbish. As we sought out Death. When I should have been back at the bungalow, drinking merlot, and grafting with Detective Keller.

This night got better and better. Yes, that was sarcasm.

"So, how do we find Death?" Keller asked, moving closer to me as Rawlins shambled along behind us.

Empress appeared on my left, padding along beside me, leaping, and prancing through the cold sea grass as she chased insects and moving things in the soft breeze.

"I wish I knew," I said. "If he were a dog, I'd just call his name. But honestly, I have no clue. It seemed like Death was present in the cemetery last time because of those disturbed grave sites. I guess we'll try calling for him and see if that works. I don't intend to disturb other grave sites and cheese him off. Might not go well for the lot of us."

It's not like I could text Death. Call him on my mobile. At least Neville Ryan and his father wouldn't think to look for me and Keller here again. Even with Rawlins along for the ride.

At least, I didn't think so.

"Whatever we do, we'd best make it quick," I said as I picked up my pace. "Just in case Neville Ryan and his father—or someone else that wants to kill us—shows up."

Keller's gaze was intense, taking in every movement, every sound.

"I like that idea," she said, hand still on the grip of her Glock.

She matched my pace, but Rawlins struggled to keep up. He'd catch up in his own time.

Ahead, fog began to roll in from the ocean, the wind rising as rain misted the night. The perfect evening to find Death—or some other dangerous immortal entity prowling through graveyards. Keller had no idea what lurked out here.

I moved closer to Keller as a figure materialized out of the fog ahead, black smoke swirling around it.

Death stepped out of the smoke, that bloody black bathrobe tied tight around his waist. He gripped his Ginsu knife.

"About time you got here," Death growled, glaring at me as he pointed a finger in my direction.

"What does that mean?" I replied.

"I heard you call for me all the way up the coast," Death said, crossing his arms against his bathrobe, obscuring the Statler Hotel logo on the left breast. "Took you long enough."

I frowned. "Unlike you," I said, motioning behind me, "we had to come by Kia Soul, not as a soul. Quite a bit easier to travel that way, wouldn't you say?"

Death shook his head, glaring.

"Kid, you're the biggest smart-ass I've met in months. Maybe all year. Best curb that mouth around some of these immortal beings or you're going to be in a world of hurt."

"Me? I didn't start this," I snapped and pointed toward the starry night sky. "Necromancers started this and Hecate joined in the fray. I'm just trying to clean up the mess and make sure no more innocents get hurt in the process." I shook my head, glaring right back at Death. "Innocents like Andy Keane who were murdered because of it."

In an instant, Death was in front of me, a hand pressed against my mouth.

"Do you actually think these immortals care about mortals?" His tone was quiet but heavy. "Well, first lesson about these beings, kid —they don't care. And they despise mortals. So, get that through that thick blond head of yours. You go spouting off about mortal injustice at Wraith's, they'll eviscerate you at worst. At best, they'll ignore you and you'll be fighting the Ryan's necromancing network all alone."

"Necromancing Network? Is that better than the home shopping channel?" I asked. "I'll have to add that one to my lineup next month."

Death shook his head, lips curling. "Well, add this to your lineup, kid."

He hit me in the chest with his upraised palm and I flew back a good thirty meters or so, and rolled over and over until a massive marble tombstone stopped my trajectory. Hard. The machete fell out of my hand.

"Greysen!" Keller cried, drawing her Glock.

Rawlins had the long knife raised.

It had to be a fear reaction. Keller knew that gun had no effect on Death. And the long knife was laughable.

Death was in my face again as I grabbed my machete and struggled to my feet.

"That was only a taste of what they can do to you, kid," he said, appearing and disappearing in a puff of black smoke around me. "If you really want me to take you to Wraith's, you're going to have to learn this lesson. Now."

"I get it already," I said with a sigh. "I'll watch my mouth while we're there."

I'd try. It was the best I could do.

Death pointed a finger at me.

"Remember. That was only a warmup of what those—deities can do to you. Understand me?"

I nodded. "I get it."

Death whirled around and stared at Keller and Rawlins. "They get it, too?" he asked. "Because if they don't, those deities will fry them."

"Keller?" I called to her. "No smart-arsery. Is that clear? I won't be able to speak."

Keller chuckled, relaxing her grip on her Glock. She slid it back into its holster.

"I've never seen him quiet before, Death," she replied. "Should be interesting."

Death hovered in front of Keller now.

"It is imperative that all of you choose your words carefully while we're at Wraith's. Understand?"

Keller nodded and glanced at Rawlins who also nodded.

"And I'll warn you, Neville Ryan and his father, Gilbert, will most likely be there. Now, that they're working for Hecate."

"Hecate?" I cried. "Well, sod it all! Now, we've got to fight through her to get to that dodgy little prat, Neville. Bugger."

Death was nodding in agreement.

"She's gonna be looking for more minions when I run into those little pricks and pull their souls out their pie holes."

I laughed. I wanted to witness that.

"Regardless," Death continued. "Saying nothing to those slimeball necromancers is a much better choice. Let them open their mouths and piss off the gods and goddesses. Not you. We want them on your side. Not these idiots that think death's a toy they get with their cheeseburgers."

"I'd rather just end them," I replied.

He floated back toward me, squinting.

"And believe me, kid, I will momentarily cut off your air to stop you from saying something that will get you and your friends here hunted for the rest of their days."

For the rest of their days? That was quite melodramatic, wasn't it? I wasn't going to argue. I'd never been inside this club, but Death frequented it. So, I would defer to his wisdom without question.

Rawlins chuckled as he let the long knife fall against his side.

Death rounded on him.

"And I will drop you to the ground like dominoes, undead. It'll take you the rest of the day to reassemble your skeleton. Got me?"

Nodding, Rawlins shrank back, the smile sliding off his greying face—along with a patch of skin. His cheeks and eyes looked hollowed, his face thin.

Death frowned, sniffing the air. "I smell death and pine trees."

I shrugged. "Thought it might help Rawlins at Wraith's. Not sure that many undead ever reach that bar."

Death was quiet for a moment or two, contemplating the air freshener, and then finally nodded at Rawlins.

"Yeah, might help."

"We'll keep quiet and let you handle everything, Death," said Keller.

"What if Neville Ryan—or his bloody family—starts something at Wraith's?" I demanded.

"The gods and goddesses will put them in their place," said

Death, looking less anxious now. "But they'll put you in your place fast, kid, if you come in there with an attitude, looking for a fight."

Fair enough. I wouldn't start any fights, but I'd bloody well finish them.

"But I will need a private space," I said. "So, I can examine one of Andy Keane's personal effects. I have to know what got summoned that night, but I need a safe, neutral place to do it. Without necromancers and undead interrupting me—besides Rawlins here."

Rawlins smiled, standing up straighter.

Death took in everyone's comments, including mine, and finally, he nodded. He understood what I needed and why. But he had to lay down the law. Make sure I wasn't going in there to start something. He knew I was an immortal and I could hold my own—unless I acted like I was better than the patrons who frequented Wraith's.

Which I wasn't. The one thing I knew about my past was that I'd been executed for witchcraft. Apparently, I'd been a criminal low life —with magical abilities. Like the bounties I pursued. I had no idea what I'd done, but being a bounty hunter helped ease my conscience a little.

"Getting you out of earshot of those deities fast would greatly please me, kid," he said, laying a hand against his chest. "If you behave and don't start any realm wars, I'll make sure you have a private place to examine that item."

Accused of starting another war? Like I was bloody Napoleon or something?

"Realm war? Me? I'm a bloody bounty hunter. I mostly hunt criminal supernaturals. Why is everyone accusing me of starting wars? I'm not a soldier!" I took a deep, calming breath. "Fine. I said I'd keep my mouth in check and I will."

Death slapped me on the back.

"Guess we'll see if you can keep your word and your mouth shut. If not, you'll need my services."

I cast a dark glare at him, but didn't say anything as Empress wound around my legs, rubbing against my calves.

Death motioned Keller and Rawlins over to him. Keller looked amused as she moved beside me. Rawlins shambled over, long knife hanging at his side.

"You are not bringing knives into Wraith's," Death ordered as his gaze flicked from my machete to Rawlins' long knife.

I rolled my eyes. "Fine," I said and started to turn toward the vehicle.

Death waved his hand and my machete and Rawlins' long knife disappeared. He saw the angry look on my face and pointed a finger at me.

"I know that look," said Death. "You'll get your toys back when you show me you can play nicely with gods."

My gaze narrowed as I glanced at Keller who was grinning, Glock still in its holster.

"You didn't take her weapon," I snapped.

Death's hands snapped to his hips.

"What are you, two years old?"

"At least five," I replied as Keller laughed. "And my favorite word is why."

Death shook his head and turned away from me.

"Blade, you're gonna get all of us erased from the universe. I just know it. All right, move in close and hold onto my robes. I know I'm going to regret this."

I gripped the soft black, terrycloth robe with both hands as smoke enveloped us. And we began to rise.

WRAITH'S VERSAILLES-LIKE exterior appeared out of the darkness and mist, the gold neon burning bright as I materialized behind Death. Keller looked alarmed in her quiet way as she glanced around her, a mixture of shock and awe burning in those piercing blue eyes. Rawlins looked like he'd just had a seizure, tilting his head a bit too far to the left, staring toward the sprawling, massive marble palace, its black mansard roof twinkling with Christmas lights. Wreaths hung on the black double doors leading inside, the distant thrum of music hanging in the air.

"Already decorating for Christmas? It's not even Thanksgiving yet?" I replied.

Death whirled around and clapped his hand over my mouth, fury in those dark eyes. He gritted his teeth.

"We aren't even inside yet and you can't resist shooting off your mouth." He glared at me. "Am I going to have to gag you to keep you quiet? I swear, you're gonna get all of us erased, Blade."

Keller gave me that cop look of hers. That annoyed, *don't make me lock you up* sort of look, her eyes narrowing, mouth pressing into a firm line, nose scrunching.

Rawlins nudged me with his bony shoulder, looking irritated.

"You trying to end up like me?"

I held up my hands.

"I'm sorry!" I sighed. "I can't do it, all right? I can't keep my mouth shut."

Shaking his head, Death pointed a finger at my mouth and suddenly, I couldn't make a sound. Not even a squeak came out.

I slapped my hands against my side and shouted at Death, but nothing came out. Making any agitation worse.

"Relax, kid. I only muted you. As much as I'd like to make that sweet silence permanent, I'd probably miss the conversation. Hate to admit it, but I do find you entertaining." His dark eyes narrowed and he gave me a dismissive swipe of his hand. "Mildly entertaining, so watch your ego."

Keller broke into a musical laugh, her face lighting up, making my sudden, forced silence almost bearable.

"My entire police post would have killed for that ability when I brought Greysen in for questioning," said Keller.

"Impressive to annoy that many people in such a short time, Blade," said Death, a smile on his misty face. "You got real talent, kid."

Was I that bad? I looked pleadingly at her and held out my arms.

"What?" she asked, still looking amused. "Is he right?"

I winced and nodded.

She looked at me and then at Death. Finally, she shook her head.

"He's not that bad, Death," she replied finally and I sighed in relief. "He calms down after you've been around him a while. And I enjoy his wit."

I frowned. Like I was a bloody border collie. I had a lot to say about that but couldn't. Was the most annoying feeling ever. Frustrated, I crossed my arms and turned away.

"I'm sorry," said Keller, her hand on my shoulder, kneading. "I made you sound like a new puppy, didn't it?"

I glanced back at her and gave her a decisive nod.

"I like his conversation," said Rawlins in a quiet voice. "And his accent. He's never boring."

Smiling, I turned around and gently patted his shoulder. At least Rawlins still liked having me around.

"Besides, he could have wasted me at his bungalow, but he listened to me. I appreciated that. Even got me a burger. Most people would have ended me as just some random undead. Even before I became undead, nobody listened to me. He did. Thanks...Blade."

I gave him a sharp nod.

Keller took hold of my hands and I wanted to melt into the heat of her fingers. Her smile was brighter than the summer sun.

"Well, I like him, too," she said, fixing me with those piercing blue eyes and I almost turned into a puddle at her feet.

She liked me. Things were looking up.

"And I agree with everything Rawlins said." Then she gave me that sobering cop look again. "But you said that you couldn't control your mouth. So, Death's just trying to protect you from yourself—and the rest of us. As soon as he gets us into a private space, you can say anything you like."

"Almost!" Death shouted. "Don't give him carte blanche like that! When you're at the bar I frequent—that's filled to the teeth with gods—you play by my rules. Or someone's gonna lose a soul. Everybody got me?"

I rolled my eyes at his over-dramatic monologue and motioned him forward. Toward this approximation of the Palace Versailles—and all its imagined vices. At least I was finally going to see the inside of this place. Under the guise of being another mortal like Keller. Keeping my secret safe.

"All right, we're going in," Death replied in a hushed voice. "Keep your mouths shut and follow my lead. Got it? I go first no matter what."

As he turned toward Wraith's, I shook my head and mocked him by mouthing his words. Making Keller snicker and Rawlins laugh out loud.

Death whirled around, giving me a hard, accusatory look.

"Am I gonna have to send you home, boy? In a box?"

I mimed a belly laugh and then waved him off in disgust. Making Keller and Rawlins both chuckle.

"I don't believe this," said Death as he started toward the doors. "You're gonna get us all erased without saying a word. Can't take you anywhere, Blade."

I mocked him all the way to the double doors. He turned around, grabbed me by the throat, and shook me.

"Heed my warning."

He didn't let go until I gave him my most emphatic nod. I wanted to bonk him in his stupid, smoky Death face, but I refrained as he opened the doors.

Electronic dance music with a thumping base beat thrummed from inside the neon-lit club that smelled like gardenias and citrus. Once inside, even the outer walls turned translucent, allowing us to see between the worlds. The first floor was all open concept, the floor made of clear glass or whatever immortals use, showing stars and planets orbiting about us.

It was breathtaking.

I rushed over to one of the walls, staring at the cosmos laid out before me. Comets shot across space, stars twinkling and glowing as planets turned on their axes in a haze of multi-colored nebulas. Some were pastel and smoky others bright like neon in blues and reds and greens.

Keller was beside me, her eyes filled with wonder, mouth open, hand against the translucent barrier.

"It's...amazing." She could only stare, wide-eyed at the universe before her. "Is this real?"

I smiled and nodded.

Rawlins stood to her right, staring out at the endless vastness filled with stars and planets and...I looked closer. Trails of light. Blues, golds, purples. Were they comets or meteors? Or gods and immortals arriving, otherworldly beings that inhabited this strange bar between the worlds.

Finally, Death stepped up to my left, hands behind his back.

"Incredible view, isn't it?" he said, staring into the sprawling blanket of stars that stretched into infinity.

I nodded emphatically at him and then held out my arms.

A shimmery man with long, curly white hair, long brocade gold frock coat, and white breeches appeared beside us, carrying a round gold-leafed tray. He wore shiny black shoes with gold buckles that reflected back the stars and his gold eyes. He was dressed in eighteenth century clothes. Clothing I knew quite well.

"Death, good to see you," said the chap, about five foot eight and a bit thick around the middle. "What would you and your party like to drink tonight?"

Death turned to Keller first. "What'll you have, Ms. Keller?"

She smiled like sunlight on water.

"Surprise me," she said in a smoky voice, those blue eyes burning with starlight as her gaze moved from Death to me.

And suddenly, she and I were the only two people in the crowded room, her warm jasmine and cool musk scent mesmerizing. Even if I could have spoken, she had rendered me speechless.

By the cosmos, she was the most beautiful woman I had ever met. And I loved her response.

"Bring the lady…" Death glanced at me and then Keller again. "A pint of authentic Georgian English port," said Death, his rough voice bringing me back to the crowded bar that thrummed with electronic dance music. "Bottled in 1722."

My mouth fell open. Georgian port from 1722? That would have been my original time period. Was it truly an authentic Georgian port? From my time? Even though Death had no idea when I'd been born.

My eyes narrowed. Or did he?

Death turned toward me, gazing into my eyes, taking in my expression. But he didn't look like he had any great insights into my life. If he did, he hid them well. I planned to ask him about his drink choices later. When I could actually speak again.

But I wanted to try that 1722 Georgian port. I desperately wanted to taste the world I couldn't picture. Sip the life I'd lost when I was executed for practicing witchcraft in 1726. Savor the life I couldn't remember.

"Blade, you want a pint of Georgian port or a 1716 Georgian strawberry brandy?"

Strawberry brandy? From 1716? I'd been seven or eight years old. There was something so familiar about strawberry brandy.

A distant memory warmed my body, making me feel like I'd had a home once. A family.

Grinning, I nodded and mouthed both to Death.

Squinting, I reached back into the shadowy haze of my memory. Into that cold October night, my birthday, in London's dark streets. The warm ruddy glow of the pub's hearth. Fiddle and fife bright with an acrobatic tune that filled the whole place. Taste of something sweet on my lips. Before resurrectionists sold me to crimpers bound for the Americas.

Some kind of lively hornpipe. And a bard singing that night. About the darling of my heart…Sally. A chill rolled over me. The tune had been called *Sally in Our Alley*! Where had that detail come from? And why now—after nearly 315 years had passed?

Death smiled at me. That was a first.

"The kid will also have a 1722 Georgian port. And a 1716 Georgian strawberry brandy."

I mouthed thanks to him and he blinked at me, acknowledging that he'd understood me.

"Rawlins?" Death asked, turning to the undead young man.

He shrugged. "Bud Light?"

I laughed, but nothing came out. Here Rawlins had every drink that had ever existed, from any place and any time, at his fingertips. And he chooses a bloody Bud Light.

"Rawlins will have a Scottish Gruit," said Death.

Rawlins frowned. "A what?"

"A gruit," said Death, his gaze flicking from me to Rawlins.

Shrugging, Rawlins gave him a kettled look.

"A gruit is one of the oldest types of ale in the world, my undead friend," Death explained. "Ancient Gaels brewed it in Scotland from bog myrtle, malted barley, and flowers. Usually heather."

Rawlins glanced at me and I was nodding at him to try it.

"Cool," said Rawlins. "Why not."

I wanted to move into Wraith's and never leave. I'd never heard of a Scottish gruit either, but I bloody well wanted to try it.

Death turned back to the bloke in eighteenth century garb. "And I'll have my usual. Mead with a shot of ambrosia."

Ambrosia? Drink of the gods? I was gobsmacked! I wanted to try everything. All of it. Especially ambrosia.

The cocktail steward dissolved into a mist and vanished in a surge of gold light that shot through the palace Versailles' first floor.

"Well, look who's returned to Wraith's," said a loud, familiar woman's voice that carried throughout the room, vibrating deeper than the dance beat thrumming through it. "With his adorable little protégé. Who'd better have a report for me."

I glanced over my shoulder and felt a chill as Hecate sauntered toward Death, her gaze shifting to me first. Undressing me with her eyes. She wore a slinky midnight blue gown that sparkled with starlight, the pattern shifting as she moved. Like the field of stars behind me. She wore black stilettos, her hair in ebony waves around her oval face and alabaster skin. Smoky eye makeup made her deep blue eyes glow, mauve lip gloss sparkling.

Beautiful. And deadly.

Death's black eyes narrowed, but he didn't turn around.

"Hecate," he said in a flat tone. "Did anyone ever tell you that you had an uncanny way of sucking all the joy out of the room?"

"Good to see you, too, Death." Her gaze enveloped me again. "And your mortal entourage—especially your luscious blond trouble-maker. I hope you're here to give me your report, Blade."

Sod it all! I still didn't have any answers about what happened at the bail bondsmen. Just a possibility that it had been a Hell general. But I had no proof. That's why we were here. So, I could safely use my powers. I didn't know jack all about what had happened in New Jersey yet.

Death propped his hands on his hips.

Hecate held up her hands, grinning as she stepped past Death toward me.

"I acknowledge a truce as long as we're both at Wraith's. Now, let's hear your delicious report, Blade."

Her fingers tangled in my hair, sliding across my face, and down my neck. Caressing my shoulders. She slid a hand underneath my torn shirt. Stroking my chest.

Keller's expression darkened. She was miffed, glaring now at the goddess.

I stiffened and shook my head at the goddess of night and magic. I couldn't speak. Couldn't tell her to take her hands off me. Like the first time I met her. She'd paralyzed my limbs and my vocal cords. Kind of like what Death had done to me tonight. I was getting tired of gods silencing me.

"I won't start much," she said in a sultry voice, smiling, fingers tracing across my clean-shaven face. My lips. "Just a little fire here and there."

I pulled away from her touch, not knowing if my unwillingness to let her molest me would start another realm war. Not that I cared. Besides, this goddess wasn't my type.

She unnerved me. She could extinguish my life force with a breath, according to Death. As an immortal, I wasn't willing to take a chance that he was right.

Besides, I preferred my dates to be less deadly.

"Just let me borrow the hot little mortal for a short while," she said and pressed her face against my neck, nibbling on my earlobe. "And we'll call it even."

Had she forgotten that I was immortal? Or that she'd accused me of starting a realm war? I was relieved she wasn't spouting off her mouth in front of Keller. Although, Keller had already seen enough to break her brain for a lifetime. Why not toss off the story that I'm immortal, too, and really put her into a coma?

"Even?" Death turned toward her, glaring. "Your new necromancers tried to kill my entourage. More than once."

Hecate clicked her tongue. "Boys will be boys."

She'd changed her tune. A lot since she'd dragged me out of hospital and here to Wraith's the first time.

"Boys will go home in a box if they try that malarky again, Hecate. I'm Death, remember? Not one of your conquests or your minions."

"It's never too late," she said with a chuckle at Death and turned her attention back to me.

"You're gonna wake up here on Earth one morning and find all your minions in the underworld, Hecate," Death said with a growl. "You may control the night, but you don't control death. That's my department."

She slid both hands into my hair and leaned toward my face, stars swirling in those deep blue eyes that looked like the night sky.

"Oh, just let me borrow him—please," she said, staring into my eyes. "I promise to return him—like I did in Corvallis."

I glanced over at Keller. She was seething with rage, her pale blue eyes shooting bullets at this goddess.

Was it because Hecate was a massive chat up? Or was it because she was grafting with me?

Rawlins looked enchanted by the tall, waifish goddess. She commanded attention and had a way of capturing an entire room's attention. But when she spoke, it was equal parts ego and narcissism.

"Like Corvallis?" Death almost screeched. "I had to come here and get him. With you demanding his head for starting a realm war." Death pointed a finger at her. "Which he didn't start."

Her lips smashed against mine, like she was trying to suck out my soul.

I held my breath, squeezing my eyes closed. I couldn't look. Terrified that she'd leave with my immortality—and my soul—in her hands.

"I want his report."

"Been guzzling the melogion? Playing Kottabos with Mars again? Because you're high if you think I'm letting you leave with the kid here."

What the bloody hell was melogion? And Kottabos?

Hecate seemed quite different from that day in Corvallis. And at Wraith's. She'd been militant and threatening that day. She'd wanted to end me, fast, not shag me.

"Hecate, please," said Death, gently tugging her off me. "You're scaring the poor kid out of his mind."

She glowered at Death, hands on her hips.

"All these mortals should be scared to death. Bowing to me, goddess of the night, of magic, and the moon. Paying tribute." She grabbed my arm and grinned. "I'm taking him. Stop me."

Hecate disappeared in a puff of smoke, taking me with her.

16

"Greysen!" I shouted, Glock drawn, but when the smoke cleared, he and Hecate were gone.

Death was livid.

I was terrified for Greysen, but I couldn't show it, my detective senses on overload now.

"Hecate!" Death shouted above the din of electronic dance music that had turned the entire main floor into a dance club. "Bring him back! Right now!"

He turned in a circle, scattering plumes of black smoke in his wake.

"Death," I said, trying to keep calm as I laid my hand on Death's black robe sleeve. "Where would she have taken him? And why?"

This strange club had already overwhelmed every single one of my detective instincts—and all my senses. Except that voice in my head screaming none of this was real. That Wraith's was an elaborate fabrication. One of those performance clubs where the staff acted parts and used computer-generated graphics to create a fantasy experience. It looked like the Palace Versailles inside with its scrollwork gold molding on the walls and the gold gilt chairs with their elaborate swirls and leaves trimming damask, velvet, and satin in rich lavenders, pale blues and golds. Even the floor had blue and cream tiles that created movement and drama. And it smelled like rose petals and fresh-cut lilies. It was stunning. But I wondered if it was somehow an illusion. But I couldn't explain away Death or Ricky Rawlins any more than I could explain away Greysen performing magic.

I had it on video.

Back in Corvallis, Greysen had insisted that this Hecate, a.k.a. alleged goddess, had spirited him away from Good Sam's critical care unit. Even the front desk showed me where another detective had signed off on his discharge and taken custody of Greysen. She'd brazenly put her name down on the paperwork. Changed care protocols and had someone that critically injured released. And just walked out of the hospital with him. Sure sounded like someone with supernatural abilities had intervened.

And then an hour later, I found Greysen in the parking lot.

I smiled at the memory, a sigh on my lips. In nothing but boxer briefs.

Despite Greysen Mallory's body being a work of art that rivaled a Leonardo Da Vinci statues, I had to get Greysen out of the cold and into some clothes that day. The entire time, he insisted that this goddess had kidnapped him. I thought it was the morphine talking. Or more of Greysen's bullshit stories.

Death insisted Hecate was real, too, but I was still trying to explain his presence in a graveyard I'd investigated a few times since becoming a cop on the Oregon Coast. I hadn't been ready to wrap my overheated brain around the idea that an ancient goddess walked these shores. Warring with Death.

It was insanity!

But maybe it was also true?

"Knowing Hecate, he could be anywhere right now," Death said with a growl, pacing around me and Rawlins, trails of black smoke rising. "Can't believe she just kidnapped the kid right in front of me.

But the real question is why." He gritted his teeth and slid his knife out of his robes. "It sure as Hades wasn't to hear some dumb report. Kid hadn't even had a chance to finish that murder investigation yet."

I felt a cold chill brush across my heart. What if that was the whole point?

What if she or someone didn't want Greysen—or me—to complete our investigation? Because it might implicate her or her human minions somehow.

Had the Ryans been acting on her orders all along or operating their own graveyard activities in secret? Raising corpses and summoning entities according to Hecate's plans or had they tricked this goddess into getting involved? And if Greysen used this ability he claimed to have, would it be enough proof to arrest this goddess bitch? Or at least Superintendent Ryan and his son.

But what could I do to an immortal goddess?

I so wanted to arrest her for assault. The way she practically molested poor Greysen and he couldn't even say no. I saw him shaking his head, holding up his hand, and pulling away from her. His whole body recoiled from her touch.

"What if Hecate or the Ryans realized that Greysen was here at Wraith's to use his abilities to find out what happened that night in New Jersey?" I asked as Death's pacing intensified, gripping the hilt of his knife. "What if she grabbed him to stop him from using it. So, he wouldn't implicate someone. Or the Ryans convinced her to stop him?"

I wasn't sure of the who, but I was almost certain that someone didn't want Greysen to use his abilities. Was it the Ryans? Hecate? Or someone else manipulating all these events from the shadows? I couldn't help but feel manipulated. Like someone else had been orchestrating all these situations. Including abducting Greysen.

Death whirled around and grabbed me by the shoulders.

"Detective Keller, that's brilliant!" But his elation quickly faded to fear. "You may be right. Hecate's moods change like the weather on a good day. She's unpredictable. If she's listening to the Ryans, then Greysen's in a lot of danger. She may hand him over to those idiot necromancers or force him to reveal what he can see using an object from the scene. And then dispose of him herself. Depends entirely on her mood. She sees most mortals as accessories anyway. And not the crime kind."

Now, I was terrified. I didn't know how to fight a goddess. Or necromancers. My Glock was useless against Hecate, but not the Ryans. And if I had to take down my police superintendent, I'd do it.

Especially to save Greysen.

If they'd taken me, he'd have rushed out the door—probably getting himself into more trouble—and thrown himself at these people. He'd have done everything in his power to rescue me if our situations had been reversed. He'd already proven that at Crypt City —the pioneer cemetery.

I didn't know exactly what this was between us, but the attraction was white hot. And I wanted to see him again. Argue with him. Hunt bad guys with him. I sighed.

Drink wine with him and stare into those bottomless violet eyes. And more—much, much more.

My heart fell. Even if it was only until Thanksgiving. That was next week!

The thought of that made me so sad. He'd crashed right through my murder investigation and became a person of interest and pain in the ass. But now, I couldn't remember what my world was like without him. He'd even cooked for me.

No, I did remember what my world looked like before he arrived on the Oregon Coast. Darker and lonelier than I'd realized.

Rawlins stepped forward, hands balled into bony fists, a fierce look stretching the skin tighter across his thinning face.

"So, what are we going to do about it? How exactly do we take down a goddess?"

"What Rawlins said, Death," I added, turning back toward Death. "Let's take her down. Now—along with these necromancers. Rescue Greysen."

But something nagged at me about this situation. It felt contrived somehow. Like someone was moving all the pieces on the board toward this moment, trying to get Death to battle Hecate.

And I couldn't help but wonder who gained from them wiping out each other's forces. Who inherited their territories? Who was powerful enough to sweep in and steal it all in the chaos? Or overpower both of them?

Was there another rivalry we didn't know about?

Death held up his hands. "Whoa, kids, slow it down to light speed! We can't just confront Hecate head on. Believe me, I know. I've been battling her and her minions forever. She'd fry both of you like a bad batch of okra. No, we're gonna need some otherworldly help to get Greysen out of her clutches. And we may have to wait until morning."

"Why morning?" I asked, frowning.

A frown darkened Death's pallid face. "Because she's a goddess of the night. Her power's much stronger at night. Weakens with the light."

"Greysen could be dead by morning," I said, but I motioned around the first floor of Wraith's as another electronic dance beat shook the clear dance floor beneath us with a new rhythm. "But fortunately, we're surrounded by an army of that otherworldly help you mentioned."

"Exactly, Detective Keller," said Death with a nod.

Death put his hands together and bowed his head. As black smoke curled in rings around him, I wondered if he was praying. He was Death. It made sense.

Finally, he looked up.

"Did you say a prayer?"

Death shook his head. "Called for some backup. Some immortals familiar with Hecate and her tactics. Friends of Greysen's."

In a flash of gold light, a tall, attractive man with long black hair, a close-cropped Van Dyke beard, and warm brown eyes appeared beside Death. He wore a shining gold cuirass, red tunic, and carried a

Roman sword. And he had the body of a gladiator. He towered over Death, looking almost seven feet tall. Rawlins' eyes got huge as he stared up at the forbidding figure in full Roman armor before us. Like an ancient gladiator.

"Mars," said Death, extending his hand. "Good to see you."

The Roman god of war? He was beautiful, a golden sheen to his Mediterranean skin, perfect wavy dark hair, a sparkle in those warm brown eyes as he shook Death's hand with a firm, forceful shake.

"Where is that night hag?" Mars demanded in a commanding velvety voice as he cast a withering glare throughout the room, its patrons unaffected by his otherworldly entrance.

In this club, Mars' entrance was just another patron in the place.

But his gaze settled on me and Rawlins who shrank back behind me.

"Forgive me," said Mars with a deep bow of his head. "I'm Mars, former Roman god of war. Persia and the Roman Empire were my primary focuses." He crossed his arms, his biceps sculpted against his molded cuirass that reflected the colored lights from the dance floor. "Before the Great Resignation at any rate. I'm more of an independent advisor these days."

"That's godspeak for mercenary," said Death with a wry smile.

Mars offered an innocent shrug and leaned against the wall.

"If it involves war, I'm a master of it. Consulting and mercenary work pay well in these difficult times."

Death gave me an apologetic glance.

"Had to cancel our drink orders. I promise both of you—all of you —a raincheck though."

"As soon as we pull your minion out of Hecate's harpy clutches, the drinks are on me," said Mars, laying a hand against his cuirass.

I bristled, casting a glare at the former god of war.

"Greysen Mallory isn't anyone's minion. And I wouldn't feel right drinking while he was in danger anyway."

He'd looked so excited about those drinks. No, enchanted.

Almost nostalgic. Made me sad to think he hadn't even gotten to try them.

"Me either," said Rawlins, bowing his head.

Mars frowned, looking concerned, and moved away from the wall.

"Wait... Greysen Mallory? Blade Mallory?"

Death nodded. "Keller's right. Blade's not my minion, Mars. He's a bounty hunter with a—"

"Why in Hades didn't you say it was Blade Mallory?" Mars replied, looking concerned now. "I know Blade quite well. Kid's got a gift for finding things thought lost forever. I hired him once when someone stole my spear. Kid found it."

"Right now, he needs our help, Mars," said Death.

"What about the undead over there?" Mars asked, raising an eyebrow as he glanced from Rawlins to Death. "Why does he still have his head?"

Rawlins shrank back behind me, looking terrified.

Mars sniffed the air. "He smells like pine trees? That's...refreshing."

"Rawlins here got himself caught up in Hecate's scheming," said Death, motioning toward Ricky. "Her necromancers got him. Double-crossed him. Not sure why Blade spared him, but it is what it is."

"If Blade spared him, I'll stand by that," said Mars.

Rawlins sighed in relief, the fear leaving his eyes.

"Cattrell on his way?" Mars asked, his baritone voice softening.

"He's cashing out of a poker game upstairs," said Death, pacing the clear glass floor again as stars and galaxies glimmered beneath his feet. "Said he'd be here shortly."

"Who's Cattrell?" I asked.

"General Cassius Bohnefeld Cattrell the Third, at your service, madam," said a man with a lilting southern drawl behind me.

Gentile and lofty like South Carolina or Georgia.

Mars rolled his eyes. "Former general," he said with a growl. "On the losing side."

I turned to see a lanky man with shoulder length white hair and gold-hazel eyes. He was attractive with chiseled features, a strong jaw, and bright smile. He wore a Confederate general's creamy grey double-breasted wool frock coat adorned with gold buttons, flourished with gold insignia at the collar, and some sort of elaborate gold piping they called a military knot on white cuffs. The coat was unbuttoned and hanging open, revealing a grey Lynyrd Skynyrd T-shirt, faded jeans, and scuffed black boots.

I couldn't help but smile.

"Not during the War for Independence. And don't get me started on Fort Dummer."

Mars groaned. "Oh, here we go..."

"You started this, Mars. In the middle of an Abenaki ambush at the fort, some damned soldier turned me. But that was another time, another war. Like there wasn't enough blood for a dozen clans that day. Fort was littered with the dying and plenty to spare. Like the War of Northern Aggression when I led troops as a general of the Confederation. And saw Yankees and my patriots turning the wounded—not the dying. Just like the soldiers before them, I guess."

Mars shook his head. "Don't have time for your war stories, Cash."

"Well, I do have a million of them, from every war fought by this great country," the man called Cash Cattrell continued. "Including the Civil War—and I assure you, there was nothing civil about it. Wraith's is about the only place I can wear this coat these days though. Damned tired of seeing mortals wearing our battle flag as a show of southern pride, too. Most shameful time in our history."

I felt my insides shudder. Cash was a vampire? Another thing I thought was just fantasy. Was he playing a part or were vampires real, too? That thought terrified me more than the scores of undead I'd already witnessed. I may never sleep again.

Death moved over and shook Cash's hand. "Cash, good to see

you." He motioned toward me and Rawlins. "These two mortals are friends of Blade's—and my guests here. Detective Harlowe Keller and Ricky Rawlins."

The former general squinted at me and then Rawlins. He sniffed the air and made a sour face.

"Pine-scented death? Really?"

I looked closer, trying to see if he had actual fangs. And hoping that I didn't see them at the same time.

"Well, you got an undead and a very beautiful mortal," said Cash in that gentle South Carolina drawl and bowed. "A pleasure. Where's Blade?"

"That's why I called you," said Death. "I know you're one of his oldest and dearest friends."

"I'd do anything for Greysen Mallory," said Cash, eyes narrowing. "Even confront Hecate. He saved my life at Gettysburg."

I tried to hide my shock and horror. Gettysburg? That was impossible!

"But that was a hundred and sixty years ago!"

"Drunk driver," said Cash without missing a beat. "Pulled me out of the street a heartbeat before I'd have been plowed right over. Ford F-450. Would have decapitated me for sure."

Mars stepped toward Cash, arms crossed, glaring at the vampire that was about six feet tall.

"Well, your patron goddess of the night nabbed him moments after he entered this club, apparently," said Mars and thumped his fist against his gold breastplate. "I say we declare war on that nocturnal bitch and put her down. Otherwise, this war between her and Death is going to divide Wraith's right down the middle and turn it into a war zone like the Oregon Coast. Like Cash's Civil War. Peace through war is my motto."

Peace through war? Uh, no.

"I pay tribute to no goddess, my dear gladiator," said Cash. "Have patience. Wraith's will survive this power struggle like it has for centuries. Before we take up arms and make battle plans, we need to know why Hecate grabbed him and where she took him. He could be anywhere." Cash held out his arms and turned in a circle. "We *are* immortals and between the worlds here. All roads lead everywhere."

Mars glared at Cash and then turned back to Death.

"I hate it when the vamp's right. I don't know why Hecate grabbed the kid and I don't know why you and Hecate are still battling each other. Probably mistook him for one of your mortals. And there are only two reasons why she'd grab one of your mortals, Death."

"And they are?" Death asked, looking more annoyed—if that was possible.

"He has something she wants or he knows something he shouldn't," said Mars with a grimace. "Blade still as good looking as I remember?"

"Still smokin' hot," said Cash.

Mars frowned at him.

"I have eyes, you cretin," Cash snapped as he glared at Mars. "I may not be—ambidextrous, but I know beauty when I see it. And Greysen Mallory is a goddamned work of art." He pointed at me. "Ask her. She'll tell you."

Mars' intimidating gaze enveloped me.

"He right?"

I smiled. I hated to be put on the spot like this.

"Yes, Greysen Mallory is still incredibly attractive."

I held up my phone, showing them the video of Greysen carrying me and then fighting off all those undead. Mars' eyes widened.

Cash gave Mars a mocking look.

"I rest my case. But the question remains: was Hecate trying to bed him or bleed him for information?" He shrugged. "Or hell, maybe both."

"Why are his looks so important?"

"Speaking as someone who's—ambidextrous," Mars said to Cash as he gestured toward my phone. "I have eyes, too. Tall, blond, and as beautiful as I remember—Blade is Hecate's type all right. She may have wanted to make him her latest mortal toy, but Cash is still right. Regardless, she'll squeeze him like a pomegranate until there's nothing left. That's what she does to mortals."

"That's terrible news!" Death began to pace between Mars and Cash, trails of black smoke coiling around the vampire and the former god of war. "You know that if Blade sleeps with her, he'll be enslaved to her will forever."

That was terrifying. And the thought of him sleeping with Hecate made me incredibly jealous, but he and I weren't together. I had no claim on him, but the thought still upset me. I'd never been possessive, but something in me didn't want to share him with Hecate. Or Iris Cline at the Historical Association. I groaned. Or with anybody.

Cash shook his head. "She may not give him a choice, Death. Taking a page out of her buddy Hades' book, a play that Hecate knows too well. Ask Seph. She'll tell ya."

Death continued to pace. "Another entitled goddess. Thinks she can just take what she desires. Persephone might be a good goddess to consult about this mess though."

"Seph's her friend and she's been through this sort of kidnapping," said Cash. "She'd want what was best for Hecate and Greysen."

"Where do you think Hecate might have taken him?" Death asked.

"Wherever her minions operate," said Mars. "Or those necromancers she's teamed up with." He glared at Death and Cash when they gave him surprised looks. "Yeah, she posted a video of her and these necromancers to her TikTok account. I keep up with social media. But I know her. She wouldn't take him anyplace personal. In case she plans to end him. Hecate hates messes—you know that. Besides, she'd make her necromancer buddies handle that part."

Cash nodded. "Mars is right. And fortunately, as a—night owl, I know where these necromancers...shop. I think she'd take him there."

Death looked a little frazzled now. "Where would that be?"

"Manny's All-Night Subs and Souvenir Shop," Rawlins replied, stepping out from behind me. "Neville always lured in his victims with half-priced pepperoni subs."

"The undead knows the place," said Cash with a chuckle, looking smug. "Shoulda asked him first, Death. Good job there, son." I couldn't see any fangs. Yet. "If I call, it's somewhere on Highway eighteen."

Rawlins nodded. "On eighteen near Otis. In an abandoned strip mall there."

He looked suddenly apprehensive, like he'd overstepped someone's authority.

"I could take you there."

"Great job, Rawlins!" I gently patted his sleeve, making him puff out his sagging chest and smile. "Then let's go already!" I shouted, hand on my Glock. "Let's stop talking and go after Greysen before that bitch does something terrible to him. I don't care if it's day or night. Greysen's in trouble."

They all turned around and stared at me. And broke into laughter.

I glared. "What's so damned funny?"

"Even the mortals are chompin' at the bit to take down Hecate," said Cash, a smile brightening his moon-pale face. "She musta caused a ton of trouble for the mortals while warring with Death. That's definitely her style."

Mars winked at me. "I like a beautiful mortal ready to wage war on a goddess."

Cash scoffed at him. "She had you at waging war, Mars."

The hint of a smile reached Mars' warm brown eyes.

"That she did."

Death slid his arm around my shoulders. "Detective Keller gets things done, gentlemen."

I nodded and gripped my Glock tighter in its holster.

"I was a special forces sniper before I became a cop."

That came out so easily this time. After telling Greysen, it had gotten easier to say. He had such a healing way about him. When he wasn't being a pain in the ass.

Mars was smiling now. "A sniper? I think I'm in love, Detective Keller."

"I'm impressed, detective," said Cash with a deep, respectful bow to me. "It takes nerves of steel and a precise eye to be a sniper."

"Hey, I served four years in the army," said Rawlins.

Mars nodded at Death. "You got a fierce entourage here, Death. With me and Cash rounding out your forces, Hecate won't keep Blade for long."

I patted the two extra magazines for my Glock that rested in the right pocket of my purple leather jacket. They wouldn't even faze Hecate, but they'd convince Gilbert and Neville Ryan they were outnumbered and overpowered. After all, the police superintendent knew about my special forces assignment from my interview. And how deadly of a shot I was.

I was counting on that to get Greysen out of their clutches before they made him an undead. Or killed him outright.

"Death!" I called. "What about that mute you put on Greysen?"

"You muted Blade?" Cash replied with a smirk. "Wish I'd been here to see that."

"Had to," said Death, looking worried. "Was afraid he'd start a realm war with that mouth of his."

Then the corners of Death's mouth turned upward into a devious grin.

"But that magic was only active here in Wraith's. After she takes him out of the bar, it'll start to break. And so will the kid's floodgates. She won't know what hit her."

Cash grinned and leaned against the wall.

"Oh, I wish I could be there to witness that. Might just be the secret weapon that takes Hecate down. Let's get goin'. I don't want to miss this."

I couldn't help but laugh. After Greysen had been forced quiet for so long, he'd have a lot to say to that bitch.

I just hoped it didn't get him killed. Or undead.

Mars motioned behind him.

"I just need to summon my spear and then we ambush Hecate at this sub shop."

Cash gave him a sharp nod and held open his Confederate general's coat. Revealing a collection of knives arranged on both sides. Daggers mostly. One had a gold hilt decorated with a crouching dragon. Another one, silver, had a wolf's head. Others had Celtic knots, Viking rune symbols, and Japanese characters. He selected one with a blackened bronze hilt depicting the moon and stars.

"And one dagger attuned to Hecate's brand of night magic," said Cash in his soft southern drawl.

Death lifted his Ginsu knife into the air and waved his hand over it, mouth moving in a silent prayer—or maybe an incantation—as black smoke roiled around the blade.

A grin curved across Cash's pale, handsome face. "That ol' night hag won't know what hit her."

Death cast a withering gaze at Cash and then Mars.

"This isn't about revenge, so get that garbage out of your heads right now." His voice was gruff, his tone short. "We're going in to free the kid. That's it."

Mars was frowning. "But if we have a chance to cripple her operation, Death, we take it."

"Mars is right, Death," said Cash, flipping the dagger into the air and catching it in his fist. "We gotta think about at least slowin' that devil woman down, otherwise she'll overwhelm us with necromancers and undead her first chance. Or maybe even block our escape."

Already, Death was shaking his head.

"Cash, all we got going for us right now is a swift surprise attack. Hit her fast, grab the kid, and go. We stay to fight, we'll all lose."

All three of them spoke at once, arguing tactics and strategy. I stepped between them, but they ignored me as the discussion turned fiery, Mars' eyes hardening like granite. Death's eyes were as black as midnight and roiling with smoke. Cash's hazel eyes had a fire in them matched by his rising voice as he sided with Mars.

I swear, if this came to blows, I'd handcuff all three of them to the wall and go after Greysen alone. Every minute we wasted gave Hecate time to do him more harm. I shuddered. Or kill him outright.

Rawlins whimpered, drawing my attention.

I turned.

His eyes were huge, his thin lips parting as he stared past me, toward the black double doors off to the right.

"What's wrong, Rawlins?" I asked, confused by his weird reaction.

The grey cast to his face turned milky white, terror shining in his dull eyes, like he'd just seen a massive asteroid hurtling toward us.

His mouth bobbed open and he pointed with a frantic shake of his bony hand.

I turned in the direction where he pointed.

A herd of undead shuffled across the dance floor as the dance beat quickened.

The sea of immortals writhing and leaping to the music parted, unaffected as they let the swarm shamble past them.

Headed right toward us.

17

On some bloody desolate motorway west of the Oregon Coast, the world reappeared around me. Hecate, the goddess of night and magic, hustled me through the cold and rain toward a dark, abandoned retail park far off the motorway.

I couldn't move. I couldn't speak. This time, I was worried about surviving this vengeful goddess and her new army of necromancers. Built to take down Death and his army—which apparently, Hecate thought included me.

The chill was sharp in the air, tires hissing against damp pavement as a lone car headed into the night, away from the coast. And this abandoned retail park.

The last set of headlamps for miles. Bathing this godforsaken place in cold darkness. And me in a world of hurt.

Fog swirled and eddied along the ground as Hecate shoved me toward the brightly lit shop ahead. The intense light clung to the distant fir trees framing the Cascade Mountains' dark presence to the east. The warm white glow was a beacon in the cloying darkness.

Maybe Death would take pity on me and come find me? Leaving my soul in my body.

Then I saw it.

An old, old cemetery with its wrought iron fence and broken gate askew, leading toward four rows of old marble tombstones, crooked, and sunken into the ground. The mist roiled and undulated through the cemetery that gave off a strange glimmer in the darkness that writhed around this old retail park.

Necromancy Central. I was so buggered.

Looked like I'd be joining Rawlins as his undead best mate before this night was over. Already, I was imagining weekly cemetery crawls with dozens of my smelly, bony compatriots hunting for half-price wings night among the locals. Until someone lopped off my bloody head.

My anxious breaths fogged the air, the only sound in this isolated place so far off the motorway. Almost hidden behind a stand of Douglas firs and shrouded in mist.

I was alone. No cavalry to help me escape from Hecate's clutches this time. My belly ached. I had just begun to get to know Detective Keller. I didn't know her well yet, but I doubted that she dated undead.

Sod it all! How was I going to survive a goddess hell-bent on ending me? And I didn't even know why.

I hadn't bought into her seduction for a moment. She wanted something from me and it wasn't a good shag. Besides, sleeping with gods and goddesses was a terrible idea. It was akin to shagging Satan. There were always strings attached.

To your soul.

The asphalt car park was mostly potholes, a rusted shopping trolley beneath a glowing yellow sign that read, Manny's All-Night Subs and Souvenir Shop. The rest of the retail park was dark, dusty windows covered in brown paper. Except for the sub shop at the far end.

The shop was long and narrow, scalding white lights casting a glare against white tiled walls and floors that reminded me of the loo at the local bus station. The stainless-steel counter had a sub-making station to the right and a small till to the left. A single Blodgett cooker stood behind the sandwich station, its hot surface yellowed, oily, and dull. And a flat screen telly hung above the counter, displaying a take-away menu.

One bossman managed the shop. A middle-aged bloke in a dirty white pinny that clung to his white polo shirt and white trousers. He stared wide-eyed at Hecate and froze at the till, dull blue eyes filled with fear.

Bloke was bloody terrified of her. And I understood why.

In front of the counter, shelves lined the left-hand wall with mugs, books, T-shirts, and keychains. Small wicker baskets of seashells and tiny bottles of sand sat beside small watercolor prints of the ocean and little plush seals embroidered with Oregon Coast on their backs.

The whole place smelled like pepperoni and onions. The only good thing about this absolute shite sub shop.

Hecate pointed her finger at the neon open sign that burned in the window and it went dark.

"You," she demanded and pointed at the bloke behind the counter. "Leave. Now."

The sub maker didn't wait to be told twice. He bolted around the counter and shot out the front door that chimed when it was open.

She pointed at the door and the lock clicked.

Bollocks! I didn't have a machete to defend myself. Or even a harsh word. Death's mute had locked my mouth up tight and I still couldn't utter a sound.

Of course, none of those things worked on a goddess. I was so buggered.

Hecate turned to me, black hair and now green eyes filled with stars as she smiled and reached out to cup my face in her cold moon-pale hands. Did she change her eye color by the occasion? Her eyes never seemed to be the same color twice.

"Why'd you have to be so cute?" she said with a pout.

"Cute? Me?" I said and the words suddenly blared out.

I could speak again!

But her calling me cute had rattled me. I'd been called many things over the centuries, but cute hadn't been one of them.

She pecked my cheek, her blood-red nails sharp against my skin.

"Yes, the cutest little mortal I've ever seen." She let go of my face. "I have half a mind to keep you after you've told me what I need to know."

I frowned. "Told you bloody what?" I snapped. "I'm a bounty hunter. I hunt mostly supernatural beings, in case you didn't know. And believe me, I don't know sod all what Andy Keane saw that night."

Only a suspicion that I didn't intend to share. When she got what she wanted from me, she would end me. So, I had to hold onto this suspicion as long as I could.

She laughed, dismissing me like I was a prattling school boy.

"And yes," I added. "I've hunted plenty of necromancers and mages, in case you're wondering. Never a goddess though."

She shoved me toward a white wooden door that led behind the sub shop counter.

"Adorable," she said with a glare. "Now, shut up and do exactly what I tell you or I'll exterminate you right now—adorable or not."

I opened the door. "Oh, thank God," I said with a sneer. "I was afraid you wanted to shag."

"Can't get it up, Blade?" she said and shoved me past the cooker, smell of heat and baking bread rising around me.

She pushed me through an open doorway, into a dimly lit back room that was long and narrow. That smelled of ozone, decay, and formaldehyde.

And sulfur. Making me uneasy.

Necromancers worked back here—and maybe a demon or two. I just hoped it wasn't a Hell general.

I turned toward Hecate.

"Sorry. Can't get a rager for dull ex-goddesses past their prime."

The tremendous blow knocked me more than a few meters forward, into a metal table reminiscent of an autopsy slab.

"Keep that up and I'll paralyze your vocal cords, Blade. Permanently."

"You want me to teach him some manners?"

The loud voice filled the cavernous space that was concrete block walls and cement floors. The only light in the room hung above the table and its scalding presence reminded me of an operating room.

"Not yet, Neville," said Hecate, hands on her hips as the door behind her slammed shut and locked. "He won't survive my...interrogation anyway."

She glanced behind me into the dark edges of the room where a shadow moved between shelves and tables.

"Gilbert, keep working."

"Yes, mistress," the voice called through the darkness.

So, that was Keller's boss? The police superintendent? A slave to Hecate? Hadn't expected that.

Neville Ryan stepped toward me, stocky, shaggy brown hair, and those black eyes that quite frankly, gave me the chills. He grabbed hold of me and I shoved him backward.

Hecate held up her hand as Neville started toward me again.

"Call off your mutt, Hecate," I said with a glare, glancing from her to Neville Ryan. "Or he's going to get hurt."

"I'm going to tear you apart, Mallory," Neville said through gritted teeth. "That's a promise."

I rolled my eyes. "Tell me, Neville...how does it feel to be an absolute failure?"

Hecate pushed Neville back when he tried to lunge at me.

"Patience, Neville."

Hecate sauntered toward me and laid her hand on my chest. Sliding it into my bomber jacket, she grabbed hold of the lapels with both hands and peeled the jacket over my shoulders, immobilizing my arms.

I struggled as she slammed me onto the table and grabbed my throat with her taloned fingers.

"No more foreplay, Blade," she said. "No more introductions or discussion. Now, I want to know what Andy Keane saw that night and I want to know now. Your existence is hanging by a thread."

I hadn't a feckin' clue what Andy saw because I hadn't had a chance to use my temporal magic on his lighter yet. That was back at Wraith's in Detective Keller's pocket. I only had bits that Rawlins heard from that saddo, Neville Ryan. But whatever Andy saw, Hecate was doing her best to erase all traces of it from mortal memory. Why?

"The moment I tell you what he saw, you'll merc me. It's that simple," I said with a glare. "Forget it!"

She bent closer to me. "I was so hoping you'd resist," she said in a dark sultry tone. "Neville, go help your father."

Neville hesitated.

"Now," Hecate ordered.

Neville crept into the back room, leaving Hecate alone with me.

Silvery bursts of light erupted above my chest and legs, securing me to the table. I couldn't move.

She grabbed hold of my jacket and yanked my arms over my head as the jacket slid free.

That silvery light wrapped around my arms and wrists, pulling them tightly over my head.

She smiled and laid her hand against my face.

"Now, let's try this again, shall we, Blade? What did Andy Keane see?"

Her cold fingers traced along the edge of my jaw and down my neck to the torn black T-shirt I wore. Her nails raked across my bare chest, slicing deep, drawing blood that dripped from the four gouges.

I winced, biting my lip. It hurt, but it wasn't the worst pain this goddess could inflict. How did a goddess go about killing an immortal? Would she try to lop off my head? I had no clue, but no matter what, I had to make her think I knew something.

Something worth keeping me alive for.

She got in my face, her nose touching mine, those starry green eyes turning deadly.

"I know you've got some kind of temporal magic, Blade," she said, stroking her fingers across my bleeding wounds like she was finger-painting. "And a big mouth. Now, I need to know what Gilbert Ryan's sister conjured up that night in New Jersey. And I can't trust him—or Neville—not to protect her. So, I need to know who she's working for."

"Why don't you bloody well ask her then? Or him?" I gritted my teeth, my gaze burning holes into her cheery expression. "Don't you bad guys talk to each other? Or are you too busy trying to make enough undead to populate Scotland—like anyone would bloody notice anyway."

Hecate slashed her nails across my rib cage and leaned close to my face again.

"Because I'm asking you, Blade Mallory," she said in a quiet, sweet—but deadly—voice. "Kerrie claims that she didn't summon anything that night, but Andy Keane saw it. Jumped bail because of it. And her husband hired you to find him. See, Kerrie Ryan knew better than to summon something for her new husband without the express permission of the cabal. And me. Which she chose to ignore when she left for the other coast. That's Circe's territory. And if I don't fix this, I'll be at war with Death and Circe. And whatever dangerous entity Kerrie Ryan brought into this world."

"I couldn't care less about your little necromancer soap opera, Hecate," I said, shaking my head. "Give Circe my regards."

She shook her head.

"Oh, but you will, Blade," she said in a sensual voice as she ran her fingers across my lips and down my neck to my chest. To my jeans.

My muscles corded, nerves seizing. Now, she was just playing dirty. I struggled against the magical bonds but couldn't release my hands or legs.

"See, that's why Beckerman hired you," Hecate continued. "Because only you and your temporal magic could tell us what Andy saw—and who he told. So he could take care of it—and you—before I got wind of it. And it would have already been handled if someone hadn't called the cops to your bungalow that morning. To pick up one body instead of two. Who called the cops, Blade?"

"How cheeky and callous I was for not dying that morning?" I shouted at Hecate. "Such an inconvenience I've caused. I'm an absolute knob for not popping my clogs like the rest of your coffin dodgers."

"But it gets worse, Blade," she said and stabbed me in the lower gut with those taloned nails.

I gasped, everything turning white for a moment, but the dark back room that smelled like sulfur and ozone returned like a bad streaming video.

"Worse than a has-been ex-goddess, peeling me like a banana because she's too skivvy to do her own research?"

She moved around to my right shoulder. And slapped my face. With cutting force. Then she pressed her cheek against mine, smiling.

"Andy Keane contacted you, asking for help. And told you everything he saw that night. You agreed to help him disappear. He planned to stay the night at your bungalow where you'd make the arrangements. Except that someone got to him first. They were steps away from your bed when the cops arrived, Blade. I need to know if it was Beckerman or Circe's people?"

"Are you daft?" I snapped. "The Ryan's necromancers got to him first. Don't you know what your own people are doing, Hecate? Going around killing people willy-nilly. Like they almost killed me at the pioneer graveyard."

"What? My people?" Genuine surprise lit her face. "No. My people had orders to grab Andy Keane. And you that morning. Alive."

She thought that Andy Keane had already told me what he saw.

Andy refused to tell me that day. Said it would be better if I didn't know. He had no idea that I had temporal magic that could show me exactly what he saw that night. By holding one of his personal items in my hands.

Like I'd planned to do at Wraith's.

I wondered if Death knew what Hecate had been planning. Now, I understood why she'd accused me of starting a realm war. She was planting the seeds. Because she intended to pin all of this on me, so Circe would see me as the instigator and blame me for what happened in New Jersey (in Circe's territory). So Circe wouldn't declare war on Hecate and her necromancer cabal. Both goddesses claimed magic and the night as their territories, so they had been enemies from the beginning.

Great, I'd stepped into the center of the mother of all cat fights. And I was their catnip mouse.

Hecate twisted my ear. "Go over it again."

"Being almost correct doesn't count, Hecate," I said, wincing. "Your premise was bang on. I do have a strange magic called temporal magic. That I can't control. It helps me find things lost in time though. Takes me to them. But I never got the chance to use my magic on Andy Keane."

"Liar! He's lying, Hecate!"

I glared at Hecate and then glanced over her shoulder at her squawking parrot, Neville Ryan who reappeared in the room. He seemed cheesed off that he had to wait to kill me.

"See," I said, nodding toward Neville Ryan. "When you hire minions from the Budget Minion Store, you get quid-quality minions. Parrots not pirates. Who knew?"

"Shut up, Mallory!" Neville growled.

"Your minions killed Andy before I had a chance to see what he saw. And without his personal effects—or the body—I can't use my magic to find out. So, good luck with your realm war with Circe. I've heard that she mostly plays fair. And Hermes may be free to help you overpower her magic. I'm sure it's not stronger than yours. By much."

Hecate slapped my face again.

"No, Blade!" she shouted. "I can't believe that Andy died before he told you what he saw. You know what he saw. Now, I need to know. And I need to know who else you told. It's the only way to clean up this mess so Circe doesn't come after me and the cabal."

She held out her fist and twisted it over me, tightening all of the magical bonds until they cut into my skin.

I flinched, fighting back a shout.

She kept up the pain for what felt like an hour, and then she snapped her fist up and splayed her fingers.

The magical bonds relaxed.

My chest heaved as I gasped for air, my muscles going slack. Pain burned across my arms and wrists, the thighs of my jeans darkening with blood. Another deep cut furrowed across my belly, bleeding onto my T-shirt.

Neville was beside Hecate now.

"Let me turn him," he said, grinning like a prat. "If he's undead, I can compel him to tell us."

She reached down and ran her fingers through my blond hair and then caressed my face. The feel of her cold touch made me recoil.

"He's much too pretty to make undead," she said with a moan. "Besides, there's an incantation that will make him tell me everything." She glanced at Neville. "Neville, bring me a torch lit from the magical flame."

"You gonna set him on fire?" Neville asked, grinning.

She shook her head slowly. "That's a magical flame, idiot. It will force him to shed light on my question." She giggled, still staring at me. "Or his brain will burn."

I couldn't help the fear creeping into my face. If she used that magical flame, then she'd know I was full of shite and knew absolutely nothing. Just what Rawlins said he heard. Hecate would know that I'd been bluffing and stalling her this whole time.

Or I'd have to suffer through some prolonged, painful burns.

Maybe some cranky old immortal in a bathrobe would feel my distress and come help me?

Before Hecate made me undead. Or worse. Dragged me into her bed. She was beautiful, radiant even, but being enslaved to her for eternity wasn't my idea of a fun first date. Apparently, Gilbert Ryan had already had that bit of fun.

"Yes, Blade," she said with a twinkle in those starry green eyes. "This is going to hurt. But you will tell me what I want to know. Don't make me turn you into a cockroach. Talk. And I'll spare you the truth flame."

A cockroach was infinitely better than being undead and maybe someone at Wraith's could reverse a spell like that? But undead? As far as I knew, that was irreversible.

I pressed my lips together and shook my head.

"Talk, damn you!" she shouted, shaking me until my teeth rattled. She looked flustered. "And I'll know if you're lying."

Damned straight she'd know. Because that's all I'd done since I'd gotten here. I'd lied to her about everything. And I had no clue what she'd do to me when she found out. They didn't call her the Goddess of Madness for nothing.

"Neville!" she shouted, losing patience when I refused to speak. "The flame. Now!"

I was so buggered.

18

Fifty or more undead lumbered across the dance floor at Wraith's, lights flashing, casting confetti colors across their grey faces and empty eyes. They stumbled toward us, looking hungry. And the club wasn't even playing *Thriller*.

Rawlins shuffled backward and slammed into the translucent wall behind us as cold space drifted past.

"Death..." I called out, backing away from the horde as they emerged through another tangle of immortals.

Who seemed unaffected by the undead's presence. This was Wraith's immortal bar after all.

"Death!"

"One second, detective," he said in a sharp tone, still arguing with Cash and Mars.

"Out of seconds," I replied.

But they didn't hear me. Still shouting about Hecate.

I snapped my Glock out of its holster, backing up until I was against the wall beside Rawlins.

I pointed my gun toward the ceiling. And fired off three shots.

The music's volume dropped. Conversations stopped. Death, Mars, and Cash turned toward me, looking puzzled and annoyed.

"Detective, you trying to be like your partner and get us thrown out of here?" Death said with a growl.

I pointed at the undead rapidly closing the distance between us.

"Better than being torn to pieces by undead."

Everything moved in slow motion as Death turned, his eyes filling with shock. Cash shouted something and slid his dagger back into his coat, grabbing two others, one in each hand, and faded into the room.

Mars twirled his spear like a buzz saw in front of him and with a battle shout, lunged into the swarm of undead.

Cash moved like the wind, on one undead with both daggers, and slicing off its head while Death wrapped them in smoke, corralling them for Mars and Cash to decapitate.

One by one, heads dropped and rolled across the translucent floor. When the last one fell, the bodies and the heads went up in a burst of blue flames and turned to dust.

In the moments of silence, immortals moved around the pile of dust on the floor, and then turned away. A heartbeat later, the music returned, the dance beat scattering the dust until Death swept through it in his smoke form and all of it floated away. Disappearing.

"That night-walking bitch is trying to slow us down," Death said as he took his business form (as Greysen called it) again.

Only then did I slide my Glock back in its holster.

Greysen would have had all of those heads on the floor in record time with his machete, but Cash and Mars handled them well. Cash materialized in front of me as Mars moved beside him, thumping the end of his staff against the translucent floor.

"All right," said Cash, putting away his daggers. "I'm changing my mind. We hit her fast and free Greysen. Anything else is gravy."

Mars nodded. "Agreed. We can't afford the time to fight through armies of undead. Grabbing Blade Mallory is priority one."

Death had an evil grin on his face.

"Then we lay waste to her necromancer's playground."

I moved beside Death. "I'm all in, Death. Can't wait to burn her operation to the ground and arrest Gil and Neville Ryan. After Greysen's safe."

Death held out his hand and Greysen's machete materialized in his hand. Along with Rawlins' long knife.

"I think the kid should have the honor of striking the first blow, don't you?" Death said as he studied my face a moment.

I took the machete from his hand.

"It's only fair."

Rawlins shuffled over, hesitated, and then took the long knife. He looked as scared of those undead as I felt.

"I call second strike," said Rawlins.

Death smiled. "Done, Rawlins."

"I do hope there's lots of gravy served with a big, heaping helping of crow at this banquet. In Hecate's honor," said Cash.

Mars patted Cash on the back and gripped his spear in his right hand.

"And I look forward to watching her choke on it."

"So do I, Mars," said Death and motioned everyone toward him. "All right, mortals, grab hold of my robes. The rest of you, too. It's time to god-travel out of here."

Mars and Cash both shrugged and took hold of Death's black robes. Death gave them a funny look.

"We get it, Death," said Cash.

"It's important that we all arrive at the same time this trip," said Mars.

Rawlins grabbed hold and moved in close to Death, taking hold of his robes. I gripped Greysen's machete in my left hand. Guess I'd have to learn how to use it without his teaching this trip.

"Hang on tight," said Death, lifting his arms into the air. "If Hecate was bold enough to send a herd of undead at us here, in Wraith's, then there's no telling what will greet us at this sub shop."

My stomach did a somersault and I held my breath as coils of thick black smoke rose around us, wrapping us tight in his grasp as he opened a smoky tunnel and the five of us careened into the smoke and shadows. Shooting like a bullet toward Manny's Sub and Souvenir Shop.

When the world stopped turning and the black smoke lifted, the five of us stood in the parking lot of an abandoned strip mall just off Highway 18. The quarter moon's pale crescent gleamed low on the horizon, turning half its face away in the crisp, cold greyness.

My breath fogged the salt-tanged air, a trace of wood smoke clinging to the clear night. It was almost seven A.M. The sun would rise soon.

But the scrape and shuffle of footsteps caught my attention. I jerked my gaze toward the single illuminated shop across the pocked and cracked asphalt. The other store windows were dark and covered in brown kraft paper, torn at the corners.

Shadows lurched through the retreating darkness above the hiss and wheeze that carried in the cold and silence. The sound and the shapes too damned familiar.

Another herd of undead shuffled toward us.

I gripped Greysen's machete tight in my fist. Guess this would be my first lesson in taking off heads. Rawlins looked disturbed by the approaching corpses as the night began to recede.

"Damn her!" Cash shouted. "She's gonna keep us away from Greysen as long as she can. What's she doing to him anyway?"

"Wish I knew," I said, setting myself as the hissing and wheezes got louder. "If she's killed him, I'll take her apart if it's the last thing I ever do."

Cash flashed me a smile.

"Couldn't have said it better, Detective Keller."

Mars' eyes narrowed, the warmth turning steely cold as he spun that spear in wide arc in front of him.

"Ready when you are, Death," said Mars, glaring at the approaching undead.

"Take down these puppets fast," said Death as black smoke coiled around him. "Before she's done irreparable damage to Blade."

Before I could raise my machete, Rawlins let out a wild shout and leaped at the undead mob shambling toward us.

"Take this, you bastards!" he shouted, raking that long knife across the nearest two undead.

Severing both heads.

Cash grinned. "I like that boy's style." He let out a whoop, daggers in both hands, and dived into the fray.

Mars joined him, a smile curving across his chiseled face, squared jaw set as he spun the spear to his right and then to his left.

When I looked up, an undead was only a foot away from me, teeth clacking.

Shouting, I lifted the machete and swung it with both hands in a wild arc. Slamming it against the shriveled grey neck of a once middle-aged man, brown hair in wisps across his mummified face and dead grey eyes.

The head tilted at an odd angle.

As he kept coming at me.

I pulled back the machete again and hacked at its neck. Severing the head.

It bounced and rolled across the asphalt, collapsing in a plume of dust. The undead's body folded like a deck of cards and exploded into another burst of dust.

Turning, I raked the machete across another one's neck and kicked it with the toe of my black pumps.

It came at me again.

Again, I hacked at it. Kicking it like a football.

It scrabbled back across the pavement toward me.

Third swing took its leathery skinned head off and it collapsed in a burst of dust, the head shattering into dirt particles.

No wonder Greysen had such sexy muscles. It was hard work lopping off their heads.

"Press the attack!" Mars ordered with the wave of his hand as he and Rawlins cut a path through the hissing horde.

"We need to get to the door of that sub shop fast!" Death shouted.

Death grabbed my arm and pulled me beside him, wrapping me in the cover of black smoke as he drove through the mass of undead like a linebacker. He moved close behind Mars and Rawlins, Cash slashing and hacking undead at the rear of our assault.

As we made our way across the parking lot. Toward the well-lit sub shop.

Until the sound of hissing echoed behind us.

Death and I turned.

Another burst of undead rushed at us from behind.

"We've been flanked!" Mars shouted.

"Cash, Mars, close ranks!" Death ordered. "We fight through them together. And we don't stop until we're at the sub shop door."

Cash and Mars moved in close, putting Rawlins between them. Cash let out another whoop, grinning as both daggers flashed through the stifling cloud of stink and decaying bodies surrounding us on all sides.

I held my position on Death's right side and turned into the horde.

And raised Greysen's machete high.

"Bring it, you brain-dead bone bags!" I shouted, raising Greysen's machete above my shoulder.

The first undead that got in range met the razor-sharp blade as I took off its head. I smirked. Just like weeding the flower beds.

I swiveled around as the sound of hissing hit my left ear.

Three undead. Right in my face.

19

BLUE FIRE DANCED IN HECATE'S HANDS AS SHE CARRIED THE large writhing flame away from a bronze brazier across the room. Smiling like I was her bloody prom date, she sauntered toward me.

"Do you know what this is, mortal?" she asked, looking so sodding smug.

She knew I was trapped and there was jack all I could do about it, either.

"Oh, please tell me it's the flame to the wood-fire pizza shop down the motorway," I said, struggling against the magical bonds holding me on the table. "At least buy me a bloody sub before you torture me and ruin my entire evening. I'd settle for some crisps and few cheese savories at this point."

Her bored look told me that she wasn't amused by my first guess. Or my menu choices.

"No? Did I guess wrong?" I replied, yanking hard against the silvery magical ropes, but they didn't budge, immobilizing me on this cold morgue table. "Unfortunately, my next guess will also involve food because I'm bloody starving, Hecate."

"Good," she snapped and leaned toward me, the fire crackling against my right ear. "It will keep you focused on answering my questions."

I felt the cold blue flame's magic aching to consume me. I pulled away from it as far as I could slide on this bloody autopsy table.

"Oh, you do know what it is, don't you?"

She laughed as the blue flame guttered in her hand, roiling like a possessed spirit.

"This gets better and better. For me—not you, Blade."

Of course, I bloody knew what it was! I'd done enough supernatural bounty hunts to recognize one of Hecate's torture instruments. I'd seen her handiwork up close, but I'd never encountered her until this trip to the coast. And she loved using this stolen truth flame, leaving damaged mortals all across the world because of it.

It wasn't a mere a magical creation. It had once belonged to the rogue god Prometheus. I'd never encountered him either, but he continued to elude Zeus and champion human causes whenever possible. He and that eagle that had to keep eating his liver had escaped during the Great Resignation and had actually become best mates. It traveled with him, also hunted by Zeus. Unfortunately, one of Prometheus' attempts to help humans ended in a weapon for the gods.

Prometheus created the truth flame to compel humans to tell the truth or face a painful burn against our brains until we told it. Prometheus' flame had been yellow. It left no physical damage—except the memory of the pain. And that worked bloody well to get at the truth.

Until Zeus got hold of it.

And forced Hephaestus to reforge the fire into a weapon causing ten-fold more pain than Prometheus' truth flame ever could.

Yes, there were a few gods still on the job out there. With a vendetta against humanity.

Hecate giggled and patted my head like I was her favorite Springer Spaniel. "Oh, you're going to enjoy this, Blade."

"Like having my tonsils removed through my nostrils," I muttered.

The reforged truth flame, now cold and blue, was excruciating to mortals now—and anyone that suffered Zeus' wrath.

During the Great Resignation, Zeus stole the truth flame when the gods extinguished the torchlights on Mount Olympus. As gods everywhere scattered to the winds, he absconded with the harmless truth flame. After he'd had it reforged, the flame quickly got away from him.

Other gods and immortals passed it around. Selling it. Trading it for goods. Using it on mortals for their own gain. Until most of the former gods knew who to go to obtain the altered truth flame. Which had mutated into something horrible and excruciating for humans.

It was a bloody commodity now. Like ambrosia. Greek fire. A bottle of Bacchus' finest wine.

"Last chance, Blade," she said and held the fire above my head.

I glanced around the room, trying to find an escape route. A way to sever these magical ropes. A weapon. Anything to escape that writhing flame in her hands.

To prevent her from uncovering all the lies I'd told her.

Neville Ryan stood off to the right, leering at me with those black, demon-possessed eyes. Enjoying every moment of my squirming.

Somehow, I had to stall her. Draw this out without having her turn my brain to ash.

If I knew Keller, she'd already pushed Death into mobilizing a rescue operation for me. They were my last hope of surviving this torture. Being an immortal with a brain fried like pork rinds would be a miserable existence. I had to keep her from using that fire on me.

I glanced past her, at the bronze brazier guttering on the other side of the room, most of its fire in Hecate's hands. Where she housed Prometheus' mutated truth flame.

Could I somehow use my temporal magic to touch that flame and send my consciousness across the room to the brazier, where the flame originated from, and avoid her stir-frying my brain into chop suey? And if I siphoned its magic, could I send it back to my body as a shield? It wouldn't block all of it, but enough to retain my faculties.

Right now, I had no other option. If that didn't work, I was doomed. I'd have to confess all the lies I'd told.

And then she'd end me.

I sucked in a breath, stiffening as she came at me with the fire.

"Burn him to the ground," said Neville, sodding prat.

Hecate halted her hand and glanced over her shoulder.

"Neville, go and get the sacrificial knives—and some buckets. We can use his blood to summon Sisyphus from the underworld." She cast an evil glare at me. "I have need of him. And his rock."

"Boulder," said Neville.

She whirled around, that flame crackling in Neville's divvy face.

"Whatever. Get the knives. Now!"

Like a crab scrabbling away from seagulls, Neville rushed off to the shadowy back of the room.

Leaving me alone with Hecate. Who now planned to siphon my blood to summon Sisyphus and his boulder. That wasn't the kind of crush I'd hoped for from Hecate. Feckin' perfect. Hadn't I already given up enough blood fighting these tossers?

I struggled against my bonds again, but they refused to budge. Bollocks.

Her cruel smile returned as she moved back to me, blue flames extended toward my face.

With a sharp inhale, I pulled in a breath and held it, closing my eyes as I summoned my temporal magic and focused on the brazier in my mind. I maneuvered my right hand up from the magical ropes and thrust it in front of my face. It was only a momentary protection, but it would stall her for a precious breath or two.

But a sharp, burning pain slashed across my wrist, cutting deep.

I gasped, eyes snapping open.

Neville Ryan hung over me, a gold ceremonial knife glinting under the fluorescent lights. Hecate reached down and touched my wrist with her finger and my right arm slid free of the magical bonds.

Neville Ryan jerked my arm downward until it hung off the table, warm stickiness collecting across my skin, smell of rusty iron in the air as Hecate bound my arm to the table again.

I felt the warm, sticky blood dripping down my palm and streaking down my fingers. Steady tick of droplets plunked against a plastic bucket below.

Hecate turned toward Neville, her green eyes turning dark.

"Now, leave us."

Neville frowned. His gaze turned pleading as he glanced at her again.

"But I've just started—"

"Leave. Us. Now!"

Neville shrank back.

"As you say," he said and slinked out of the room, back where his father worked on some dark and twisted project for the former goddess of night and magic.

Hecate waited until Neville was out of the room before she turned back to me. She laid her hand against my face and stroked my cheek with her long, delicate fingers. Tipped with spiked black fingernails sharp and pointed enough to poke out my eyes.

She leaned down until her lips were a breath away from mine. Full, mauve lips shimmering with moonlight and poor choices. And right now, I had no use for either.

Wait! Moonlight...she was the goddess of night. She ruled the dark, her magic at its strongest during moonlight and evening. In the morning, when the sun rose, her magic weakened. It was already long after midnight when Death had brought us to Wraith's. And I'd been here for hours.

Could I stall her until morning? Until sunrise? When her magic weakened with the sun. Would her magical bonds weaken, too? I had to outlast her until morning. With my temporal magic.

"You're just too adorable to sacrifice," she said and laid a finger to her lips, shushing me.

Like I was going to bloody shout for that wanker Neville to come slit my other wrist? Had she lost the plot?

Goddess of Madness, I reminded myself. Yes, she had. She'd lost all perspective, too. All she could focus on was some conjured Hell general from New Jersey. And the one person who had apparently seen it, wasn't planning on doing anything but disappearing. She'd convinced herself that this thing would start a coast-to-coast realm war with her and Circe on the East Coast. And probably royally piss off Death even further, intensifying her turf war with him here. But only I could tell her what Andy saw for certain.

Poor Andy Keane died for that information.

"Why torture me?" I asked and nodded behind her toward her back room. "Why not torture Gilbert Ryan for this information? After all, his sodding sister's the one that did the summoning."

She pecked my cheek. "I already have, Blade, dear," she said with a grin. "And he didn't know. Now, I could just pop out to New Jersey and torture her for the information—like she's expecting." She leaned down and softly kissed my lips. "But with you right in my backyard, it's so much more convenient to torture you to find out what our little bail jumper saw."

Logic was sound. It was bollocks, but it was sound.

"I suppose I'll have to go there if my truth flame kills you," she said, caressing my face again.

She kissed her index finger and pressed it to my lips.

"So, please don't be rude and die before I get my information. Blade."

I glowered at her.

"Oh! Well, now—I'd hate to skive off in the middle of you torturing me. Or pop my clogs."

"Good!" she cried, stepping back from me. "Now, that that's settled, let's get started."

Well, that's taking the piss right out of my plan to stall her until morning.

One last time, I glanced over at the brazier as she gathered the blue flames she carried into both hands and shifted them toward me.

I smashed my eyes closed and called up every last bit of my temporal magic. Focusing on the brazier.

Red sparks coiled around the fingers of my left hand as I shifted it into the blue fire that engulfed my shoulders and neck. It seeped into my chest and shot into my face, searing my forehead, and singeing my frontal lobe.

I tried to block the fire. And the pain. But it bore into my brain like the first stifling moments of a brain freeze worming its way through my mind, chewing through grey matter and all my thoughts until I could swear that I smelled my hair burning.

"Tell me what Andy Keane saw!" Hecate shouted into my right ear. "Now, Blade!"

Already, my consciousness throbbed with a terrible pain akin to a lava-hot ice pick piercing my brain stem and punching out through my amygdala.

"Now!" she demanded, her voice sounding tinny and funneled. "The longer you resist, the more it will damage that sexy little mortal brain of yours."

Forcing my body to remain on the table, I closed my eyes, clenching my left hand into a fist, and let my consciousness shoot forward. Past the blue flames. Past Hecate as it hovered around the bronze brazier. Where I channeled its protective magic back toward my body.

The distance was short, but it was enough to blunt the pain. Block the damage.

It was brutal watching from a distance while she screamed in my face and shoved more magical fire at me.

I glanced around the space, searching for a clock. There were no windows, so I couldn't tell how close it was to sunrise.

Finally, I located a small digital clock glowing blue on a shelf in the far corner.

Seven sixteen A.M.

Absolute magic! The sun had to be rising soon. It had been rising around twenty past since I'd arrived on the coast. Maybe it would rise soon enough to save me from permanent brain damage?

The minutes ticked past until Hecate glanced down at my right arm and the bucket below it. She made an annoyed face and snapped her head up, swiveling that blue truth flame away from my face.

"Neville!" she shouted, the shrill sound enough to shatter crystal as she turned toward the back room. "Get in here and take care of this blood sacrifice."

She waited, but no response came from the back room.

"Neville!" she shrieked.

No answer.

"Dammit, Neville!" she said with a growl and jerked the fire away from my body as she stormed into the back room.

I glanced at the clock. Seven twenty-two.

It was a risk, but I had to take it. Now. Before she returned to finish me off with that damned truth flame.

I unclenched my left fist, releasing my hold on the magic, letting the red sparks slip through my fingers.

My consciousness shot away from the bronze brazier, slingshotting across the room. Back to my body.

The leading edge of pain washed over me like a knife blade and began to ease as I grabbed hold of the silvery strands of magic wrapped across my body.

And yanked with all the strength I had left.

They shattered in puffs of smoke, falling away!

I threw myself forward, breaking the rest of the bonds, and rolled off the table into the floor, my head throbbing.

Blood still leaked from the slashed veins in my wrist, dripping down my hand and fingers as I stumbled toward the door into the sub shop. I gently pulled it open and staggered through the threshold.

Lurching toward the other door that led to the front of the sunlit store.

Glorious tarnished gold light of autumn sun poured into the

windows as I pitched forward at the front door, smearing blood across the glass as I yanked it open and pushed myself through the narrow opening.

Into the crisp morning cold.

I stumbled into the car park, my boots slapping against the asphalt.

The crowd startled me. I halted in my staggering lope and glanced up.

Seeing Detective Harlowe Keller's beautiful face and those piercing powder blue eyes.

"Keller!" I shouted, unable to hold back my grin. "You found me!"

"Greysen! Oh, thank God!" she cried, the most concerned smile I'd ever seen brightening her face.

"Death!" I said when I caught sight of his black robes. "And Rawlins!"

They were all here.

Then I saw the smiling face of one of my oldest and dearest friends, Cassius Cattrell. Who went by Cash. An immortal like me. Well, a bit like me. He was a vampire after all. We met in New York City in 1726, shortly after I'd been dumped there by crimpers. Beside him stood Roman former god of war and good friend, Mars. The only god I'd ever met before I came out to the Oregon Coast.

"Cash!" I shouted, gripping his shoulder, dripping blood all over him. "Mars, good to see you, I..."

I held out my right hand to shake his and bled all over the asphalt as Mars slid back. But not Cash. His eyes twinkled and I could see the conflicted look in those gold-hazel eyes. My blood gave his eyes a bright twinge of hunger. He was a vampire after all.

"Greysen, you're bleeding like crazy!" Keller cried, reaching toward me.

Her hand was on my right arm, her touch so hot and encompassing that I wanted to melt into her heat.

Reaching out, I brushed the fingers of my left hand against her arm, feeling lightheaded.

But the world began to turn blizzard-white around me. Sparkling with sunlight as consciousness left me.

I pitched forward into Cash and Keller as the lights went out.

20

It was an eternity until the whiteness fled. Like a blizzard tapering off, the world took shape around me. And I could feel my arms and legs again.

But I was no longer at the abandoned retail park. I was in...Greece? I frowned, gazing around the spacious room. Where was I?

Rich Aegean blue silks draped snow-white stone walls. Lanterns guttered around the outdoor space, casting a warm glow against the white marble floors framed by a ring of capitals topped with skeins of night-blooming jasmine that sweetened the air with its familiar soft scent. And the savory scents of herbs growing in small cobalt blue urns scattered around the capitals. Basil, thyme, and oregano mixed with salty sea air and sweet jasmine, the sound of the sea whispering through the space.

The bed linens, a bright, deep cobalt blue, smelled like salt water and jasmine as I shifted under the covers, feeling a hand gripping my right wrist and warmth spreading through my palm and fingers.

"Gash is deep," said the bright and commanding baritone voice. "Sacrificial knives slowed the healing and coagulation with magic.

Will take some time to close this wound, but I've gotten the bleeding to stop at least."

Then I recognized the voice.

Mars. Former Roman god of war. He was a seasoned warrior with a god's healing touch. I was lucky that he'd been here.

"So, Hecate used Prometheus' mutated truth flame while bleeding him dry? Monstrous." That rich southern drawl belonged to Cash.

"I don't care if it can kill her or not," said the familiar smoky alto voice. "I want to shoot her in the face with my Glock. Wouldn't kill her, but it'd make me feel better. Poor Greysen."

My heart beat faster. She was ready to take on a goddess because of me. And not just any goddess. Hecate—who was as powerful as former Greek god Zeus.

I opened my eyes wider as Death floated around the bed in a trail of black smoke.

"She'd probably enjoy that too much, Detective Keller," Death said with a snarl as he moved around the bed. "Don't waste your bullets."

"Where am I?" I asked in a weak voice, sounding more kettled than I'd expected.

"Greysen!" Keller cried, rushing over to the bed when her gaze met mine.

She dropped down beside me and laid her hand against my face. And I wanted to drown in her softness and heat.

"Keller," I said, my voice a raspy half-whisper, sounding much weaker than I'd hoped.

But the colossal headache from the truth flames did not disappoint. It pounded against my skull and my temples like the Royal Highlanders. Forcing me to lay back down.

Her pained smile radiated, her gaze looking apologetic.

"You're in a lot of pain, aren't you?" she said and I felt cold when her fingers left my cheek.

I nodded and that hurt more than I wanted to admit.

"Didn't think...I'd survive the—truth flame."

She reached out and gently stroked my hair. And I'd have endured that truth flame all over again to feel Keller's touch.

"We tried to get there sooner," she said, "but Hecate kept sending hordes of undead at us. To keep us busy."

Death stood over me on her right, nodding.

"She put up a good fight to keep you, kid," he said, his voice rough like burlap. "But you managed to escape her on your own."

"Where are we?" I asked, my voice so quiet I barely heard it.

Cash sat down on the other side of the bed and leaned over me.

"We're in Mars' suite at Wraith's," said Cash, holding out his arms. "It's massive."

I frowned. But everything about it looked Greek not Roman.

"Why does it—look like we're in...Greece?"

Mars looked amused as he stepped behind Keller.

"Because this is the Prometheus Suite, Blade. Not making that up."

I gave him an annoyed stare.

"How coincidental."

"The universe has a strange sense of humor sometimes," said Mars as Cash rubbed my shoulder, nodding.

"Does it ever," Cash added. "That's what I said at Fort Dummer when that soldier turned me in the middle of an Abenaki ambush. With a field of soldiers and Abenaki dying around us. Sombitch could have drunk his fill that day, giving some dying boy immortality, but no, he decided to turn the man next to him. Out of sheer laziness. Bastard."

I smiled. "Is that why you hired me to stake that wanker like a rose bush? Because he turned you?"

"Indeed I did," said Cash with a smirk as he settled back beside me on the bed and leaned against the headboard, arms behind his head.

Death materialized beside Cash as black smoke trailed over the bed.

"So, how'd you escape getting your brains fried with Zeus' truth flame, kid? Or Hecate killing you for lying?"

I started to remind him that I was immortal when the obvious dawned on me. Immortal or not, Hecate could have ended me tonight. As a god, she could have zapped me from existence. A sobering thought that I hadn't realized until right now. Besides, Keller sat on the other side of the bed, against my legs, and I couldn't let her discover that fact.

I shifted the pillows higher beneath my head, trying to hide my shaking at that realization.

"Greysen, what's the matter with you, boy," said Cash, sitting up as he gave Mars a concerned look. "You look like you just saw a spirit or something."

"Just my own mortality, Cash," I muttered, glancing at Death and then Keller.

She smiled and laid her hand on mine a moment. And for a moment, I couldn't breathe, her touch shuddering through me. I wanted to wrap her in my arms and kiss her.

But I couldn't. I didn't want to complicate this case for her. Besides, I had no idea how she felt. We had only known each other for a few days. And even if she was interested, I was immortal.

Why was everything so sodding complex?

"You escaped a powerful goddess trying to sacrifice you, Greysen," she said, her tone encouraging. "That's cause for celebration."

"Celebrate that she was trying to sacrifice him or that he escaped?" Death asked with a snort.

Everyone laughed, including me.

"Probably a little of both," I replied as Cash patted me on the back and Death ruffled my hair.

"Seriously, kid," said Death, a lighter expression on his moon-pale face, "we're glad you're okay. We were moments away from taking Hecate and her minions apart to save you."

The fact that they'd risk themselves to challenge a goddess as powerful as Hecate choked me up and I pulled in a deep breath. Death squeezed my shoulder. Keller's hand tightened around mine and then let go.

"Thank you," I said in a half-whisper.

I needed to be more careful around gods. I'd gotten so complacent dealing with mortals that I'd forgotten there were more powerful beings that could snap me like a twig.

"A humbling experience," I said in a raspy voice. "Thank you. All of you for coming to rescue me." I bowed my head when my voice broke. "It meant a lot to me."

"I think Hecate scrambled his brains," said Death with a chuckle.

Cash frowned. "Why's that?"

"Never heard the kid so humble before," he replied. "Or quiet."

They all laughed.

I hadn't ever intended to appear arrogant. I'll admit, I'd been a bit overconfident, used to coming out of skirmishes and bounty hunts unscathed because I was immortal. Until tonight when I realized that former gods could still destroy me. Immortal or not.

"I have a much healthier respect for former gods now," I replied.

"A wise attitude, Blade," said Mars.

The former god of war bent down and lifted my right arm, frowning at the rusty bandage wrapped around my wrist.

"Wound's still bleeding," he said and let go of my arm. "Need to rebandage it and apply more healing."

He studied me a moment. Scrutinizing me.

"How do you feel?"

I looked up at him, feeling my eyelids drooping.

"Tired," I said.

"Understandable," said Mars as he reached for some lily-white bandages and hit them with a burst of blue light from his fingertips.

Sterilizing them.

He sat down on a chair beside the bed not three inches from where Keller sat and gently unwrapped the white cloth from my wrist. The more he unwound it, the bloodier it got.

When he'd removed it all, he destroyed it with a burst of fire from his fingertips and it turned to ash, floating away.

With a flicker of orange light, he pressed his fingers to the puffy gash on my wrist and held them there until the light traveled from my fingertips, to my wrist, and up to my shoulder. Warm and pulsating.

Keller's mobile singsonged and she rose from the bed.

"It's the police post," she said to me. "I've got to take this."

"Of course," I replied.

She walked over to one of the capitals framing the edge of the terrace-like platform where the bed stood, a warm breeze fluttering through the room.

"Keller," she said as the mobile pressed against her ear. "What's up?"

She paced with slow steps, an intense look on her beautiful face.

"Finally!" She paused, like someone had spewed a bunch of things all at once at her. "All right, what's wrong. I hear that hitch in your voice. What's wrong?"

Her face turned white and her mouth bobbed open, eyes wide.

"Keller..." I said, my voice too quiet for her to hear me. "Keller, what's wrong?"

"What? Are you sure?" she demanded. "Check again."

More pacing.

"What do you mean you did and the results are the same?" Her voice rose, sounding frightened. "Check it again. That can't be right. It can't be!"

I watched her pace and my heart began to race. Something was very wrong.

"If it's not him then who the hell is it?" Keller was shouting into her mobile now. "Run it again!"

Mars began wrapping my wrist in a new, clean bandage.

"Go easy on this hand for the next week, Blade."

"But I'm right-handed," I said with a frown, still trying to listen to Keller's broken, one-way conversation.

"I said run it again, Smitty!"

Fear crept into those large, powder blue eyes as she licked her lips and paced back and forth in front of two capitals about three meters from the bed.

She halted in mid-stride.

"How many times did you run it?"

Her voice was quieter this time. Sounding kettled. And still fearful.

"Then whose prints are they?" she asked finally.

Her eyes smashed closed as the mobile fell away from her ear. She stared into the corner, looking far away now.

"Keller, what's wrong?" I asked.

Finally, she put the mobile back to her ear.

"Thanks," she said in a quiet, defeated voice.

"Keller, what is it?" I said again.

She put the mobile back in her pocket, looking gobsmacked as she turned around.

With unsteady steps and Cash and Mars yelling at me to stay in bed, I staggered to my feet and moved over to her. I gripped her forearms.

"Keller?" I said. "What is it?"

Her gaze moved toward me and she stared past me a moment.

"Just got Andy Keane's records from New Jersey," she said and fixed me with her gaze.

"And?" I replied.

"The body," she began. "The body outside your bungalow isn't Andy Keane."

"What?" I cried.

How could it not be Andy Keane? He had his mobile open to one of my emails. My name was in his bloody contact list. I met him at the Portland airport. The same bloke lying dead in my front garden the next morning.

"How is that possible? That's the bloke I met at the airport, Keller? I'm certain."

She shook her head. "I...I don't know."

"Then who is it?" I asked.

Her face scrunched into a kettled look and she shook her head.

"Brian Beckerman."

I grabbed hold of one of the capitals to steady myself as the wave of shock rolled over me.

Brian Beckerman? I was gobsmacked.

21

BRIAN BECKERMAN. I COULDN'T HOLD BACK MY SHOCKED response from Greysen.

He was unsteady as hell, standing there in front of me, looking so devastatingly hot with his lean body, that messy blond hair, and those hypnotic violet eyes so intense and filled with surprise. He had such an innocent look on his face, eyes wide, and lips pursed.

He had nothing to do with this mess. I had zero doubt now.

God, I wanted to kiss him. To forget about this damned phone call and this insane case. Kick everyone out of Mars' suite and be alone with him.

Here he was with a debilitating headache from Hecate's magical truth fire and weak from that bitch-of-a-goddess siphoning blood from him like a firehose to use in some dark, demented necromancer's ritual. Yet, he was out of bed and at my side, worried about me.

I stared into his eyes, wanting to fall into them (and into his bed). But I couldn't completely ignore the fact that I'd only know him a few days.

Every part of me trusted him with my life, with the truth, and with finding the real killer, but this tiny little voice in the back of my head nagged, reminding me that I'd only known him a few days. And I wanted to strangle that voice with those blue silk scarves on the wall. After I'd made love to Greysen Mallory.

But I couldn't just fall into bed with a man I'd only known a few days. Damn that voice of restraint. Besides, we were far from alone.

And now, with Thanksgiving only days away, my case had been turned upside down and dumped on the ground. Like it or not, Greysen still had a connection to Brian Beckerman, the man that hired him, but it was a much more distant connection. Which made me happy, but he was still a person of interest because Beckerman died outside his rented bungalow.

My brain had already been speculating how the murder happened.

Beckerman must have hired Greysen to find Andy Keane and then shadowed Greysen out to the coast, intending to kill Keane and then Greysen. Erasing any trace of this entity-summoning bullshit that everyone kept harping on—especially Hecate.

Most of the crimes I'd dealt with were about greed or passion and deep down, I expected this one to be no different. Instead of some supernatural tall tale about spirits and entities. But we were still sifting through evidence to find the greed or passion angle.

What did Andy Keane gain by killing Beckerman? Had he somehow turned the tables on Beckerman? Shot him first—in self-defense? If so, why did he run? And take Beckerman's identity?

But there hadn't been a weapon on Beckerman. No gunshot residue on the victim's fingers. No traces of blood spatter on the victim's hands. Just a big hole in his chest. Had Beckerman been killed in self-defense or did Andy Keane—or someone else—murder Beckerman?

And the big question: where was Andy Keane?

He'd switched credentials with Beckerman and fled, posing as the New Jersey bail bondsman. The BOLO had already gone out, but no leads yet. Not even a single sighting.

Until we found him, I needed to see the footage from that security camera outside Greysen's bungalow. With the holiday so close, it took extra time to locate the out-of-town owner of the camera and obtain the footage. Still hadn't received the results of that trace on the anonymous call to the post the morning we found the body either. Thanksgiving had slowed my case to a crawl.

As soon as I got Greysen back in bed, I'd call Smitty and get a look at that camera data.

Greysen slumped against the capital, trying to act nonchalant about the fact that he was ready to pass out.

I grabbed him around the waist before he pitched into the floor.

"Whoa, that's enough exercise for one day, Mallory," I said as I steered him back toward the bed. "Time to rest."

"I'm fine, Keller," he said, protesting.

Cash and Death got involved and forced him back into bed. He sat back against the headboard, looking annoyed, those violet eyes beginning to steam.

I sat down beside him on the bed and his anger softened.

"Greysen, did you ever meet face-to-face with Brian Beckerman before you took this bounty?" I asked.

He shook his head.

"No, it was all handled through my mobile. And I never got a look at the body. Smitty and his baton had been too anxious to cart me off to the police post in only my joggers that morning. With a slight head wound. I only saw it from a distance. And it was night when I briefly met Andy Keane at the Portland airport. He didn't linger. I gave him the address to my letted bungalow and he said he'd meet me there when it was safe. Then he scampered off into the night like a randy jack rabbit."

I studied his face. His eyes looked so tired, his face paler than usual.

"Smitty said he'd have that security camera footage for me today," I told Greysen and that lightened his expression a little.

"Finally, we'll see who was lurking about that morning while I was sleeping," he replied, the hint of a smile on his face.

"And," I said, patting his arm. "In the *here's good news* department, we finally got a trace on the number used to report the dead body outside your doorstep, Mallory. Should have an identity on that caller any time now."

"I hope it gives us some concrete information to go on," said Greysen as he rubbed his forehead with one hand.

That headache was really getting to him and he'd refused to take anything for it.

"Mars," I called and the tall, dark, and handsome former god moved over to the bed. "Can you heal anymore of his headache?" I asked.

His flowing dark hair and Van Dyke beard framing his mouth gave Mars a commanding appearance. Along with his nearly seven-foot-tall, muscular frame.

"I'll see if I can ease the pain a little more," he said and bent over Greysen, pressing his fingers against Greysen's forehead.

Orange light washed over the stubborn Brit, but I saw some of the pain leave his eyes after Mars' healing session ended.

My phone rang again. I yanked it out of my pants pocket. Smitty.

"Smitty!" I cried, jumping up from the bed and pacing back toward the capitals. "Talk to me. What you got for me?"

"Keller," said Smitty in a reticent voice, his tone a little more nasal than usual. "I...did another follow-up on Andy Keane like you asked."

Why did I know that I already didn't want to hear this?

"And..."

"Andy Keane is in East Jersey State Prison, serving a three-year sentence for burglary. Went in November first."

Stunned, I couldn't even speak for a moment.

We'd checked all of Keane's records the day we found the body. We'd verified everything, run it through all the databases. Keane had been out on bond, pending sentencing. Beckerman's Bail Bonds had covered the bail, pending his court hearing when Keane left the state and jumped bail.

"That's impossible," I snapped. "Smitty, we checked all of that. According to New Jersey court and police records, Keane was out on bond. Bail had been covered by Beckerman's Bail Bonds."

"Sorry, detective, I don't understand it. The records say something else now. Whoever came out to the coast, pretended to be Andy Keane, and hid their tracks like a pro. Probably used that bail bonds business to falsify all the database records. Then reverted them back."

And that pointed to Brian Beckerman. Might be why someone killed him, too. But I couldn't even arrest him for it. He was dead.

But the big money question was: who had come out here impersonating Andy Keane? The same person that called with the anonymous tip about a dead body in front of Greysen's bungalow?

All of this had something to do with Greysen Mallory and right now, I was more inclined to believe that he'd been the target not the perpetrator. But why? What did Greysen Mallory have that they wanted?

That nagging little voice wormed its sliver of doubt into my brain again. Was Greysen part of it? In on...whatever was happening here?

"Any reports from our BOLO yet?" I asked and Smitty sighed.

"Not yet."

And now, I wondered who's lighter I had in my pocket. The one that Greysen was going to use his *ability* on to find out what Andy saw.

That lighter didn't belong to Andy Keane. I was certain now. Was it Beckerman's lighter? Or someone else's that had been pulling all the puppet strings from the shadows?

Andy Keane hadn't seen anything. Because he wasn't there. He was in jail when the event supposedly happened.

Regardless, I wanted Greysen to look at this lighter. And tell me whatever he could, so I could unravel this case. Maybe whoever killed Beckerman still hadn't wanted Greysen to use his talent on it—for a reason we hadn't uncovered yet.

Either way, I had to know.

"Detective," said Smitty in a hesitant voice. "I'm uh, sending you the links to the security camera footage. Forensics made it as clear as they could. Let me know what you want done after you've viewed it."

My stomach roiled. What would I see on this footage? It had still been dark around four A.M. that morning, so the footage would be hazy at best. I just hoped we could uncover something important from it.

Enough to catch a killer.

I couldn't help but worry about Greysen though. My gut was ignoring that little nagging voice inside my head and telling me that he'd been the intended target all along.

I just had to prove it before these necromancers killed him.

"Thanks, Smitty," I said. "I'll be in touch after I've reviewed the footage."

I slid my phone into my pocket and moved back to Greysen who stared at me intently, frowning, looking unsettled.

"What was all that about, Keller?" he asked in a quiet voice.

I sat down in front of him again and took hold of his hand. So soft and smooth that it surprised me. His heady, smoky vanilla oak scent washed over me with distracting warmth and I wanted to lose myself in its intoxicating rush. And in those violet eyes. Had to work to pull myself out of them.

"Greysen," I began, trying to find a way to tell him all this without making his head explode.

His expectant stare flicked from my face to my hand.

"Everything's bodged, isn't it?" he said in that soft, velvety British accent that made my heart do flips in my chest.

I tried to hold onto to my neutrality, but it drifted away in the hollow of those expectant violet eyes burning through me.

I nodded. "We ran all of our suspects through the databases again. Turns out that Andy Keane was already serving a three-year sentence in East Jersey State Prison before Beckerman called you about this bounty."

His eyebrows shot up, mouth bobbing open, those violet eyes filling with shock.

"What?"

And for the first time since I'd met him, Greysen Mallory was speechless.

"Whoever you met at the airport wasn't Andy Keane, Greysen. But they've been systematically eliminating everyone involved in this bounty. And you're the last loose end."

His gaze fell to the bed, his focus a million miles away now. I could almost see him tracing every step and every conversation in his head, trying to unravel this Gordian knot.

I squeezed his hand and his gaze flicked back to me.

"Greysen, I'm afraid for you," I said as we stared at each other.

Did he feel the heat radiating like I did? He was so hard to read and I had no idea if he felt this electric connection that I'd felt between us since he arrived on the coast.

"Whoever eliminated Beckerman will come back after you," I said, my tone sounding dire, but I needed him to take this seriously. "I'm certain of it."

Finally, he exhaled and the distance receded from his gaze.

"What do you suggest?" he asked in a quiet voice.

I pulled the plastic bag with the lighter out of my pocket and dropped it on the deep blue comforter in front of him.

"Let's start with this lighter," I said. "I want you to use this ability of yours on it. Tell me who this lighter belongs to and what images are attached to it."

He started to reach for it when my phone rang again.

I laid my hand on his, halting him from opening the bag and pulling out the lighter, and mouthed wait as I pulled my phone out of my pocket. I groaned at the caller.

Smitty again. With more bad news.

"Keller. Talk to me, Smitty," I said.

Greysen laid his hands in his lap, impatience in his gaze as it flicked from the lighter to my phone. But I felt his tension rising.

"Got back the trace on that call reporting the body," said Smitty, his dark tone making me uneasy.

"Spill it, Smitty," I said.

"Call originated from...Brian Beckerman's phone."

I smashed my eyes closed. Great. So, the dead man called in his own murder.

I was beginning to hate the supernatural.

22

My bloody head was spinning after Keller's series of bombshells dropped on me. I could barely process all of it. This whole sodding time, Andy Keane had been in the nick and we didn't know it! How was that even possible? Like the corpse turning out to be Brian bloody Beckerman.

I had two conversations with the bloke about Andy Keane jumping bail and Beckerman being out seventy-five thousand quid because of it. And how urgent it was to nab him before the sodding Thanksgiving holiday. Could hardly wait to get back to New York for that day and eat my cold, bland turkey sandwich alone.

All I remember was how bloody urgent this case was and how desperate Beckerman sounded. Bloke offered me seventeen thousand quid to do the job fast and quiet. Beckerman probably never intended to pay me. Just hook me into the case, so he could shadow me and off us both.

But someone merked him first. Someone posing as Andy Keane. I cringed. Someone who'd given me their sod all sob story about protecting kids and a wife. A sob story about being on the run for his life. And like a bloody plank, I'd believed him.

Who in their right sodding mind would impersonate a bail jumper? And why? It was bonkers! It made no sense to me.

I glanced at Keller who'd paced over to the capitals spread about the room, having an intense conversation with Smitty on her mobile.

"Greysen," said Cash, his voice low and quiet as his gaze encompassed the room. "This whole case is beginning to smell like your undead friend over there beside Death and Mars—pine scent notwithstanding."

"Worse, I'm afraid," I replied and my gaze returned to the lighter.

Rawlins had been unusually quiet throughout this whole piss parade. I wondered why. Did he know something else or was he still afraid we'd off him for being undead? And manky.

Cash nodded toward the lighter and nudged my shoulder.

"Now's your chance to find out who owns that hardware." His voice was low, southern drawl intense. "While your beautiful detective is otherwise engaged—and won't see your magic spark off when you use it."

I smiled. Cash had a very good point.

I had no intention of telling Keller about my magic any more than I planned to tell her I was immortal. If I had any chance at all of seeing Keller once this case was over, she couldn't see my magic. Not in person.

"Right," I said and opened the plastic bag.

I slid out the lighter.

I gripped it tight in my right hand as sparks began to gleam red like embers at my fingertips, drawing me into a hundred different directions.

Smashing my eyes closed, I held up my right hand and fought against the tides of time to keep my body in place, allowing my consciousness to float above all the possibilities laid out before me.

From the 1960s onward.

I pushed past the lighter's origins. Past the bloke that first bought it. I shot past the ripples of his life that gleamed in the darkness. Seeking the most current undulations.

Time was like a great dark ocean at the center of the universe. Enclosed. Cavernous. Encased in darkness.

Neon bright trails of light danced above the turbulent ocean's luminescence, shooting off toward the distant sprinkle of stars on the horizon.

I hovered over the brilliant colors that vibrated in the indigo blackness until I located the most current thread in the chain.

And grabbed hold of it with both hands.

Like a meteorite, my consciousness shot along the neon wash of light. Into a dank, high-ceiling cellar. Torches guttered along the walls like some medieval castle. The air was so cold it burned as I entered the space like a phantom.

Staring at eight or so blue robed hooded figures ringing a blood-red circle that covered the cellar's dirt floor.

A circle made of blood.

Creating an intricate design consisting of sigils and runes that glistened in the torchlight as a drum kept time, creating a beat for the bass humming that resonated through the dim-lit chamber.

Chanting. Because they were summoning a god.

I edged closer to the gathering until my consciousness hovered at the shoulder of two people in flame red hooded robes. They faced the circle of blue robes, arms outstretched and held high as a female voice began to chant.

As I slipped behind them, the torchlight brought the cinder block walls into focus.

All four walls were covered in an array of symbols drawn in blood. Sigils. I swallowed hard.

From the Underworld.

I'd had enough dealings with demons and the underworld to recognize those symbols painted in some poor sods' blood. They were calling something out of the underworld to materialize in that circle of blood on the dirt floor.

A chill raked my spine.

And not any random demon. Not just a Hell general.

All of them.

Every last one of Hades' Hell generals, his high-ranking entities that kept the titans and other prisoners locked away in their prisons. Prisons that Hades guarded, making sure all these powerful creatures remained caged. And harmless to humanity.

It was Hades' job.

Did he know that someone was summoning his generals? Or was he on the dole? Looking the other way? Or working with Hecate to make use of these generals stateside?

The woman in the red robes stopped chanting. She lowered her hood, revealing shoulder-length dark curls and glossy black eyes as the sigils along the wall and within the circle began to glow.

I groaned, recognizing her from the website image. That marriage announcement.

She was Kerrie Ryan Beckerman.

Beside her, the man slid off his hood, dark hair short, dull blue eyes washing dark. I couldn't quite see his face though as something began to materialize in the circle.

My body began to vibrate as the bloke reached into his pocket and slid out a stainless-steel lighter.

The lighter!

He snapped open the lighter's lid with his left hand, revealing a silver wedding band that matched the one that Kerrie Ryan Beckerman wore. Both had strange carvings and symbols on the bands dotted with tiny blood-red garnets. He moved toward an unlit brazier at the edge of the circle and lit it with his lighter.

Brian Beckerman! It had to be him.

The chanting began again, thrumming above the beat of a single drum as the sigils all over the walls began to pulse. Both Beckermans joined in the chanting.

As the staccato drum beat's rhythm quickened, the blood circle began to churn with life, smoke coalescing in its center.

A dark figure began to emerge in the smoke. All teeth and horns and eyes burning with red flames as it stepped out of the haze, cloven hooves thumping against the dirt floor. Its smoky skin was covered by black metal armor that gleamed in the torchlight.

On the dirt floor, a paper map materialized out of the smoke beneath the brazier that Beckerman had lit.

I moved closer, frowning. A map of the Oregon Coast.

I followed a coil of dripping red blood across the map as it flowed into a tiny puddle along Highway 18. In the spot where that abandoned retail park stood. Where Hecate had kidnapped me and tried to siphoned away all my blood while she tried to burn my brain to cinders.

But the blood on the map pointed behind the abandoned retail park. Centered on that old cemetery that had haunted the back side of it.

"Welcome, General Adramelech," said Kerrie Ryan Beckerman in a dramatic voice. "The map is yours to command."

The smoky-skinned demon bared pointy teeth, its curved horns glinting in the torchlight as it thumped its hooves onto the map and stepped into the stream of blood running across it.

Disappearing.

Bollocks! That wasn't just a map. It was a blood magic gateway. They were summoning demons out of the sodding underworld and transporting them to the Oregon Coast using blood magic.

The Beckermans were forming an army. And that general had been the very first wave.

Why? It made no sense to me. What war was she trying to fight? Was this part of the immortal war being waged between Hecate and Death? Or was she trying to take over all the sodding territory for herself? Or Circe?

Regardless of what I thought, this whole picture looked like an offensive assault, not someone trying to defend anything. These greedy prats were trying to control the immortal realm. I felt it.

But I knew jack all how to stop it.

I gazed around the room, traveling the length and width of it.

Andy Keane was not in this dark, musty cellar. Furthermore, he'd never been in this room. Ever. I felt no trace of him.

The Beckermans lied to me. Made up the story of a bail jumper, promised me a large bounty, and sent me to find someone already in the nick. They'd never intended to pay me either. But then they ensnared me into Andy Keane's bleeding sob story about his two lads and wife being in bloody danger and I'd downed it like a pint of Smithwick's on Boxing Day.

Why? It made no sense.

Maybe I'd been the bait to lure Kerrie Ryan's new husband into a deathtrap? So she could off him?

Inherit his money? His business? I gasped...his magic? With the right set of spells, magic could be absorbed at death by someone else. And by spells, I meant necromancy.

Now, I had more questions than answers.

I wasn't worried about one Hell general loose in the world. I was worried about *all* of them being loose in the world. And based on these blood sigils all over the walls, Kerrie Ryan Beckerman intended to bring all of them up from the underworld. While she gathered all the magic she could nick.

At that graveyard behind the abandoned retail park. Did Hecate even know Hell generals were being ported behind that place or were they being summoned on her orders?

I needed to go back there. Fast. And find out where in that graveyard they were hiding demon generals that had escaped their duties in the underworld.

Something felt off kilter here, but I didn't have time to ponder or analyze it. There was no telling how many dark things Kerrie Beckerman had conjured out of the underworld and hid in that graveyard.

I had to get out there. And stop it. Before the Oregon Coast became the undead demon capitol of the immortal and mortal realms. Run by dictators, Kerrie Beckerman and Hecate.

I released my grip on the lighter and it slid out of my grasp as I spiraled out of the dark New Jersey cellar below Beckerman Bail Bonds. And returned to the balmy pervasive blue of Mars' Prometheus suite in Wraith's.

Keller and Cash were seated around me where I'd slumped against the headboard. For how long, I had no idea.

"Greysen Mallory!" Keller said with a growl. "What were you thinking? Examining that lighter without my input."

It took me a few moments to acclimate back to the suite and the bed. And into Keller's angry blue eyes. Cash sat between us, smirking.

"I needed to know who owns this lighter," I said to Keller who sat with arms crossed, eyes narrowed.

"Did you find out?" she asked.

I nodded. "It was Brian Beckerman's."

As the detective pondered that outcome, which didn't seem to surprise her at all, I grabbed hold of Cash's grey general's coat and shook him.

"Cash, there's no time," I said, staring into his bright gold hazel eyes. "Beckerman's wife summoned a Hell general into this world. Used blood magic to send him through a map to the coast."

When he didn't respond, I shook him again. Harder.

"Cash, she's planning to summon more!"

Cash raised an eyebrow as he cast an uncertain glance at Keller and then me.

"How many more?" he asked, sounding indignant.

"All of them," I said.

Stunned, Cash fell silent. Keller looked worried.

"Death, we've got an—an issue over here," said Cash finally.

Suddenly, Death materialized beside me, looking pissed off.

"Kid, what do you mean they're summoning Hell generals?"

"I watched Kerrie Beckerman summon one. She used blood magic on a map to transport him here. Directly from New Jersey to the coast. Before I got this bounty hunting job."

Death's dark eyes narrowed.

"That had to be a week or more ago." He exhaled and stared past me, a hand on his chin. "I wonder if Hecate's behind this. Trying to take over the mortal and immortal realms both."

I had no answer for him. I had no idea who was behind it. I just knew we had to hurry out to that abandoned retail park and find out what they'd hidden in that cemetery.

Before I woke up with a Hell general sitting on my chest some morning. Eager to execute me. And undead outnumbering tourists five to one.

"Well, there's only one way to find out, Death," said Cash as he got to his feet and stretched. "I'd say we'd best get out to that cemetery and investigate this map. Find out where this Hell general went, wouldn't you say?"

Mars stepped over to the bed, clutching his spear, looking fierce.

"I couldn't agree more," said Mars. "Let's go battle these demons and send them back to Hades to deal with. After all, this thing escaped on his watch."

Death cast a pensive look around the room and began to turn into smoke.

"Wait!" Rawlins shouted.

The undead thief edged closer to the bed, scent of pine and decay settling around him, and I sat up straighter and motioned for him to speak.

"What's the matter, Rawlins?" I asked. "Something to add?"

He nodded, looking frightened.

"Something you need to know about Hecate." His sigh ended in a wheeze, grave dust rising around him.

Death's gaze narrowed and he let go of his smoke form.

"Speak up, undead," said Death.

"What about Hecate, Rawlins?" I asked, trying to sound patient and encourage him to continue.

Rawlins seemed almost too frightened to speak up, but he pulled in a hiss of breath and fixed me with his dull gaze.

"Neville Ryan is in love with Hecate," he said.

I frowned, pondering that statement a moment. On one hand, why did I care? On the other hand, Neville Ryan fancying Hecate made him much more dangerous to deal with—total devotion to a goddess. Especially if he'd slept with her.

"Unrequited, pining for the goddess love?" I asked. "Or *I slept with a goddess because I'm a bloody nob who's been enslaved now* love?"

Like Gilbert Ryan, Neville's father.

"Definitely a nob," said Rawlins in an anxious tone.

His response made me laugh harder than I'd expected.

"So, ol' Neville slept with Hecate like his father?" I said, still laughing. "That means he's her own personal slave now. What a bellend. She'll use him up like a bag of cheese savories and toss him. So, that's why he's been an absolute nob. She's controlling him."

Keller gave me that cop look of hers.

"I don't think I understood a word of that, Mallory," she said. "Can you Americanize that a little?"

"Neville fancied Hecate. Neville slept with Hecate. Now, Hecate's controlling the stupid prat—because that's what happens when you sleep with a goddess that powerful. End of story."

"Well, that cleared it right up," said Keller, sighing as Cash and Death laughed. "I think I got the gist of it. Hecate's been controlling Neville this whole time."

I glanced over at Rawlins and gave him an encouraging smile.

"Good work, Rawlins," I said. "Important information to know about Neville. Which also gives us his weakness. Thank you."

Rawlins preened, looking pleased, like he'd contributed something to the case. And he had. We knew Neville Ryan worked for Hecate and that Neville fancied her. But not that he'd slept with her. That meant we couldn't appeal to his humanity now. Because he had none while Hecate controlled him.

"All right," I said, sliding my feet into my brown loafers that sat beside the bed. "Let's go investigate another bloody graveyard, shall we?"

I stood up and everything shifted.

Keller grabbed me around the waist before I pitched into the floor. My face was inches from her lips and I wanted to smash my mouth against hers, frantically snogging her. I didn't even care who saw me either.

But she set me back onto my feet as Cash moved to my left to steady me. Breaking the moment.

Keller stared into my eyes for a moment or two and then turned toward Mars.

"Mars, is Mallory all right to travel?" she asked.

Asking him not me? That annoyed me. Like I was a sodding child.

Mars nodded toward me.

"He's unsteady and will be for the rest of the day. But he'll be fine tomorrow."

"Is he able to investigate this graveyard?" Keller asked.

"I'm still in the room," I replied. "Might try asking me for a change."

Of course, they didn't. They ignored me. Again.

"No worries, detective," said Cash, patting me on the back. "I'll keep watch on Greysen. He'll be fine."

"Yes," I snapped, giving all of them my most annoyed look. "I'll be fine. Thanks for asking." I mumbled the rest under my breath. "Bloody prats."

Keller bit her lip and I know it was to keep from laughing at me as Death turned to smoke again and hovered beside Mars.

"All right then," said Death, motioning with both hands around the room. "Everyone crowd into the smoke and we'll god-travel to this graveyard. That way, I'll know that no one's been kidnapped by Hecate again."

He gave me the evil eye when he said that.

"Like I had a sodding choice," I replied.

He ignored me.

Nodding, Keller laid her hand on my forearm and led the way

into Death's smoky black form. I moved as close to her as I could and we exchanged a couple of grafty smiles (that's flirting again for all you Yanks) as we stood against each other.

I could get used to her this close to me all the time.

After Rawlins crowded in beside Mars, Death swept the entire group out of Mars' suite at Wraith's, tunneling between the worlds, until we materialized in the misty graveyard in the desolate dark behind the abandoned retail park near the number 18 motorway that led back to Portland from the coast.

Douglas Firs surrounded the back of the retail park and framed the cemetery on three sides. The scalding white lights from Manny's Subs and Souvenir Shop burned into the night, a hint of pepperoni in the salt air. But it was still too dark to see the snow-capped Cascades towering to the east now. Only the glow of the sub shop sign lit the crisp indigo darkness beyond the retail park. The occasional hiss of tires against damp asphalt filled the quiet, the air cold and hinting of onions as we got closer.

As Cash and the others stepped out of the smoke and surveyed the old graveyard, I stood with my body still against Keller and stared into her powder blue eyes, wanting to wrap her in my arms and snog her.

She patted my sleeve and turned away, her gaze shifting to the graveyard ahead.

Her response—and her distance—stung.

Had I been deluding myself this whole time that she had some interest in me...beyond being a person of interest in this case. Now that the body had been ID'ed as Brian Beckerman, she seemed less interested in me.

And that made me feel sad as I walked behind her underneath a rusting wrought iron arch into the old cemetery.

A specter-like mist clung to the grass, crawling across the ground, and nestling against eight rows of broken and shifted tombstones scattered throughout the fog. A black wrought iron fence framed the small cemetery, the gate rusted open and hanging at an odd angle.

"So, what are we looking for in here, kid," Death asked as he hovered beside me, taking my mind off Keller's disinterest.

Cash, Mars, and Rawlins clustered behind Keller who scanned the surroundings.

"I saw the Beckermans summon a Hell general," I said, holding out my arms. "He stepped on a map with a blood trail on it that created a gateway and he disappeared through it. The blood pooled on the map here—on top of this cemetery."

Cash looked pensive, a hand against his chin as he stared out at the rows of tombstones. Rawlins looked distracted, nervous, glancing behind him and then at Death. And Mars looked hungry for battle. Keller looked frustrated, a hand on her Glock, and her gaze on me now. Death looked miffed. I hoped it wasn't at me this time. That would take the piss right out of this whole graveyard investigation.

Death scratched his head a moment, a trail of black smoke coiling around him as he gazed up and down the rows of headstones and then back at me.

"So, we split up and search the graveyard," he said. "But what do we look for, kid?"

That was an excellent question. And I hadn't a clue.

I scrutinized the misty plot of land with its broken marble tombstones, many of them toppled over or leaning at a sharp angle, the text looking almost sanded off by wind and time. This whole place looked forgotten, like no one had been inside here in decades. But someone had. A Hell general. And Hecate's minions. Where was the gateway? Was this just a landing zone or did this graveyard conceal something else more sinister?

"My gut tells me that this is still Necromancy Central, so we look for anything out of the ordinary."

"Son, everything about this graveyard is out of the ordinary," Cash said as he propped his hand on his hip and shook his head. "It looks like Stephen King fought Steven Spielberg and ended up in the M. Night Shyamalan version of Weekend at Bernie's."

I shrugged. A bloody good summation.

"All right then. Look for either a trail of bodies, ghosts, or Bruce Willis." I waved Cash into motion. "Go. Investigate. And something to ponder: not all these headstones may be real."

Rawlins muttered to himself as he lurched into the mist. Mars followed behind Cash who shook his head and headed toward the far side of the cemetery. Death turned to smoke and floated into the dark, disappearing among the tombstones. Keller looked over at me.

"I'll follow you," she said. "Lead the way."

I couldn't quite hide my smile as she stepped closer to me. I nodded toward the easternmost edge of the cemetery.

"Let's start at the far edge and work our way back to the gate," I said.

"Good plan," said Keller.

I so wanted to know what was going through her head right now. Had I completely slid off her radar now? Or did she feel that spark that I felt?

I turned to the right and crept through the dark cemetery, feeling the detective close on my right.

Movement whispered from all directions, the air crisp and cold, stars spilling overhead, a sliver of moon low on the horizon, about to set. Cash moved like the fog, being a vampire, so I had no idea where he searched inside the graveyard. Death was in his smoke form, so he made no sound either. Mars crept on kitten feet, being a god of war. Only the whisper of Rawlins' bony shuffling echoed above the occasional rush of a car along the nearby motorway.

Even Keller moved like the wind, her footsteps whisper-quiet as she moved beside me. I had none of these supernatural abilities—or special forces training—to move without noise. My loafers crunched against the cold grass as I walked from tombstone to tombstone, expecting a Hell general to materialize in front of me and skewer me with his horns. I touched the grip of my machete, still tucked in the hidden pocket of my bomber jacket, knowing my weapon would only cheese off a Hell general, but it was all I could use with Keller beside me.

Keller's gaze was intense, focused on every sound and every movement around us, hand on her Glock. Her steps were careful, deliberate, and she did her best to make minimal noise.

We covered all the tombstones at the cemetery's edge and moved toward the center, mist swirling around our ankles, wind sharp and cold as it bit through my bomber jacket. Keller fastened the collar of her motorbike jacket, but she was still shivering. At least she had on boots tonight instead of those pumps she normally wore, but she still looked miserable. And apprehensive.

I shielded her with my body as I reached over and rubbed my hands up and down her sleeves, trying to warm her up. She looked cold and miserable. And surprised. I cringed. Or was that annoyance? Blimey, I felt sick at how she'd suddenly lost all interest in me.

"Sorry," I said and pulled back. "You look frozen. Was trying to—"

"No, it's fine," she said, gazing right then left, like she expected to be mobbed by undead at any moment. "And I'm freezing out here."

With a tentative touch, I rubbed her arms again, afraid she'd pull away or tell me to stop.

"We need to get you out of the cold soon," I said in a whisper. "Can't have you catching your death out here."

My feet flew out from underneath me and I tumbled into the mist, my chin hitting the cold, hard ground.

"Greysen?" she cried. "Are you all right?"

"Tripped over this bloody stone," I said with a groan and scrambled to my feet.

The tombstone had fallen forward, turning at an odd angle. Clods of dirt were strewn across the frosty grass. I frowned. Like it had been freshly disturbed.

Reaching out, I gripped its cold, pocked surface, trying to shift it, but it wouldn't budge.

But the thin ray of gold light threading through the fog beneath it caught my attention.

"Keller, look," I said and pointed at the light.

Her brow furrowed. "Where's that light coming from?"

Then it hit me. This tombstone was exactly where it was meant to be. Because it was a hidden entrance to something below it.

I scrabbled around in the dirt, looking for a switch, or a button—even a bloody lever. But I didn't find one. Finally, I nudged the stone with my foot. When that didn't work, I grabbed hold of the stone and leaned down on it. Until it tilted beneath my weight and shifted toward the ground.

A grinding sound moaned through the night as a metal plate covered in grass and dirt lurched open. Revealing four stairs leading into a dark cellar.

Keller gasped and we exchanged an incredulous expression and I turned away toward the graveyard.

"Here!" I called out. "Found an entrance."

Cash was beside me like a rush of wind. Death hovered beside Keller in a smoky translucent form as Mars crept up behind him. Rawlins shuffled toward Cash and stared down into the stairwell.

"That's good work, kid," said Cash, patting me on the back.

"I tripped over it," I answered.

Cash smirked. "Either way, you got results, son. That's what counts." He bowed and extended his hand to me. "After you, Blade."

Keller grabbed hold of my arm. "I'm on your six, Mallory," she said.

Was she being protective or making sure her person of interest didn't fade into the night? After all, the dead bloke hired me, so like it or not, I was still connected to her case.

With one hand on the handle of my machete, I crept down the four stairs, Keller at my back.

As soon as I cleared the last stair, lights snapped on throughout the long, narrow room. Motion activated.

A lab stretched out through the scalding white lights. A work bench on either side of the concrete room with three grey metal stools on either side. Beakers, Bunsen burners, and even a microscope scattered across the black work benches, the stale air pungent with an array of sharp chemicals that I didn't recognize. Except the bleach smell that permeated everything.

The coppery scent of blood was as unmistakable as the collection of bright red blood sigils painted on the lab's far wall.

Keller gasped. "What the hell is this place?" She glanced around. "And please tell me that's not blood on the walls."

"Afraid it is, Keller," I said as I moved toward the closest sigil.

The longer I studied these symbols, the faster I came to the realization that something was...off about them. They looked rough around the edges. Like an uncertain hand had drawn them on the walls. Not shaky and frightened. Unsure if they were correct.

"Cash," I called out. "Take a look at these sigils. They seem— badly drawn."

"I'm quite familiar with these particular sigils," he said as he steered Mars toward the wall beside me. "And so is Mars."

Mars was quiet, but Cash speculated on how they'd been drawn.

"Looks like whoever put these up used a long stick or even a rag. Must not like to touch blood." He chuckled. "Guess that lets out me and all the vampires in the area."

"Agreed," said Mars. "Look at the ragged edges of the symbols. They aren't crisp. Like they've been...traced or something."

"Good call, Mars!" Cash called out. "Death, come take a look at these. Tell us if Mars is right."

Death materialized behind them and moved toward the symbols, his hand extended.

Keller and I walked through the silent lab, looking at everything.

"Uh, Greysen," said Keller suddenly, sounding quite apprehensive. "What the hell is this?"

I turned toward her.

Bloody boot prints tracked across the concrete floor and disappeared in mid-stride at the back of the lab.

"Blimey! What the bloody hell?"

I followed the tracks alongside Keller.

Taped to the far corner was a copy of the map I'd seen on the floor in New Jersey. The images from the lighter. But this map was different.

A digital timer affixed to the wall ticked down the minutes in a glare of big red numbers above the paper map. A map of the Oregon Coast.

I moved closer.

A collection of three, small red symbols, like they'd been stamped in blood onto the map, were painted above the cities of Newport and Lincoln City. A big red circle had been drawn around Depoe Bay.

Then I realized what I was looking at. It was necromancy bomb. Set to go off in one hour. And these red symbols weren't summoning sigils. They were the parts of a necromancy ritual. Had the Ryans or Hecate painted these symbols in blood throughout those two towns?

When that clock counted down, a dark ritual would fire, and turn both towns into undead wastelands. With Depoe Bay being the safe zone.

That meant the Ryans were cowering in Depoe Bay, ready to turn the coast into Undeadland. As crafters of the spells and sigils, they had to be in close proximity of the locations for the necromancy rituals to complete.

"Death...we've got a big problem," I called out.

"We sure do," said Death, his black bathrobe swishing through the lab as he appeared beside me, Ginsu knife glinting from his right-hand pocket. "Those sigils over there are forgeries. Someone changed them after a blood magic ritual put them on the wall." He groaned. "And as much as I'd love to blame Hecate for it, those base symbols are hers. And they've been tampered with."

"Good to know," I muttered. "But we have other pressing matters, I'm afraid."

"Like what?" Cash asked, moving up behind Death in his grey Confederate general's coat.

"Like all of Newport and Lincoln City turning into undead in an hour unless we interrupt a blood magic ritual."

"What?" Death shouted, fury beneath his voice.

I motioned to the wall, at the timer, and the blood magic splayed across the map. Especially the sigils representing real ones drawn in blood somewhere in these two towns. We had to find the sigils and destroy them in each location. I sighed.

Or we'd be fighting hordes of undead for a very long time. And Christmas on the coast was about to get Medieval.

23

"What are we gonna do?" Rawlins cried, trembling as he ran his hands across his face, staring at me and then Keller in terror. "Everybody's going to be undead now. Everybody!"

Bloke was off his trolley.

Keller grabbed him by the shoulders and shook him.

"Rawlins! Get hold of yourself."

Her shout got his attention and he turned his gaze toward her, still shaking, bones rattling. Sighing, he nodded, looking calmer, the skin not stretched quite so tightly across his skeletal face. Only then did she let him go.

Cash and everyone else turned to Death.

"Well, Death," said Cash. "What say you? How do we stop this necromancy ritual from ruining our beautiful coast?"

"I say we fight them head on," Mars said with a growl, lifting his spear into the air. "Don't stop until the streets run red with their blood."

"Mars, as much as I admire your battle prowess," said Death, squinting at the huge and fierce gladiator. "Taking this fight into the streets will create chaos and casualties. Not to mention a massive headache for Detective Keller and her police post."

Mars set himself and thumped his spear against the concrete floor.

"Less casualties than when this undead ritual gets set off, wouldn't you say, Death?"

"Less corpses, maybe," Death replied. "But still an unacceptable body count. We need to find Hecate. Get her to stop this mess before it starts."

Cash frowned. "Hecate? She doesn't even realize it's happenin', Death. She's probably off at the bar at Wraith's or on the dance floor, oblivious to what's about to happen in both your territories."

Wait a moment! Blimey, Cash was right! I hadn't realized it until just now, but these two affected coastal towns were part of the central coastline, straddling both Hecate's and Death's territories.

Who gained from Death and Hecate continuing to fight? Or who gained from them eliminating each other's forces? Circe perhaps? That was the real question.

"But she's the only one that can stop all her people in time," Death countered, hands on his hips as he glanced from the timer to Cash. "It'd take me all night to stop all those human hearts."

"No need for that, Death," said Keller. "The state police will put out BOLOs on the Ryans—yes, even the superintendent. We'll send out patrols to arrest these people on sight, but like Death, it'll still take all night. That timer will go off long before that."

She jumped, acting startled, and then pulled her mobile out of her trouser pocket, answering it. Must have had her mobile on vibrate.

"Keller," she said in a sharp voice. "Not a good time, Smitty. Yeah, I went over the security camera footage. Yeah. I saw a dark, grainy image of someone wearing jeans, a black peacoat, and a black New York Yankees ball cap. Shooting Brian Beckerman." Keller sighed. "Yes. Yes! The suspect was dressed exactly like Brian Beckerman. And no sign of the murder weapon? Right. Give the footage back to forensics and have them go over it again, Smitty. Right. Keller out."

I frowned, pondering that statement. Whoever killed Beckerman knew what he was wearing that night and they dressed exactly like the bloke. To kettle the security cameras?

"Detective," said Cash, "Might not be a bad idea to round up these bastards and arrest them, but you're right. Would take more time than we have."

All of them started talking at once, but no one was addressing the problem head on. Those sigils in both towns had to be destroyed. Fast. Before the ritual's magic ignited.

"We have one hour. So, we need to have Death take us to each town," I announced, talking over the lot of them and forcing them to listen to me. "Then we split into three groups, each finding and destroying one blood sigil, repeat the hunt in the other town, and Bob's your uncle."

"Which one?" Rawlins asked.

I frowned. "Which one what?" I asked.

"I have two uncles named Bob. Which one?"

"I think that's just an expression, Mista Rawlins," said Cash, smiling.

"Right," I said. "Let's take care of these tossers' sigils and stop this sodding ritual. And then hunt down whoever gains by either wiping out Death's and Hecate's forces or keeping them fighting for bloody eternity."

Death appeared in front of me. He studied me a moment and then hugged me. And no one was more surprised by his hug than me.

"Kid, that's brilliant," he said, letting me go. "Best plan we've got." He turned to face the others. "All right, Keller and Greysen, you're team one. Cash and Mars, team two. Rawlins and I are team three. We'll all god-travel to Newport where we each hunt down a sigil and destroy it."

"Uh, Blade, refresh my memory," said Cash, turning toward me. "How does one destroy these sigils?"

Everyone turned to stare at me.

I had only handled two cases with necromancers before and none of them were this powerful.

"All right, listen up. Necromancy relies on the eight magical elements," I said. "But they cast rituals in blood, fire, or fragrant ash. Blood is the strongest magic. Water counters fire. Metal counters ash which is one state of wood. And bone counters blood."

Cash was already shaking his head.

"Gonna have to spell it out for the dumb vampire in the group."

I smiled. "You're not dumb by any means, Cash," I said and turned back to the tense, wide-eyed expressions encompassing me. "No, to counter blood, we have to rub the sigils with grave dust. Which comes from the bones of the dead. I figure Death can get us a quick supply of grave dust—which is bone dust. The bone dust will absorb the blood and the sigil."

Death floated toward Cash. "You figured right, Blade," he replied and zipped over to the work benches.

He closed his eyes, turned to black smoke, and circled one of the benches until piles of bone-white grave dust shimmered along the bench top. He moved away from the dust, back toward me.

"All right, grab some of those containers and fill them with grave dust," Death ordered, pointing toward the work bench. "And hurry, we only have fifty-six minutes to stop this ritual."

"And please—no one sneeze," said Keller.

I rushed past the remnants of Death's smoky trails and grabbed a clear plastic container small enough to fit in my jacket pocket. I snapped open the lid and carefully scooped up several handfuls of grave dust, placing them inside the container. When it was full, I snapped the lid closed. And filled a second one.

Everyone gathered around me, filling containers, and stowing them in their pockets and satchels.

"Let's have a go at spoiling this beach party for these wankers, shall we?" I said with a wry smile and moved back beside Death.

When everyone had filled their containers, Death swept all of us into a tangle of black smoke and launched us into a dark tunnel between the worlds. We came out on Newport's shoreline, the cold night windy and inky black and smelling of brine.

"How do we find these sigils?" Keller asked, moving closer to me.

"Cash, you can sniff out blood better than anyone I know," I replied. "As you locate the sigils, we'll follow behind, and snuff them. You and Mars will destroy the third one. Then we move on to Lincoln City."

Cash grinned. "You got this all figured out, don't you, Blade?"

I shrugged. "I don't know if it'll work and I don't know if it'll be in time, but it's the best I can do for now."

Cash patted me on the back and then turned his face to the wind. "Then let's find those blood sigils."

Closing his eyes, Cash held out his arms and took deep breaths until a smile curved across his angular face again.

"And there's one close by," he said and pointed to the beach below. "Blade, you and Keller head down to that pier. At the edge of it, on the last pylon, I can smell blood. It's a rare type. B negative. Bitter with a hint of bile and a touch of insulin."

I motioned to Keller and we broke into a run down a winding sandy path through sea grass. Down to the beach where a long pier hung above the dark, gunmetal waters. Two pristine white boats were moored on one side as Keller grabbed hold of my arm. Our footsteps hissed through the dry sand, onto the damp, wave-smoothed beach, and onto the sun-bleached planks of the pier.

Our footsteps were hollow as we pounded down the old dock boards until we reached the end.

Keller slid out her container of grave dust as I leaned out around the pylon, locating the red glimmer of blood and magic clinging to the wood.

"Found it!" I cried.

She extended the open container of grave dust to me. It sparkled white in the darkness, the light glinting off the waves with a pale blue phosphorescence.

"Here," she said. "Do you just rub the dust on it?"

I nodded as I scooped out a handful and smashed it against the waterlogged, barnacle-encrusted pylon. A cold, clammy orange starfish began to inch away as the grave dust absorbed the blood until the sigil vanished. I scattered the used grave dust, which had turned pink from the absorbed blood, into the sparkling ocean waves below.

Keller snapped the container closed and slid it back in her jacket pocket.

"Let's go," she said, her eyes so bright and inviting.

I nodded and together, we ran back down the pier, across the beach, and back up the trail to where Cash and Mars stood.

"Death and Rawlins are taking care of the second sigil," said Cash, a twinkle in his eyes, fangs flashing as a car's headlamps passed over us. "I'm searching for the third one now."

Mars paced along the dark shoulder of the road, spear in hand.

Death and Rawlins returned in about fifteen minutes. By then, Cash had located the third sigil.

"Got it! It's by a bank ATM. What in the world?" He shrugged. "You ready to spear an ATM machine, Mars?"

Mars glanced at his spear and then at Cash, a grin brightening his intense features.

"If it's the only fight in town, I'll take it. Let's go." He motioned to Death. "Take the others on to Lincoln City. Cash and I will catch up."

Death nodded. "Rawlins and I popped back into the lab to check the time. We're down to twenty-two minutes, people. Hurry!"

Mars gripped Cash's shoulder and they vanished into the night as Death turned into his black, smoky form.

Keller followed Rawlins into the smoky coils and I hurried behind her. As everything turned dark, Death tunneling between the worlds to get to Lincoln City, I felt Keller lay her hand against my arm, making my heart swell. But I couldn't help wondering whether it was for balance or because she was interested in me beyond this case.

It seemed like forever before we materialized in front of what Yanks called an outlet mall that stood up the road from my bungalow in the Nelscott neighborhood. It was long after midnight, so everything was dark and locked up tight.

"Sure hope Cash and Mars hurry," said Death, pacing along the sidewalk on the quiet side street, streetlights pooling against the damp pavement. "We're running out of time fast."

Behind the outlet mall, the usually packed car park was empty. Not a single car present. Only the occasional hiss of cars and lorries against damp pavement filled the late night as a cold mist hung in the air that smelled like brine and a hint of motor exhaust.

In ten minutes, Cash and Mars materialized on the sidewalk.

"Newport's sigils are gone," Cash declared as he turned his face into the wind. "Now, let's find the ones here in Lincoln City."

He was quiet, arms outstretched, head raised, long white hair fluttering as he searched for the sigils.

"Death, Rawlins, there's one behind the caboose at Streetcar Village. A ways away from us to the south."

Death wrapped Rawlins in black smoke and disappeared as Cash searched for more sigils. He was quiet for what felt like an eternity until finally, he spoke.

"Found the other two. There's one on the bench at the public turnaround, Nelscott beach area. The other's outside the post office way up north. Mars will take you and Keller to the turnaround, Blade, and then he and I will head north to destroy the last sigil."

I moved over to Mars and Keller followed, Cash right behind her.

"Hurry," I said. "We're almost out of time."

With a nod, Mars swept all four of us into a wash of gold light and we began to rise. We shot across the sky in a blur and suddenly, Keller and I were standing on a half-moon shaped concrete observation platform overlooking the beach and the Pacific Ocean. The waves were wild along the beach, kicking up foam, and lifting huge driftwood logs off the sand. They floated in the foam and ropey green seaweed as the ocean covered the entire beach.

"The bench," I whispered to Keller in the dark, only a thin gold beam from a security light washed over the concrete bench.

But even in the darkness, the blood sigil gleamed like a red beacon.

"Here!" Keller cried, dropping onto her knees as she pointed to the sigil on the left side of the bench, almost underneath it.

I fumbled my grave dust container out of my jacket pocket and handed it to Keller. She snapped open the lid, but the sound was muffled beneath the hiss and shuffling sounds echoing from the stairs leading up from the beach.

At least a dozen undead lumbered up the stairs toward us.

I turned, sliding my machete out of the hidden pocket in my jacket and raised it high.

"Destroy the sigil," I said to Keller. "I'll cover you."

She glanced left and right, looking horrified. Another line of undead lurched toward us from the other side of the beach.

"There's too many!" she cried.

"Hurry!" I shouted as I swung my machete, decapitating the first undead to reach me.

I fell back behind the bench as Keller picked up a handful of grave dust, and I swung my machete like a wild man. But Keller was right. There were too many. I couldn't swing my machete fast enough to take them all down. And I was out of tricks.

Something razor-sharp bit into my forearm.

Shouting, I whirled around, machete slicing through the air. Another head rolled down the steps.

Another set of teeth bit into my thigh. Tearing. Rending.

My blade tore through the air, separating undead limbs and heads, but as fast as I dropped them, more shambled up behind them.

"Sigil's gone!" Keller shouted.

"Get behind me!"

Another undead clamped down on my forearm. I shook it off, gritting my teeth against the pain. They were like piranhas and if I didn't stop them, they'd strip the flesh from my bones.

I groaned. Our bones.

"No, you need help fighting them!" Keller shouted.

"You don't have a blade!"

I grabbed hold of her, shoved her behind the bench, and shielded her with my body as the swarm of undead closed around us.

I kept her between me and the bench, taking bite after bite, until they had us against the railing.

Below, the sea churned onto the beach, wild and powerful. There was nowhere to run. There was no beach to run to right now. It was covered by the ocean swells. That were rising.

I kept swinging my blade and shoving undead backward, the bites coming fast and furious.

But the roar of the surf filled my ears. I turned.

A wave of water rolled up the stairs and surged across the turnaround.

"Hold on!" I shouted and Keller threw her arms around my legs.

I dropped to my knees and held onto her with every bit of strength I had left as the water knocked us to the concrete. Soaked and freezing, we rolled across the ground, but I wrapped my legs in the railing and held onto it.

Icy sea water rushed over us, but the powerful wave didn't pull us down the stairs and onto the flooded beach.

But the receding rogue wave took all of the undead with it into the churn of surf below.

"Blade! Keller!"

Cash's desperate voice pierced the surf's roar as Mars scooped Keller and I off the turnaround. Together, we shot across the sky. Landing at my bungalow. Where Death paced in front of Rawlins who looked terrified.

"Well?" Death shouted as Mars set Cash, Keller, and I down in front of the bungalow. "Did we succeed?"

Cash nodded. "We sure did."

Dripping water like a bloody sprinkler, I leaned against the bungalow, my chest heaving, and blood dripping from more than a dozen bite wounds.

"Keller and I were almost overrun by undead," I said, trying to get my breath. "But we destroyed our sigil."

Keller was beside me now, a hand on my back as she glanced from Cash to Death, grinning.

"I thought we were finished when a rogue wave blasted up the stairs and wiped all the undead off the turnaround. Dragging them out with the tide. Greysen held onto the railing and kept us from following them."

I nodded and began to sink.

But Cash was beside me in a blink, holding me up.

"Easy there, kid," he said and slid my machete out of my hands, leaning it against the front stoop. "They carved you up good."

Exhausted, all I could do was nod again.

Keller was on my other side now as Cash walked me toward my bungalow door.

"Come on, son," said Cash. "Let's get you and Keller some dry clothes while Death, Rawlins, and Mars talk about where we take this fight next."

Rawlins perked up, looking pleased that he'd been included as I let Cash lead me into my bungalow.

"I'll be right back, Mallory," said Keller and hurried toward the other bedroom.

To change her clothes.

Cash got me into my bedroom. I'd just gotten my jacket and boots off when Keller returned. Dressed in dry jeans and a dark blue sweater that looked as soft as her eyes.

"Now, let's get you out of these soaked clothes," she said as she reached up and began to unbutton my drenched shirt.

Turning my skin to gooseflesh and setting it alight at the same time.

I wanted to take her in my arms and make love to her, but she'd been so distant, I didn't even feel confident about snagging her.

Besides, Cash was still there, pulling clothes out of my luggage for me. I pulled off my soaked shirt and draped it over the back of a chair and snaked off my jeans.

Keller's face was bright and intense, but I couldn't read her expression. Or the emotion. Did she like what she saw or was she bored? Or a million miles away, focused on this foiled necromancy ritual—and the Brian Beckerman murder?

I couldn't tell, even when I stood there shivering in my black boxer briefs.

Cash was all over me with ointment and plasters, Keller helping him.

After they'd treated all the bites, Cash handed me an armful of clothes. I unfolded a grey V-neck sweater and yanked it over my head. With dry jeans and pants (blue boxer briefs), I limped into the loo to change.

In a few moments, I stepped out to an empty bedroom. After locating my black hiking boots, I hurriedly put them on, lacing them up. Then I grabbed my long black and red frock coat (that I'd had since they put me ashore at the New York port in 1726), and put it on, still shivering. My bomber jacket was soaked and it needed some repairs after all those bloody coffin dodgers had yammed it up.

When I opened the bedroom door, Cash and Keller were just outside it, leaning against the wall. She moved toward me, taking hold of my arm. She gave me a funny look.

"What?" I said.

"That's a...very unusual...coat."

I nodded. "Had it a long time."

Gently, she steered me toward the sitting room instead of out the door.

"Where are you taking me?" I asked.

"To sit down and rest," said Keller. "Cash and the others are on their way inside."

I relented and let her sit me down on the tan sofa that sat perpendicular to the window. She sat down beside me.

"You really got chewed up by those undead," she said.

I nodded. "Those teeth bloody hurt."

"I'll say," she replied. "I took a few bites, too, but you took the brunt of them. I want Mars to take a look at you."

I fixed her with my gaze as the front door opened and the others rushed inside, and I tried to figure out if her concern was for my well-being or her case.

"Need to make sure I'm upright enough to cuff for the murder of Brian Beckerman?" I asked.

Her eyes widened. "What are you talking about?" she said.

I started to elaborate, but Death swirled black smoke through the bungalow as Cash dropped down beside me on the sofa. Rawlins slid into a wooden chair against the wall and Mars and Death shared the loveseat.

Keller started to respond, but her mobile buzzed. Bloody calls. She slid the mobile out of her pocket and answered it.

"Keller."

She rose from the sofa and moved toward the short hallway.

"Good news! I've located Gilbert and Neville Ryan," said Death. "We're heading there next so Detective Keller can arrest them."

"That's excellent news," Cash replied, a grin rising on his face. "Can't wait to see their surprised faces."

"Me neither," I replied. "Although I'd rather punch up Neville Ryan. I owe him a bit of violence after he nearly bled me out at that sodding sub shop."

"You got the trace?" Keller's voice echoed through the room. "Excellent! Give me the location where it originated and I'll head right there. Right. I'll hold."

Keller leaned back into the room.

"Guys, we've pinpointed an address for whoever called in Brian Beckerman's murder. On Beckerman's phone. Smitty? Yeah, I'm here. Go ahead."

The room went silent and so did Keller, the mobile smashed

against her left ear as she nodded and wrote information down on a small yellow pad of paper.

"Got it! Thanks, Smitty!"

She cleared the call and glanced from the paper to the screen, typing information.

"Call was traced to an old motor inn near Gleneden Beach," said Keller as she stepped back into the room. "It's currently closed for the season, but whoever has Beckerman's phone is there right now. Phone's pinging off the towers. Along with Gilbert and Neville Ryan's phones."

Huddling together like sewer rats. And that was an insult to rats.

I leaped to my feet.

"Now, we'll finally know who merked Brian Beckerman and took Beckerman's identity."

Keller nodded and hurried toward me.

"Exactly. And as a bonus, it's time to arrest Superintendent Gilbert Ryan and his son, Neville. After we unmask whoever's posing as Brian Beckerman. Let's go!"

And I wanted to know why they were impersonating the dead bail bondsman.

Death sighed. "Let's god-travel. It's faster."

I crowded into the thick coils of black smoke beside Cash and Keller as Mars and Rawlins stepped in close and gripped the folds of Death's black bathrobe. Keller laid her hand on my arm as the room disappeared into a swirling black tunnel.

But I couldn't help feeling unsettled. Like this had been a trap from the beginning and this killer was about to launch the final act of their own personal Scottish play.

Where I'd been their final target. And now, I was wrapping myself up and giving them an early Christmas present.

Through the blackness and smoke, we hurtled toward the old motor inn. To finally unmask a killer.

24

T RAVELING BY D EATH ' S GOD-TRAVEL MADE ME QUEASY. I WAS A cop, not an immortal or a god. I wasn't used to all this magic and strangeness. As a cop, I was used to weirdness, but only when it involved mortal humans. Greysen's level of weirdness was in a whole different realm, and I admit, I struggled with it at times.

Like how he knew that lighter belonged to Beckerman. Or how he knew all of that information about destroying these magical blood symbols. Like a gory crime scene.

He knew so much, but there was a vast ocean of things he wasn't telling me. Things he was hiding. I couldn't help it. It made me suspicious, and I couldn't help searching his name and social security number in every database I could access.

I just wanted the truth. That was it. Why couldn't he trust me enough to tell me the truth?

When the black smoky trails dissipated, only four of us stood in a dark parking lot nestled in the trees between the shoreline and Highway 101. A dark blue tarp lay in the middle of the parking lot, weighed down with a cinder block.

"Cash, what happened to Mars and Rawlins?" I asked as Greysen gazed around at the isolated, closed inn.

Frowning, Death looked puzzled.

"I don't know. They were right beside us."

Death closed his eyes a moment as if communicating with the former god of war. After a few seconds, his eyes snapped open.

"Mars said he's frozen in place at the bungalow alongside Rawlins."

"That's impossible!" Greysen shouted. "Something feels very wrong with this place."

Greysen was right about that. It didn't look out of the ordinary, but the motor inn felt—off somehow. Like a crime scene when the perps were still onsite, lying in wait for the police. Liked we'd arrived in the middle of the action.

Despite the growing discomfort, we pressed on across the parking lot. Toward the closed motor inn.

The old, single-story motel huddled in the shadows of the surrounding trees, mostly concrete, metal, and glass. With ten rooms that opened onto the parking lot. Like an old 60s Travel Lodge or a 40s motor inn as they used to call them. This place had been painted in shades of pale blue and green with murals along the front of the inn. Of mermaids and orcas and porpoises riding the ocean waves. Starfish and clams and even an octopus decorated the edges of the mural.

It was campy and a little cartoony and I loved the look of it. But the feel of this place made my skin crawl. It felt dead-end road isolated. Horror movie abandoned. And evil in that way when a dark alley suddenly exploded into gun fire and violence.

My heart bounced into my throat when all the security lights dimmed and buzzed, flickering now as we approached room ten at the far end of the building. Where the call had originated from, the one that reported the body outside Greysen's bungalow that morning.

On a phone registered to Brian Beckerman. The murder victim.

Death cast a smoky mist around me and Greysen that was barely visible in the strange dusk that had engulfed this old motor inn.

"Won't stop everything, but it'll make the two of you harder to hit," said Death.

"Thank you," I said.

"Yes, thanks, Death," said Greysen.

He moved with reticent steps beside me as we approached the last room at the motor inn. He had that machete in a death grip, his violet eyes intense, his handsome face taut, mouth drawn into a tight line. His muscles were corded.

I wanted to reach out and soothe his angst and tension, but stopped myself. If the person in this room was our killer, my case would be closed. I sighed. And he'd be leaving.

A day before Thanksgiving.

I couldn't handle him leaving—and finally getting to love him would only make that pain worse.

Still, my cop senses were on overload. Something felt very wrong here.

I drew my Glock and worked my way from light pole to light pole. Past closed dark rooms with shadowy, dark windows that captured every slight movement of the trees.

Toward the farthest room, the one by the dark treeline surrounding the motel that had been shut down for the season.

Not a single car haunted the empty parking lot. Other than room ten, not one light shone through the building. It was all dark.

Cash and Death had faded into the dark and shadows, letting me do my job. But I felt relieved that I had some supernatural backup just beyond this sketchy closed motel with one room lit up in an otherwise dark and closed motor inn.

As we got close to the door to room ten, warm orange light flooded beneath the cheap plastic beige shade and blackout drapes that hung heavy in the window.

A shadow hovered in front of the window with another shadow

passing behind the closest one. I could clearly make out the bill of a baseball cap on the figure in front of the window.

Still dressed like Brian Beckerman.

Why? It made no sense.

I motioned Greysen toward the left side of the door as I moved toward the room. My gold detective's badge was visible on my purple leather coat now. By law, I had to display it when approaching suspects. And identify myself.

At least there was no door out the back where these people could escape into the woods. Or circle around and ambush us.

Tonight, this case would finally be over.

I glanced over at Greysen who stood at the left side of the door, machete raised, waiting for my orders.

He'd listened for once, but I knew if things got heated, he'd do something risky. That was Greysen Mallory. I knew even now that I could never change this man. And honestly, I didn't want to change him. I liked him the way he was—even though he made me crazy sometimes. But I preferred his secrets exposed. At least the important ones. Like his name. Where he came from? Whether he had feelings for me?

My heart began to race, breath coming quicker now as I approached the ocean blue door with a tarnished gold number ten affixed to it.

With my foot, I thumped on the door, Glock drawn with both hands.

"Oregon State Police. Open the door and step outside with your hands in front of you. Now."

The light snapped off in the room, sounds of feet shuffling through the paper-thin walls.

Dammit. They were going to resist.

Again, I thumped the door with my foot.

"This is Detective Harlowe Keller with the Oregon State Police. I am ordering you to step outside with your hands in front of you. Now! Or I'll be forced to enter this room. You are illegally occupying a room in a closed establishment that is classified as private property. You are trespassing. Step outside. Now!"

Not even a hiss of movement echoed in the chilly night air.

I turned toward Greysen and he watched me, still waiting for my instructions, I realized.

I pointed at the door and then twirled my index finger in the air, telling him to mobilize and get ready.

Greysen gripped his machete in both hands, nodding, as he pressed his back against the painted wall, ready to follow me inside.

"Last warning!" I called out to the room, keeping my body turned against the pole, so I wasn't an easy target. "Either step outside or we're coming in to arrest you."

They needed to know I wasn't alone.

When I got no response, I held up my left hand, three fingers in the air, counting down to zero.

I waited a heartbeat. Then two fingers.

No response.

Then one finger.

When no one responded, I motioned toward the door with two fingers.

Gripping my Glock in both hands, I pulled in a breath. Held it. And rushed the door.

I kicked it twice at the doorknob until the lock gave.

Inhaling another sharp breath, I held it. Grabbed the doorknob. And shoved open the door.

I threw myself to the right of the doorjamb as bullets popped through the stillness, sizzling past like hailstones from the half-open door.

Waiting, I listened for sounds of reloading and then swung around the casing and into the threshold, kicking open the door.

Greysen was immediately behind me as we entered the room and both hit the floor. We rolled behind the first double bed as more bullets fanned through the dark room.

"Oregon State Police. Drop your weapons and surrender. Now!"

More bullets pounded the stillness.

Pinning Greysen and me behind the bed.

I held my gun above the bed and returned fire.

Things shattered throughout the room. Probably a big mirror giving me seven years or more of bad luck.

Like right now.

Greysen popped up like a gopher for a quick look, but more guns joined the fight, forcing him back down on the musty, cigar-smoky gold carpet. But Death's mist still clung to our skin.

I was trying to figure out how to get past the storm of bullets when a shadow flitted past me, disappearing into the room.

Moments later, a thick trail of black smoke coiled through the space.

I smiled. Death and Cash had joined our little chat with the bad guys. This would be over fast.

In the darkness, someone whimpered. Neville Ryan?

"No, stop!" shouted a familiar voice I'd heard on many conference calls and on the news.

Superintendent Gilbert Ryan. My boss. The necromancer.

The lights in the motel room snapped on. Mars stood in the doorway, spear at his side, hand on the light switch.

Cash hustled Neville Ryan out of the bathroom and toward the broken door.

"Got this little dirtbag," Cash said with a grin as I stood up from behind the bed.

"And I got your boss," said Death as he gripped Superintendent Ryan's arms, immobilizing him as Death. pushed him toward the door.

I had three sets of handcuffs in my pockets, two reserved for my boss and Neville Ryan.

Greysen got to his feet as I approached Neville Ryan and slapped the cuffs on his wrists. And read him his rights.

I moved toward my boss who wouldn't look me in the eye now, his head bowed. I cuffed his hands and read him his rights.

Greysen yanked the man in a black peacoat, jeans, and a black Yankees baseball cap out of the closet. The bill nearly covered the man's entire face and I couldn't see anything from where I stood.

"Got you banged to rights, you absolute knob," Greysen said and grabbed the ball cap, yanking it off the man's head.

But my mouth fell open when a shock of long brown hair fell out from underneath the cap.

Kerrie Ryan Beckerman stood there, dressed in her dead husband's clothes as she glared at Greysen.

"Why couldn't you have just died?" she shouted at Greysen. "I knew when Brian hired you that you'd be trouble."

Greysen's violet eyes narrowed.

"Well, pardon my refusal to bloody pop my clogs at your sodding command, you stonking sea hag!"

I had no idea what most of that meant, but Greysen was furious.

"Why did you call the feckin' rozzers and report your husband's body?" Greysen demanded. "After you merked him."

Kerrie laughed. "I didn't."

What? But the call traced back to Brian Beckerman's phone. The one she currently had on her. I grabbed it and put it in a plastic bag.

"I called," said a voice from the doorway.

Hecate stood in the flickering gold light, hands on her hips.

"You?" Greysen shouted, his gaze snapping toward the goddess.

She shrugged. "Thought you were too cute to let her off you. So, I called the police and made it look like it came from the phone this traitorous bitch carried. Because this whole time, she's been stabbing me in the back, trying to take over my Oregon Coast territory because Circe refused to even work with her."

Something glinted in the light.

I turned as something flashed toward Greysen's arm.

"Greysen, look out!" I shouted.

Kerrie Beckerman's knife sliced across Greysen's wrist, cutting deep.

Blood dripped down his arm and onto the carpet as she broke free of Greysen's hold and barreled past Hecate.

A horrified look burned on Greysen's face. But he had his back to the door.

"Bollocks!" he shouted, clutching his arm as Death turned to smoke and surged past Hecate, rushing outside after Kerrie Beckerman.

I thought Greysen was talking about the wound on his arm.

Still training my Glock on Neville and Superintendent Ryan, I moved toward Greysen to see how bad Kerrie Beckerman had cut him. But his gaze was locked onto the room's far wall. On the mirror that covered it.

"What is it?" I asked him.

He pointed toward the mirror.

Blood sigils covered it, glistening with an eerie red glow, pulsating.

Cash was at Greysen's side now.

"She's trying to summon *all* the Hell generals," Greysen said in a low voice, looking shocked. "Right now. With that."

"Greysen," Cash moaned and motioned toward the sigils. "I hate to tell you this, but those sigils are written in your blood."

"What?" Greysen cried, his gaze snapping to the white-haired vampire beside him. "My blood?"

"That's right, Mallory," Kerrie Beckerman said with a snarl from somewhere outside. "Gilbert took your blood after Neville siphoned it. Right under Hecate's nose. Gave it me."

The air shimmered beside Cash and something knocked him across the room.

Grabbing Greysen around the neck.

A hulking, ashen skinned creature with large curved horns materialized, its thick arms yanking Greysen into a headlock.

And pulled him outside as Cash got to his feet.

I cuffed Neville and Superintendent Ryan together to the bed and rushed outside after them.

With a wave of her fingers, Kerrie snatched my Glock out of my hand, leaving me without a weapon.

Outside, Hecate and Death were trapped in a blood circle that gleamed beyond the doorway as what could only be that Hell general dragged Greysen across the parking lot toward the blood circle.

Where Kerrie Beckerman had painted another larger circle in blood across the asphalt. Where the blue tarp lay in a tangle now. After she'd pulled it off the blood circle on the parking lot floor.

Both circles had been hidden beneath that tarp.

Dammit, why hadn't any of us thought to check under it!

"You got played, Mallory!" Kerrie Beckerman shouted, laughing as she poured blood from what looked like a red gas can into whorls and sigils within the large circle. "I forged Hecate's magic signature at every cemetery and at every location I led you to, so you would escalate the war between her and Death. I planted that lighter in Brian's pocket for you to find. So, your ability and your cop sidekick would lead you here."

"To a dodgy closed motor inn? You people have no sense of drama and imagination. A bloody motel—really? Stephen King did it much better. Much."

"This motor inn is where the coastal Ley lines are strongest," Kerrie said, holding out her arms.

"She's right," said Hecate from across the parking lot.

The goddess crossed her arms and glared at the Beckerman woman.

"And she's going to be erased from all existence when I get out of this circle, but she's right about the Ley lines."

Kerrie chuckled as she shook the last bit of blood out of the can and tossed it aside.

"Why me?" Greysen demanded as he struggled against the Hell general's hold. "When you had your bloody pick of supernaturals?"

"Because I needed your...unique blood. And you for a unique blood magic ritual." Kerrie motioned to the Hell general. "General Adramelech, bring him to the circle, please."

"Unique how?" Greysen demanded again as the Hell general shuffled him across the pavement toward the circle made from his own blood.

And I was powerless to help him.

"When Neville told me that you had a connection to resurrectionists and those papers, I decided to test you. We planted that page in the grave you investigated. It's real. And when I learned that you were able to read that planted page, that it had turned blue at your touch, I knew that the universe had handed me a gift."

The general shoved Greysen into the circle and Kerrie stepped outside it as the circle began to glow bright red. Trapping Greysen within the glowing lines of his own blood.

"What does that even mean?" Greysen shouted, fighting against the force that held him in the circle.

Kerrie shook her head. "Don't you even know?"

When Greysen didn't respond, Kerrie laughed.

"It means your blood has rare magical properties," she said. "Magical enough to summon a powerful god."

Hecate screamed as the blood circle around her began to contract. Death turned to smoke and hugged the ground. Hecate turned into a raven, giving her more space inside the collapsing circle.

"Soon, the magic in the other circle will crush Death and eventually Hecate," said Kerrie. "But not before they witness the arrival of the most powerful god in existence."

She lifted her arms into the air.

The ground beneath Greysen began to shake, a thunderous rumble echoing around them as the Hell general joined hands with Kerrie Beckerman, strengthening the magical pull on the circle.

Greysen's agonizing scream pierced the night as he dropped to his knees, shaking, teeth gritted. Like some tremendous force was weighing down his body.

"Stop it!" I shouted. "You're killing him!"

"That's why we call it a human sacrifice, Detective Keller," Kerrie Beckerman said with a laugh.

One by one, each of the security lights sparked, popped, and went out as something dark and powerful rose around the motor inn.

"Hecate!"

A voice shouted from somewhere behind me as a shadow rushed through the night.

A man with long blond hair stepped out of the shadow and crouched beside the circle where Hecate huddled in her raven form.

He grabbed hold of the force compacting the circle and held it back, keeping it from crushing Hecate and Death.

"I'll be damned, its Hades!" Cash cried.

Hades glanced around the scene, looking horrified.

"Hecate, I came to warn you. When I checked all the underworld cells, his was empty. Empty, Hecate! And *Theoktónos* is gone. You know what that means, don't you?"

An explosion of red light shook the surroundings, knocking all of us to the parking lot's cracked asphalt.

Hecate let go of her raven form, gasping as a forbidding shadowy figure stepped out of the smoke and flicker of red light that went dark. Where Greysen lay spread eagle in the middle of the circle.

The hulking form turned solid. Taller than Mars. Muscular, sharp jaw line, square face, wild dark eyes. And even from this distance, I felt the evil radiating from this being.

"By the gods," Death said with a hiss, staring in horror at the massive man.

"Kronos!" Hecate cried, skittering back from the edge of the circle.

The titan moved toward her. With his powerful arm, Kronos hit Hades in the chest, knocking him backward. The titan towered over Hecate and raised a shiny, ornate gold knife with Greek symbols above his head.

Hecate threw her hand in front of her face, trying to ward off the blade.

A red fireball slammed into the titan, staggering him a moment.

"No!" Kerrie Beckerman shouted. "No, no, no! She's supposed to die, too!"

Kronos looked up.

As a shadow slammed into him full force.

Kronos staggered, the knife skittering across the parking lot.

I couldn't believe it! It was Greysen, hands glowing red with fireballs.

Kronos turned, but the red fireballs had weakened him somehow.

In an instant, the Hell general was beside Kronos as he slumped forward. With an ashen sweep of his arm, the general whisked Kerrie Beckerman between them.

Kronos glared at Greysen, pointing a finger as they began to disappear.

"Boy, you've made a powerful enemy today," said Kronos. "I will see you again. This isn't over."

The trio faded into the night as the circle surrounding Hecate and Death collapsed in a wash of red light.

I rushed over to Greysen as the red fireballs dissipated. He was on his knees, dizzy, and panting.

Hecate appeared beside him, smiling, a hand on his face.

"You just saved my life, Blade," she said in an almost humble tone. "I think we just declared a truce, you and me. Thank you."

Greysen flashed a weak smile at her as I got him onto his feet. "You're welcome."

She turned her gaze to Death who was beside Greysen now.

"With you, too, Death. We've got bigger things to worry about."

Death nodded. "Kronos escaping his prison changes everything."

Hades moved toward Hecate and gripped her hand. He carried the dagger that Greysen had knocked out of Kronos' hands. The one they called *Theoktónos*. Godkiller.

"It will take him a long time to regain his power," said Hades, god of the underworld. "But when he does, he'll try to insert himself over the entire immortal world. Come, Hecate, we have much to discuss."

"Of course," said Hecate.

With that, Hades and Hecate vanished into the darkness.

Leaving me, Greysen, Cash, Mars, and Death in the dark car park.

Standing beside Greysen, I reached up and brushed a smudge of dirt off his cheek.

"Come on, hero," I said and gently pecked his cheek. "Let's get Neville and Superintendent Ryan off to jail. Then you can explain what just happened here."

"You always know how to have fun, detective," said Greysen as he moved slowly between me and Cash, toward the motor inn's room ten. "It's quite simple, really. Ley lines and blood magic amplified my temporal ability." He smiled. "Kronos is the old god of time. Add a match made in the Underworld. And Bob's your uncle."

Shaking my head, I pulled my phone out of my pocket and called in the arrest, alerting them that our superintendent of police was among my alleged perps as I gave them a list of the charges. I identified Kerrie Beckerman as the killer, requested a BOLO on her, and a warrant for her arrest.

"We still need to deal with that damned weapon," said Death as he coiled around us in a protective stance.

I frowned. "That weapon that Kronos carried?"

Death nodded. "Theoktónos. Or godkiller in Greek. It can kill immortals, Detective Keller. We need to find it and secure it."

Great. Another loose end. Another danger. And another supernatural case. I'd cite the weapon in my report as a stolen Greek antiquity that needed to be recovered, request Greysen Mallory as an antiques expert, and put it with my other open case files. A pile that was already huge.

"I think Hades took it with him," said Greysen.

"Let's be sure," Death replied.

Nodding, Greysen mumbled something about reluctantly checking with Hecate. From a long distance.

I picked up my Glock off the asphalt and stepped inside the motel room, Greysen behind me as we waited for backup to process this crime scene and take custody of the Superintendent and Neville Ryan.

25

THE DAY BEFORE THANKSGIVING, IT RAINED BUCKETS AS I STOOD
on the stoop of my formerly letted bungalow, luggage in hand.
Wishing for my Wellies and my Macintosh. It's a jacket, you Yanks,
not a bloody laptop. If you must know, I'm more of Windows bloke.
That's got to hurt, I know.

Keller stood in front of me under the porch eaves, looking droopy,
her powder blue eyes glassy, frowning as she glanced at my luggage
and then at me.

"So, you're headed home to New York?" she asked.

I started to reply, but she pressed on with whatever cop spiel she
had prepared. She looked pale. Nervous. Even sad.

When I first met Detective Harlowe Keller, she couldn't wait to
get me off her coast and back to New York, but standing here now in
the pouring rain, she looked like she wanted to plead with me not to
go. Like maybe there was something between us, something that
made her want to ask me to stay.

And not arrest me.

But she was still that hard as nails cop that I was attracted to and wanted to get to know much, much better. And certainly much longer than one week. She continued with her wrap up of the case.

"Judge issued an arrest warrant for Kerrie Beckerman for the murder of her husband, Brian Beckerman, so you've been officially cleared of any and all wrongdoing, Mallory."

I sighed. Back to Mallory again, were we?

"I'm so relieved not to be a suspect any longer," I said. "And now that this bounty hunt is over—and I'm out seventeen thousand quid —I need to find another bounty. And get paid this time."

Keller squinted.

"Back to New York then," she said.

Again. The second time she'd said that.

Was she relieved to be rid of me or sad that I was no longer a person of interest on this case? I winced. Judging by her stony expression, I was no longer *her* person of interest either.

That hurt.

I forced a smile, wanting to unwind that long, sable braid and run my fingers through her silky black hair. She still wore that purple motorbike jacket but with black jeans and a cropped black T-shirt that gave me a delicious peek at her smooth, flat belly. I sighed. And her glorious navel.

"Not your person of interest anymore, am I?" I said.

And that made me sad.

She didn't smile.

"Not for this case anyway," she said in a quiet voice.

Was that a glimmer of hope I heard or was that a polite way of telling me to sod off?

"Since bounty hunting is illegal in Oregon," I continued. "It would be difficult to work bounties without getting arrested, wouldn't you say, detective?"

She forced a smile onto her face, but she still looked miserable.

Was it the rain or because our case together had been solved? Perhaps the arduous task of apprehending Kerrie Beckerman was upsetting her?

"If I even get a whiff of you hunting bounty on this coast, you'd be looking at time in county jail, Mallory. Could be months. And if it becomes felony kidnapping..." She paused a moment, her gaze on me again. "You could be here for a lifetime."

"Is that a good or bad thing, detective?" I asked in a quiet voice, wanting to reach out and stroke her face, take her into my arms, and kiss her.

But I needed to know that she fancied me. Personally. And that she wanted me to stay. Assuming I hadn't bollocked everything.

"Maybe a little of both," she said and brushed a thick lock of that silky sable hair out of her eyes.

We stared at each other a moment, the silence mounting as her powder blue eyes glistened. Like every part of her body wanted to beg me not to go.

But she said nothing.

"What time's your flight?" she asked finally, her voice cracking a little as she tried to sound matter-of-fact.

Was that the weather or a chink in the detective's armor I'd heard?

"What flight?" I asked, frowning, as I opened the door into my bungalow and pushed my luggage toward it.

She grimaced and pointed at the luggage inside the door, looking rather kettled.

"But your suitcase and—"

"Oh, I was taking it out of the car. I left it in the boot the first night I arrived and hadn't unpacked it yet."

I couldn't hold back my smirk any longer, but she still looked kettled. Confused for you Yanks.

"Keller, I bought the bungalow, remember?" I reminded her. "I've decided to stay on the coast for a while. You've got an international airport in case I have another bail jumper to hunt. I've got easy access to Wraith's. And my antiques business is online."

"So, you're staying?" she cried, her gaze brightening.

"Yes, detective," I said with a grin. "I'm staying. I've arranged for an office at Wraith's to hunt bounties."

Her eyes narrowed.

"Don't worry, detective," I said. "My office will be between the worlds and out of Oregon's jurisdiction. Death has a case for me and Cash has a friend that needs a treasured possession found. And there's some research at the historical association I need to complete—a possible lead on another page from the Resurrectionist Papers."

Keller stepped closer to me, relief burning across her face.

"And now that you mention it," she said. "There's this case that came in this morning. It's a little...out of my wheelhouse and—"

"Don't tell me, it's another bloody cemetery," I said with a groan.

She nodded and gripped my forearm, her touch bonfire-hot against my sleeve.

I pulled in a breath.

"I'll cook you the best Thanksgiving dinner you've ever had if you help me investigate. I'll invite Cash, Mars, and Rawlins, too. Even Death. And Hecate, if you really want me to invite her."

"Bugger," I said with a sigh. "Another sodding graveyard. All right, you cook Thanksgiving dinner, including the turkey, stuffing, and that cranberry pudding I always see on the telly...with some Yorkshire puddings—and I'll help you with this case."

She grinned and rubbed my arm, the heat radiating. She had no idea that I'd have done it for free—just to be near her.

"Deal! Thanksgiving dinner. Your place. Four o'clock tomorrow? And for the record, Mallory, it's cranberry sauce not pudding."

She turned away and rushed across the pavement toward her red Honda SUV as the rain began to fall.

"Whatever," I called to her. "But this case better not involve a Ryan or a necromancer!"

"It doesn't!" She shouted and opened the CR-V's door, but then she turned back toward me.

"Oh, by the way," she called. "The new case file report said something about...werewolves?"

"Werewolves?" I shouted, making a sour face. "Bollocks!"

She nodded, laughing.

"See you tomorrow," she said and started the engine.

In a moment, she pulled onto the motorway.

Bloody hell. Werewolves? I hated werewolves. Discovered I was allergic on my first werewolf case—manky bloke made me sneeze for days and made my eyes water until I couldn't see anything.

Still, I would investigate the hairy bloke. Because I loved investigating alongside Detective Keller.

Happy Thanksgiving to me—at last. I got to spend it with Keller and friends.

But now, I needed to stop at the chemist's and get a boatload of some sodding allergy medicine. And a bloody rabies jab. Bollocks!

***The end of Grave Reckoning, Book 1: The
Resurrectionist Papers***

***The story continues in...
Stiffed Again, Book 2: The Resurrectionist Papers***

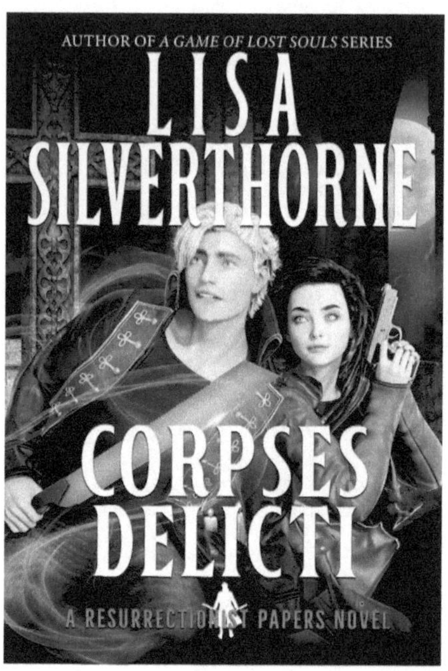

AUTHOR OF *A GAME OF LOST SOULS* SERIES
LISA
SILVERTHORNE
CORPSES
DELICTI
A RESURRECTIONIST PAPERS NOVEL

Subscribe to the Reader's Club

An exclusive reader club dedicated to the fiction of Lisa Silverthorne, including her series: **A Game of Lost Souls, The Resurrectionist Papers, The Spiral,** and **Experiencing True Purple**.

When you subscribe to the reader's club:

- *Receive exclusive updates from Lisa on Ream*
- *Influence future works through Reader Polls*
- *Get early access to new books*
- *Read stories only available on Ream!*
- *Acquire Book swag!*
- *And more!*

JOIN THE CLUB AND SUPPORT A WRITER!

NOVELS BY LISA SILVERTHORNE

Standalones:

ISABEL'S TEARS

LANDFALL

PACIFIC BLUE TATTOO

A Game of Lost Souls series:

THE CINDERELLA HOUR

THE PRINCE CHARMING HOUR

THE EVER AFTER HOUR

THE FALLEN HEARTS SEASON

THE RISING SPIRITS SEASON

THE ETERNAL SOULS SEASON

THE ROYAL WEDDING HOUR

THE HEAVENLY HONEYMOON HOUR

THE DIVINE NEWLYWEDS SHOW

THE CELESTIAL COUPLES SHOW

THE ENOCHIAN APOCALYPSE SHOW

The Spiral series:

BETWEEN

REPRISE

AVENGE

The Resurrectionist Papers:

GRAVE RECKONING

Short Story Collections

THE SOUND OF ANGELS

THE MAGIC OF ORDINARY THINGS

Science Fiction writing as L.S. Silverthorne

Standalones:

REDISCOVERY

Experiencing True Purple series:

RECOMBINANT, Book 1

HELIX, Book 2

SPLICE, Book 3

FORTHCOMING

A Game of Lost Souls series:

The Angelic Anniversary Hour, Book Twelve

The Perdition Picture Show, Book Thirteen

The Spiral series:

Ruin, Book 4

Descent, Book 5

The Resurrectionist Papers:

A ROMANTIC FANTASY MYSTERY SERIES

Corpses Delicti

Stiffed Again

SCIENCE FICTION WRITING AS L.S. SILVERTHORNE

Experiencing True Purple series:

Cipher, Book 4

Renascence, Book 5

SHORT STORY COLLECTIONS

Timeless: 8 Time Travel Romances (January 2024)

About the Author

LISA SILVERTHORNE has published over 20 novels and 150 short stories and novelettes in many genres. She is the author of *A Game of Lost Souls* series, *Experiencing True Purple* series, *The Spiral*, and the upcoming series, *The Resurrectionist Papers*. She lives in Las Vegas, Nevada.

Before you go, you are invited to please leave a **review of this book**!

Reviews are a wonderful way to help an author. They are also an exciting opportunity to share your honest thoughts with other readers, so **please post yours,** in as many places as possible!